Delores Fossen, a *USA Tod*[...] written over 150 novels, with [...] books in print worldwide. She's received a Booksellers' Best Award and an *RT* Reviewers' Choice Best Book Award. She was also a finalist for a prestigious *RITA*® Award. You can contact the author through her website at deloresfossen.com

Juno Rushdan is a veteran US Air Force intelligence officer and award-winning author. Her books are action-packed and fast-paced. Critics from *Kirkus Reviews* and *Library Journal* have called her work 'heart-pounding James Bond-ian adventure' that 'will captivate lovers of romantic thrillers.' For a free book, visit her website: junorushdan.com

Also by Delores Fossen

Saddle Ridge Justice
The Sheriff's Baby
Protecting the Newborn

Silver Creek Lawman: Second Generation
Last Seen in Silver Creek
Marked for Revenge

The Law in Lubbock County
Maverick Justice
Lawman to the Core
Spurred to Justice

Also by Juno Rushdan

Cowboy State Lawmen: Duty and Honor
Wyoming Mountain Investigation
Wyoming Ranch Justice

Cowboy State Lawmen
Wyoming Mountain Murder
Wyoming Cowboy Undercover
Wyoming Mountain Cold Case

Fugitive Heroes: Topaz Unit
Disavowed in Wyoming
An Operative's Last Stand

Discover more at millsandboon.co.uk

TRACKING DOWN THE LAWMAN'S SON

DELORES FOSSEN

WYOMING CHRISTMAS CONSPIRACY

JUNO RUSHDAN

MILLS & BOON

First Published in Great Britain 2024
by Mills & Boon, an imprint of HarperCollins*Publishers* Ltd
1 London Bridge Street, London, SE1 9GF

www.harpercollins.co.uk

HarperCollins*Publishers*
Macken House, 39/40 Mayor Street Upper,
Dublin 1, D01 C9W8, Ireland

Tracking Down the Lawman's Son © 2024 Delores Fossen
Wyoming Christmas Conspiracy © 2024 Juno Rushdan

ISBN: 978-0-263-32256-9

1224

This book contains FSC™ certified paper and other controlled sources to ensure responsible forest management.

For more information visit: www.harpercollins.co.uk/green

Printed and Bound in the UK using 100% Renewable Electricity at CPI Group (UK) Ltd, Croydon, CR0 4YY

TRACKING DOWN THE LAWMAN'S SON

DELORES FOSSEN

Chapter One

Deputy Luca Vanetti ran through the ER doors the moment they slid open, and he made a beeline to the reception desk. The nurse on duty saw him coming and got to her feet. Luca figured the concern on her face was a drop in the bucket compared to his.

He tried to tamp down the worry and fear that were firing through him. Tried not to jump to any bad conclusions, but Bree and his baby boy could be hurt.

Or worse.

No, Luca couldn't deal with *worse* right now.

He just needed to see Bree McCullough and his two-month-old son, Gabriel, and then try to get to the bottom of what'd happened. Bree and he might barely be on speaking terms, but they both loved Gabriel, and Bree would know what a gut punch it was for Luca to get a report that she'd been in a serious car accident.

"Where are they?" Luca demanded before he even reached the reception desk.

The nurse, Alisha Cameron, was someone he'd known his whole life. Something that could be said about most people in their small hometown of Saddle Ridge, Texas, where there weren't many degrees of separation.

Alisha motioned toward the hall. "The exam room on the right. Slater's already here."

Slater McCullough was not only a fellow deputy at the Saddle Ridge Sheriff's Office, but he was also Bree's older brother. Luca had expected him to be here since Slater was the responding officer who'd arrived on the scene of the single car accident, only to learn his sister was the driver.

"Gabriel wasn't in the vehicle with Bree," Slater said the moment he spotted Luca. "I just got off the phone with the nanny, and Gabriel's with her."

Some of the tightness eased up in Luca's chest. Some. His baby boy wasn't hurt. "And Bree?" Luca managed to ask.

"She's in with the doctor now," Slater said after he swallowed hard. "She has a head injury, and they're examining her."

"How bad?" Luca wanted to know.

Slater shook his head. "I'm not sure. When I arrived on scene, she was trying to get out of the car, but her seat belt was jammed, and she couldn't reach her phone. There was blood," he added. "Some scrapes and cuts, too, on her face, but I think most of those came from the airbag when it deployed."

"What happened?" Luca wanted to know. "Why did she crash?"

"I'm not sure what caused the accident." He paused, his gaze meeting Luca's. "Her car went off the road right before the Saddle Ridge Creek bridge, and she slammed into a tree. If she hadn't hit the tree, her car would have plunged into the creek."

Hell. That was where his parents had been killed, so Luca knew firsthand that a collision like that could have been fatal because the creek was more than twenty feet deep in spots. But crashing into a tree could have killed her, too.

Luca studied Slater's eyes that were a genetic copy of not only Bree's but of Gabriel's. "Why did she go off the road?" he pressed.

Slater shook his head again. "I don't know. Like I said, she was woozy, and I arrived on scene only a minute or two before the ambulance got there. The EMTs loaded her right away and brought her here."

Because Luca knew Slater well, he could see that Slater was worried. And troubled. "You said Bree has a head injury. How bad?" Luca asked.

"I don't know," Slater repeated. He scrubbed his hands over his face. "Other than what I've told you, the only other thing I know is a delivery driver traveling on that road spotted Bree's car and called it in. There were tread marks nearby, but I have no idea if they were from her vehicle or not. The delivery driver didn't see any other vehicles around."

So, maybe she'd gotten distracted or something and had lost control of the car. That wasn't like Bree, though. She was usually ultra-focused. A skill set she needed for her job as legal consultant for the Texas Rangers. But she was also the mother of a two-month-old baby, and it was possible lack of sleep had played into this.

That possibility gave Luca another gut punch. Because he could see how this would have played out. Even if Bree had been exhausted, she wouldn't have asked him for help. In fact, he was probably the last person in Saddle Ridge she would have turned to. Ironic, since they had once been lovers.

Had.

That was definitely in the past, and as far as Bree was concerned, it wouldn't be repeated. Luca was learning to live with that even though they'd had an on-again, off-again thing since high school. The *off* had become permanent eleven months ago when they'd landed in bed after Bree's father had been murdered.

That brought on gut punch number three of the day.

Because Bree's late father, Sheriff Cliff McCullough, hadn't only been Luca's boss, he'd been his surrogate father after Luca's parents had died in a car crash when Luca had been just sixteen. Luca had been grieving and on shaky emotional ground following Cliff's murder. Bree had been, too, and they'd spent the night together.

The night when she'd gotten pregnant with Gabriel.

Bree hadn't told him that though until four months ago when she'd moved back home. Only then had Luca learned he was going to be a father. Luca hadn't quite managed to forgive Bree for shutting him out like that, but she apparently didn't want his forgiveness.

The door to the exam room opened, and Dr. Nathan Bagley stepped out. Another familiar face but not an especially friendly one. Well, not friendly toward Luca anyway. Luca knew Nathan had always seen him as a romantic rival. During Bree and Luca's off-again phases, Nathan and she had dated.

"How is she?" Luca immediately asked.

The doctor didn't get a chance to answer though. "I'm fine," Luca heard Bree say.

Nathan's sigh indicated he didn't quite agree with his patient, but he stepped back out of the doorway, and Luca saw another nurse who was in the process of washing her hands.

And Bree.

Her short dark brown hair was tangled and flecked with powder from the airbag. And she was pale. So pale. She was also getting up from the exam table. Not easily. She was wobbling a little, and Luca immediately went to her, took hold of her arm and steadied her.

There was blood on her cream-colored shirt. A few flecks of dried blood, too, on her right cheek by her ear. That had no doubt come from the cut on her head that was now stitched up.

Bree dodged his gaze, but that was the norm for them these days. "Thanks," she muttered, and stepped out of his grip. "I'm fine," she repeated, her gaze pinned to Slater.

"You're sure about that?" Slater questioned. He went to her, gently cupped her chin, lifting it while he examined her.

"Sure," she insisted at the same moment that Nathan added his own comment.

"She doesn't appear to have a concussion, but I'd like to run some tests," the doctor said. "I'd also like to admit her for observation for the head injury."

All of that sounded reasonable to Luca, but Bree clearly wasn't on board with it. "I'm fine. I want to go home and check on Gabriel."

"Gabriel's okay," Slater assured her. "I called the nanny just a couple of minutes ago."

Now it was Bree's turn to study her brother's face, and it seemed to Luca that she was making sure he was telling her the truth.

What the heck was going on?

Slater and Bree were close, and Slater wouldn't have lied to her. Well, not under these circumstances anyway. And not about Gabriel. Slater might have downplayed the truth though if Bree had been in serious condition, but that wasn't the case.

"I need to go home," Bree repeated. "Can you give me a ride?" she asked, and then moved away from Slater. She went to the small counter where the nurse was now standing and picked up her purse.

"Hold on a second." Slater stepped in front of her to stop

her from heading for the door. "What happened? Why did you wreck?"

Her pause only lasted a couple of seconds, but it was enough to make Luca even more concerned about her. "A deer ran out on the road in front of me," Bree said. "I swerved to miss it and lost control."

There were indeed plenty of deer and other wildlife in the woods around the creek, and drivers did hit them from time to time. But something about this still felt, well, off.

"Why were you on that road?" Luca asked. It wasn't anywhere near Bree's place. Her house was one she'd inherited from her grandparents when she'd turned twenty-one, and it was on the outskirts of the other side of town.

"I was going to Austin for a business meeting," she said.

That didn't seem off. Bree was a lawyer who did legal consultations for the Texas Rangers and some state agencies. Most days, she worked from home, but she sometimes had meetings in nearby San Antonio or Austin.

"I thought I was going to end up in the creek," she added in a mutter.

Now she looked at Luca. Or rather glanced at him, and he saw the apology in her eyes. She no doubt knew it always hit him hard to be reminded of his parents' deaths.

"A deer," Slater muttered, a question in his tone.

"Yes," she verified, and Bree suddenly sounded a whole lot stronger. She didn't look it though. She still seemed plenty unsteady to Luca. "And now I need to go home and see my baby."

This time, it was Nathan who maneuvered in front of her. "You hit your head. You really should stay here for observation. You need to have medical supervision."

"I can get someone in my family to stay with me," Bree insisted right back. "I need to check on Gabriel."

Nathan huffed and turned to Slater to plead his case. "Head injuries can be dangerous. She shouldn't be alone."

A muscle flickered in Slater's jaw, and he volleyed glances at both his sister and the doctor. Slater must have seen the determination on Bree's face because he sighed.

"She won't be alone," Slater told Nathan. "I'll make sure someone is with her for the next twenty-four hours."

Nathan repeated his huff, but his obvious objection didn't stop Bree. "I'll phone in a script for pain meds," he called out as Bree headed for the door. Slater and Luca were right behind her.

"Where are you parked?" she asked without looking back at them.

"By the ambulances," Slater provided. It wasn't far, but Luca's cruiser was closer.

"I'm right by the ER door," Luca said. He'd left his cruiser there when he'd been in a near panic to check on Bree and their son.

"Your cruiser then," Bree said, and her glance was just long enough for Luca to confirm she was talking to him.

She was obviously shaken to the core so Luca understood her urgent need to see Gabriel. The baby would likely steady her nerves. Again though, it seemed like more than that.

"Slater, why don't you ride with us, and I can give you a statement about the accident?" Bree asked when they stepped outside. She fired glances around as if looking for something.

Or someone.

"Sure," Slater said, sounding as concerned and skeptical as Luca was. He opened the passenger's side door to help Bree in, and he slid into the back seat.

"Drive," Bree insisted the moment Luca got behind the wheel.

Luca didn't press her to explain what the heck was going

on. He pulled out of the hospital parking lot while he, too, glanced around.

"All right, what's wrong?" Slater demanded once they were on the way.

Bree dragged in a quick breath and squeezed her eyes shut for a moment. "Someone ran me off the road." Her voice cracked. "I think someone tried to kill me."

Chapter Two

Bree knew she had plenty of explaining to do. No way could she just drop a bombshell like that on two cops and not tell them more.

Especially these two cops.

Slater, because he was her brother, and Luca, because of their history together. Of course, their history was playing into their present since she'd given birth to Luca's son.

"Drive slow," she instructed Luca since it would normally only take about five minutes to get to her house. She needed a bit more time than that. "I don't want to talk about this in front of Coral." Coral Saylor, the nanny. Bree trusted her, but she needed to keep this just between the three of them.

For now, anyway.

Because it was possible anyone she involved in this could end up being in danger.

She hated that. Hated that she had to bring them into this, but after today's attack, Bree didn't see a way around it.

"Who ran you off the road?" Slater asked. "Who tried to kill you and why?"

The first part was easy to answer. Well, the info was easy anyway. Reliving it sure as heck wasn't.

"I didn't see the driver," Bree admitted. "He came flying out from the dirt turnoff by the bridge and rammed into me. It was a large silver truck with heavily tinted windows." She shook her head and winced, which caused the fresh stitches to pull. "I didn't get a chance to dodge him or see the license plates."

"Had you ever seen the truck before?" Luca asked.

"I don't think so, but, uh, for the past couple of days, I've had the feeling that someone was watching me."

Both Slater and Luca cursed. "And you didn't think to tell one of us that?" Slater demanded.

"No." She stretched that out a few syllables, annoyed that he was using his big brother tone. "Because it was only a feeling. It happened twice when I was in town. First at the grocery store and late yesterday when I went to the post office. I glanced around, but I didn't see any unfamiliar faces."

Still, she should have trusted her gut. If she had, she would have been more careful. That had to stop. Careful had to be at the top of her priorities because of Gabriel.

"All right," Slater said a few moments later. He was making a visible attempt to rein in the big brother stuff. "Tell us why you think this truck driver maybe followed you and then rammed into your car."

Bree dragged in a long breath. Where to start? There were so many pieces to this so she decided to go back to the beginning.

"I've been investigating Dad's murder," she said, knowing that in itself wouldn't be a bombshell. They were all investigating her father being gunned down by an unknown assailant eleven months ago.

A date that she had no trouble recalling.

Because it was also when she'd gotten pregnant with Gabriel.

She'd ended up at Luca's that night, and they'd both been in shock and grief-stricken not just over her father's murder but her mother's disappearance. Her mother, Sandra, had simply vanished without a trace, and there was the worry that she, too, was dead. Or that she'd killed her husband and fled. That theory had some juice since her mother's wallet, phone and car had gone missing as well. None of the items had yet been recovered.

Both of those possible scenarios had shaken Luca and her to the core, and with their defenses down, they'd fallen back into their old routine of landing in bed.

"What does Dad's death have to do with what happened to you today?" Slater pressed.

"Getting there," she muttered and returned to the beginning. "As you know, Dad called me the day before he was killed. I was a legal consultant for the state prosecuting attorney back then, and Dad wanted me to check through my resources to see if I could find any info on one of his cold cases."

"Brighton Cooper," Luca readily supplied. "The young woman who was murdered five and a half years ago."

She made a sound of agreement. It didn't surprise her that Luca would remember that. Or know how much the unsolved murder had troubled her father. Luca had been a deputy for over a decade and had been on duty when the twenty-three-year-old waitress had been found stabbed to death in her apartment in Saddle Ridge. The case had gone cold, but the sheriff's office, and especially her father, had continued to investigate it.

Her mother, Sandra, had done some unofficial investigating as well since Brighton had been the daughter of Sandra's late friend, and Sandra knew that Brighton was often impulsive and prone to getting into trouble. Brighton also had a track record of getting involved with the wrong men.

Something that Bree could definitely relate to.

"Dad was frustrated that he hadn't been able to find anything new on Brighton," Bree went on, "and he knew I had access to a lot of different databases and law enforcement resources. He wanted me to see if anything about Brighton popped. *Anything*," she emphasized.

"Did you find something?" Luca asked.

"Not then. And maybe not now, either," she added in a mutter. "After Dad was killed, I continued to dig though."

It was hard for her to spell out, but the digging felt as if she was helping to fulfill her father's last wish. Added to that, diving into work temporarily helped her set aside the grief and her worries about her missing mother. Well, it had when she wasn't using those databases to hunt for her mom. Something she did at least weekly in case anything new turned up.

"For months, I did facial recognition searches, a lot of them, looking for any sign of Brighton," Bree went on. "And yesterday, I saw a woman I believe could be her on security camera footage of a fight outside a bar in Austin. The footage was recorded two nights before she was murdered, and the only reason it hadn't been erased was because the footage was used in a civil lawsuit."

"Brighton was assaulted in this bar fight?" Luca immediately wanted to know.

"No, if it was indeed her, then she was a bystander, along with about a dozen or so people who were trying to break up the fight that started inside the bar and then moved out onto the sidewalk. It was one of the men involved in the fight who filed the lawsuit."

A lawsuit he'd lost and then had posted the footage on social media.

"I contacted the officers who were called in," Bree continued, "but neither of them took a witness statement from anyone matching Brighton's description so I'm guessing she left before they arrived on scene. The man who filed the lawsuit didn't remember her either."

Bree's phone rang, and she groaned when she saw her sister's name on the screen. Joelle would have almost certainly heard about the accident by now and would want to know how she was doing. And Bree would tell her. First though, she had to finish filling in Slater and Luca so she let the call go to voicemail.

"Using facial recognition, I matched another face in the bar crowd footage to a bartender and contacted her," Bree went on, trying to hurry since they'd be at her house soon, and she had so much to tell them. "She didn't recall seeing Brighton so I dropped by the bar and spoke to the owner to ask him to give me receipts for that night. He said it would take a while since it was years ago but that he'd get them for me."

"We checked Brighton's credit card," Slater reminded her. "And she hadn't recently charged anything at a bar."

Bree made a sound of agreement. "I wanted to see if I recognized any names of customers who might link to Brighton."

"Did you?" Luca asked.

"I don't have the list yet. But this morning I got a call from the bar owner, and he said someone tried to run him off the road."

Both Slater and Luca cursed. "I want his name," Slater demanded.

"Manny Vickery," she quickly provided. "He owns the Hush, Hush bar in downtown Austin. It's one of those not-so-secret trendy gin joints. Not seedy though, and I didn't uncover anything illegal going on there."

"But someone tried to kill both him and you," Slater was equally quick to point out.

Hearing it spelled out like that gave her a new jolt of fear and worry. Bree wanted to believe it was all a really bad coincidence. Or an accident. If it'd only been Manny's incident, she could have believed that, but coupled with hers, both attempts had to be intentional.

But who had done this?

It was something she needed to find out and soon.

"What did Manny say when he called you this morning?" Slater asked.

It wasn't hard for her to recall it since she'd mentally gone over the conversation several times. "Manny told me he was driving to the bar from his house, which is apparently in a rural area about twenty miles outside of Austin. He was on an isolated road when a silver truck rammed into his car from behind. The truck had one of those rhino bumpers and tried to push him off the road. Manny said he managed to keep control, and the driver of the truck sped off when another car came along."

"Did he get the license plate?" Luca wanted to know.

She shook her head. "He said he was too shocked by what'd happened to even think of looking at the plate."

"Was he hurt?" Luca pressed.

Bree shook her head again. "And his car only had some minor damage. He reported it to the local cops," she added since Bree knew that would be Luca's or her brother's next question. "Manny said he'd spoken to the cops right before he called me. He wanted to know if someone was after him because he was gathering those receipts for me. I said I wasn't sure. And I'm not," she quickly tacked on to that. "I'm not sure of a lot of things."

"You were on your way to see this Manny Vickery when someone tried to run you off the road?" Luca pressed.

Bree nodded. "And, yes, I've considered that Manny knew

I was coming so he could have said something to someone who was waiting for me. Or he could have done it himself if he lied about being attacked and wants me to back off the investigation."

They sat in silence for a moment, all of them obviously processing this. "I'll need to check your car," Slater finally said. "If the silver truck broadsided you, there could be some paint flecks we can use to try to trace the vehicle. I'll need to check the bar owner's vehicle as well."

Luca stopped the cruiser at the end of her driveway, and he turned in the seat to face her. "I'll also make some calls and see if anyone's brought in a vehicle like that for repair. I could ask around, too, to see if anyone spotted it in the area." He paused. "You didn't want to say anything about this in front of Dr. Bagley. Why?"

She had so hoped not to get into this, but Bree doubted Luca was just going to drop it, and if she tried to stonewall him, it might make him dig for the answer on his own.

"Because Nathan has been pressuring me to go out with him, and I didn't want to give him any excuse to…insinuate himself into my life."

She stopped, groaned, and knew she obviously had to spell that out a little better.

"As you know, Nathan and I briefly dated a couple of years ago when I was home for the summer, and when I broke things off, he didn't take it well. He kept calling and texting, kept sending me flowers. When I went back to Dallas, he showed up at my office there, and I had my version of a showdown with him. I made it clear he'd better back off."

As expected, Luca and Slater cursed. It was Luca who responded though. "And you didn't tell us he was stalking you?"

"No, because it stopped." Bree locked gazes with Luca's

intense brown eyes and went ahead with her explanation. "Added to that, I wouldn't have felt comfortable blabbing to you because of our history together."

Luca's jaw tightened. "It's not blabbing. It's reporting a stalker to a cop." He stopped, muttered more profanity. "If you didn't want to tell me, you could have gone to one of the other deputies. Or to the Dallas PD. You should have said something both back then and today. By that, I mean, you could have asked for another doctor instead of being treated by a man who stalked you."

She'd considered doing that. Mercy, had she, but Bree had just wanted to get the stitches and get out of there. She certainly hadn't wanted to dish up any of what'd happened since it would have ended up being juicy gossip. Even though she had no idea what was going on, Bree figured it was best to work this quietly behind the scenes.

"There's more," Bree went on, and this part was not going to be easy. "After I saw the woman I believe was Brighton on the video, I expanded the search to other cameras in the vicinity. Of course, most had been erased since it was over five years ago, but I found this."

She pulled up a picture on her phone and realized her hand was shaking when she held it up for Slater and Luca to see.

"It's footage of that same fight outside the Hush, Hush, but it was filmed by another customer who also posted it on social media." She paused. Had to. "I examined the footage frame by frame and saw this." She used her fingers to enlarge the still image she'd culled from the video.

"Hell," Slater said, and he not only moved in even closer, he took the phone from her, repeated his single word of profanity and then handed it to Luca.

Luca shook his head. "That's your mother."

Yes, it was, and when Luca handed her back her phone,

she took yet another look at it. Because she was in the mix of the other bystanders, only her face was visible, but it was enough for Bree to see the familiar short brown hair, and the eyes and mouth that were so much like Bree's own features.

Either her mother had a doppelgänger, or that was indeed Sandra McCullough.

"I don't recall Mom ever mentioning going to a bar in Austin," Slater muttered.

Nor had Bree. And their mother hadn't seemed to be the bar-going type. Then again, maybe she hadn't actually been in the Hush, Hush. It was possible she had just been walking by and had been filmed.

But it didn't feel like that.

This felt like some kind of important clue. But what? This had happened five and a half years ago, long before Bree's father had been murdered and her mother had disappeared.

"This morning, I went back through Mom's old credit card statements," Bree added. "No charges to the bar or anywhere else in Austin. And since Mom's not around, I obviously can't ask her about it."

"You're not thinking Mom had something to do with Brighton's death?" Slater questioned.

"I can't think that," Bree admitted in a whisper.

She couldn't wrap her head around her mother committing a crime of any kind. But then, Bree knew she wasn't impartial about this.

"I'd like to check on Gabriel now," she murmured.

Luca stared at her. And stared. She wasn't immune to that look. Nor to him. And that caused her to silently curse. She couldn't handle another on-off with Luca. No bandwidth for it. Even though she couldn't deny that the heat would always be there between them.

"You two can go in and see Gabriel," Slater suggested.

"I'll drive the cruiser to the crash site and look around. And I want to check out Bree's car. After I get back, we can figure out how to handle the rest of this."

Yes, *handling* was indeed required, and it wouldn't be just the three of them for long. They'd need to brief Joelle and her husband, Sheriff Duncan Holder. And Bree's other brother, Ruston, who was a San Antonio cop. All of them would want to know what'd happened and if it was connected to Brighton's and her father's murders.

Luca drove along the driveway to the house and parked near the porch. A reminder that he didn't want her to be out in the open any longer than necessary. And that was a reminder that she could be in danger. Bree wanted to hang on to that "could be," but she didn't plan on taking any unnecessary risks either. That's why she hurried into the house after she used her phone to unlock the front door.

"It's me," Bree immediately called out to let Coral know she was there.

As soon as Luca and she stepped in, Bree closed and relocked the door. Moments later, Bree heard footsteps coming from the laundry room.

"Didn't figure you'd be back this soon," Coral said, coming into the entry. She was carrying a clothes basket, and the baby monitor was on top of the folded pile of laundry.

As usual, Coral was wearing loose sweatpants and a T-shirt that was equally loose, and she'd pulled up her dark blonde hair into a messy ponytail. She had one of those faces that made her look a good decade younger than her thirty-eight years.

"Oh, hi, Luca," Coral greeted. "Gabriel's still napping," she said, smiling. At least she was smiling until she saw Bree's face.

Coral gasped. "You're hurt."

"A minor car accident," Bree was quick to say. "I'm fine, really."

But she would need to say plenty more because she wanted Coral included in that better-safe-than-sorry mode. It sickened her to think of that truck driver coming here, but it was too risky not to prepare for it. That meant locked doors and using the security system. The house was rigged with one, but normally Bree only turned it on at night. That would change.

"You're sure you're okay?" Coral pressed.

"Yes. It's just a few stitches." Which were starting to sting now that the numbing meds were wearing off.

Bree glanced at the baby monitor and checked the time. Since she'd put Gabriel down for his morning nap before she'd left, that meant he'd been asleep for nearly three hours. That was slightly longer than his usual, but then his sleep pattern was nowhere near consistent.

"I was going to put this laundry away and go take a peek at him," Coral explained, and she handed Bree the camera monitor.

Gabriel was indeed still asleep in his crib, and just seeing that precious face performed some magic. Bree felt some of her nerves start to melt away.

"He'll probably want a bottle soon," Coral remarked. "You want me to go ahead and fix that so Luca can feed him?"

That had more or less become their routine. Luca had been coming over daily to give Gabriel at least one bottle, sometimes two. Bree hadn't been able to nurse because of a nasty bout of mastitis when Gabriel had only been a week old, so that meant she hadn't needed to be in the nursery during those feedings.

A good thing.

She'd learned the hard way that too much time with Luca

triggered the memories of their last night together, which in turn triggered memories of her father's murder. It was ironic that her son didn't have that same effect on her despite Gabriel being the spitting image of Luca.

"Yes, please make the bottle," Bree instructed, and she was about to head to the nursery when Luca touched her.

She jolted when his fingers brushed over hers, but then she realized he wasn't actually touching her. He was taking the monitor, and he had his attention pinned to it and not her.

Her nerves returned in full force. "Is something wrong?"

Luca shook his head, but the gesture didn't seem very convincing. "Look," he said, pointing to the screen. She saw a bird zoom past one of the nursery windows.

"A blue jay," she muttered and was about to dismiss it. Then, a few seconds later, a bird flew past again.

No. Not "a" bird. It appeared to be the same bird, flying at the exact speed and angle. This wasn't live feed but rather a recorded loop.

Bree bolted toward the nursery. Luca was right behind her, and he actually passed her before she reached the nursery door. He threw it open, and together they rushed into the room.

And her heart stopped. Just stopped.

Because the crib was empty.

Chapter Three

Everything inside Luca froze. At first, his mind couldn't register what he was seeing, and then the reality slammed into him.

The baby was gone.

"Where is he?" Bree asked, the panic rising in her voice. "Where's Gabriel?" She ran to the crib, and since there were no toys, pillows or blankets, it was easy to see it was empty. Still, Bree felt around the sheet as if she expected him to be there.

The cop in Luca kicked in, and he took hold of Bree to pull her back. If someone had taken Gabriel, then he needed to try to preserve any evidence.

If someone had taken Gabriel.

Those words knifed into him, robbing him of his breath and nearly sending him to his knees. But none of those reactions were going to help this situation, and he tried to focus on fixing this. On finding his precious son.

"What happened?" Coral asked as she ran into the room. She gasped and put her fingers to her mouth when she saw the empty crib.

"Where's Gabriel?" Bree demanded. "Why isn't he here?"

Coral frantically shook her head. "He has to be here. You put him in the crib and left for your meeting."

Luca fired glances around the room, taking it all in, but other than the missing baby, he didn't see anything out of place. There were no signs of a break-in, and the windows were all closed.

While Coral and Bree ran to search the closet, Luca looked at the baby monitor again. On the screen, Gabriel was exactly where he was supposed to be, and the sickening realization hit him. This was a loop, a repeated recording of when Gabriel had actually been sleeping in the crib.

And that meant someone had hacked the monitor.

"We need to search the rest of the house and the grounds," Luca insisted, taking out his phone to call the dispatcher. "This is Deputy Vanetti. I need backup." He rattled off Bree's address. The next part wasn't nearly as easy to say. "Issue an Amber Alert."

He heard the sound, not footsteps, but a heart-crushing moan, and he knew it had come from Bree. She wasn't crying, not yet anyway, but that would no doubt soon happen.

"Search the other bedrooms," he told her and then shifted to Coral. "You look through the rest of the house. Check to see if any windows are open." Since it wasn't a huge place, that wouldn't take much time.

The grounds though were another matter.

This wasn't a small city lot by any means. The house that had once belonged to Bree's grandparents was situated on about a dozen acres with a barn and pastures for horses. He would need backup to cover the entire area, and every minute counted right now. Especially since there were two country roads within a quarter of a mile of the place.

"Coral, were the doors all locked?" Luca called out as he headed toward the kitchen so he could access the back porch.

Coral hurried into the kitchen with him, but she was clearly still in shock, and it took her several seconds to answer. "I think so. I don't know," she amended with a sob. "Where is he? Did someone take him?"

Someone clearly had, but Luca didn't voice that. Wasn't sure he could. He definitely didn't want to think of his son in the hands of someone who might hurt him.

"What about keys?" Luca pressed, trying to tamp down his own building panic. He drew his gun but prayed he didn't need it. "Who has keys to the place?"

Coral shook her head again, and their conversation must have gotten Bree's attention because she, too, hurried into the kitchen. "Me and my family," Bree said. "Coral, too, of course."

Since her family members were all cops, they'd likely kept the keys secure. He'd need to make sure Coral had done the same. For now though, Luca checked the back door for himself. His gut clenched, and he cursed under his breath.

Because it was not only unlocked, it was slightly ajar.

"Did you leave this open?" he asked.

"I didn't," Coral said.

"Neither did I," Bree insisted, "but I can't swear it was locked either. I had my coffee out there this morning, and I got distracted by the phone call from Manny."

Now, the tears came, flooding her eyes, and Luca wished he had time to comfort her, to try to reassure her that they would find their baby. But time was critical now so he used his elbow to open the door wider in the hopes he wouldn't destroy any prints that might have been left there. Then, he hurried out onto the porch.

He understood why Bree would want to have her coffee out here. The October temps weren't scorching hot as they could sometimes be in this part of Texas, and there was a picture-postcard view of the still green pastures, a pond and two grazing horses. But there was nothing picturesque about it for Luca at the moment. He took it in like a crime scene.

And he cursed again when he saw nothing out of the ordinary.

He needed clues. Evidence. He needed anything that would point him in the right direction to where his son had been taken. Then, he could catch up with the kidnapper and get Gabriel back.

"Don't go in that part of the yard," he instructed when Bree headed down the porch steps. "There might be footprints."

Since it probably wasn't a route a kidnapper would have used, Luca ran to the side of the porch and checked the yard below. As expected, there were no indications anyone had recently walked here so he vaulted over the railing, dropping down the three or so feet to the soft ground.

"Did you get any visitors this morning?" he asked while he searched that side of the house. Nothing visible there either, but there were shrubs so he had a close look around those.

"No," Bree answered. Luca heard the sound of footsteps behind him and saw that she, too, had jumped over the porch railing. "I only got that phone call from Manny."

Yes, that. Luca certainly hadn't forgotten about it. Or about Bree's, and possibly Manny's, run-ins with a truck driver who might or might not have wanted them dead. It was probably all connected.

But how?

If those attempts had been some kind of threat to ward them off, then why hadn't they gotten a lesser warning? A *back off or else*. Maybe because their attackers and the kidnapper hadn't wanted to alert them as to why this was happening. As a cop though, he had to believe this was connected to Brighton's murder. It didn't seem like a coincidence that all of this had started shortly after Bree had come across that video.

"Coral, did you see any vehicles near the house after Bree left?" he called out while he ran to the front porch so he could check it. Bree was right behind him.

"No," the nanny was quick to say. "I swear, nothing happened, and I didn't see or hear anything."

He believed her, but she had obviously been in the laundry room, and it was on the other side of the house from the nursery. If the washer or dryer had been going while she was in there, Coral might not have heard someone come in through the back door and take the baby.

There was a problem with that theory though.

A stranger would have had to search through the house for Gabriel. Of course, that search could have happened by peering through the windows, but Luca wasn't seeing any signs of footprints to indicate that. There was also the question of where a kidnapper would have parked so that Coral wouldn't have noticed.

Luca immediately shifted his attention to the barn.

"You think Gabriel's in there?" Bree asked, obviously following Luca's gaze.

"I can't rule it out," he settled for saying. "I want to check the other side of the house first," he added and headed in that direction just as his phone rang.

Because his mind was narrowed in on Gabriel, his first thought was that this was the kidnapper with a ransom or some other demand. But it was Slater's name on the screen.

"What the hell's going on?" Slater immediately demanded. "There's an Amber Alert?"

"Gabriel's missing. I don't know who, why or how," he added while he combed the side of the house for any potential clues. "When Bree and I went inside her house, he was gone, and it's possible he was taken as long as three hours ago."

Bree made another of those ragged sobs, and Luca knew she was thinking the same thing as he was. If it'd been that long, if the kidnapper had taken Gabriel within minutes of Bree leaving the house, then their baby could be anywhere. Three hours was a lifetime when it came to something like this.

"I'm on my way," Slater insisted. "I'll call Duncan, Joelle and Ruston and fill them in."

That meant the four of them would also soon be on their way here, too. Well, maybe not Joelle since she was on maternity leave and had a baby of her own. Still, she would likely find a way to join the others. So would any available deputy. And Luca had to believe that would be enough help for them to find and recover Gabriel.

"Uh, how's Bree?" Slater asked. "Never mind. She's a wreck. I'll be there soon," he added before he ended the call.

Bree was indeed a wreck. She was strong and had survived going through hell and back, but that didn't mean she couldn't break. This was enough to break even the strongest person. That's why he needed to help her focus on the things that could be done rather than letting the fear take over. Luca tried to do the same for himself.

"Look for any signs of footprints," he instructed. "Especially beneath the windows."

She did, pinning her gaze to the ground as they hurried along the side of the house, but there was nothing to indicate the kidnapper had been here.

"Stay right behind me as we go through the backyard," he told her. Because there was a strong possibility of footprints being there.

"We're going to the barn," she muttered.

They were, and Luca knew it wouldn't do any good to ask Bree to stay in the house while he did that. If their situations had been reversed, he sure as hell wouldn't have stayed put and neither would she.

But it could be dangerous.

If they cornered a kidnapper, then Gabriel's captor might do anything and everything to escape. Still, there was no other option, not even waiting for backup. Luca intended to do everything possible to find his son now, and then he'd have to deal with whatever they were about to face.

"Look for tracks," he reminded her.

Luca did the same, but he didn't take the direct route across the yard. He stayed on the perimeter, hurrying, while he made his way through the flower beds and shrubs and toward the barn. They reached the wide metal gate, and Luca slowed down to check for footprints.

And he saw something.

Of course, that something could be Bree's own tracks since he knew she tended her two horses. Still, Luca skirted around them, climbing over the fence and approaching the barn from the side.

"Are the barn doors usually shut like this?" he asked Bree in a whisper.

"Yes. I open them if bad weather is coming."

Since there was no such weather in the forecast, then this was the norm, but Luca hoped Gabriel's abductor had ducked in and shut them. That way, his son would be nearby, and he'd be within seconds of finding him.

The horses whickered and lifted their heads, but they must have picked up Bree's scent because they went back to grazing. Luca and Bree went past them and ran to the barn. There were no footprints on the side of it. None that Luca could see anyway, but there were also enough patches of grass that anyone could have used them like stepping stones.

When he reached the door, Luca lifted the latch to ease it open, and he winced at the creaking sound it made. No way to sneak it with that noise. Then again, the spears of sunlight would have alerted anyone inside, too.

They stepped in, and Luca paused so his eyes could adjust to the dim light and so he could listen for any sounds. Nothing.

Not at first anyway.

Then, he heard something or someone rustling. It came from the far corner of the barn where there were some stacks of hay bales. Bree must have heard it as well because her attention zoomed in that direction while she took hold of a muck fork rake that was propped against the wall. It wasn't a gun, but it could be an effective weapon if it came down to it.

Luca was praying it didn't.

Keeping his footsteps as light as possible, he made his way toward those bales. Not approaching them directly where Bree and he would be easy targets. Again, he kept them to the side of the barn so he could approach from the side.

Of course, there might not be a kidnapper. The sound could have come from a mouse or some other critter that had gotten inside. Still, Luca moved as if their lives depended on it.

Since they could.

Luca stopped when he heard another sound. More rustling. Followed by what could be a whimper. That got Bree and him moving even faster, and he had his gun aimed and ready when they reached the stack of hay bales. Bree moved to his side, the muck fork raised.

And then they both froze.

There, seated on the floor was a woman, and she had Gabriel cradled in her arms. Not a stranger. Far from it.

Because the woman was someone who'd been missing and presumed dead for nearly a year.

Bree's mother.

Chapter Four

Bree's breath stalled in her throat, and the only sound she managed to make was a strangled gasp of raw shock. That shock anchored her feet in place. Her mind, too. She just couldn't grasp what she was seeing.

Her mother.

With Gabriel.

What the heck was her mother doing here in the barn, and why had she stolen Gabriel?

Her mother didn't say anything. She just stared at Bree with her own stunned silence. She was pale. No color except for some red scratches on her right cheek. Her hair looked as if it hadn't been combed in a very long time.

Gabriel made a sound, a soft whimper that yanked Bree right out of her stupor. Her maternal instincts kicked in. Mercy, did they. The boiling anger and urgent need to protect her baby slammed through her, and despite who was holding him—a woman she'd once loved and trusted—everything inside her screamed for her to get to her son.

Bree flung the muck fork aside to hurry to Gabriel. She didn't even acknowledge the woman holding him. Bree just reached down and took him.

Her mother didn't resist. Just the opposite. Her grip on Gabriel melted away as Bree's own grip gathered him into her arms. Cradling Gabriel against her chest, Bree stepped back.

Luca moved in front of Gabriel and her. Protecting them. And giving Bree a jolt of a different kind. Luca and she were a unit. Parents. Together. For this nightmare anyway. Even though she was holding their son, the fear of him being kidnapped was causing adrenaline to fire through her, and the only person who could understand what she was feeling right now was Luca.

Or rather, he could understand what she was feeling about finding their son.

He probably couldn't grasp what she was going through over seeing her mother. Then again, Bree couldn't quite grasp it either.

"You're hurt," her mother said. "Were you attacked?"

Bree had forgotten about her fresh stitches and the nicks on her face, and it definitely wasn't a high priority for discussion right now. "You took my son," Bree managed to say.

Her mother nodded, and tears spilled from her already red eyes. "Yes. To protect him."

Nothing about this felt like protection. But Bree immediately rethought that. Just an hour or so ago, someone had run her off the road and had possibly tried to kill her. Was that connected to her mother?

"To protect him," Luca repeated. "Explain that," he snapped, and it was obvious from his tone that he was still getting some adrenaline jolts of his own. Equally obvious, too, was that he wasn't just going to dole out a welcome home to the woman who'd stolen their child.

Her mother opened her mouth but didn't get a chance to answer before there was the sound of running footsteps. "Bree?" Slater called out. "Luca? Where the hell are you?"

"Here," Luca said.

That brought on more running footsteps, and he wasn't alone. Coral was with him.

"Did you find…" Slater's words trailed off when he saw them. He, too, had his weapon drawn, and his gaze swept from Gabriel to Luca and Bree.

And then to his mother.

Slater shook his head, clearly not able to process what he was seeing. Coral was having a similar reaction. The nanny didn't know Sandra well, but it was obvious she recognized her.

"What are you doing here?" Slater asked Sandra.

"Sandra's the one who took Gabriel," Luca supplied.

"I did it to protect him," her mother insisted. She moved to get to her feet, a gesture that caused Luca and Slater to take aim at her.

"Are you armed?" Luca demanded.

Luca and Slater were clearly treating her mother like a kidnapper, and Bree didn't object. Too many things weren't clear right now, and she didn't want Gabriel in any more danger than he might already be.

Her mother shook her head, and she lifted her hands while she stood. She staggered a little but kept her hands raised.

"I don't have a gun, and I wasn't going to hurt Gabriel," her mother said. Her face was a mix of shock and fear. "I'd never hurt him or any of you." She added that last part when she shifted her attention to Slater.

Slater swallowed hard. "What are you doing here? Where have you been all this time?"

Those were both very good questions, but Bree had another question of her own. "Why did you feel the need to kidnap my son to protect him?" She didn't ask it nicely either, not with the terror of nearly losing her son still coursing through her.

The sigh that left her mother's mouth was long and weary. "Because someone else was going to take him."

"Who?" Luca and Bree asked in unison.

Sandra shook her head. "I don't know." She repeated that while she shook her head again and continued to cry. She took a step toward them, staggered a little and caught onto the barn wall.

"Are you hurt?" Slater asked. He lowered his gun but didn't holster it.

"Just my ankle." Sandra squeezed her eyes shut for a moment. "I twisted it when I escaped."

Bree was trying to grasp each word her mother said. Trying to examine her body language, too. But *escaped* flashed like a neon sign in her head. Luca picked right up on it, too.

"Escaped from who and from what?" Luca still sounded like a cop interrogating a suspect.

Again, her mother didn't get a chance to answer because there was a shout from outside the barn. "Bree?" someone called out.

Joelle.

And judging from the sound of more footsteps, her sister wasn't alone. Bree was betting Duncan was with her. Moments later, she got confirmation of that when Joelle and Duncan hurried in. Since they didn't have their baby with them, Bree figured they'd left Izzie at home with the nanny.

"We came to help look for Gabriel," Joelle said.

Bree looked back at her sister. Their gazes connecting, for a couple of seconds anyway, before Joelle saw Gabriel in her arms. Relief flooded her face, but it, too, passed quickly when Joelle's attention landed on Sandra.

"Mom," Joelle muttered on a rise of breath. Unlike the rest of them, Joelle didn't stand back. Just the opposite. She hurried to their mother and pulled her into her arms.

"She could have a gun," Bree was quick to point out.

Joelle's shoulders went stiff, and she shifted from worried daughter to cop in a blink. She stepped back, way back, volleying glances at Slater and Bree. "What's going on?" Joelle asked.

Bree wanted to know the same thing. Clearly, so did Duncan, Luca and Slater, but Slater obviously wanted to make sure they weren't about to be attacked.

"I'll check her for weapons," Slater volunteered, stepping forward.

Joelle's mouth dropped open, and it seemed as if she was about to object to their mother being frisked. She didn't though. It must have occurred to her that they needed a whole lot of answers before they could trust the woman who'd given birth to them.

"She's not armed," Slater relayed. "She doesn't have a phone or a wallet. Just some keys." Slater lifted out the keys and held them in the air. "There's one here marked with a B."

Bree was pretty sure that was the key to her house. Her mother had had one like that anyway. But Bree didn't recognize the rest of the keys. Or the clothes her mother was wearing. Loose jogging pants and a baggy T-shirt. Definitely not her mom's usual fashion choices, especially since she was barefoot. And she'd clearly lost some weight. All possible signs of, well, Bree couldn't be certain, but she wanted to know.

"What happened?" Duncan demanded. "Is Sandra the one who kidnapped Gabriel?"

Luca nodded. "She hacked into the baby monitor—"

"No," her mother interrupted. "I didn't do that. The kidnapper did."

That got their attention, and all of them pinned their attention on Sandra. She sighed again. "Eleven and a half months ago, I was kidnapped, and I've been held all this time."

Bree had to admit that fit with her mom's appearance. Well, maybe it did. But it could also fit with someone who'd been on the run.

"Did you kill Dad?" Bree came out and asked.

Her mother's eyes widened. "No." She sounded stunned but adamant. "Of course not." The tears began to spill again, and a hoarse sob tore from her throat. "I think the person who took me killed him."

"And who would that be?" Slater demanded.

Sandra shook her head. "I don't know."

Bree and Slater both groaned, but Duncan cursed. Maybe because of Sandra's answer but also because his phone dinged with a text.

"Someone reported seeing a silver truck that matches the description of the one we're looking for," Duncan relayed. "It was near here."

Bree automatically pulled Gabriel even closer to her. Oh, mercy. Had the hit-and-run driver come back for another attack?

"I drove a silver truck here," her mother volunteered.

Again, that got their attention. Not that it had strayed too far from her mother. "You're the one who ran me off the road?" Bree asked.

Her mother flinched. "No." She used that same adamant tone. "I drove the truck here, that's all, and I parked it on a ranch trail." She pressed trembling fingers to her mouth for a moment. "Did someone try to hurt you?"

"Someone did hurt me by running me off the road so I'd crash into a tree," Bree clarified. "And that someone was driving a silver truck."

Sandra staggered back and sank down onto the floor. "I

didn't do that. I wouldn't do that," she amended. "But my kidnapper would."

"I'll want to hear all about the kidnapper," Duncan stated. "For now, tell me where you parked the silver truck."

Sandra fluttered her fingers toward the pasture. "It's on the old ranch trail just on the other side of the fence. I left it there and walked to the house."

"Because you didn't want the nanny or Bree to spot you?" Duncan pressed.

"No, because I didn't want the real kidnapper to see me," her mother was quick to say. "I wanted to get Gabriel away from the house before she had a chance to show up and take him." She stopped, her forehead bunching up. "I should have figured out another way. I shouldn't have scared you like this."

Bree glared at her. "Yes, you should have figured out another way. If you thought Gabriel was in danger, you should have called me."

Sandra shook her head. "I didn't have a phone, and when I didn't see your car in the driveway, I figured you weren't home."

"I wasn't here, but Coral the nanny was," Bree was equally quick to point out.

"Coral," she repeated, and her gaze drifted to the nanny. "The woman in the laundry room. I only saw her back so I didn't know who she was. I wasn't sure I could trust her so I decided better safe than sorry. I took Gabriel, sneaked out the back door and waited in the barn, hoping you'd show up and start looking for him."

Bree mentally went back through that. "You said you'd been held all this time so how did you even know about Gabriel?"

"From her. From the woman who held me," Sandra clarified. "I overheard her talking to someone about Bree and her baby. I don't know who she was talking to, but it was clear they were planning on kidnapping Gabriel."

"Who is this woman?" Duncan pressed.

"I don't know. I don't," Sandra insisted when Duncan groaned. "She always wore a mask whenever she was around. I didn't even know where I was until I escaped."

Now it was Bree's turn to groan when her phone rang, and she yanked it from her pocket and answered it without taking her attention off her mother. She instantly regretted not looking at the screen for the caller's ID though when she heard the man's voice.

Nathan.

"Bree," he said, and there was a frantic edge to that single word. "I just heard about your son being missing. I can come and help look for him."

"No," she couldn't say fast enough. She definitely didn't want to have to deal with the clingy Nathan right now. "We found him. He's safe."

And she hoped that was the truth. Hoped that her little boy wasn't still in danger. But if what her mother was saying was true, then he possibly could be.

"Oh, thank God," Nathan said, punctuating that with what sounded like a breath of relief. "Are you all right? You must have been shaken to the core when you realized he was missing."

"I was. And I'm fine," Bree added, ready to hang up.

Nathan spoke before she could. "I can come over and give the baby a checkup. You know, just to make sure he's really okay."

That gave her another jolt of fear. She hadn't checked Gabriel after she'd taken him from her mother, but she intended to do that now.

"I have to go," she told Nathan, and she ended the call so she could put her phone away and open Gabriel's onesie.

Her movements must have been frantic because Luca holstered his gun and moved closer to help her with the onesie zipper. Gabriel objected to that by frowning and whimpering, but other than that, there appeared to be nothing wrong with him. She wanted to do a more thorough check soon. First though, she needed to deal with her mother.

"I didn't hurt him," her mother insisted. "I wouldn't. I stopped him from being hurt. If the kidnapper had taken him…" She stopped, dragged in a few clipped breaths. "I don't know what would have happened. And I couldn't risk it." Sandra paused. "We should take the baby inside the house and I can tell you how I ended up here. I can tell you what happened to me."

Bree very much wanted to know that, but she didn't budge. Neither did the rest of them.

Duncan's phone dinged again, breaking the silence. "The CSIs are going with one of the deputies to locate the silver truck. If it's where Sandra says it is, then we should know within the hour if there are paint flecks on the truck that match Bree's and Manny's vehicles."

"Do you mean Manny Vickery?" Sandra asked. "The owner of the Hush, Hush bar in Austin?"

Once again, they all turned toward her mother. She had managed to surprise them once again. "You know him?" Luca asked.

Sandra nodded. "I talked to him when I was helping your dad investigate Brighton's murder." She stopped, gathered her breath and opened her mouth to continue.

The sound stopped Sandra cold. A loud blast. And Bree instantly knew what it was.

A gunshot.

Gabriel jolted from the sound and began to cry. Bree instinctively pulled him back to her body while she stooped to go to the floor.

Luca helped her with that. He got her down in a blink, positioned himself over them and drew his gun. Joelle, Slater and Duncan did the same, and they took cover behind the hay bales.

"Move away from the wall," Duncan told Sandra, and the woman scrambled closer to Joelle. Duncan then called for backup. "Carmen and Woodrow were already on their way out here to look for Gabriel," Duncan relayed to them a moment later. "They'll be here in less than five minutes."

Carmen Gonzales and Woodrow Leonard, both veteran deputies. Good. Bree wanted all the help they could get.

There was another blast, but it didn't seem to hit anything. At least Bree hoped it hadn't.

"I think both shots came from the direction of the road," Luca muttered. His gaze met Bree's for a split second, and she saw the renewed fear that was there. Fear for their son's safety.

She doubted the shots had come from a hunter who'd strayed too close to her place. Not with everything else that had gone on. Someone was after her, and that someone didn't care if they put her baby at risk. That both sickened her and terrified her. Bree could deal with someone coming after her. She was a cop's daughter after all. But she didn't want her baby involved in this.

Keeping low, Slater made his way to the barn door that was still open, and staying to the side, he peered out. "I don't see anyone, but if the shots are coming from the road, the shooter could be hiding in the trees."

There were certainly plenty of those by the country road. So many places for a gunman to hide. But maybe Carmen and Woodrow would be able to see the shooter when they arrived. Maybe they'd even be able to arrest him, and Bree might be able to get those answers she so desperately needed.

The seconds ticked by, and her heartbeat and breathing had just started to level when there was another gunshot. This one blasted through the wall of the barn, creating a hole where light speared through it.

Another shot.

This one tore through the barn as well and smacked into the wall on the opposite side. The shots weren't low but rather at the height if the target had been standing. That changed though because the next shot came in low. It ripped through yet more wood, sending splinters flying.

Bree ducked her head, putting her face right against Gabriel's to shelter him. He continued to cry, loud wails now because he was obviously afraid.

In the distance, she heard another sound. A police siren. Obviously, Carmen and Woodrow weren't going with a silent approach. Part of her was thankful for that because it might cause the shooter to stop. But it might also cause him to run.

Duncan's phone rang, and he answered it while he ran to the barn door next to Slater. "The deputies don't see a shooter or a vehicle on the road."

The vehicle could be on the ranch trail. Perhaps even the one where her mother had left the silver truck. But there were trails that threaded all through this area. What likely hadn't happened though was the shooter had come on foot. Her place was too far off the beaten path for that.

The wailing of the sirens got closer. But there were no more gunshots.

"Luca and Joelle, wait here with the others," Duncan instructed. "Slater will come with me. Stay put," he added to Bree.

She didn't ask what Duncan and her brother were doing. Because Bree knew. They were going to go in pursuit of the person who'd just tried to kill them.

Chapter Five

Luca set the bag of baby supplies on the floor next to the sofa in the break room of the sheriff's office where Coral was feeding Gabriel a bottle. Bree was right there, clearly not wanting to take her eyes off their son, but Luca also knew she would soon have to do that. Because there was no way she would miss her mother's interview.

Bree, her siblings and every cop in the building—including Luca—wanted to hear what Sandra had to say. It could be critical for not only the events of the past eleven months but also for what'd happened today. Bree being run off the road, Sandra taking Gabriel.

And the shooting.

That was at the top of Luca's list of things he needed to know. Since Duncan and Slater hadn't been able to find the shooter, it meant there was a possibility it could happen again. This time, they might not get so lucky, and someone could be hurt. Luca didn't intend to let that happen, and it was the reason he hadn't let Bree and Gabriel out of his sight since those shots had been fired into the barn.

Of course, he'd have to allow it eventually because he didn't want the baby in the interview room where tempers might flare, but Coral would stay just up the hall with Gabriel. No baby monitor, not after what'd happened to the one at Bree's. But if there was any trouble, Luca would be able to get to Gabriel in a matter of seconds.

"It's time?" Bree asked him.

Luca nodded. After they'd all arrived at the sheriff's office, Duncan had told them to take thirty minutes so they could get Coral and the baby settled. So they could settle their own nerves, too. That would also give Duncan time for an EMT to come in and give Sandra a quick exam. Other than some cuts and bruises and the sore ankle, Bree's mother hadn't seemed injured, but if she was telling the truth about being held captive for eleven months, then she needed at least a cursory exam that would no doubt be followed by a complete physical once she'd given her statement.

"Your mother, Slater, Joelle and Duncan are already in the interview room," Luca added. He knew that because he'd glanced in the room after he'd retrieved the baby supplies from Carmen, who'd picked them up from Bree's place. Everyone was sitting and waiting for the EMT to finish. "Ruston is on his way from San Antonio, but he said for us not to wait for him."

Since Ruston was a San Antonio detective, he understood the urgency of getting any and all info. In this case though, there were plenty of emotions mixed with that urgency. Yes, Sandra could possibly give them answers, but she was still Joelle, Bree, Slater and Ruston's mother. A woman who'd been missing for almost a year.

A woman who, despite her denial, could have murdered their father or at least have knowledge of that murder.

Yeah, no way to take the emotions out of that.

Bree brushed a kiss on the top of Gabriel's head. Luca did the same. And after giving their son one last look, they left to go to the interview room. Luca stopped just outside the closed door and looked at Bree to gauge how worried he should be about her.

Worried, he decided.

She looked exhausted and no doubt was. Spent adrenaline was a bear to deal with and sapped plenty of energy. Added to that, she still had those stitches from her car crash. There'd been way too little time for her to process that before they'd realized Gabriel was missing. Then, the gunshots had added to the hellish day.

And it wasn't over.

Bree still had to deal with her mother, and the nightmarish memories the woman's reappearance would stir up for her. Then, there was the part he'd go ahead and tell her now.

"I'm staying with Gabriel and you," Luca spelled out. "You can consider it protective custody, but I'm staying." He steeled himself for an argument where she could point out that one of her siblings could provide that protection.

But no argument came.

"Good," she muttered. "No one will protect Gabriel better than you."

"I feel the same way about you," he assured her.

Their gazes connected. Held. He saw the faith she had in him about this. And he hoped she saw the same in him. They would indeed do whatever it took to keep their son safe. But like a hit of adrenaline, there'd be a price to pay. The close quarters were going to test barriers that Bree likely didn't want tested. Still, no price was too high to pay for their little boy.

The door opened, breaking their connected gazes, and Luca and she stepped back so the EMT, Shaun Gafford, could come out. Luca knew him well since they'd been in the same grade at school.

"She's got some bruises on her arms, hands and legs,"

Shaun explained, "but other than that, she's good." He paused, looked at Bree. "How about you? You got meds in case those stitches start to throb?"

Bree nodded. "Dr. Bagley phoned in a script."

At the mention of Nathan's name, Luca remembered the call Bree had gotten from him shortly after they'd found Gabriel and her mother in the barn. Maybe Nathan had just been concerned about Bree and Gabriel, but after what Bree had revealed about the doctor's stalking, Luca made a mental note to keep tabs on Nathan to make sure he didn't resume those stalking attempts.

They stepped into the interview room that was a decent size, but usually there weren't this many people present. Duncan, Slater, Joelle, Sandra, Bree and him. Then again, there was nothing "usual" about this situation. Sandra was seated with Joelle by her side, but Duncan and Slater were standing. Bree and Luca stayed on their feet as well.

"I just got a call about the silver truck," Duncan said. "Woodrow and Carmen found it where Sandra said it would be. And they saw paint flecks on the bumper. It's being taken in now for processing. According to the plates, the vehicle belonged to a man named Alan Smith, but Woodrow says the guy's been dead for nearly a year now, and that his son sold the truck to a woman who paid cash for it. Woodrow has the buyer's name. But it's Ann Wilson so it's probably bogus."

Probably. But it was something Luca would check for himself.

"Still no sign of the shooter?" Bree wanted to know.

Duncan shook his head, and the frustration of that was all over his face. "But there were other tire tracks on the trail so it's possible the shooter parked there and then escaped after he or she fled." He made eye contact with Luca. "There were some indications that someone had tried to set fire to the silver truck."

Hell. Luca hoped no evidence had been destroyed. They needed anything and everything in that vehicle to help them make sense of what'd happened. He was hoping though that the making sense would start right now with Sandra.

"I'm going to Mirandize you," Duncan said, shifting his attention to Sandra.

Sandra didn't object. She only sighed as Duncan recited the warning. He followed that up by stating his name, the time and the names of others who were present. All very official, but it didn't mean Duncan was anticipating that he might have to arrest Sandra for anything. This was just a legal formality and a way of covering themselves.

"I didn't kill my husband," Sandra said the moment that Duncan had finished. Her voice cracked, and more tears filled her eyes. Joelle handed her mother a box of tissues that she took from the table. "Cliff was alive the last time I saw him," Sandra insisted.

"Start from the beginning," Duncan instructed as he took the seat across from her. "You said you were kidnapped. When and how were you taken?"

Sandra gathered her breath. "It was November first of last year. Cliff had already left for work, and I went to my home office to try to do more searches on Brighton. She'd been dead for four years by then, and Cliff was frustrated that he hadn't been able to find her killer. He wanted me to search through old social media posts to see if I could come up with something."

Cliff had asked Bree to dig as well. And Luca. So, Luca could attest to his former boss being frustrated. It was understandable, too, that he would ask his wife to help since Sandra and Brighton's late mom had been best friends.

"Someone knocked at the door while I was working," Sandra went on. "At first, I thought it was Cliff, that maybe he'd locked himself out or forgotten something since he'd only been gone about twenty minutes so I opened the door without looking. A woman wearing a ski mask jabbed me with a stun gun. She dragged me out of the house and into a car, and then she gave me some kind of injection in my arm that knocked me out."

Luca thought back to the scene of Cliff's murder. There'd been no signs of a struggle. No signs of Sandra either, and her purse and phone had been missing.

"Describe the woman and the car," Duncan said.

Sandra nodded, but then paused for a couple of seconds. "Like I said, she wore a mask so I never saw her face. But she was tall, maybe five foot ten, and she had an athletic build. She didn't have any trouble dragging me to the car. She just put me in and drove off."

"But she took your purse, keys and phone?" Luca questioned.

"Yes. I had my phone in my pocket, and she got that right away and took out the SIM card. But she also grabbed my purse, and it had my keys in it." She paused again. "I've had a lot of time to think about that, and I think she took my purse to make it look as if I'd voluntarily left. I didn't," she insisted. She repeated that while she made direct eye contact with Joelle, Bree and Slater.

"What happened after this woman kidnapped you?" Duncan pressed, clearly anxious to get some answers.

"I'm not sure how long I was unconscious," Sandra admitted. "When I woke up, I was in a bedroom with log walls, and it was attached to a small bathroom. There was a window in the bedroom, but it'd been boarded up." She stopped, shook her head. "Believe me when I say I tried to tear off those boards, but I was never able to do that."

"Where was this place?" Duncan asked.

Sandra pulled in another of those long breaths. "I didn't know at the time, but after I escaped in the silver truck, I realized the cabin was only about twenty-five miles from here. It's off an old farm road between Bulverde and the Guadalupe River." Her eyes went wide. "It'll be in the GPS. I didn't know where I was, but the GPS was working so I told it to navigate to Bree's address."

Duncan took out his phone and made a quick call to Woodrow, instructing him to check the truck's GPS right away and then to have local cops go out to the scene immediately.

"Okay," Duncan said to Sandra when he'd finished with the call. "Go back to the kidnapper. You're sure you never saw her face, never got any indications as to who she was?"

"I'm sure," Sandra insisted. She stopped, and it seemed as if for several moments, she got lost in the memories of what'd happened. "She only came in every three days or so, and one time she brought me a newspaper with the article about Cliff. That's how I learned my husband was dead." Her voice broke. "I read about in a newspaper that horrible woman brought me. Did she kill him?" Sandra asked.

Most of them shook their heads. Bree went with a verbal response. "We don't know. We're all investigating it. Did the woman ever say anything about Dad?"

"Nothing. Just that article. I asked…no, I begged her for more information. I begged her to let me go, to tell me why she was holding me. She never answered." There was a world of genuine heartbreak in her words, and Luca didn't think any part of it was fake.

"Did your captor stay there with you the whole time?" Duncan asked, obviously shifting the interview back to the abduction.

Sandra shook her head. "No, she wasn't around that much. Like I said, she'd come every two to three days and always had on a mask. She'd put a bag of groceries in my room. Sandwich stuff and chips mainly. Toiletries, sometimes." She wiped away more tears. "A couple of times, I tried to jump her when she came in, but she always had the stun gun with her and would hit me with it."

"Not this last time though," Luca reminded her.

"No," Sandra murmured. She stopped when Duncan's phone dinged with a text.

"Woodrow called the county sheriff's office, and they're sending out deputies now to check the cabin," Duncan relayed after he read the message.

Good. The sooner they got there, the better, and with any luck, the kidnapper would still be there so they could arrest her.

"You were telling us about how today's encounter with your captor was different from other times," Duncan prompted.

"Yes," Sandra verified. "A couple of times before today, I'd heard her talking on the phone to someone. It sounded as if she was getting instructions or orders because she said things like, 'I can do that' and 'Understood.' The call I heard today though was different." Her voice cracked again.

"How?" Duncan pressed.

"She said she was worried about someone noticing the damage to the truck, that she didn't want to be pulled over by some local yokel when she went after the kid. Then, I heard her say Bree's address, like she was repeating it to make sure she had it right." A bite of anger trickled into her voice. "She said she'd get out there and get the kid before Bree was back from the hospital." Sandra shifted her gaze to Bree. "I didn't even know you'd had a baby."

Bree nodded. "Gabriel. He's two months old, and Luca's his father." She didn't add more, but Luca could see for himself that Sandra was working this out in her head. Especially the fact that Gabriel had been conceived shortly after Cliff's murder.

"Duncan and I have a daughter," Joelle said. "Elizabeth Grace. We call her Izzie. You can meet her after, well, after," she settled for saying. "For now, we need to know how you ended up at Bree's and anything else you can tell us about what happened to you."

Sandra stared at Joelle for a moment, and there was another flood of emotions. One that looked as if it might cause Sandra to lose it, but she reined herself in and continued. "When I overheard the woman saying she was going to take Bree's baby, I knew I had to do something. I couldn't let my grandbaby be taken and locked up like I was."

Now the rage flared in Sandra's eyes. Luca had rarely seen any show of temper from her over the years, but it was there now.

"I crammed everything I could into the last plastic grocery bag she'd dropped off two days earlier," Sandra explained. "My shoes, toothpaste, even the bar of soap, and when she came in, I bashed her upside the head with it. She fell, the stun gun clattering to the floor so I used it on her. While she was jittering and flopping around, I ran. The truck was parked out front, and the keys were in the ignition so I got in and drove away as fast as I could."

"You didn't think to take off her mask and see who she was?" Duncan asked.

"No. I just ran. I had to get to Bree's. I had to save her baby."

Duncan shook his head. "But if you took your captor's truck, then why did you believe she would still come after Gabriel?"

"I thought once she was able to move, she'd call her boss or partner and that he or she would rush to Bree's and take Gabriel. I couldn't risk that." Sandra stopped again to wipe away more tears. "If she killed Cliff, I didn't want to think what she could do to a baby."

Neither did Luca, and if all of this was the truth, then Sandra had stopped something horrible from happening. Luca was beyond thankful for his son's safety. But without the identity of the kidnapper, there could possibly be another attempt to take him.

But why?

Did someone want to use Gabriel for leverage? If so, that brought Luca right back to another why? It was possible someone wanted to use him to sway the outcome of an investigation, but at the moment, there were only two unsolved murders on the books. Cliff's and Brighton's. So, did that mean one of them was connected to this?

"Why do you think this woman kidnapped you? Why did she want Gabriel?" Bree asked, taking the questions right out of Luca's mouth.

"I don't know," Sandra said through a hoarse sob. "I've obviously had plenty of time to think about it. To think about losing my husband, too. Did he suffer?" she asked Slater. "Did your dad suffer when he was killed?"

Slater shook his head. "The ME said death was almost instantaneous after he was shot."

Almost. Like Slater and the rest of his family, Luca had read the ME's report countless times, looking for anything that would lead them to his killer. So far, all they had was that someone had gunned down the sheriff, and he'd bled out.

"If the woman kidnapped me," Sandra went on, "she must have had something to do with Cliff's murder. Did she try to frame me? Did she do something to make me look guilty?"

"With you missing, you became a suspect," Duncan admitted. "But we also had to consider that the killer had murdered you as well."

Sandra flinched a little. "But she didn't kill me. Why?"

Again, the big question. Too bad they didn't have a good answer. But maybe there'd be clues in the cabin where she'd been held. Maybe in the silver truck, too.

"You said you used the stun gun on the woman who kidnapped you," Duncan continued. "So, she would have been incapacitated for a while. For at least five minutes. Was there another vehicle at the cabin that she could have used to come to Bree's and fire those shots?"

Sandra's forehead bunched up. "Maybe. I didn't look behind the cabin. I guess a car or motorcycle could have been parked back there. You think she's the one who tried to kill us?"

Duncan shrugged. "I'm considering it." He glanced down at a notepad. "Tell me about Manny Vickery," Duncan threw out there, obviously trying a different angle. "How well did you know him?"

"Not well at all. In fact, I've never met him. I just knew the name because I talked to Brighton a couple of weeks before she was killed, and she mentioned she'd been going to the Hush, Hush. She was upset, but the only thing she'd say about it was that things weren't going well with some man she'd been seeing. She was very upset," Sandra emphasized. "So, I went to the bar to see if I could find out what was going on."

"That's how you ended up on the video outside the Hush, Hush," Luca commented.

"Video?" Sandra questioned.

"Several people posted recordings of a fight, and I saw you on one of them," Bree explained. "I saw Brighton on another. It's possible though you weren't there at the same time, that Brighton left before you showed up." She stopped, gathered her breath. "Did you find out what was going on with Brighton when you went there?"

Sandra shook her head. "No. I talked to a couple of people, just to get a sense if anyone there knew Brighton. I talked to a bartender, Tara…"

"Tara Adler," Bree provided. "I spoke to her, too," she added when her mother gave her a questioning look. "She said she didn't know Brighton."

"She told me the same. I tried to talk to Manny, but he had Tara tell me he was too busy to see me. And there was that fight. A regular brawl, and it scared me so I left." She squeezed her eyes shut. "If I hadn't, if I'd stayed and found out what was going on with Brighton, she might still be alive."

"Wait," Sandra said a moment later. "You think Manny's the one who had me kidnapped? You think he had something to do with your father's murder?"

"We're looking into that," Duncan assured her. "We're looking into a lot of things. But in light of what happened to Bree and to you, I want you in protective custody. I could arrange for a safe house." Now it was Duncan who paused, and he looked at Joelle as if maybe confirming—or questioning—something they'd discuss.

Joelle nodded and turned to her mother. "You can go home if you'd like. Duncan, Izzie and I live there now."

What Joelle didn't spell out was that it was the place where her father had been killed. If Sandra had read the article about his death, she would know that, and it might not be easy for her to deal with it.

There was another side to this situation though. Luca believed Sandra was telling the truth about her abduction, but there were still plenty of blank spots as to what had happened. And why.

Especially why.

Sandra apparently wondered that as well, and she came up with the same concern that Luca and Duncan had. "I want to be there with you. All of you," she amended, glancing at Slater, Duncan, Bree and Luca. "But what if that woman comes after me again? It'd put you in danger."

No one could dispute that. As long as her captor was at large, the threat was there. And not solely for a kidnapping either. Those shots were proof that this person could and would kill. If the woman hadn't been the shooter, then the likely suspect was the person she'd been talking to on the phone. So, two people who could come at them anytime, anyplace.

"We'd have to take precautions," Duncan said. "Lots of them."

"One possibility is that Slater and I could be at the ranch with you," Joelle explained. She glanced at Slater, and he nodded, indicating this was something they'd already discussed. No doubt when Bree had been in the break room with Coral, Gabriel and him. "We could also ask one of the reserve deputies to stay with us as backup."

Duncan's attention shifted to Bree. "But you're in danger, too. Which means so is Gabriel."

Yeah, Luca had already gone there. Obviously, so had Bree because she made a quick sound of agreement.

"We could all be at the ranch," Joelle spelled out. "All," she emphasized, glancing at Luca. "We could conduct the investigation from there while putting security measures in place."

Luca thought of the McCullough ranch and the house. It was big, with five bedrooms, but there were a lot of adults and two babies. Added to that mix would be Sandra, a woman he wanted to trust but wasn't sure he could.

Bree turned to Luca, and she lifted her eyebrow. "Well?"

"I'll be wherever Gabriel and you are," he assured her.

Bree nodded. "All right. Then, we'll all go to the ranch."

He heard the worry in her voice. Saw it even more on her face. And he knew something else. Bree hadn't been back there since her father's murder so this was going to be an emotional avalanche. Then again, the same could be true for Sandra.

Slater took out his phone. "I'll make arrangements for Gabriel's baby things to be moved to the ranch."

Luca would need to pack a few things as well, but before he could even consider a mental list, the door opened, and Ruston came in. His gaze fired around the room and landed on his mother. Unlike Joelle though, he didn't rush to pull her into his arms.

"Does she know anything about Dad's murder?" Ruston immediately wanted to know.

"No," Sandra said at the same moment Bree, Duncan and Joelle indicated with headshakes that she didn't.

The disappointment seemed to wash over Ruston. Obviously, he'd hoped his mother would be able to give them that closure.

"We have a lot to fill you in on," Bree said, going to Ruston and giving him a quick hug. Their gazes met. "There's trouble."

"Yeah, I heard. Are you all right?" Ruston asked.

"I've been better," Bree muttered. She took in a breath through her mouth. "I'm going to check on Gabriel."

Luca moved to go with her, but before they made it to the door, Duncan's phone rang. "It's Woodrow," he relayed, taking the call. He didn't put it on Speaker, but after just a couple of seconds, Luca knew Duncan was getting bad news.

"What?" Duncan asked the caller. "You're sure?" He paused and a moment later muttered, "Hell." Duncan scrubbed his hand over his face and repeated the single word of profanity when he ended the call.

"The local cops went to the cabin," Duncan explained, "but it was on fire. The fire department's on the way, but they won't get there in time."

Luca groaned, and it blended with the other negative reactions in the room. With the cabin gone, they'd lose any critical evidence that might have been inside.

"There's more," Duncan added a moment later. "Woodrow checked, and the cabin was on a two-year lease to someone local." His gaze met Bree's. "Dr. Nathan Bagley."

Chapter Six

Bree watched from the back seat of the cruiser as the house came into view. She'd never thought of her childhood home as cramped quarters, but it certainly felt like that now. Still, she knew this was their best chance at keeping everyone safe.

Well, hopefully it was.

Until they had answers about her mother's kidnapper and the shooter, they'd never actually be safe. And some of those answers might come from Nathan.

It twisted at her to think of her former boyfriend having a part in this. Or rather *maybe* having a part in it. Woodrow had verified that Nathan's name was indeed on the lease for the cabin, but so far, they hadn't been able to question Nathan about that since he was tied up with a patient in the ICU. Once that was finished though, he'd be given the message to contact Duncan right away.

Rather than wait at the sheriff's office for Nathan's response, Duncan had proceeded with the move to the ranch. No easy feat with plenty of moving parts. Literally. She watched as Duncan's cruiser stopped in front of the house, and Joelle, Slater, their mother and Duncan all got out. Izzie's nanny, Beatrice Walker, opened the door for them.

Luca pulled up behind Duncan's cruiser, and as Ruston and he had both done on the drive over, they glanced around, looking for threats. Bree did as well, but she didn't see anyone other than some ranch hands milling about.

Luca's gaze met hers in the rearview mirror, and she saw the concern in his eyes. She was no doubt sporting plenty of concern of her own, but somehow they had to make this situation work. They had to do whatever it took to keep Gabriel safe.

Even share a bedroom.

Yes, that was the plan. The house had five bedrooms, but one was being used as a nursery and another had been converted to the live-in nanny's quarters. Joelle and Duncan had the main bedroom attached to the nursery. That left two rooms, and since her mother would need one of them, Luca and Bree would be roommates along with Gabriel.

That way, they wouldn't have to be far from Gabriel.

Thankfully, Luca and she wouldn't actually have to share a bed. Ruston had come ahead of them to set up a cot for Luca and a portable crib for Gabriel. Since Ruston was recently married and had an adopted daughter, he wouldn't be staying at the ranch but rather at his own house on the outskirts of San Antonio. Slater, however, would and had claimed the sofa in the family room. Coral had offered to use a cot or sofa as well, but since the nanny hadn't actually been threatened, Bree had decided to give her some time off.

"Go ahead and get Gabriel out of the car seat," Luca instructed while they were still in the cruiser, and Bree understood why he wanted that. It would minimize their time outside.

She unbuckled a sleeping Gabriel who stirred when she picked him up. It was at least another hour before he would normally want another bottle, but with his schedule thrown off, Bree wasn't counting on much of anything being normal today.

Ruston and Luca gathered up the diaper bag and baby supplies they'd brought with them and got out of the cruiser. Bree steeled herself for the punch of grief from seeing the spot where her father had died. And it came. It came with a vengeance and momentarily robbed her of her breath. She didn't give in to it, though. Couldn't. Because even a slight hesitation could turn out to be a deadly mistake. Gathering Gabriel close to her, she hurried inside.

Joelle and Duncan had kept the furniture. In this part of the house anyway. But for the time being, they'd turned the large formal living and dining areas into a makeshift squad room. Someone had moved in small tables that were serving as desks, and there was even an incident board, and Slater was in the process of pinning up three photos.

Brighton's, Sandra's and Bree's.

There'd no doubt soon be other photos and notes, and the visuals might help them better connect all of this. Duncan was already in work mode, too. He was talking on the phone while he gathered up papers that were churning out from a printer. Luca set down the diaper bag to go help him with that while Ruston carried their things upstairs.

"I've put Luca, Gabriel and you in your old bedroom," Joelle explained to Bree. She was holding her infant daughter who was fussing and clearly ready to eat because she kept turning her mouth to Joelle's breast. "And Mom will be in Ruston's old room. Beatrice is up there now, getting everything ready."

Her mother actually seemed relieved about that. Maybe because Sandra had thought she might end up having to sleep in the room she'd shared with her husband.

"You holding up okay?" Joelle asked their mother.

Sandra's nod was shaky and not very convincing. "So much happening," she muttered.

Yes, and Bree figured this was just the start of it. There were five veteran cops in the house, and she knew Duncan was thorough. This would be a *leave no stones unturned* kind of investigation.

"I could cook if anyone's hungry," her mother volunteered.

"Food is on the way from the diner. Lots of it," Joelle clarified. She studied her mom's face for a moment. "But if you could put out paper plates and cups in the kitchen, that'd be great. Also, maybe make a fresh pot of coffee."

Sandra nodded and seemed eager for something to do. Or maybe she was just eager to get a moment to herself to try to wrap her mind around all of this. She certainly didn't waste any time heading toward the kitchen that had once been hers.

Though technically it still was.

Even though the ranch and the house had belonged to their father, Sandra was his primary beneficiary. Bree knew that since she'd been the one to prepare his will. There'd be legalities and such to work out later about that, but Bree didn't want to deal with it now.

"Once Duncan finishes with his latest call to Woodrow, he wants to do a briefing," Joelle added to Bree. The baby's fussing became more insistent. "But I might be late for that since I need to feed Izzie."

Joelle hurried upstairs, and Bree glanced down at Gabriel to see if she would need to feed him as well, but he'd gone back to sleep. So, she made her way to the sofa and watched Slater as he added Nathan's picture to the board. Slater looked back at her.

"You know him fairly well," Slater remarked. "Is Nathan capable of something like this?"

Bree took a couple of seconds, trying to picture Nathan orchestrating her mother's kidnapping and the shooting. Also arranging for Manny and her to be run off the road. She couldn't quite make herself see that.

"Nathan might have the means and opportunity," she said, "but I can't figure out a motive...unless maybe it all goes back to Brighton."

She realized Duncan had finished his call, and along with Slater, both of them were listening to her.

"As far as I know, Nathan has no connection to Brighton," Bree said. "But this is a small town so he likely knew her."

"Trust me, I'll be asking him about that when he's available," Duncan assured her. He walked to the board, and sighing, he put up a picture of what she realized was the burned-out cabin. "There's good news and bad news. I'll start with the good. Two people came forward and said they'd seen a woman driving a silver truck in the area of the cabin over the past couple of months. They're working with sketch artists right now."

That was indeed good news. Even if they didn't recognize the woman from the sketch, they could put it out to the media and maybe get some hits.

"Now, for the bad," Duncan went on. "The cabin's owner never met Nathan or the person posing as Nathan. The rental agreement was all done online and secured with a credit card that has Nathan's name on it, but it can't be traced to him. It's linked to an offshore account under the name of a dummy company."

Bree groaned. Not only was that sort of account hard to unravel, it also meant Nathan probably hadn't actually been involved. If he had, he wouldn't have used his real name. Well, unless this was some kind of reverse psychology deal.

"So, someone wanted to set Nathan up?" Bree asked.

Duncan shrugged. "Maybe. Or it's possible the kidnapper

just used his name. Maybe because the owner of the cabin wouldn't think twice about renting the place to a doctor."

Yes, that made sense as well. Then, if things fell apart—like the victim escaping—there'd be nothing to point back to the real culprit. Yes, they'd interview Nathan, but with no actual proof to link him to the crime, he wouldn't be arrested.

Duncan shifted his attention to Bree. "I need to interview Manny, but since the incident with his vehicle didn't happen in my jurisdiction, I can't force him to come here, not without a warrant. I thought maybe since he already knows you, you could talk to him."

"Of course," Bree readily agreed, already taking out her phone. Though she wasn't sure Manny would actually be willing to come to Saddle Ridge. Still, he might if he thought it would prevent him from being attacked again.

"See if Manny will agree to having the call on Speaker," Duncan added. "That way, I can hear if he has anything to say about his attack."

She nodded and made the call. However, it wasn't Manny who answered with a "Yeah?" It was a woman.

"Tara Adler?" Bree questioned.

"Yes," she verified, and she paused. "Who is this?"

"Bree McCullough. I spoke to you, remember? I asked you about Brighton Cooper."

"I remember." There was plenty of uneasiness in her voice. "Like I told you, I didn't actually know her. You're calling for Manny?" she quickly tacked onto that. "Because I can get him for you. He left his phone out here on the bar so that's why I answered it."

"Oh, I didn't realize you were open this early," she commented.

"We're not. I'm training some new waitstaff. Let me get Manny," she insisted.

Tara hadn't been exactly friendly when Bree had spoken to her before, but the woman seemed on edge now. Maybe because of Manny's attack? Tara might be worried she could be at risk, too. And she might be if this was indeed connected to Brighton's murder.

"It's that lawyer who asked about the dead woman," Bree heard Tara say, and several moments later, Manny came on the line.

"Bree," he said, sounding just as uneasy as Tara. "Did they catch the guy who tried to kill us?"

"No, not yet. Manny, I want to put this call on Speaker. Is that okay? I'm with Sheriff Duncan Holder and some of the other deputies from Saddle Ridge. They're all looking for the person who attacked us, and anything you can tell them might help find him or her."

"Sure," Manny said after a brief hesitation. "But I've already told the Austin cops everything I know."

"Yes, and they're looking, too," Bree assured him, switching to Speaker. "But the more people searching, the better."

Manny made a sound of agreement. "All right. But I don't know what more I can say. Someone in a silver truck rammed into me, that's it."

"This is Sheriff Holder," Duncan said. "And we believe we've found the truck. It's being examined now by CSIs to see if there are any paint flecks on it that match your vehicle."

"You have the driver?" Manny quickly asked. "You know who tried to kill me?"

"No, we don't have the driver, but we might have a description soon that'll help with that," Duncan explained. "What will help, too, is if we know why the attack happened."

"I don't know why." Manny's voice took on an agitated edge. "But since the same thing happened to Bree, I have to figure it's got something to do with all the questions she was asking about the dead woman."

Duncan didn't confirm that. "Who else knew Bree was asking questions about Brighton Cooper?"

Manny muttered some profanity. "Well, I didn't exactly keep it a secret. Anyone who works for me knew. And my financial guy, too, since I asked him to get the old credit card statements Bree wanted."

Bree sighed. She'd hoped that Manny and Tara had kept this close to the vest, which would have significantly narrowed their pool of suspects. But when Bree had spoken to them, she hadn't known there'd be attacks. If this was all connected, then someone had gotten spooked and wanted to silence Manny and her.

That, however, still didn't explain her mother's kidnapping.

"It's possible I'll soon have sketches of your attacker," Duncan told Manny. "I was hoping you'd be willing to come to Saddle Ridge and have a look at them and so I can get a statement about what happened to you. Then I'll compare it to Bree's statement to see if it can help with an arrest."

Manny certainly didn't jump to agree to that. "I guess," he finally said. "I can't get there today though, but I can come in the morning, maybe around ten. I should have those old credit card statements by then and can bring them with me."

"Good," Duncan said just as his phone dinged with a text. "We'll see you at the sheriff's office in the morning."

Bree thanked Manny, ended the call and kept her attention on Duncan while he read the text he'd just gotten.

"The CSIs have found no prints other than Sandra's in the silver truck," Duncan explained. "There was a box of plastic disposable gloves on the passenger seat."

So, the kidnapper had gloved up. That shouldn't have

surprised her, but Bree had hoped the woman had left some part of herself behind. And maybe she had. It would likely take the CSIs a while to go through the entire truck and then process whatever they found. Including those paint flecks that Woodrow and Carmen had seen.

Luca walked toward her and sank down on the sofa next to Bree. "It's been a hellish long day," he pointed out. "If you want to try to get some rest, I can watch Gabriel." He brushed his fingers over Gabriel's hair.

It had indeed been hellish, and since she was exhausted, Bree didn't want to turn down his offer, but she figured Luca was worn-out as well. Plus, she didn't want to pull him away from the investigation.

"I'll put Gabriel in his crib for the rest of his nap, and then I'll lie down," she said to offer a compromise, though both knew Gabriel might wake up the second she tried to put him down.

Luca sighed and went with her out of the room and toward the stairs. "Are you okay about being here with your mother?" he asked, keeping his voice barely above a whisper.

"Yes." That was the truth. Mostly, anyway.

"You believe everything she said about what happened to her?" he pressed.

She considered her answer while they went up the stairs. "I want to believe her. That's not the same thing."

His quick sound of agreement told her they were of a like mind on this. "Sandra had no obvious motive to kill her husband. No reported marital problems. No history of violent tendencies."

"All true. But that doesn't mean the unthinkable hadn't happened. An argument that went horribly wrong. An affair that none of us knew about." She stopped. "But that doesn't feel right."

Luca made another sound of agreement. "This is a wild what-if, but what if your dad learned your mother had something to do with Brighton's death? That could have spurred a violent confrontation."

She considered it and dismissed it just as Luca added, "But that doesn't feel right either. Your mother was looking out for Brighton. She was almost like another of her children."

Again, that was true, and hearing it spelled out like that helped convince Bree that her mom had been a victim in all of this. Just as her father. And it was connected. It had to be. She just didn't know how yet.

Luca and she were halfway up the stairs when she heard a flurry of movement on the ground floor. She turned to see Duncan and Slater moving fast toward the front door.

"What's wrong?" Luca asked.

"One of the hands alerted me that Nathan just drove up," Duncan explained.

Bree's first reaction was to groan. Or curse. She was beyond exhausted, but Duncan needed to question Nathan about the lease on the burned-out cabin. She hadn't figured though that the interview would happen here but rather over the phone or at the sheriff's office. Still, since he was here, she'd be able to listen while he gave his statement.

The nanny, Beatrice, appeared at the top of the stairs, and she'd obviously heard they had a visitor. "Joelle and your mom are with Izzie so I can take Gabriel if you like," she offered.

Bree glanced down at her sleeping baby and then over her shoulder out the sidelight windows of the front door. Nathan was pulling his car to a stop in the driveway.

"Yes, thank you," Bree said, and she eased Gabriel into the nanny's arms.

"You don't have to deal with Nathan," Luca let Bree know after Beatrice had taken Gabriel upstairs.

Bree nodded. "But I might be able to tell if he's lying." Of course, that was a long shot. She certainly hadn't picked up on any overly possessive behavior until it'd started to happen.

"Still," Luca said, "you don't have to put yourself through this."

"I never had sex with him," she blurted out and then immediately wanted to take it back. Good grief. Luca didn't need to know that.

Luca didn't seem pleased. Or surprised. Then again, Luca and she had dated for nearly four months before they'd had sex the first time. Nathan and she had only gone out for a couple of weeks.

"I think that's why his possessiveness was such a shock," she went on. Since she'd launched into this uncomfortable subject, she might as well get some things clear. "We weren't lovers, and I certainly hadn't made any kind of commitment to him. I never mentioned anything about being exclusive. I was just testing the waters, that's all."

He nodded. "That happened when I was dating Shona Sullivan. And, yes, I know your dating Nathan had nothing to do with that," he was quick to add. Maybe because he saw the flash of annoyance in her eyes. "I mentioned it because of the timing. Nathan might have thought Shona and I were in a 'together forever' kind of deal, so that could have been why he thought he had a clear path to a long-term relationship with you."

The annoyance vanished because Luca was right. Everyone knew Luca and she were an item. Heck, they even thought it now. Bree could see the *aha* look in people's eyes now that Luca and she had a child together.

She pushed all that aside for now when Nathan knocked at

the door, and Duncan opened it. "I got your message that you needed to talk to me right away," Nathan said. "I went by the sheriff's office, but the dispatcher told me you were home."

Nathan looked past Duncan, his gaze settling on Bree as she came down the stairs.

"Are you hurting?" Nathan asked her. "Is that why Duncan called me?"

"This isn't about anything medical," Duncan was quick to say. "Come in." He stepped back, his cop's gaze focused on Nathan as he came in. Like Luca and Slater, Duncan was probably checking to see if there were any signs Nathan was about to try to attack them.

Bree certainly didn't see anything like that. If she had to put a label on his expression and body language, it'd be moony-eyed. Nathan always managed to seem as if she held his heart in her hands. She definitely didn't want that or the look he was giving her.

"Are you sure you're all right?" Nathan asked her. "I called the pharmacy on the way over, and they said you hadn't filled the prescription I wrote you for the pain meds."

She certainly hadn't forgotten about the pain but didn't intend to fill the prescription. She didn't want her mind to be numbed. "I'll take something 'over the counter,'" she settled for saying.

Nathan opened his mouth, probably to advise her to get the prescription, but Duncan motioned toward the living room. "In here. Slater, will you turn the board around while we talk to Nathan?"

Slater nodded, hurried ahead of them, and she heard the movement as Slater did as Duncan asked. There wasn't a lot on the board at the moment, but Duncan still probably didn't want to display an investigative road map to someone who was still technically a suspect.

"Is this about Bree's accident?" Nathan asked, looking and sounding very concerned.

"Not exactly," Duncan said once they were in the living room. "I need to ask you some questions, but I'm going to read you your rights first. It's just a formality," he insisted when Nathan snapped back his shoulders. He didn't give Nathan a chance to voice his defensiveness. Duncan just proceeded to Mirandize him.

"You can't possibly think I'd have something to do with Bree's car accident," Nathan said when Duncan had finished.

"Are you familiar with a hunting cabin about twenty-five miles from here?" Duncan asked, obviously not addressing Nathan's comment. Duncan then provided the exact address.

Nathan's forehead bunched up. "No. I don't hunt, so I don't usually go to places like that. Why?"

"Because it was leased in your name," Duncan supplied while he watched for Nathan's reaction. Bree, Luca and Slater did the same.

"What?" Nathan snapped. He reached into his pocket, causing Duncan, Luca and Slater to all put their hands over their weapons.

Nathan froze, and his eyes widened. "Obviously, you think I've done something wrong. I haven't," he assured them. "If someone used my name to lease the cabin, then my bank account has been hacked or something. I was just going to take out my phone and see if any money was missing."

"Do that," Duncan instructed, but he didn't take his hand from his gun until he saw for certain that Nathan was pulling out a phone.

Nathan muttered something under his breath and started typing in something on the app he pulled up. It took him at least a minute before he shook his head. "No. There are no missing funds, no fraudulent charges on my credit card. Who said I leased that cabin?"

"The owner," Duncan answered. "Someone used a credit card in your name to secure it and paid for the lease."

Nathan cursed. "Well, it sure as hell wasn't me. Someone must have stolen my identity." He groaned, cursed again. "I need to report that. Do you investigate it or is that something my bank does?"

"We'll be investigating it," Duncan said, tipping his head to Slater and then Luca.

Judging from the sudden tight set of his mouth, Nathan wasn't a fan of having Luca dig into his financials. "I'm guessing something illegal happened at this cabin?" Nathan snarled.

"We're investigating that, too, but yes, something happened there," Duncan verified. He didn't add any specifics though. "We're also looking at a Ford F-150 silver truck that was involved in several incidents. Have you ever owned or driven a vehicle like that?"

"No. I drive an Audi." Nathan looked at her again. "Bree, what's going on?" he asked, but he didn't wait for her to respond. "Certainly, you've told them I haven't done anything wrong."

She hadn't meant to give him a flat look but it came away. After all, Nathan had stalked her. Nathan not only noticed her expression, he also responded. His mouth tightened. His eyes narrowed. And he aimed a glare at Luca.

"I don't appreciate you trying to turn Bree against me," Nathan said. "If you're jealous of her and me—"

"I'm not," Luca interrupted and stepped to Bree's side. "And Bree can make up her mind for herself how she feels about you."

Nathan's scowl stayed in place, but it was obvious he

didn't have a good comeback for that. "All right," Nathan said through clenched teeth, indicating that things were far from all right. His expression softened a bit when he shifted back to her. "Bree, if you need me for anything, you have my number. And remember, I care about you. I wouldn't do anything to hurt you."

He reached out as if he might try to hug her, but Bree stepped back and landed right against Luca. The impact put her off balance just enough that Luca's arms came around to steady her.

That intensified Nathan's glare. "Remember what I said," he muttered. "I care about you."

With that, Nathan walked out. Or rather, he stormed out. And Bree found herself releasing the breath that she'd been holding. She hated that Nathan could still annoy her like this. Hated, too, that it had felt so reassuring when she'd landed in Luca's arms. She eased away from him and stood on her own two feet.

"I swear, I've told Nathan many times that nothing will ever happen between him and me," she muttered. "And, no, I don't need to do a restraining order," she added to Slater. "Nathan hasn't called or texted me in months."

But she was worried that Nathan would use her injury and this interrogation to try to wheedle himself into her life again.

"I plan on doing a deep background check on Nathan," Luca said, going to the front door to lock it. "It's possible he has a history of stalking women. Maybe other things, too, that he doesn't want us to know about."

"You believe he could have been the one who leased that cabin?" Duncan asked.

Luca shrugged. "On the surface it wouldn't be the smartest move to use his own name. But criminals aren't always smart. And sometimes that sort of move might have us thinking he's not guilty."

That was true, and Bree tried to play out that scenario. "Even before I went out with Nathan, he was obsessed with me. I didn't see that until afterwards," she added. "But I know now, it's an obsession. It might be far-fetched, but maybe he kidnapped Mom to try to punish me."

"Or maybe he hoped you'd turn to him while you were vulnerable and grieving," Slater supplied.

That settled like a fist of ice in her stomach. Because it didn't seem so far-fetched at all.

"I'll do that deep background check," Luca repeated. He looked at her. "You want to try to get some rest now?"

She would have definitely agreed to that, but Duncan's phone dinged again. "It's Woodrow," he said, glancing at the screen. "The artist just finished with the first sketch of the woman seen driving the silver truck." He looked at it, shook his head and then turned his phone for them to see. "I don't know her."

Bree went closer. She didn't get an immediate jolt of recognition, but it came the longer she studied the image. "I think I might know who that is," she muttered. "She looks like the bartender at the Hush, Hush bar. I think that's Tara Adler."

Duncan, Slater and Luca all exchanged glances. "Do you have her number?" Duncan asked.

She shook her head. "I can call Manny and ask to speak to her."

"Do that," Duncan said. "I want to see if I can get Tara to come in with him tomorrow morning for an interview."

Bree called Manny and put it on Speaker. She thought Tara might answer again, but this time it was Manny.

"This is Sheriff Holder again," Duncan said. "I'd like to speak to Tara Adler."

"Tara?" Manny questioned. "Why?"

"It's routine," Duncan answered, which, of course, wasn't an actual answer at all. "May I speak to her?"

"You could if she was here," Manny grumbled. "Right after I got off the phone with you, Tara claimed she was sick and had to leave."

Bree couldn't believe that it was a coincidence. Was Tara really the one behind her mother's kidnapping and the attacks? If so, this had to be connected to Brighton's murder. And maybe her father's.

"She didn't look sick to me," Manny added in a snarl. "You want her number so you can talk to her?"

"Yes, I do," Duncan verified.

Once Manny had given them the number, Bree ended the call with him, and Duncan used his own phone to call Tara. Or rather, to try to call her. Bree's stomach sank when she heard the recorded message that she didn't want to hear.

Tara's phone had been disconnected.

Chapter Seven

Luca hurried in the shower. Along with not wanting to hog the bathroom, he also didn't want to leave Bree and Gabriel alone for long. Added to that, there was plenty of work to do, and a long shower was a luxury he couldn't afford.

He turned off the water and listened to make sure everything was well in the adjoining bedroom. The bedroom he'd shared with Bree and their son the night before and would continue to share as long as there was a potential threat. He could hear Bree murmuring something to Gabriel, but that was it. No sounds of distress or phone conversations that might or might not deliver more bad news.

So far, the bad news was winning out over the good. There was no sign of the gunman who'd fired those shots into Bree's barn. No sign of Tara either, which meant they couldn't question her about the sketch that matched her description. Since Manny didn't have any idea where she was either, it could mean Tara had gone on the run. It was possible she was the one who'd held Sandra captive, but it could also point to Tara meeting with foul play.

When Duncan had shown Sandra a photo of Tara, Sandra had said she recognized her from the Hush, Hush, but that she had no idea if Tara had been the one who'd kidnapped her. That wasn't much of a surprise since Sandra had been adamant about not knowing who'd been responsible for taking her.

The bad news had continued on the forensic side of the investigation as well. Other than the gloves and Sandra's prints, the CSIs hadn't found anything in the silver truck. Manny might be able to help with that though during his interview if he could tell them anything else about the truck or the driver. Especially if the driver could possibly be Tara.

There had been some good news though in the burned-out cabin. No DNA results yet, but there was evidence to support Sandra's account of the boarded-up window and multiple locks on the interior door where she'd been held. That was a huge validation for Bree's mother.

And a relief.

There were enough unknowns in this investigation without adding Sandra to the mix. Now, she could be ruled out as a suspect, and they could focus on Tara. Nathan, too, since Luca was keeping him on the list. Maybe that had more to do with Nathan's history with Bree, but Luca wasn't dismissing Nathan's possible involvement in all of this.

Luca dressed in the clean jeans and shirt he'd had brought to the ranch, and he went into the bedroom to find Bree sitting with a very alert Gabriel who'd obviously just finished a bottle. Bree had the baby against her chest and shoulder and was patting his back, no doubt to get him to burp.

Bree's gaze immediately went to Luca's, and he saw the tension in every bit of her expression. It was understandable and wouldn't be going away until they had a suspect in custody.

Or as long as they had to share such close quarters.

That was definitely causing her some stress. Him, too. They'd been on-and-off lovers for a long time now. Over a decade. His body couldn't forget that kind of history and neither could Luca. He still wanted Bree. Still cared deeply for her. And that must have shown on his face.

"It's not you," she muttered. Then, she shook her head. "I mean, you're not the reason I get this slam of memories about my dad."

He was glad to hear that, but there was a flip side to this particular coin. "You get them though," he said.

She nodded. "So do you."

Luca had to go with a nod as well and admit it was true. In fact, he'd had a dream about her father's murder in the handful of hours he'd managed to sleep. Judging from some of the things Bree had muttered in the night, she'd done some dreaming as well.

He wanted to say more. A whole lot more about hoping that one day they could look at each other and not see the past. But the sound of an approaching vehicle had him going to the window.

"It's Coral," he relayed to her.

Luca sighed. "If you're still going to the sheriff's office for Manny's interview, we'll have to leave soon."

He already knew though that Bree hadn't changed her mind about this. If she had, she would have already called Coral to cancel. But like him, Bree wanted to be at the sheriff's office to hear what Manny had to say. Bree wouldn't actually be in the interview room though. Duncan had made an exception when they'd questioned Sandra, but with Manny, they had to play by the rules.

Bree stood, giving Gabriel a kiss before she handed the baby to Luca so he could do the same. They made their way downstairs where Duncan was already letting Coral into the house. Coral immediately went to Bree and hugged her.

"I've been so worried about you," Coral said, but she

conjured up a smile when she looked at Gabriel. "And I've missed this little man. How is everything?" she asked.

"The investigation's still in progress," Bree said. It was the standard response cops often doled out, but in this case, it was the truth. And about all that could be said since they couldn't voice suspicions about a local doctor. Not without proof anyway, and at the moment, they didn't have that.

Joelle, Sandra, Slater and Ruston were all downstairs, and Sandra was holding Izzie. Woodrow was there, too, and he was no doubt waiting to make the drive with them to the sheriff's office.

"I made Mom an appointment to see her doctor at the hospital clinic," Joelle volunteered. "I talked to him, and he wants to run some labs on her just to make sure she's okay."

Luca and Bree both made quick sounds of agreement. Not Sandra though. She was obviously reluctant.

"Woodrow can stay with Sandra at the hospital, and Carmen will meet them there," Duncan explained, glancing at Luca and Bree. "Then, the three of us can go to the sheriff's office."

It'd be a snug fit in the cruiser with five people, but it was better than making two trips. They were leaving backup at home with the babies, too, since Joelle, Slater and Ruston would be staying behind.

Luca wished they'd had a dozen cops available to guard his son and Izzie. Not enough manpower for that, but the ranch hands had been put on alert to keep an eye out for anything suspicious.

Sandra handed Izzie back to Joelle and kissed Gabriel as Luca was passing the baby to Coral. Bree's mother patted Luca's arm in a gesture she had done many times before she went missing. He muttered a thanks. Then silently said a prayer that they'd make this trip without incident. That included nothing going wrong at the ranch, either.

Duncan said his goodbyes to Joelle and his daughter, and he quickly got them out of the house and into the cruiser parked at the foot of the porch steps. Sandra, Luca and Bree went in the back seat with Bree in the middle. Duncan took the wheel with Woodrow at shotgun.

"I asked Austin PD to go ahead and put out an APB for Tara," Duncan explained once they were on the road. "They'll check with her family and friends, too."

If the woman had truly gone on the run, she might not go to places where she'd readily be found. But what had spooked her? Had it simply been Bree's phone call, or had something else alerted her? Luca was hoping Manny might be able to provide some insight.

All five of them kept watch as Duncan made the short drive to the hospital where Carmen was indeed waiting for them, so Woodrow and Sandra got out. Then, Duncan continued up the street to the sheriff's office. They breathed a whole lot easier once they had made it to the private entrance outside Duncan's office.

The moment they stepped in, Luca saw the man in the small waiting area. When he immediately stood, Luca slid his hand over his gun until he got a good look at the guy's face and realized it was Manny. Luca recognized him from his driver's license photo and the background info he'd accessed.

Tall and with a lanky build, Manny was only thirty-three which made him the same age as Luca. He'd owned the Hush, Hush for seven years, since the death of his father. He didn't exactly look the part of a business owner though, more of a rocker with his blond hair that fell past his shoulders. His faded, ripped jeans and plain black tee had that rocker vibe as well.

There were two deputies in the squad room, Sonya Grover and Ronnie Bishop, and even though they were both on their computers, Luca could tell they were also keeping an eye on Manny.

"He's already gone through the metal detector," Ronnie volunteered. "And he consented to a search. He's not armed."

Good. Though it wouldn't have been very smart for Manny to come in here armed.

"I'm early," Manny muttered. He also seemed nervous and was rubbing his hands down the sides of his jeans. "Bree," he greeted. "Please tell me you've found Tara and the person who tried to kill us."

She muttered an "I'm sorry" and shook her head. Luca noticed her wince a little from the movement. She hadn't said anything about being in pain, but he figured the stitches had to hurt.

"This is Sheriff Holder and Deputy Vanetti," she explained. "They'll be conducting the interview."

"And you'll be there, too, right?" Manny asked.

"No—" she started.

"But I want you there," Manny insisted, glancing at Luca and Duncan to plead his case. "Bree's the only one who knows what I'm going through right now. Someone tried to kill us," he spelled out.

"Yes, but I'm not a cop," she reminded him.

"You're a lawyer," Manny argued. "And I can have a lawyer with me, right?"

Bree sighed. "I can't be your lawyer."

Because it would possibly be a conflict of interest, but she didn't spell that out. No need to make Manny defensive when they brought up the possibility that he could have faked his attack and could be the person responsible for this current nightmare. That was a long shot, but it was still on the radar.

Manny glanced around as if trying to figure out what to do. His nerves seemed to be building.

"Tell you what," Duncan said. "Why don't we talk here in my office for now and Bree can stay with us. I'll still Mirandize you," Duncan tacked onto that. "It's procedure," he said when Manny's eyes widened, and he started shaking his head. "When we catch the person who tried to run you off the road, we want to be able to use anything you say to help with the prosecution. If your statement's official, then it makes things easier."

That was all true, but Luca knew there was another reason for the Miranda. If Manny said anything incriminating, Duncan would be able to use it without Manny claiming he hadn't been read his rights.

Duncan waited for Manny to nod before he motioned for Manny to come into his office. When all four of them were inside and seated, Duncan shut the door and Mirandized him.

"I'm going to record this," Duncan continued, turning on the recorder and stating the time, date and attendees. "Now, Manny, I want you to tell us what happened yesterday when you were driving."

Manny glanced at Bree, and even though there was still plenty of uneasiness in his expression, he began. "Like I told Bree and the other cops, I was driving from my house into Austin so I could meet with a supplier. A big silver truck came up from behind and rammed into me. The driver tried to push me off the road. I think he was trying to kill me," Manny added in a hoarse mutter.

"And from what I understand, you didn't get the license plate?" Duncan asked.

Manny shook his head. "I didn't even think to do that. I

was just so shocked. And I didn't think to try to follow the truck or anything."

"Who knew you'd be traveling on that road at that particular time?" Duncan pressed.

"Lots of people." Manny shrugged. "I live alone, but I had the appointment on my big wall calendar in my office, so anyone who came in there could have seen it."

"Tara would have known?" Luca asked.

Manny gave another nod, and the sigh that came from his throat was hoarse and filled with emotion. "You think she could have done this. You think that's why she disappeared. But why?" Manny asked.

"Why do you think she would have done that?" Luca countered.

"I don't know. But if she did it, it must have something to do with Bree since the same thing happened to her." Manny stopped again, groaned. "It's just hard for me to believe Tara would try to scare us. Or kill us. But if she did, it could be connected to the questions Bree was asking about that murdered woman. I can't remember her name," he said to Bree.

"Brighton Cooper," Bree supplied. "I found out Brighton had gone to the Hush, Hush shortly before she was killed—"

"Yes," Manny interrupted, and he reached into his pocket to take out a memory stick. "You wanted the old credit card receipts, and I finally got them from my finance guy. I didn't have your email address so I put them on this."

Bree didn't take the drive though. "Why don't we go ahead and enter this into evidence?" she suggested. "To preserve the chain of custody."

Duncan was already moving to do just that. He took out an evidence bag from his desk, dropped in the memory stick and then sealed and labeled it. Luca knew they'd soon be going through that.

"Did you look at the receipts?" Bree asked Manny.

"I glanced through them. You know, just to see if anything jumped out at me. It didn't. We had a DJ in for the nights you asked about so business was good. Lots of customers, lots of credit card charges. The cash receipts are on there, too, but obviously there aren't names on those."

If Brighton's killer had been there that night—and that was a big *if*—it was possible one of the cash charges might belong to him or her. But Brighton's murder didn't seem planned so maybe her killer's name was indeed on those receipts.

"Look, is there any way to keep me out of all of this?" Manny asked. "I mean, I know it's important to find who did that to the woman, but I don't want to get mixed up in it. I want to be able to drive to work without someone trying to kill me."

Duncan gave a sigh of his own. "Your name's already connected to this," he said. "Of course, I won't advertise that you came in today for an interview, but someone might find out about it." He tipped his head to the bag. "Especially if there's anything on here to link to a killer."

Manny groaned and pressed his hands against the sides of his head. He stared down into his lap, muttering some profanity.

"Did you get the sense that anyone followed you here today?" Duncan asked.

"No," Manny said.

Duncan continued to press. "How about any unusual visitors at the bar?"

That got another "no" from Manny. "The cops said they could do patrols on the road near my house, but that won't stop a killer. Do you think I should hire a bodyguard?"

"If that'll make you feel safer, then do it," Duncan agreed.

"It's probably a good idea not to put your appointments on your wall calendar for a while. Also, shake up your routines if possible. Do you have a security system for your house?"

Manny nodded, but then he glanced at the large window that looked out onto the squad room and reception. All of them did. Because the front door opened, and they saw a woman come in.

Tara.

Luca was sure of it, and she did indeed bear a striking resemblance to the sketch. She seemed just as nervous as Manny and was disheveled, too, in her wrinkled gray shirt and jeans. She'd scooped back her long brown hair into a ponytail, but there were just as many strands pulled back as were falling onto her shoulders.

Both Sonya and Ronnie were on their feet now, and Sonya started toward their visitor.

"Tara," Manny muttered. He walked toward her as well. Then, he stopped. Probably because he remembered Tara might have been the one who'd nearly run him off the road.

"Wait here, Manny," Duncan instructed, and he went into the squad room. So did Bree and Luca. "Tara Adler?" he asked.

She nodded. "I'm looking for Bree McCullough…" Her words trailed off when she saw Manny. "And you," she muttered. "Manny, I think someone's trying to kill me." With that, Tara broke into a sob.

Despite Duncan's warning for Manny to stay put, the bar owner came out into the squad room, but Duncan stepped in front of him. Just as Luca had done to Bree.

"Tara, I want you to go through the metal detector," Duncan instructed.

She looked more than a little startled at the request, but

she complied. No alarms went off, and when Sonya searched Tara's purse, she didn't find anything.

"I'll call to have the APB dropped," Sonya said, returning to her desk.

Volleying glances at Bree and Manny, Tara made her way through the squad room toward Luca, Duncan, Manny and Bree. "Why are you here?" she asked Manny. "Did someone try to run you off the road again?"

He shook his head. "The sheriff wanted to talk to me… about you, among other things. Where the hell have you been?"

Duncan motioned for her to hold back on answering that, and as he'd done with Manny, he read Tara her rights.

"I'm a suspect?" Tara blurted once he was finished. She frantically shook her head. "I'm a victim. Someone followed my car this morning. Not a silver truck," she added. "This was a black one."

Duncan led her into his office. "Did you report it?"

"No." Tara suddenly seemed flustered. Or else she was pretending to be anyway. She sank down into a chair in Duncan's office. "I thought someone was following me," she clarified, "but I'm not sure. I'm hoping I'm wrong. Am I wrong?" she pleaded.

"I don't know," Duncan answered. "Now, tell me why you're here and where you've been for the past eighteen hours."

Tara certainly didn't launch into an explanation, but she handed Duncan her phone and pointed to a text from an unknown number. "I got this yesterday, right after Bree talked to Manny."

"'Talk and you die,'" he said, reading the text out loud.

"Did you report this?" Duncan repeated.

Tara shook her head. "I was terrified," she insisted. "And

I panicked. My instincts were to run, to get away from the bar. I didn't want to end up like that dead woman Bree asked about, or have her killer track my phone, so I took out the SIM card."

That explained why the cops hadn't been able to find her, but most people wouldn't have thought to do something like that. Especially if they were in a panic as Tara had claimed.

"It's the woman's killer who wants us dead, right?" Tara asked. "He wants to silence us all for good."

Bree made a sound that could have meant anything. Obviously, she wasn't going to volunteer that to Tara.

"Sonya," Duncan called out to the deputy. "I need phone records for this number. See if you can find out who sent that text." He passed Tara's phone to Sonya and then turned his attention back to Tara. "We're looking into connections between the recent attacks and the murder of Brighton Cooper," Duncan said. "Did you know her?"

"No," Tara was quick to say. "I told Bree I didn't remember her, but after I got to thinking about it, I think I recall her coming into the bar. *Think*," she emphasized, "but I'm not positive."

Luca didn't read much into that. Witnesses often recalled things long after being questioned.

"And you didn't know Brighton either?" Duncan pressed, shifting his attention to Manny.

"No." Manny's response was equally fast.

Duncan drew in a breath as if that wasn't the response he wanted. "Well, we know Brighton was in the Hush, Hush shortly before her murder."

"And that's why her killer is coming after us," Tara concluded.

"Maybe," Duncan muttered. "Where did you go after you got that text?"

It took Tara a couple of seconds to shift gears in the conversation. "Home first. To my apartment. I packed a bag, grabbed the emergency cash I keep on hand and then went to a motel. I put the SIM card back in my phone this morning so I could call Manny and ask him what I should do," Tara went on. "It went straight to voicemail so I called the bar. Otto answered, and he said he heard Manny talking on the phone about coming to Saddle Ridge for an interview. So, I came here, too."

"Otto?" Duncan questioned.

"Otto Gunther," Manny supplied. "He's the janitor."

Luca immediately took out his phone to do a quick run on the man. The guy was seventy-three and had no criminal history. That didn't exclude him from being a killer though, so Luca requested a background check. While he was at it, he ordered that for all of the Hush, Hush employees.

"You can't think Otto would try to run someone off the road," Manny protested. "He's a good man. He'd give you the shirt off his back, which is why I've kept him on long after normal retirement age. He loves his job, and the rest of the staff love having him around."

"Manny's right," Tara piped in.

Duncan didn't address their comments. He opened a folder on his desk and took a printed copy of the drawing that the sketch artist had done. "This woman was seen driving the silver truck that was involved in the incidents with both Bree and you," he said to Manny.

Manny's eyes widened, and he turned to Tara. "That looks like you."

Tara fixed her gaze on the drawing, but she was also shaking her head. "It's not. There must be a mistake. I've never driven a silver truck, and I wouldn't try to run anyone off the road."

"Then why does that look so much like you?" Duncan

asked, going full cop mode. The muscles in his face had tightened, and his eyes were narrowed.

"I don't know..." Her denial trailed off, and her gaze shot to Duncan. "Is it my sister, Shannon?"

The moment she asked the question, Luca started the background check on Tara's sister. He silently cursed when Shannon's DMV photo came up because while she wasn't Tara's twin, the two women did look a great deal alike.

Luca showed the photo to Duncan, and Luca was betting he did some silent cursing as well. They'd believed Tara was their suspect, but now that was in serious doubt.

"Where's your sister?" Duncan demanded.

"I'm not sure. We've lost contact," Tara said. She paused, then sighed. "Look, Shannon's a trouble magnet. Always getting involved with the wrong guy. Always in and out of messes. I washed my hands of her about a year ago. Last I heard, she was seeing some lowlife from Bulverde."

The burned-out cabin was near that particular small town.

"You know this lowlife's name?" Duncan pressed.

"No. I didn't want to know," she insisted. "Like I said, I'd washed my hands of her." She stopped again, and this time she groaned. "Oh, God. Is Shannon the one who sent me that text? Is she the one who tried to kill Manny and Bree?"

Luca figured that fell into the "to be determined" category. "Do you have your sister's phone number?" Luca asked.

Tara shook her head again. "She never had the money for a good phone so she always used cheap disposable ones."

Burners. Which would be next to impossible to trace.

But if Shannon was indeed behind this, then she probably hadn't been acting alone. Her low-life boyfriend would also need to be questioned.

"Where were you both yesterday morning starting at nine and going past noon?" Duncan asked, and Luca knew Duncan was trying to see if either had alibis for the incident with Bree and the shooting.

"I was home," Manny said. "Well, I was after I reported the silver truck to the cops. Why?"

Duncan ignored the question and turned to Tara. "And where were you?"

"At my apartment," Tara answered.

"Alone?" Duncan pressed, glancing at both of them.

Manny and Tara nodded.

"Did you see or speak to anyone during that time?" Duncan continued.

"No," Tara was the first to say, and then Manny repeated it. Manny also repeated his, "Why?"

Before Duncan could answer, there was a knock on the side door of the office. "It's me," Woodrow announced. "Sandra's appointment was quick so I brought her back here."

Duncan unlocked and opened the door. He got Sandra in as quickly as possible.

"The doctor did some blood tests," Sandra said. "And I should have the results soon." She stopped when she glanced at the others in the room. "Oh, I'm sorry, I'm interrupting—"

Sandra gasped when her attention landed on Manny.

"It's you," Sandra muttered, and the color drained from her face.

"You know Manny?" Duncan was quick to ask.

Sandra nodded. "He's the man who was having an affair with Brighton." She swallowed hard. "I think he might have been the one to kill her."

Chapter Eight

Bree certainly hadn't expected her mother to say what she had. And apparently neither had anyone else in Duncan's office.

Especially Manny.

He jumped to his feet, and for a moment Bree thought he might try to run, but Luca and Duncan prevented that. Duncan, by stepping in front of the side door, and Luca by blocking the path toward the squad room. Manny cursed and dropped back down into the chair.

"It's not what you think," he insisted, aiming that at Luca and Duncan. "I didn't kill Brighton. I've never killed anyone."

"But you had an affair with her?" Duncan asked. "And you lied about it during an official interview?"

Tara, who was now also standing, spoke before Manny could respond. "You had an affair with her?" She was clearly upset.

Jealous, maybe?

It was hard for Bree to tell, but it seemed to her that Manny wasn't the only one who'd lied.

"You said you didn't know Brighton either," Bree pointed out to Tara.

Tara opened her mouth, closed it and then huffed. "I didn't

know her name. But when you asked about her, I went to Manny to see if he knew her. He said he didn't," she practically spat out.

Oh, yes. Jealousy. And Duncan picked up on it. "I take it Manny and you had a personal relationship around this time?" he asked Tara.

Again, she hesitated, and it was Manny who answered. "Not a relationship," he insisted. "We had sex, and yes, I know that was stupid since I'm her boss."

"It was more than sex," Tara muttered, but then she seemed to freeze. Maybe because she'd realized she was spelling out a motive for killing Brighton. "Manny and I were together for about six months, and we agreed to end things."

"I broke things off with you," Manny corrected. "And it wasn't because I was having an affair with another woman," he was quick to add. "I ended things with Tara before I started seeing Brighton."

Duncan huffed, and glared at Manny. "I could charge you with lying to a police officer. And I still might do that if you don't tell me everything about Brighton and how her murder connects to what's going on now."

Manny got that panicked look again, and he dragged in some quick breaths. So quick that Bree thought he might hyperventilate. Duncan must have also thought that was a possibility because he got the man a bottle of water from the small fridge behind his desk.

"Talk," Duncan demanded after Manny had taken some long drinks. "Start with your affair with Brighton."

Manny nodded. "Like I said, I was having sex with Tara, but it was causing the other waitstaff to gossip. It was hurting morale so I ended things. About a week or so later, Brighton came into the bar, and we started talking. That led to us seeing each other. Not for long," he quickly tacked on to that. "And I don't think it was exclusive for her."

"Brighton was involved with someone else?" Luca pressed.

"I don't know for sure, but Brighton would get texts when we were out together, and I think the texts were from another man. It was just a feeling I got. She never confirmed it."

"How long were the two of you involved?" Duncan asked.

"Only about a month." Manny shut his eyes for a moment. "I'd made dinner reservations at a place in Austin, and Brighton didn't show. She didn't call or text so I figured she was ghosting me."

"And you didn't call or text her?" Duncan wanted to know.

He shook his head. "I just assumed she was done with me." Manny paused again. "Then, about two weeks later, I saw something online about her being murdered. The cops were asking anyone to come forward with information, but I didn't know anything."

"You should have let the cops decide that," Duncan snarled. "You should have let us know about the relationship."

"I didn't kill her," Manny snarled right back. "And I didn't want to get caught up in an investigation."

Bingo. That was the bottom line, and Bree had to wonder if he hadn't wanted to be involved because he'd killed Brighton and didn't want to be on the police's radar. But he'd come on their radar when she had spotted Brighton on the video outside the bar.

Manny looked at Sandra. "How'd you know I was involved with Brighton? Did she tell you or something?"

Sandra took in some deep breaths as well. "Brighton's mother and I were best friends, and after she died, I tried to keep an eye on Brighton. I was at her apartment and saw a photo of the two of you on her phone. I asked who you were, but she dodged the question. Why would she do that?"

"Well, it wasn't because she was afraid I was going to kill her," Manny protested. "Maybe she just didn't want to talk to you about her personal life."

"Possibly," Sandra admitted. "During that visit with Brighton, she mentioned she'd been going to some interesting bars in Austin. Hush, Hush was one of them, but she named a couple of others. Then, a week or so later when I went to visit her, she was crying. Sobbing, really. And again, she wouldn't get into specifics, but I think she was having trouble with a man she'd been seeing."

"Again, it wasn't me," Manny insisted. "Brighton and I didn't have that kind of relationship. It was casual, barely more than friends with benefits."

Of course, they had no proof that was true. At least, Bree didn't have proof. Except...

"If it was so casual, then why would Brighton have a picture of the two of you on her phone?" Bree asked.

He leveled his gaze on her. "Who knows? Maybe she liked the way she looked in it, or, hell, maybe she was just in the mood for taking a picture and then didn't bother to delete it. There's all kinds of reasons for pictures to be on someone's phone."

True, but the photo could be an indicator that the relationship wasn't as casual as Manny was making it out to be.

Bree turned to her mother. "You went to the Hush, Hush shortly before Brighton was killed. Did you hear anything about her involvement with Manny then?"

"No," Sandra said. "And I didn't see Manny either. I went to try to figure out what was going on with Brighton, but then that fight started, and I got spooked. I left." Her mouth trembled. "If I'd stayed, I might have figured out who'd wanted to hurt her." She looked at Manny. "I didn't know who you were, so I couldn't give your name to the police during the investigation."

Manny jumped to his feet again. "This inquisition is over," he snarled to Duncan. "If you want to talk to me again, go through my lawyer. Am I free to go, or do you plan on arresting me right now?"

Duncan took his time, though Bree knew what his answer was likely to be. There wasn't enough evidence to arrest Manny. Yes, he'd lied, and Duncan could charge him with that, but it was probably best if Duncan used that for leverage to bring Manny back in if anything else did come to light.

"You can go," Duncan finally said. "For now," he immediately tacked onto that.

Manny stormed out, and Tara kept her eyes on him until he was out the door. "He wouldn't have killed Brighton," she muttered.

"You're certain of that?" Duncan challenged.

Tara didn't issue a quick, resounding yes. In fact, she didn't verify that at all. She merely shrugged. "What about me? What if someone wants me dead?" Her gaze drifted to the door again where Manny had just made his exit, and Bree wondered if the woman was actually thinking—what if Manny wants me dead?

"I can't provide police protection to you in Austin," Duncan explained. "But I can call Austin PD and explain the situation. If they feel it's warranted, they'll assign someone to watch you."

Bree figured the cops there wouldn't consider it warranted, not when the only threat had been the text from an unknown number. Still, that seemed to placate Tara because she nodded.

"Thank you," she muttered. "I'll need my phone back, too."

Duncan motioned for Sonya to bring it back in and the deputy did. "Did you get anything from it?" he asked Sonya.

She shook her head. "The text came from a burner."

That surprised absolutely no one, not even Tara who sighed and slipped the phone into her pocket.

"Manny and you had a relationship," he spelled out to Tara. She'd already started for the door, but she stopped. "He broke up with you and yet you still continued to work for him. Why?"

"Because I'm in love with him," Tara admitted. "Because I want to be near him. Manny wouldn't have killed that woman," she repeated as she walked out.

"You think Tara believes that because she's in love with Manny or because she was the one who murdered Brighton?" Luca asked, taking the question right out of Bree's mouth.

"She's definitely a suspect for all of it," Duncan concluded. "And not just for the murder but for the cover-up attempts that I think are going on now."

Yes, a cover-up. Bree thought that was what was happening as well. And if so, the cover-up had started with her mother's kidnapping.

"Tara bears a strong resemblance to the sketch, and both Manny and she have means, motive and opportunity," Duncan summarized, and then he looked up at Sonya. "Try to find out if either of them own a gun or have had firearms training. I also want their phone records to see if either made calls anywhere near Saddle Ridge yesterday."

Sonya nodded and went back to her desk in the squad room.

"If we can get their financials, we can check and see if either bought burners or supplies we can maybe match to those taken to the cabin where Sandra was being held," Luca suggested.

Duncan nodded and looked at Woodrow. "I can request a warrant for that. Everything we've got is circumstantial, but it might be enough," Woodrow said.

"Go for it," Duncan agreed, and Woodrow stepped to the side to make a call.

Duncan picked up the evidence bag with the memory stick. "You two want to work on this back at the ranch?" he asked, directing the question to Bree and Luca.

They both nodded. Bree was eager to get started on that since it might give them a vital clue. Of course, it could take a lot of searching to find anything, but it'd be worth it if only to close off that particular investigative thread.

"I'll get this to the techs, then," Duncan said, "and I'll have them copy what's on it and forward it to you as a secure email attachment." He shifted his attention to Sandra. "I'd like for you to take a look at it, too, in case anything pops for you."

Sandra nodded and made a soft groan. "Am I responsible for what's happening? Are all of you in danger because I was digging into Brighton's murder?"

"I was digging into Brighton's murder, too," Bree assured her, and because she hated seeing those fresh tears in her mother's eyes, she went to her and pulled her into her arms. "We aren't responsible for what a killer's doing," she added, hoping that she would start to believe that as well. It certainly felt as if she'd set all of this in motion, especially since she'd been investigating Brighton's murder at the time her mother had been taken.

When Bree eased back from the hug, her mother attempted a smile. She failed miserably. So did Bree, but the moment still felt like some kind of turning point, and it was so very good to have her mother back.

"I love you," she whispered to her mom.

Now Sandra really did smile. "I love you, too."

Bree hadn't actually forgotten that they weren't alone, but then she noticed Luca, Woodrow and Duncan were all looking at them. Not with impatience though she figured they had to be feeling some of that. The investigation had to take priority. Had to. But Bree was hoping they could all have a proper homecoming once the danger was over.

"I'll have Woodrow and Ronnie accompany all of you back to the ranch," Duncan explained, motioning for Ronnie to come out of the squad room and into the office. "I want to wait here until the techs have picked up the memory stick, and then I'll head home, too."

"Not alone," Sandra was quick to say.

"Not alone," Duncan assured her.

He walked with them to the side door, opened it and glanced around the parking lot. He must not have seen anyone suspicious because he stepped back to let them all out. The cruiser wasn't far, only about ten feet away, and Woodrow and Ronnie went out first. Bree and her mother followed with Luca behind them.

When they reached the cruiser, Bree caught the strong smell of gasoline. The scene barely had time to register in her head before there was a sharp sound, like someone blowing out a huge candle.

And the flames shot up around them.

THE MOMENT LUCA heard the sound, he hooked his arm around Bree and yanked her back from the cruiser. Thankfully, Woodrow did the same to Sandra, and they fell back on the ground.

Not a second too soon either.

Because the fire blazed over the cruiser and the pavement beneath it. And the flames were spreading, too.

Ronnie, who'd been the closest to the cruiser, had a harder

fall than the rest of them. The impact knocked him back, and Luca could hear his fellow deputy's sharp groan of pain.

"Get back," Duncan shouted from the doorway.

With his left arm still around Bree, Luca drew his gun and started to bolt toward the still open office door. He stopped though when he saw the fire snaking along a trail of gasoline that stopped there. It had barely had time to register in his mind when the flames shot up there, too, forcing Duncan back into his office.

Luca yanked Bree away from the door. Away from the cruiser and toward the front of the sheriff's office.

And into what he knew could be extreme danger.

He couldn't see who'd ignited the gasoline, but he knew the person could be nearby, ready to gun them down. That's why he moved in front of Bree. Woodrow did the same to Sandra, and he practically dragged the woman toward Luca. Once Woodrow had her there, Luca got to a crouching position.

"Wait here," Luca told Woodrow. "I'll get Ronnie."

Ronnie groaned in pain again, and Luca knew that moving might make his injuries worse. Still, it couldn't be helped. If he stayed out in the open like that, he'd be an easier target. Luca ran toward him, the heat from the fire stinging his face. He couldn't see any gasoline in this particular spot, but the liquid and the flames could easily spread.

Something they were already doing.

Luca had no idea how much gasoline had been spilled, maybe only a gallon or two, but it'd obviously been more than enough to create this blaze that could be a cover for another attack.

While he tried to keep watch around him, Luca hooked his left arm around Ronnie, helping the deputy to his feet. Not easily. Ronnie outsized Luca by a good thirty pounds, and Luca had to take the man's weight so he could get them started across the parking lot.

Each step felt as if it took an eternity, and it didn't help that everything inside Luca was telling him they could all be gunned down at any moment. Telling him, too, that Ronnie could have serious internal injuries from the fall.

Thick black smoke billowed up from the fire, cutting across his path to the building. For a few terrifying moments, Luca lost sight of Bree, and his mind immediately went into some worst-case scenarios. Maybe this wasn't a murder attempt but a kidnapping. The killer could be trying to take her.

That possibility gave Luca an extra shot of adrenaline, and he fought his way through the smoke and heat so he could reach the side of the building. He finally saw Bree. Saw the fear and worry that was there, and he cursed their attacker for putting them through this.

Whatever this was.

Bree reached out for him, taking hold of Luca's arm and pulling both Ronnie and him closer until they were all in a huddle.

"Tara or Manny could have done this," Bree muttered.

Yeah, they could have, and it wouldn't have been especially hard if they'd already had the gasoline with them. Manny and Tara had arrived separately and would have used this parking lot. If they'd parked on the other side of the cruiser, the side that wouldn't have been easily visible from the street, one of them could have poured the gasoline from the door while seated in their vehicles. That theory worked.

But there was a problem.

He didn't see either Manny or Tara, and their vehicles weren't in the lot right now. So, how had the flames ignited?

Luca soon came up with the answer.

There were clusters of trees and shrubs at the far back of the parking lot, and one or both of them could have poured the gasoline, driven away and parked somewhere up the street. They could have then made their way back to the trees and shrubs and waited. If the stream of gasoline was nearby, all it would have taken was lighting a match and tossing it. Then the person could have run away and taken up the vantage point to fire some shots.

"An ambulance and the fire department are on the way," Duncan called out.

Luca glanced at the front corner of the building and saw Duncan and Sonya. Both had their weapons drawn and were firing glances all around. Clearly, they'd braced for an attack, too.

"Try to get inside," Duncan instructed.

Since that wouldn't happen from the side door where the fire was still blazing, it meant going through the front. The sheriff's office was on Main Street and there were buildings on each side as well as across the street. Places for a gunman to hide and take aim. Still, it wasn't safe where they were either.

Woodrow hurried to the other side of Ronnie and, along with Luca, they hoisted up the deputy. "Stay against the side of the building," Luca told Bree and Sandra.

At least that way, a gunman would have to shoot through Woodrow, Ronnie and him to get to them. Maybe though the threat wouldn't come from a gunshot. Luca realized that when he looked at the fire shooting up the front of the cruiser.

Hell.

Luca knew it was rare for a vehicle to actually explode during a fire, but it was possible their attacker had added something to the mix. Like maybe some other chemical that could be toxic to breathe in.

"We need to evacuate the area," Luca shouted to Duncan, and he tipped his head to the cruiser to let him know what was going on.

Duncan cursed and made a frantic motion for them to move faster. They did, but it wasn't easy. Ronnie was unconscious now so Luca hefted him over his shoulder in a fireman's carry so he could put some distance between them and the cruiser.

Bree and Sandra thankfully stayed against the wall of the building, and they all moved together. All keeping watch as best they could, considering the slashes of smoke that kept coming their way.

It seemed to take a lifetime or two before they finally reached the door, and the moment they did, Duncan got Sandra and Bree inside. Luca moved to do the same to Ronnie, but he caught some movement from the corner of his eye and whipped around in that direction.

Luca caught just a glimpse of Tara running from the scene.

Chapter Nine

Bree just wanted to stop feeling as if she were about to jump out of her own skin. She wanted her heart rate to go back to normal. She wanted to stop being afraid for her precious little boy.

But none of that was likely to happen anytime soon.

She was back at the ranch with Luca, Woodrow and her mother. Away from the fire and smoke-filled parking lot. Away from immediate danger. But nothing felt safe right now.

Probably because it wasn't.

If their attacker could come at them in the parking lot of the sheriff's office, then he or she could come after them here. Luca obviously understood that was a possibility because the ranch was on high alert with the security system activated and ranch hands patrolling the grounds.

Bree watched the laptop screen as Duncan was finishing up his interview with Tara. Not at the sheriff's office. That entire area had been evacuated so when they'd seen Tara running from the fire, Duncan had gone after her, caught her and ultimately taken her to an office in city hall. He'd then set up a laptop to do a live feed of the interview so Luca, Woodrow, Joelle and Bree could watch from the ranch.

So far, Tara wasn't saying anything Bree wanted to hear.

"I didn't start that fire," Tara insisted for the umpteenth time. "I told you that I was walking to my car that I'd parked up the street. I saw the fire and ran."

"We've requested the camera feed from the bank," Luca muttered to Bree while he stood right next to her. Right next to her had been his default position since they'd escaped the fire.

And Bree wasn't complaining.

As bad as her frayed nerves were right now, she knew they'd be even worse if Luca wasn't there. Ditto for Gabriel. Even though the baby was asleep, she was holding him because she wanted him as close as possible.

"The angle of the bank camera won't help with the parking lot," Luca added, knowing that Tara couldn't hear him, "but it might be able to confirm or disprove what Tara is saying."

Bree considered the location of the bank, which was more than a block away from the sheriff's office. It was the only security camera in the area. Still, they might get lucky and be able to see Tara's movements. If she had indeed parked up the street, then it wasn't likely she'd spilled that gasoline and ignited it. Well, not likely unless she'd spilled it before she'd ever parked on Main Street and then come into the sheriff's office. It was possible she'd done just that, but it might be hard to prove unless Tara had left behind some evidence that pointed to her guilt.

Bree continued to watch as Duncan pressed Tara, trying to trip her up with different versions of the same question. But Tara was staying steady, insisting she was innocent.

Luca's phone dinged with a text, and when he lifted it, she saw Sonya's name on the screen. Ronnie's conscious, the deputy texted. Doctor says no serious injuries but he'll be admitted for an overnight stay.

Bree latched on to the "no serious injuries" part. They'd

gotten lucky. With a fire of that size, all of them could have gotten burned, literally.

Luca texted back to thank Sonya for the update, but his phone dinged again before he could put it away.

"The tech picked up the memory stick and copied it," Luca explained. "He just emailed me the bar receipts."

Bree glanced at the laptop screen with the interview, then at Gabriel who was deep into his nap and would no doubt still be asleep for at least two hours. "Let me put him down in his crib, and maybe we can go over the receipts in the guest room." That way, they'd still be able to watch Gabriel while they worked.

Luca took one of the laptops scattered around the room and told the others what they were doing. Woodrow assured him if anything came up in the remainder of the interview with Tara that he'd let them know. They agreed to do the same if they found anything in the receipts.

Bree and Luca made their way up the stairs to the guest room, which was now empty since Coral had already gone home. Bree welcomed the quiet. For a couple of seconds anyway, and then the flashbacks came.

Mercy, did they.

There was a whirl of images of the attack on the road, the shooting into the barn and the fire, all mixed with the memories of her father. It was a volatile combo, and her hands were already starting to tremble when she crossed the room toward the crib.

Luca set the laptop aside and steadied her by slipping his hands beneath hers, and together, they eased the baby onto the mattress. Gabriel stirred just a little but stayed asleep.

"Thank you," Bree whispered. And it wasn't just gratitude for helping her with this but also for what he'd done during the fire. "You put yourself in front of me again. You shielded me."

"I'm a cop," he said as if that explained everything. Maybe in his mind it did. Maybe he would have done that for anyone. After all, he'd run out into the parking lot to rescue Ronnie.

It was a bad time for her to make direct eye contact with him, but Bree found herself doing it anyway. As usual, things passed between them. Unspoken but still intense. Things always seemed intense between Luca and her.

Yes, the eye contact was a mistake, but she made it much worse when she stepped toward him. And into his arms. Luca pulled her to him, brushing a kiss on the top of her head. A kiss of comfort. So was the hug when he tightened his embrace. It was wrong to take this from him, but Bree couldn't make herself back away.

She stayed there where it felt so safe. So right. The first part was the truth. The second, wasn't. Luca and she weren't together, and this was not only playing with fire, it was wrong. As if she were leading him on.

That gave her the steel to move back, and he eased his grip to let her do that. But it was another mistake. Because now they had the intense eye contact and the body-to-body touching. Definitely not good.

Bree felt the heat slide right through her. Of course, it did. There was always heat whenever she was around Luca. Heat and need. Another bad combo. Still, she stayed put, looking at him. Holding her breath.

Waiting.

Luca didn't stay put though. He lowered his head and brushed his mouth over hers. This was not a gesture of comfort. No. This was about the fiery attraction. And she felt it. Felt it not only on her mouth but in every inch of her.

He pulled back, looked at her, no doubt gauging her reaction, and he muttered some profanity. She didn't think his reaction was because he saw any objection on her face but because he probably saw the invitation she could feel her body sending out to him. An invitation that could complicate an already complicated situation.

Did that stop her?

No.

Bree moved in and kissed him. Really kissed him. Hard pressure of her mouth on his. Then, more. She was the one who deepened the kiss, the one who slid her hand around the back of his neck to pull him down to her.

Luca certainly didn't resist. Just the opposite. He made a sound that came from deep within his throat, and he snapped her to him. Not that she could get much closer, but instead of merely touching, they were now pressed against each other. Like lovers.

Her body knew just how to react to the feel of his chest against her breasts. Everything inside her went warm and soft. Then, hot. Everything inside her pushed her to take more, more, more. She had no doubts, none, that Luca would give her that more, but there was another sound.

Gabriel whimpering.

That sent Luca and her flying apart, and both of them whipped their attention to their son. Gabriel stirred, stretching and making a face before he sucked at a nonexistent bottle and went back to sleep.

Luca and she stood there. Breaths racing. Heartbeats, too. She knew that because she could see Luca's pulse on his neck. A neck she wished she could kiss. Heck, she wished she could do a lot of thing with Luca, but the timing was all off. Might always be off if she couldn't set aside the horrible flashbacks.

"Saved by a whimper," he muttered. Luca shook his head.

Then, he surprised Bree by smiling. "I'm not sure I want to thank Gabriel for the interruption."

He seemed to be waiting for her to agree. Which she did. That whole not being sure was front and center in her mind. But so was the heat. Since she didn't want to give in to that heat, which might lead them straight to the bed, Bree motioned toward the laptop instead.

"The receipts," she reminded him, keeping her voice at a whisper.

Luca nodded, sighed and picked up the computer. He took it to the small seating area in the corner, booted it up and set it on the table that was between the two chairs. The email was indeed there with the large attachment of the receipts. Bree's heart dropped a little when she realized it was well over a hundred pages, and each page had at least two dozen transactions.

"These are for the three weeks before Brighton's death," Luca pointed out.

So, Manny had been thorough. Or it appeared he had been on the surface anyway. If he was the person who'd murdered Brighton and was now responsible for the attacks, then he might have turned over the receipts only because he knew they wouldn't incriminate him.

"Neither Tara nor Manny have alibis for the attacks," Bree said, "but we didn't ask them where they were when Brighton was murdered."

Luca nodded. "I'm sure Duncan will do that. If anything pops in their background checks, he'll have cause to bring them back in for interviews. The same could happen if we get that warrant for their financials. If one of them held your mother captive for all these months, there could be a money trail."

True, and that was a trail they'd have to find since neither Tara nor Manny would likely confess to something like that. Kidnapping and imprisonment were serious crimes that would carry long jail sentences. Ditto for the attacks. Added to that, if the kidnapping and the attacks could be linked to Brighton's murder, then life with no parole could be doled out. Heck, even the death penalty.

First, they had to find evidence to prove their guilt or eliminate them as suspects. They probably weren't going to be able to do that based solely on the receipts, but it was something that needed to be investigated.

"Email me a copy of the list," she said, standing so she could get her laptop she'd had brought over from her house. "I'll start at the bottom. You can start at the top."

Luca pulled his computer onto his lap to send her the email. "Flag anything that seems suspicious," he muttered.

Bree made a sound of agreement and settled back in the chair to get busy. Since she had no idea what the usual daily revenue was for the bar, she flagged large charges, those over a thousand dollars, just in case Manny or Tara was using the Hush, Hush to launder money. Still, she supposed charges that high wouldn't necessarily be anything sinister but rather a single payment for large group.

"Your mom's on here," Luca said, snagging her attention.

She leaned over and looked at the charge. Less than five dollars, which meant it was likely water or club soda. The date matched Sandra's account of being at the Hush, Hush the night of the fight.

"And here's Brighton," Luca added a moment later.

"Clearly, you got the good end of the list," she muttered. "So far, I haven't recognized a single name on mine." And she leaned toward Luca's laptop for another look. "Twenty-three dollars, and this would have been the same night Mom was there."

"Does the bar serve food?" he asked.

"A few items. When I was researching it, I looked at the menu on the website. Typical bar stuff. Sliders, nachos, that sort of thing."

Of course, they had no way of knowing if Brighton's bill had been for food or drink. And maybe it didn't matter unless twenty-three dollars was to pay for her drink and that of a companion.

"Funny that Manny didn't give her the drinks or food on the house," Luca pointed out.

"Manny will probably say he'd broken things off with her by then. Tara might be able to say otherwise though." Unfortunately, Bree wasn't anywhere near certain they could believe what Tara would tell them.

"I'm going to flag the bar tabs paid around the same time Brighton paid hers," Luca said. "Then, we can maybe contact these people and see if they remember her."

"Good idea," she said and continued with her list. Finally, she got a hit. Maybe a huge one. "Another charge from Brighton, for eighteen dollars. And this was the night she was murdered."

That got Luca's attention, and he leaned over to take a look. "Definitely flag the other receipts within an hour of that."

Bree started doing that, using a highlighter function on the laptop, but her fingers froze when one name practically popped off the screen at her.

"What?" Luca questioned.

He'd obviously heard the sharp sound of surprise she'd made, and he leaned in again. Then he cursed. Because the customer's name was one they both recognized.

Nathan.

LUCA STOOD AT the window, waiting and watching. It definitely wasn't standard procedure to interview a suspect at the ranch, but with the CSIs and fire department clogging up the parking lot of the sheriff's office, Duncan had decided to hold the interview here. Luca didn't especially care where they questioned Nathan. He just wanted it to happen.

They needed answers. And this just might be the break they'd been looking for.

"Even if Nathan's guilty of murdering Brighton, he won't confess," Bree said. She was right next to Luca, keeping watch as well while Sandra was upstairs with Gabriel.

Luca agreed. But sometimes confessions weren't intentional. And it was possible that Nathan being at the bar had nothing to do with Brighton. The timing was suspicious though, and the receipts could put Brighton and Nathan together at the bar at the same time. Since they were from the same small town, they would have likely recognized each other. Yet, Nathan hadn't said a word about seeing Brighton mere hours before she'd been murdered.

And that gave Luca an idea.

He took out his phone. "I'm going to text Nathan's picture to Manny and Tara to see if they recognize him. I won't mention Brighton, but it's possible one of them remembers seeing him with her. If so, Nathan won't be able to deny knowing that Brighton was at the bar the same time he was."

Bree made a quick sound of agreement, and Luca sent off the first text to Manny. When the man would answer was anyone's guess. Manny might want everything to go through his lawyer. Ditto for Tara, but Luca sent her an identical message anyway.

The moments crawled by with no response, so Luca put his phone away and continued to keep watch for Nathan.

While still standing right next to Bree. With their arms pressed against each other. It wasn't anywhere near the embrace they'd had upstairs, but any contact with Bree was a mental distraction for him.

So was the memory of that kiss.

Hard to forget that, and that sensation of heat and need. He'd been on the verge of losing control with Bree. Again. Apparently, he hadn't learned his lesson about that from eleven months ago. He'd surrendered to the kiss knowing full well that it was a bad idea, that there'd be a serious loss of focus. But that hadn't stopped it, and he had to figure out a way to make sure he kept this heat in check so he could keep Bree safe.

She looked up at him. Their gazes connecting. And he cursed. She muttered some profanity, too, so he knew they were on the same page here. A page that likely would have involved them talking about it if his phone hadn't sounded with a text.

"Manny," he said when he saw the screen.

Once again, Luca had to push aside thoughts of Bree and that amazing kiss and nail his attention to this investigation. Well, to this response anyway, which Luca knew could be Manny lashing out to demand to be left the hell alone.

But it wasn't.

Yeah, I've seen him before, Manny texted. He was in the bar with Brighton a couple of times.

Bingo. They now had the verification they needed in case Nathan lied to them. Of course, this was still just hearsay, but it'd be strong hearsay if Tara confirmed seeing Nathan as well.

Do you know if Brighton was dating him? Luca messaged back.

They were together, that's all I know. They weren't like having sex on the bar or anything like that, but I did see her kiss the guy. I figured she was doing that to try to make me jealous because I'd recently ended things with her. Why? Are you going to grill him the way you did me?

Luca definitely intended to do some grilling when it came to Nathan. For now though, he reread Manny's text. Bree was obviously doing the same thing.

"Interesting," Bree said.

It was indeed, and Luca could see one way this might have played out. "If Brighton was truly using Nathan to make Manny jealous and Nathan found out, Nathan wouldn't be happy about that. In fact, he could have been so angry that he attacked her."

Of course, there was no proof of that, not yet anyway. And it was equally possible that Manny was lying. The bar owner might say or do anything to point the finger at someone other than himself.

Thanks, Luca texted to Manny. Please let me know if you remember anything else about the guy in the picture.

He didn't get an immediate response from Manny, but Luca did see something else he'd been waiting for. Nathan's car as he pulled into the driveway. Duncan must have heard it because he, too, went to the window to stand behind Bree and Luca.

"I want you to do the interview," Duncan told Luca. "I figure if the doctor has any hot buttons, you'll be able to push them better than I could." He looked at Bree. "And I want you close to Luca while he's questioning him."

Bree's eyebrow lifted. "You want Luca and me to pretend to be together so that it'll rile Nathan?"

Duncan gave them a flat look. "Just sit close to each other.

If Nathan's not an idiot, he'll pick up on the vibe between you two, and it could set him off."

Luca could tell Bree wanted to deny there was any *vibe*. She couldn't though because it was indeed there.

"I just got these texts from Manny," Luca said, passing his phone to Duncan. "I'm waiting to hear from Tara."

Duncan smiled when he read Manny's responses. "Definitely use this," he insisted.

When Nathan parked and got out of his car, the three of them stepped away from the window to go to the front door. Bree must have taken Duncan's advice to heart because she stood arm to arm with Luca while Duncan ushered in Nathan. Duncan also immediately riled the doctor by checking him for weapons and reciting the Miranda rights.

The annoyance was building on Nathan's face. Until he turned his attention to Bree. Then Luca saw the quick change. Worry and concern rather than anger.

"Are you all right?" Nathan asked Bree. Completely ignoring Luca, he went to her and laid his hand on her shoulder. "Are the stitches hurting?" He proceeded to examine them.

"I'm okay," Bree said, stepping back and aligning herself with Luca again.

And, yeah, Nathan noticed all right. It'd been a good call on Duncan's part to go with this ploy since it caused a spark of fresh anger to flare in Nathan's eyes,

"Good," Nathan muttered, but his tone indicated her actions were anything but. "I'm betting you'll be glad when you can get back to your own place," he said, speaking to Bree. "It can't be easy being cooped up here in a house that holds so many horrible memories for you."

Luca silently cursed because the remark had hit pay dirt. Bree flinched, but it was obvious to Luca that she was trying to suppress her reaction. Hard to do though when there were indeed bad memories here of her father's murder.

"Not all bad," Bree said. "I grew up here so there are plenty of good memories, too."

Bree's remark hit pay dirt as well because she coupled it by brushing her arm against Luca's. A subtle gesture, but it obviously packed an emotional punch for Nathan. He practically snapped to attention toward Duncan.

"So, where are we doing this interview?" Nathan asked him.

"Actually, Luca will be conducting it in the living room," Duncan was quick to say. "I've asked Bree to stay in the room as well as an observer." He'd no doubt added that to cover any legal bases. "Hope you don't have a problem with that," Duncan added like a challenge.

"No," Nathan muttered, his response in direct contrast to his expression. It was obvious he did have a problem, but Luca figured it wasn't because Bree would be there but rather that Luca would be the one doling out the questions.

They went into the living room where Duncan had already turned around the incident board and Slater was working on his laptop at a makeshift desk in the corner. Duncan motioned for Nathan to sit in one of the chairs that he'd obviously positioned like a hot seat directly across from the sofa and chair that Duncan, Bree and he would be using. Duncan revved up the tension some more by turning on the recorder and putting it on the coffee table only a couple of inches from Nathan.

For the record, Luca read in the date, time and those present, and he added, "Dr. Bagley has consented to Attorney Bree McCullough being present as an observer for this interview. Could you state your consent for the recording?" Luca added.

Nathan's teeth came together. "Bree can be here," he said.

Good. With that formality out of the way, Luca jumped right to the heart of the matter. "Tell me about your relationship with Brighton Cooper."

Nathan seemed to do a mental double take. "Brighton?" He shook his head. "I was aware of who she was. She'd come into the hospital a couple of times, but there wasn't a…" He stopped, studying Bree's and Luca's expressions.

The doctor had been about to lie. Luca was certain of it. But Nathan must have sensed this could be a trap.

"Has that bar owner and bartender said something about me?" Nathan asked.

"You mean Manny Vickery and Tara Adler?" Luca prompted when Nathan didn't add anything.

Nathan nodded.

"How did you know we'd interviewed them?" Luca pressed.

Nathan's jaw went tight again. "Word about that sort of thing gets around. Did they say something about me?" Luca didn't respond. He just stared at Nathan until the doctor huffed. "Manny or Tara probably told you I occasionally went to the bar. You might even have proof of that if you looked over old credit card charges. Is that it? Is that why I'm here?"

Luca felt as if some of the wind had been taken out of his sails. He'd been hoping that Nathan would deny even being at the Hush, Hush, but if word had indeed gotten around about Manny and Tara being questioned, then Nathan might have realized it'd be stupid for him to lie.

That didn't mean the doctor was innocent though.

"And your relationship with Brighton?" Luca repeated.

Nathan huffed. "It was hardly a relationship. We didn't exactly travel in the same social circles or anything."

The man's snobbery was coming through so Luca gave that a nudge. "What do you mean by that?"

Nathan huffed again and looked at Bree. "I swear, I didn't have anything to do with Brighton when I was seeing you. I didn't cheat on you."

Bree shook her head. "We dated, and that wasn't exclusive, so even if you were with Brighton or anyone else it wouldn't have been cheating."

Oh, Nathan didn't like that, but instead of doling out a verbal blast to Bree, he turned his frosty gaze on Luca. "All of this feels like a witch hunt and a gross violation of my privacy."

"Not a witch hunt," Luca said. "But interviews can definitely take pokes at privacy. Especially if the interviewee has something to hide. Did you want to hide your relationship with Brighton?"

"It wasn't a relationship," Nathan practically yelled, but the outburst was short-lived, and he made a visible effort to rein in his temper. "Brighton and I hooked up a few times, that was all. She wasn't my type, and she was six years younger than me."

"Hooked up?" Luca questioned. "Does that mean sex or just hanging out at the bar together?"

If looks could have killed, Nathan would have finished Luca off then and there. "Both. Briefly," he quickly tacked on to that. "I was only with her a couple of times and never when I was with Bree."

That was probably meant to give Luca a dig, to be a reminder that Bree and this jerk had once dated, but Luca didn't get the jolt of jealousy that Nathan was likely hoping for. Luca felt nothing but disgust over Nathan's behavior once Bree had ended things with him.

"Did you hook up with Brighton or hang out with her at the bar at the same time she was seeing Manny?" Luca asked.

Nathan did a double take, part flinch, part raised eyebrow. "Maybe. I don't know when she was involved with Manny. I'd stopped seeing her long before she died. Months," he provided.

"Yet you were at the Hush, Hush at the same time the night she died," Luca pointed out.

"That could be true, but if so, she wasn't there with me," Nathan insisted.

Maybe. But Luca wished he had security footage of Brighton leaving the bar that night so he could see if she'd left with either Nathan or Manny. The camera footage hadn't been preserved since they hadn't known for weeks that Brighton had even been to a bar in Austin. By then, the security system had recorded over the old footage.

"I didn't have anything to do with Brighton's death," Nathan went on, talking to Bree now. "You know me. You know I'm not capable of violence."

Bree stared at him. "I know you're capable of stalking."

Nathan cursed. "That wasn't what was happening. I simply didn't understand why you said you didn't want to see me anymore. I thought maybe it was a misunderstanding and that if we just talked, you'd be able to see that I cared deeply for you. I still do," he added. "And that's why I'm so worried about you now."

Judging from Bree's stiff body language, she wasn't buying it. Caring deeply for someone didn't mesh with stalking.

"Where were you yesterday morning before you treated Bree at the hospital?" Luca asked.

Nathan pulled back his shoulders, obviously thrown off a little by the shift in subject. "I went on shift at seven, so I'd been there for a couple of hours before Bree arrived."

"Can anyone verify that?" Luca added.

"Plenty of people." Nathan had to answer that through clenched teeth. "Nurses and other doctors. If you need names, you can ask for the duty roster."

"I'll do that," Slater volunteered, earning his own glare from Nathan.

"And what about after Bree left the hospital?" Luca went on. "Did you stay on duty or did you leave?"

Nathan opened his mouth as if ready to do that blast, but he reined in again. "I had nothing to do with the shooting at Bree's. I'm not a killer."

"Did you stay on duty at the hospital or did you leave?" Luca repeated.

"I stayed on duty until I heard about Bree's son being missing. I left then because I thought I could help look for him."

"So, you have no alibi for the time of the shooting," Luca concluded. "What about for earlier today when someone set the parking lot on fire?"

Nathan got up from the chair. "Enough. You clearly have it in for me."

Duncan stepped closer. "No one here has it in for you," he stated. "This is an interview with questions that should be relatively easy for you to answer. The fire was only a couple of hours ago so you shouldn't have any trouble recalling where you were."

"I was at the hospital," Nathan snarled. "You can check the duty roster for that, too."

Luca had no doubt that Nathan's name would be there, but that didn't mean he was innocent.

Duncan's phone rang, the sound slicing through the heavy silence that had fallen over the room. He took the call, moving away from them. Luca was about to continue the interview when he heard Duncan mutter some profanity.

Alarmed that there was more bad news, Luca went to him. So did Bree and Slater, and they ended up huddled together in the corner.

Duncan put the caller on hold and looked at Slater, Luca and Bree. He cursed again before he said, "There's been a murder."

Chapter Ten

Bree watched from the window as Nathan drove away. She'd kept back because she hadn't wanted him to see her watching him and conclude that she was longing for him or anything like that. She just wanted to make sure he was gone and away from the house. She didn't want any of their suspects under the same roof as Gabriel.

"All right," she heard Duncan say after he'd finished his latest call. The third one he'd gotten since delivering the whispered bombshell.

There's been a murder.

Other than assuring Bree and the others that it wasn't a family member or one of the deputies, that was all Duncan had been able to tell them. He'd then dismissed Nathan, basically telling him to get the heck out of there, and then had started the calls. Luca and Slater had done the same, and even though Bree didn't know the specifics, it was obvious some things were happening in the investigation.

Duncan repeated his "all right" as if trying to gather his thoughts, and he slipped his phone back in his pocket. "About two hours ago, a hunter reported finding a dead body in the woods not too far from the burned-out cabin. Not on the grounds but about a quarter of a mile away. According to County Deputy Morales who arrived on scene, cause of death appears to be a single gunshot wound to the head."

That gave Bree a jolt. Even though that wasn't the exact way her father had been murdered, it still gave her the flashbacks.

"Any indications it could be a suicide?" Luca asked.

Duncan nodded. Then, shrugged. "Deputy Morales says it's set up to look that way. The gun is in her hand and positioned more or less the correct way if the shot had been self-inflicted, but Morales believes the position of the body is off. He says it looks staged to him."

Staged would equal murder as far as Bree was concerned.

"The county sheriff's office had copies of the sketches done by the police artist," Duncan went on. "The ones that the two witnesses said were of the woman they saw driving the silver truck when Sandra would have been captive. Anyway, the responding deputy says he believes the dead woman is the one in the sketch. So, it could be Tara or her sister, Shannon. I've tried to call Tara, but she's not answering."

If the dead woman was indeed Shannon, then it was possible she was the one who'd kidnapped Sandra. Sandra had said the woman who'd held her had had phone conversations with someone and appeared to be getting instructions. The person giving those instructions could have been Shannon's boss, and he or she might not want Shannon around to spill anything incriminating.

"She didn't respond to a text I sent her earlier," Luca pointed out.

Duncan scrubbed his hand over his face and seemed to consider that a moment. "Try to contact her again. If she still doesn't answer, I'll have the Austin cops go to her place and see if she's there. For now, call Manny and see if knows where she is. Find out, too, if he knows Shannon, and it's okay to tell him there's a body matching Shannon's description."

Luca nodded, and he took out his phone, moving a few yards away into the adjacent formal dining room and motioning for Bree to join him. She did, and Luca put the call on Speaker when he tried to call Tara. Bree got a very uneasy feeling when it went straight to voicemail. Maybe Tara was just dodging them, but it was also possible she was dead.

"This is Deputy Vanetti," Luca said, leaving a message. "I need to speak to you right away." He paused a heartbeat. "It's about your sister."

That might prompt Tara to return the call. If she was in any position to do it, that is.

Luca pulled up Manny's number next and also put it on Speaker. "Didn't I make it clear that you'll have to go through my lawyer if you want to talk to me?" Manny greeted in a snarl.

"I'm looking for Tara," Luca said, clearly ignoring Manny's rant.

"I have no idea where she is. She's not at work, that's for sure." He paused. "Why are you looking for her? Did you find some kind of proof that she's the one who killed Brighton?"

"No," Luca answered. "I wanted to talk to her about her sister."

"Shannon?" Manny questioned.

"That's right. You know her?"

"Yeah, I've met Shannon a couple of times," Manny confirmed. "She's the spitting image of Tara, but they're nothing alike personality-wise. Or rather they were nothing alike. Tara used to be reliable. Shannon's a train wreck. She takes that whole bad girl attitude way too far."

"What do you mean Tara used to be reliable?" Luca asked. Bree knew he wasn't dropping the subject of Shannon, but that past tense could be a red flag if Manny knew Tara was dead. "Has something changed?"

"Damn right, things have changed. Tara's spooked out of her mind and believes this whole thing of someone wanting her dead. I'm the one who was nearly run off the road. I'm the one who was attacked, not her, but you'd think she was the only one at risk here. Hell, there's no indication other than her wild imagination that someone is after her."

Bree mentally repeated all of that, and there was something about it that didn't ring true. But she didn't know what part. If Manny was the mastermind behind what was happening, then he could be setting up Tara to take the fall. That didn't feel right either though.

"Truth is, I've told Tara that she should look for another job," Manny went on. "Now watch, she'll probably pull some 'hell has no fury like a woman scorned' deal and accuse me of all sorts of things."

"Like what?" Luca pressed, and Bree realized this was turning into the interview that they hadn't been able to finish with Manny when he'd been at the sheriff's office.

"Who the hell knows," Manny grumbled. "She'll probably accuse me of murder or something. She might even claim I'm the one after her." He paused. "Wait, is Tara working with Shannon to try to smear my name or something?"

"Not that I know of," Luca assured him. "Would Tara or Shannon do that?"

"Hell, yeah. Shannon would, anyway, and it wouldn't take much of a push for Tara to get Shannon to come after me for her version of payback."

"You think Shannon could be violent?" Luca went on.

Now, Manny wasn't so quick to answer. "Did Shannon do something? Does she want Tara to bail her out of jail again?"

"No," Luca said, but didn't add more to that. "Does Shannon have any identifying marks that Tara doesn't and vice versa? Like a birthmark or tat?"

Again, Manny hesitated. "Why are you asking that? Did something happen to Shannon or Tara?"

Luca dodged those questions. "We're looking into that. Tats or birthmarks?" Luca repeated.

Manny huffed. "Tara has a shamrock tat on her right ankle. As far as I know, Shannon's not into that sort of thing."

Bree hurried back to Duncan to let him know to have the cops on scene check for an ankle tat on the dead body. It didn't take Duncan long to make the call or for the cops to respond.

"No tat of any kind on her ankle," Duncan relayed.

So, this was Shannon. Bree didn't know whether to be relieved or not. The proximity of the body to the cabin and the eyewitness accounts of the woman driving the silver truck likely meant Shannon had been involved in not only her mother's kidnapping but perhaps everything else that'd happened.

But that didn't exclude Tara's involvement.

In fact, the conversations Sandra had overheard could have been Shannon talking with Tara. Tara might be the mastermind behind the kidnapping and the attacks. Why though, Bree still wasn't sure.

She went back to Luca to let him know that the dead woman didn't have a tat and found him in the middle of another Manny tirade. Manny was now demanding that Luca tell him what was going on, and the man was peppering the demand with plenty of profanity.

Bree mouthed the info about the tat. Luca nodded and interrupted Manny's rant. "A woman's been murdered, and it might be Shannon," he said.

That stopped Manny mid-sentence. "Murdered?" he questioned. "And you think I did it?"

"Did you?" Luca asked.

"Of course not." He paused again. "This is why you want to talk to Tara," Manny concluded with a sigh. "Do you think she killed her sister?"

Luca frowned. "Why would you think that? Is Tara capable of killing Shannon?"

Manny did more cursing. "To hell if I know. A week ago, I would have said no, but I think Tara's had some kind of breakdown. There's no telling what she might do in this state of mind."

There it was again, the feeling that what he was saying just didn't ring true. Basically, Manny was throwing Tara under the bus. Maybe because he believed she was indeed capable of murder, but it felt to Bree as if Manny was trying to cover his own tracks by making them believe Tara was guilty.

"I really need to speak to Tara," Luca went on. "But she's not answering her phone. Any idea where she might be?"

"None whatsoever," he was quick to say, "but when you do talk to her, remember what I said. Don't believe anything she tells you about me. Or anything else for that matter," Manny added a split second before he ended the call.

Luca stared at his phone for a moment as if he might hit Redial, but something Duncan said must have caught his attention because he headed in that direction. Duncan was still talking to someone on the phone, but he finished his conversation just as they approached him.

"They ran the dead woman's fingerprints and got an immediate hit," Duncan explained. "It's Shannon."

Bree wasn't sure what to feel about that. With her death,

she would no longer be a threat. But the threat was still out there, and if Shannon were alive, she might at least have been willing to spill the name of her accomplice. If she had an accomplice, that is. For now, all they could do was speculate as to what her part had been in Sandra's kidnapping and the attacks.

They knew from the witnesses' sketches that Shannon, or Tara, had been at the cabin and had driven the silver truck. So, one of them had held Sandra. It was too bad that Sandra had never seen her kidnapper's face or she might have been able to verify which one.

But the proximity of Shannon's body to the cabin pointed to it being her.

Shannon had that "trouble magnet" past, and she would have had an easier time getting to and from the cabin than Tara who, according to her work schedule, was putting in fifty-plus hours a week. That didn't totally exclude Tara, but at the moment the circumstantial evidence was skewed more to Shannon. She was almost certainly the one who had brought in groceries to Sandra.

"Deputy Morales will get the body to the ME and send the gun to the lab for analysis," Duncan explained. "Her address is listed as an apartment in Austin, so Austin PD will send someone out to take a look at the place."

Duncan was scowling. So were Luca and Slater. Probably because this had turned into a three-prong investigation with three different law enforcement agencies involved. That meant red tape and possible delays.

"I checked and Shannon Adler doesn't have a gun registered to her," Slater said a moment later. "Of course, that doesn't mean she didn't buy one illegally, but we still might be able to trace the gun to someone."

True. "How about our other suspects?" Bree asked. "Do they own guns?"

"Not Tara. Again, not legally anyway," Slater answered. "Manny has a permit to carry concealed, and he owns both a Glock and a SIG Sauer."

Those were normally cops' weapons, but plenty of civilians carried them as well. Manny could probably justify ownership of that kind of firepower though by saying he'd wanted protection for the bar. Added to that, if Manny was responsible for the attacks, he almost certainly wouldn't have used one of his own weapons. However, the concealed permit was an indicator that he knew how to shoot since he would have needed classes to get that.

"Did Morales say if the shot to Shannon's head was point-blank?" Luca asked.

"It was," Duncan verified. "There was stippling around the point of entry."

Bree knew that stippling was unburned gunpowder striking the skin, and it was an indicator that the shot had been fired less than two feet away. So, if this wasn't a suicide, it likely meant Shannon's killer had been someone she knew. Or at least someone who could get that close to her anyway.

"Morales thinks Shannon was actually killed in the spot where she was found," Duncan went on. "There were no drag marks, and there was an ample amount of blood to make him believe that's where she died."

"How far from the road?" Luca wanted to know.

"About fifty yards," Duncan answered. "It was a heavily treed area in between the cabin and the river. Morales said it was the very definition of *off the beaten path*."

"So, Shannon was meeting someone or was lured there," Luca concluded.

"This is all too pat for my liking," Slater said, reading through something on his laptop screen.

That got Bree's and everyone else's attention, and they turned to Slater, waiting for him to explain that.

"Shannon had a short stint in the army before she was dishonorably discharged," he said. "She would have gotten firearms training. She also had a record for drugs and B and E. Everything I'm seeing in her background indicates she couldn't stay out of trouble and had issues with authority."

Bree figured she knew where he was going with this. "So, how could she have stayed on task for the eleven months Mom was held captive?"

"Exactly," Slater agreed. "She doesn't seem to fit the profile of someone who could have done this on her own. Yet, she also doesn't fit for someone taking orders either."

"I guess that could depend on whoever was giving the orders," Duncan suggested. "If it was someone she trusted... or loved, then maybe that allowed her to stay on task." He paused, shook his head. "And it's possible that Shannon is being used as a scapegoat in all of this."

Luca made a sound of agreement. "And if so, that points back to Tara."

It did indeed. But Bree knew they couldn't rule out Nathan or Manny. Especially Manny who'd admitted to knowing Shannon. That made Bree wonder if Nathan would admit to knowing the dead woman as well. She was on the verge of asking Luca, Slater and Duncan if they should ask Nathan that when Luca's phone rang.

"Tara," Luca said when he looked at the screen. The relief was in his voice, but the concern was still on his face. He took the call and immediately told Tara, "I've got the call on Speaker. Sheriff Holder, Deputy McCullough and Bree are here with me."

"What's so important?" Tara responded, the ice practically dripping off the question.

"I need to talk to you in person," Luca explained. "Can you come back to Saddle Ridge? If not, I can arrange—"

"I'm not going back there," Tara interrupted, "and I'm not talking to any Austin cops either. If you've got something to say to me, just say it fast because you've got exactly thirty seconds before I hang up and then block you."

Duncan nodded, giving Luca the okay to tell her about Shannon. Normally, this was something done in person, but it was obvious Tara wasn't going to consent to a visit with cops.

"Tara, I regret to inform you that your sister, Shannon, is dead," Luca stated.

There were a couple of seconds of silence, followed by a sharp gasp. "What?" she demanded but didn't wait for an answer. "You're lying. You're saying that so I'll meet with you."

"I'm saying it because it's true," Luca spelled out. "A positive ID was made of her body just minutes ago."

Tara muttered something Bree didn't catch. "Her body?" she repeated. "Shannon's dead."

"Yes," Luca verified but didn't add more. He was no doubt giving Tara some time to let it sink in.

"How did she die?" Tara asked a couple of moments later.

"We believe she was murdered," Luca said.

No gasp this time, but Tara's moan was plenty loud enough. There were some rustling sounds, and Bree thought maybe Tara was dropping down into a chair. "Who killed her?"

"We don't know yet. We were hoping you could help us with that," Luca explained.

More silence. "You'd better not be trying to pin this on me because I didn't kill my own sister."

The denial sounded adamant enough, but Bree knew that

some people were top-notch liars. She had no idea though if Tara was one of them.

"Any idea who'd want Shannon dead?" Luca asked.

"No," Tara said, and her tone had softened some. "But you thought she was involved in what was going on with Manny and Bree, so maybe Shannon got mixed up with the wrong person. That wouldn't be a first," she added in a mutter. "I want to see her body. Where are you sending her?"

"To the county medical examiner. I don't have the number off the top of my head, but if you call the Saddle Ridge dispatcher, they can connect you. Then you can arrange a time to see your sister."

"Good," she said in a hoarse whisper, and she repeated it a couple of times as if using it to try to steady herself. "Please tell me you know who killed her because I want the SOB behind bars."

"I don't know, not yet, but there are a lot of cops investigating Shannon's murder. We're—"

"Did Manny kill her?" Tara blurted out.

That caused everyone in the room to freeze. "Why would you think that?" Luca asked.

"Because he's an SOB, that's why," Tara was quick to say. "He fired me, did you know that?" Again, she didn't wait for an answer. "Manny's a lying lowlife scum, and I wouldn't be surprised if he was using my sister. Used her and then killed her." A hoarse sob tore from her throat. "If he did kill Shannon, I will bury him."

"Tara," Luca warned, "you need to calm down. And you need to stay away from Manny. Leave this to the cops. Like I said, we're investigating several possibilities. Some cops are headed to Shannon's apartment in Austin now to see if there's anything there that'll point us in the direction of her killer."

"Her apartment in Austin?" Tara questioned. "She moved out of there close to a year ago."

Bree was certain Luca, Duncan and Slater didn't miss the timing of that. It meshed with when her mother had been kidnapped.

"Do you know where Shannon had been living?" Luca asked.

"The last time I saw her, she said she was staying in a travel trailer our grandparents left her. She had it parked on a lot she was renting... Hang on a sec," Tara muttered. "I put the address in my phone." A couple of seconds later, she read it off. "It's 116 Wilmer Cranston Road, Bulverde."

Slater immediately pulled up a map on his laptop and showed it to them. It was less than five miles from the burned-out cabin and where Shannon's body had been found.

"Get someone out there right now," Duncan told Slater, and Bree understood the urgency. Shannon's killer might intend to destroy the trailer if he or she hadn't done that already.

Slater stepped into the dining room to make a call while Luca continued with Tara. "Thanks for the address."

"I hope you find something there that tells you who killed her," Tara was quick to say. "And if it's Manny, then I think I can add a nail to his coffin."

"What do you mean by that?" Luca asked, obviously just as unnerved by the comment as Duncan and Bree were.

"I mean, I might have some proof that'll help you convict Manny of murder," Tara spelled out.

"What kind of proof?" Luca demanded.

But he was talking to the air because Tara had already ended the call.

Chapter Eleven

Luca, Bree, Duncan and Slater stood in the living room of the ranch, their attention pinned to Luca's phone. They watched as Woodrow, who had FaceTimed them, approached the travel trailer where Shannon had supposedly lived.

This was not the way Luca wanted to conduct a search. Especially a search that could finally give Bree and him answers as to who was trying to kill them. But Luca also hadn't wanted to leave Bree behind while he joined the search. Duncan had agreed, and that's why he'd sent Woodrow to accompany County Deputy Morales.

Thankfully, Beatrice and Joelle had agreed to stay upstairs with the babies. Both Izzie and Gabriel were way too young to know what was going on, but neither Luca nor Bree had wanted them in the room in case something god-awful was discovered in the search.

Like another body.

After all, Shannon might not be the only loose end a killer wanted to tie up.

Woodrow panned his phone the entire length of the trailer, and Luca could see it wasn't that large, but it seemed to be in good shape with no obvious damage to the sleek silver exterior. Woodrow then turned his camera back on Morales as he went up the narrow trio of steps. He already had his weapon drawn, and he knocked on the door.

"I'm Deputy Morales," he announced. "Anyone here?"

There was no response, which wasn't a surprise since there'd been no vehicles in the gravel driveway that led to the trailer. From what Luca had been able to see so far, this wasn't the sort of campground where people normally parked their RVs and such. There were no community buildings, no pristine trails. This was basically just a partially cleared area in the woods, with an old mailbox to indicate the address. It was secluded, and with no neighbors in sight, no one would have seen Shannon coming or going, which was probably why she'd chosen this particular location.

"Anyone here?" Morales called out again, and when he didn't get a response, he gloved up and tested the doorknob. The deputy frowned and glanced back at Woodrow when the knob turned. "It's not locked."

Even though Luca couldn't see Woodrow's right hand, he knew his fellow deputy already had his weapon drawn, and judging from the movement of the phone, Woodrow was adjusting his aim in case someone inside the trailer started shooting. Morales was doing the same.

Morales eased open the door and immediately stepped to the side. A classic cop move so he wouldn't be in the line of fire.

But no shots came.

In fact, nothing happened. There was only silence and darkness in the trailer.

Still staying to the side, Morales reached in with his gloved left hand and turned on the lights. He must have not heard or seen anything alarming because he stepped in with Woodrow right beside him. Woodrow set his phone aside for a couple of moments while he, too, put on some gloves.

When Woodrow resumed the call, Luca got confirmation that the camper was indeed small, with a kitchen on one side and a seating area on the other that had been let out into a bed. An unmade one. There were clothes strewn on the floor and take-out bags on the narrow strip of counter.

The bathroom door was open so Morales headed there while Woodrow focused on going through the pockets of the clothes at the foot of the bed and on the floor. "Nothing," he relayed, moving to the small table next to the bed.

There was a phone charger plugged in but no phone or laptop, though Luca saw a charger for that as well.

"I think someone's cleaned out the place," Morales relayed from the bathroom. "I can see where some things were, but the shelf and the trash can are empty in here."

That sent Woodrow to the cabinet under the sink where he, too, found an empty trash can. Considering the take-out bags were still there, it did appear that someone had almost certainly gone through it and removed anything incriminating.

And that someone was no doubt Shannon's killer.

"Any sign that the door had been jimmied open?" Luca asked, though he believed he already knew the answer.

"None," Woodrow confirmed while he checked behind the trash can. Nothing there. He moved on to checking the bags, stopping to check the receipt that was taped to one of them. "This was a pickup from this morning at eight, and it came from the diner in Saddle Ridge."

Slater and Duncan both cursed, and Luca figured Bree was mentally doing the same. This meant Shannon had likely been the one who'd set the fire in the parking lot, though it was beyond risky of her to order takeout from the diner since it was so close to the sheriff's office.

"She must have come back here after being in Saddle Ridge," Woodrow concluded, panning the camera around again. "But there's no blood. No signs that anything violent happened in here."

"No signs of that in the bathroom either," Morales added.

The deputy started going through the fridge while Woodrow went back to the bed. He lifted it and muttered, "What's this?"

The camera angle wasn't right for Luca to see what had caught Woodrow's attention, but it obviously got the other deputy's as well because Morales joined him and took Woodrow's phone so he could aim it at a piece of paper.

"It's a torn-off piece of a white delivery bag," Woodrow explained, "and there's some writing on it." He paused, did some cursing of his own. "It's Bree's address."

Luca heard the quick breath that Bree took in. Of course, Bree had known that Shannon was likely involved in the attempt to kidnap Gabriel, but it still had to feel like a punch to the gut.

"There's something else," Woodrow went on. "It's the name *Aubrey* with a circle drawn around it. There are some doodles, too."

Morales shifted the camera so they could see it, and it did indeed look as if someone, Shannon probably, had done some crude drawings of a rifle and a baby. Now it was Luca who felt the gut punch. Because one of the doodles was another name.

Manny.

The last letter of the name had a little heart dangling from it.

"Manny claimed he didn't know Shannon that well," Bree muttered.

Yeah, he had. "If we confront him with it, he'll probably just say he has no idea why Shannon wrote his name." Luca paused. "But Manny might own up to knowing who this other woman is."

"Aubrey," Slater repeated, and he hurried to his laptop. "I've seen that name before." It took him nearly a minute before he finally got that *aha* gleam in his eye. "Aubrey Kincaid. She was arrested with Shannon about four years ago when they were caught doing a B and E. Aubrey didn't have a previous record so she got parole." He continued to type on his keyboard. "And Shannon and Aubrey were in the army together."

Bingo. That was a solid connection. "Contact information?" Luca asked, grabbing a notepad so he'd be ready. Slater rattled off an Austin address and a phone number.

"Slater, try to call her," Duncan instructed, "but block your number. If she sees a cop calling, she probably won't answer."

"True," Slater muttered, and he made the call and put it on Speaker. It was answered on the first ring.

"Shannon?" a woman immediately said. "Is that you?"

"Yes," Bree lied, making her voice a hoarse whisper.

"Where the hell are you?" the woman demanded. "We were supposed to leave for the McCullough ranch by now."

Hell. That was another gut punch. They'd planned to come here, and Luca figured that meant they'd planned another attack.

"Shannon?" the woman repeated. "Are you there?" She sounded suspicious.

It was that suspicious tone that no doubt had Slater responding the way he did. He cupped his hand over his mouth and muttered something that was indistinguishable.

"I can't hear you," the woman said, punctuating that with some raw profanity. "This is a bad connection. Where are you?" she repeated.

Slater did more of the muffled muttering.

"Hang up and call me back," Aubrey instructed. "And make it fast. We're already running a half hour late, and we're not going to get paid if we screw this up."

Luca held his breath, hoping that Aubrey was about to say who was paying them. And for what? But she merely added. "Call me right back."

Slater hung up, hit Redial, and waited for Aubrey to answer. She did. "This better be a good connection. Are you still out there in the sticks?"

Slater repeated some muttering, causing Aubrey to curse some more.

"All right, just meet me at the ranch," Aubrey said. "We can..." She stopped, and a few moments crawled by. "Shannon?" she questioned. She paused again, doled out some more profanity, and Luca could hear her suspicions skyrocketing.

Not for long though.

Because Aubrey hung up.

Duncan whipped out his phone to call Austin PD. He didn't have to spell out that they had to stop an attack on the ranch. They needed to find Aubrey now.

BREE KNEW EVERYTHING possible was being done to find Aubrey, but that didn't help settle her nerves one bit. Aubrey's words kept racing through Bree's head. Words that tightened and twisted every muscle in her body.

We're already running a half hour late, and we're not going to get paid if we screw this up.

Aubrey had made it crystal clear that Shannon and she had plans to come here. Maybe to try to kill Luca and her. Maybe to try to kidnap Gabriel. It was possible Aubrey would carry through with it even if Shannon wasn't with her.

Bree had considered taking Gabriel and just leaving in a cruiser with Luca. But that could be a huge risk, too, since Aubrey could attack them on the road. At least here they had a security system. And now that they knew Aubrey was coming, they could watch for her.

That was the reason Bree had come back to the guest room so she could be with Gabriel and keep an eye out the upstairs window. Thankfully, Luca had come with her. Just having him nearby was a reminder that they were a united front there to keep their son safe.

Luca was on the phone, getting updates from Duncan, but he was practically whispering so Bree couldn't hear what he was saying. The low voice was no doubt so he wouldn't wake up Gabriel, who'd just been fed and was now asleep in Bree's arms. Since she very much wanted those updates, she eased him into his crib and went closer to Luca.

"I think we need to move another of the hands to the back part of the ranch near the pond," he said to whomever was on the other end of the line. "One is already patrolling that area now, but it's a weak spot. There's a trail there with easy access to the road."

There was. And it was a trail where Luca and she had parked and done some heavy making out when they'd been teenagers. It probably wouldn't be an easy place for a nonlocal like Aubrey to find, but the woman could and probably had researched such things.

Luca ended the call and slipped his phone into his pocket. "That was Slater. We're working out where to put the hands and the deputies who are keeping watch."

"Good," she muttered. And it was. Any and all security measures could keep Gabriel safe. But Bree knew there were plenty of weak spots where Aubrey could get through. "I read her background. She's had a lot of firearms training."

He made a sound of agreement. Then he sighed as he pulled her into his arms. "If she decides to do this mission solo, we have more than a dozen hands and deputies to spot her. It's my guess though that she's gone on the run. Or maybe run back to her boss because she was suspicious of the two calls she got from an unknown number."

"Yes," Bree said. She had to figure that Aubrey would at least contact her boss. Whoever that was. Perhaps Manny since Shannon had doodled the man's name along with Aubrey's. No matter who it was though, during that call Aubrey might learn Shannon was dead.

"Unless Aubrey was putting on a really good act, I didn't get the sense that she was the one who'd murdered Shannon," Bree added.

"Neither did I," he said.

Bree was certain that Luca had been through every one of the woman's words many times. For such a short one-way dialogue, they'd learned a lot. Shannon and Aubrey were basically hired guns, and they were supposed to have arrived at the ranch well over an hour ago. Added to that, Aubrey must have been accustomed to having Shannon call her on a burner with an unknown number since Aubrey didn't question that. She'd simply answered Slater's call and had assumed it was Shannon.

"If Aubrey goes to her boss, he or she could kill her, too," Bree pointed out, but she figured she was voicing what Luca already knew.

His nod confirmed that, and while neutralizing such a potential threat would be good for the here and now, it wouldn't be good in the long term. If they could make contact with Aubrey, they stood a chance of learning who'd hired her. If, like Shannon, she was killed, or simply vanished, the boss could just end up hiring other would-be killers to come after them.

At that thought, she had to close her eyes for a moment. Had to try to rein in the panic that was starting to slide through her. Luca helped with that.

By kissing her.

Since her eyes were closed, Bree hadn't seen it coming, but she certainly felt it. His mouth landed on hers for what he'd probably thought was a soothing gesture. And it soothed all right. It also gave her a jolt of pure, hot lust.

The heat came, skimming right over the panic and filling her with a need that she knew was a distraction. That didn't stop her from sinking right into the kiss. It didn't stop her from wrapping her arms around Luca and pulling him closer.

So many sensations hit her at once. The feel of his body against hers. His scent that was as familiar to her as her own. The taste of him. That had always revved up the heat, and this time was no different.

Bree wanted to just keep kissing him. To get lost for a moment in the hazy heat he was creating. She wanted to hold on to Luca and never let go. But this was the opposite of a security measure so with much regret, she eased back.

"Sorry," she muttered.

The corner of his mouth lifted in a dry smile. "I'm the one who started it." He paused, brushed a chaste kiss on her forehead. "When this is over—"

He stopped at the sound. Not Gabriel whimpering this time. This was a car engine, and it was approaching the house. Mercy. Was this Aubrey? Had she decided to go through with an attack?

Luca and she whirled toward the window and saw two armed ranch hands step in front of the dark blue car that was in the driveway. Both hands took aim at the driver, and a couple of seconds later, a woman stepped out.

Tara.

She lifted her hands high in the air, and even though she was saying something to the ranch hands, Bree couldn't make out what since she was so far away.

Luca's phone buzzed, and she saw Duncan's name on the screen just as Luca answered it. "I'm guessing you weren't expecting her," Duncan said.

"No," Luca verified. "I'll call her and see what she wants. The hands have instructions not to let her close to the house."

Luca ended the call with Duncan and made one to Tara. They watched as Tara said something else to the hands, and then she got back in her car. Seconds later, she answered.

"Deputy Vanetti," Tara said. "You need to tell your goons to let me through."

"They're ranch hands, not goons, and they're not letting any unscheduled visitors through," he snapped. "Why are you here, Tara?"

"Because of Manny," the woman was quick to say. "Because I want you to arrest him." Tara's voice trailed off into a sob. "I want him to pay for what he did to my sister."

"We're not certain Manny killed your sister," Luca pointed out just as there was a light tap at the door, and Duncan announced he was coming in. He did, and he headed straight to the window with Luca and her so he could hear the phone conversation.

"Well, I have something that'll help convince you," Tara argued. "Let me in, and I'll show it to you."

Luca huffed. Clearly, he wasn't convinced this wasn't some kind of ploy or maybe even a diversion so that Aubrey could get close to the house.

"What do you have, Tara?" Luca demanded.

"Something important. A video I recorded," she added when Luca only huffed again. "Trust me, you'll want to see it."

Bree certainly wanted to see it, and if it was indeed something that could lead to an arrest, then this could be the break in the case they'd been searching for. Then again, it could turn out to be nothing, so Bree tried to tamp down her hopes.

"Text me the video," Luca said.

"No, I want to show it to you," Tara insisted.

"I'm not letting you inside, Tara," Luca spelled out. "If you want me to see the video, then text it to me. If not, then hand your phone to one of the ranch hands, and he'll bring it to me."

Tara's next sob was even louder than her other one. "All right, I'll text it to you, but swear to me that you'll arrest Manny once you've seen it."

"I can't promise that," Luca said in a tone to indicate Tara was definitely testing his patience. "But I will view it and see if there's anything that could result in charges being filed."

That seemed to appease Tara because Bree saw the woman type in something on her phone. A few moments later, Luca got the text. Once the video loaded, Luca motioned for Bree to step to the side of the window. Probably because this could be some kind of ruse to distract them while a shooter got in place to try to gun them down.

Bree did move to the side but motioned for Luca and Duncan to do the same. They did, but both angled themselves so they could keep an eye on Tara.

The video finally came on the screen, and Bree immediately saw this wasn't some kind of security footage. It appeared to have been filmed from a camera phone, and the person holding it didn't exactly have a steady hand. There was also something obstructing the view, and it took her a moment to realize the person was likely recording this through an ajar door.

"Manny," Bree muttered when she saw him. He was in an office with a desk and bookshelves, and he wasn't alone. There was a woman with him, but Bree could only see the back of her head.

"I don't want you showing up at my apartment in the middle of the night," Brighton snarled. "I'm tired of going through this because it's over."

"It's not over until I say it is," Manny lashed out.

Just as Manny said that, the woman turned enough so that Bree could see her face. Yes, it was Brighton all right, and it was hard to tell with the shaky recording, but she seemed to be crying.

"If it was over, you wouldn't have called me," Manny continued. "You wouldn't have wanted to keep having sex with me."

"It was just sex," Brighton insisted, the anger coming off her voice. "And, trust me, I regret it. You think I enjoyed that scene you just made when you showed up at my place last night?"

"It wasn't a scene," Manny snapped. "I was merely talking to my replacement."

Replacement? So, Brighton had seemingly dumped Manny and moved on to someone else.

"You were causing a scene," Brighton said like a warning, "and I want it to stop. Don't contact me again. I love this bar, and I plan on coming here in the future, but I don't want to have to deal with you, understand?"

The camera stayed on Manny's face, and Bree had no trouble seeing the rage there. Yes, rage. Apparently, Manny wasn't ready to accept this breakup. And it also meant Manny had lied to them by omission.

"Check the date of the video," Tara insisted after the recording had ended.

Luca did. And cursed. Because this had been recorded just two days before Brighton's murder.

"Well, does that convince you that Manny killed Brighton?" Tara asked.

Luca didn't respond to that. Instead, he doled out a question of his own. "Do you know your sister's friend, Aubrey Kincaid?"

"A little," Tara said after a short pause. "Why?"

"Because we're trying to get in touch with her. Do you have any idea where she might be?"

Tara paused again. "No, but Manny might. Aubrey and he dated for a while."

Bingo. There was another red flag. Well, it was if Tara was telling the truth.

"So, are you going to arrest Manny?" Tara repeated with even more venom in her demand.

Duncan nodded, not responding to Tara but letting Luca and Bree know what he was about to do. "I'll get an arrest warrant started. Arrange to have Manny picked up right away."

Chapter Twelve

Luca kept watch as they made the drive into town to the sheriff's office. He was in the back seat with Bree who was firing glances around, too. Ditto for Woodrow and Duncan who were in the front. Luca figured Slater, Joelle and Carmen were doing the same back at the ranch, along with the hands and reserve deputies who were still patrolling the ground.

They had put a lot of security in place to keep Gabriel safe while they made this trip. There were now nine armed cops or ranch hands guarding him, and Luca had to hope that the small army would be enough. Had to hope, too, that maybe this journey wouldn't turn out to be a big mistake. But pretty much anything they did at this point could fall into the "big mistake" category.

That included doing nothing at all.

Yes, they'd likely be safer if they stayed put inside the ranch house. *Likely.* But if they'd done a correct interpretation of those notes in Shannon's trailer, then no place was truly safe. And they had to do something about that for Gabriel and everyone else who happened to be in the path of this killer.

That something meant Bree and him traveling into town to the sheriff's office to have a chat with Manny.

Manny hadn't resisted the warrant and had immediately

come in for an interview, but he had demanded to speak to Luca and Bree. Luca had considered refusing, or leaving Bree at the ranch, while he went to hear what Manny had to say. Hell, he'd considered a lot of things, but this was a murder investigation and at least some of the things had to be done by the book. That included holding the interview at the sheriff's office since that's where Manny had surrendered himself. It was also procedure for Manny to have his lawyer with him—which he did.

However, it wasn't the norm for a suspect to ask to speak with two of the people involved in the attacks. Still, Luca had reasoned that Manny might finally be ready to spill all. And spilling all could finally put an end to the danger to Gabriel.

During his visual sweep of their surroundings, Luca's gaze collided with Bree's. She was worried all right. And exhausted. Too bad he couldn't do squat about either of those things.

"A few days ago, our biggest concern was how we were going to co-parent Gabriel while being at odds with each other," she muttered.

For some stupid reason, that made him smile. "Yeah," he muttered.

They had much more serious concerns now, but Luca no longer felt the at-odds things. That was something good to come out of all of this. They were solidly on the same side. But would that last? Luca hoped it would but knew there were no guarantees that Bree would ever be able to look at him and not think of her murdered father.

When they reached the sheriff's office, Duncan was forced to park out front since the main parking lot was still being processed and cleaned. However, the fire chief, Elmore Dauber, was on scene, and he motioned that he needed to talk to them. Duncan indicated for the chief to meet them inside.

They hurried into the building, but the only people Luca saw inside were the two deputies, Sonya and Brandon Rooney. "Manny and his lawyer are already in the inter-view room," Brandon explained. "Sonya searched Manny and read him his rights again."

Duncan nodded and then shifted his attention to the fire chief when he came in. Elmore was a former deputy turned fireman, with over twenty years of experience under his belt, so Luca knew this part of the investigation was in ca-pable hands.

"We're nearly finished up out there," Elmore explained, "and I'll be doing my report as soon as I'm back in my of-fice. But I can give you the high points now." He drew in a long breath. "The accelerant was gasoline, and we found the empty can behind a tree at the back of the parking lot. It could have been there for hours. Maybe even days. There were some sticks lying around so it's possible they were used to cover the can."

So, this had been planned maybe well in advance. That didn't surprise Luca, but he wished someone had seen that can before it'd been turned into a weapon.

"A simple trigger device ignited the gasoline," Elmore went on. "We've got what's left of the device, and it'll be examined, but this is something anyone can learn to make from the internet."

"Was it on a timer?" Duncan asked.

Elmore shook his head. "It was set off with a remote con-trol or maybe a phone. Again, not hard to do if you can read and follow instructions."

Luca considered that for a moment. "How close would the remote or phone have to be to ignite it?"

"Not especially close. We might be able to give you specif-ics on that once it's examined, but it's my guess the arsonist had line of sight of all of you when you exited the building and triggered it then."

That was Luca's guess as well. A timer would only be effective if the person had known the exact time they'd be leaving the sheriff's office.

"I figure we're looking for someone who was hanging around within a block of the building," Elmore added. He looked at Duncan. "You've requested footage from the camera at the bank?"

Duncan nodded. "The camera was working, but they're having trouble getting the footage off the server. The techs from the Rangers' crime lab are assisting, so we should have the recordings soon."

Luca was definitely hoping for that, and while he was at it, he was also hoping the arsonist didn't know about that particular camera and hadn't bothered to conceal his or her face. Of course, Manny and Tara would likely be on the feed since they'd been in the area for interviews. However, there would have been no valid reason for Shannon and/or Aubrey to be on scene. But it was possible that by the time of the fire, Shannon had already been dead.

"Go ahead and see what Manny wanted to tell Bree and you," Duncan instructed Luca. "I've got a few more questions for Elmore, and then I'll join you. Oh, and record everything Manny says. I don't want this to be an off-the-record kind of conversation just because Bree is there."

Luca was glad to hear that. He didn't want Manny trying to hide behind what he might consider to be private. As far as Luca was concerned, Manny's right to privacy was over.

"I'm a legal consultant for the Rangers," Bree pointed out. "Since the Rangers are assisting in this investigation, I can use that to be present during interviews of a suspect." She lifted her shoulder. "Well, I can as long as Manny's lawyer doesn't flat-out object and start some legal wrangling. I can wrangle right back, but I don't want to do anything to compromise an arrest."

Duncan stayed quiet a moment, obviously processing that and then nodded. "Get permission from Manny and the lawyer to be there," he agreed. "I haven't arrested Manny yet, but let's all hope he'll say something to the two of you that'll make that happen."

Yeah, that had to happen because if it didn't, there likely wouldn't be an arrest. There was no physical evidence to link Manny to Brighton's murder or any of the attacks. Of course, there was the recording that Tara had made, but it might or might not be able to be used as evidence. Even if it was, the video wasn't proof Manny had murdered Brighton.

Luca and Bree headed to the interview room, and the moment Luca opened the door, Manny practically jumped to his feet.

"I didn't murder anyone," Manny immediately volunteered.

Luca held up his hand in a gesture for Manny to wait, and he turned to Manny's lawyer. "I'm Deputy Vanetti, and this is legal consultant for the Rangers, Bree McCullough. Do either of you have any objections to her being here?"

"No," Manny snapped. "In fact, I want her here so I can make both of you understand that someone is setting me up."

Luca shifted his attention to the lawyer. "No objections at this time. I'm Corey Bennett," he said. He shook hands with both Luca and Bree, and Luca noted that the lawyer didn't seem anxious or ready to launch into a tirade about how they were treating his client.

"Someone is setting me up," Manny repeated, but once again, Luca gestured for him to hold off on that so he could start the recording and read in the time and those present.

"You believe someone is setting you up," Luca repeated. "Who and why?"

"I don't know." Manny groaned and dropped back into the chair. "But someone must be if there was a warrant for my arrest. Why the hell would your sheriff do that?"

Bree and Luca took the chairs across from Manny and the lawyer. "Because we recently got access to a recording of you having a very nasty argument with Brighton Cooper, a woman you claimed you didn't know well." Luca leaned in, spearing Manny with his narrowed gaze. "You knew her, and if you lie and say you didn't, then I'm arresting you on the spot."

Manny had already opened his mouth, but he closed it, huffed and leaned back in his seat. "A video," he repeated. "How did you get it and what's on it?"

"I'm not at liberty to disclose who gave it to us, but it's obvious from the recording that Brighton and you were lovers, and you were enraged when she ended things. Lie to me about that, and you're under arrest," Luca repeated.

Manny's lawyer started to speak, but Manny lay his hand on the man's arm. "Tara," Manny grumbled. "She recorded something and gave it to you. She's the one trying to set me up."

"Why would she do that?" Bree wanted to know.

Manny made a *duh* sound. "I've already told you that Tara's upset because I dumped her. She'd do anything to get back at me."

That was possible, but Luca didn't voice that to Manny. "Tara didn't make you lie to us about Shannon," Luca pointed out. "You did that on your own."

"I did," Manny admitted. "But lying about my sexual partners isn't the same as committing multiple felonies."

Maybe not. But it could be red flags.

"What about Aubrey Kincaid?" Luca pressed. "Is she a lover, too?"

Manny's forehead bunched up. "No. Why are you asking that? Did Tara claim I'd slept with Aubrey?"

Luca didn't respond to that either. He just sat quietly and stared at Manny until the man was practically squirming in his seat.

"I didn't sleep with Aubrey," Manny insisted. "I'll admit to having an affair with Brighton, and she did break up with me. But I didn't kill her, and there won't be anything on any video saying otherwise."

Luca gave that some thought. Manny could probably say something like that because perhaps he'd never come out and threatened Brighton with violence. The violence could have still happened though.

"I was in love with Brighton," Manny added, his voice lowering to a whisper. "I loved her, but she was seeing someone else."

"Who?" Bree immediately asked.

Manny shrugged. "It's all speculation. You're not the only one who investigated Brighton's murder," he said.

Luca and Bree exchanged glances. "What does that mean?" Bree pressed.

"After you called and asked me to give you those old receipts, I talked to some of the regular customers who were around back then. No one could confirm it," Manny explained, "but a few people recalled her having some conversations with that doctor."

Everything inside Luca went still. "What doctor?"

"Dr. Nathan Bagley," Manny spat out like profanity. "That snake oil quack who lives right here under your own nose."

Luca made a circling motion for Manny to continue just

as Duncan came in. Duncan announced himself for the recording and took a seat at the end of the table.

"Manny here was just telling us that he suspects that Brighton was seeing Dr. Bagley," Luca summarized.

Duncan's eyebrows rose, but he didn't get a chance to say anything because Manny continued. "I don't have proof of it so don't try to charge me for withholding evidence. And I only found out about this two days ago after Bree wanted the receipts."

"Why don't you just tell us what you do know about Brighton and the doctor?" Duncan prompted, not addressing the withholding gripe.

"I knew Brighton was seeing someone else," Manny quickly confirmed, "and like I already told Luca and Bree, a couple of people I talked to said they recalled seeing her with Dr. Bagley."

Duncan pushed a notepad Manny's way. "Jot down the names of those people."

Manny huffed, but he wrote two names and passed the notepad back to Duncan. Luca glanced at the names but didn't recognize them. Bree shook her head, indicating that she didn't either.

"So, these two people saw Brighton with Nathan Bagley," Luca went on. "Did you know she was seeing the doctor?"

Manny wasn't so quick to respond this time. "No, but once she came in the bar sporting bruises on her arm. They were clearly marks left by fingers. It was obvious to me she'd gotten them when someone manhandled her."

"Bruises?" Bree questioned. "When was this?"

"About a month or so before she died," Manny answered.

Luca had studied the photos of Brighton's lifeless body, and while there had been bruises on various parts of her torso and arms, there hadn't been any that resembled marks made by fingers. A month though would have been plenty of time for them to have healed.

Manny lifted his arm and clamped onto the fleshy part between his elbow and wrist. "There with the thumbprint underneath and the other four on top. I was furious that someone had hurt her like that, and I wanted her to come to my office so we could talk about it. She wouldn't. She said the bruises were nothing and that I should mind my own business, but then she admitted she was having trouble with someone she was seeing."

"Did she specifically say she was seeing Nathan Bagley?" Luca asked.

"No." Manny sighed. "But one of the bruises was bigger than the other, and when I pointed to it, she mumbled something about the guy wearing a class ring and that the stone in it was tilted to the side on his finger."

Luca tried to picture Nathan's hands, trying to recall if he had worn a ring with a stone, but he couldn't recall one. Apparently, neither did Bree because she shook her head again.

"I was trying to rein in my temper because I knew if I got mad, Brighton would just walk away," Manny went on, "so I tried to get her to tell me more about the bruise by saying it must have been a big ring. She said it was one of those chunky gold ones from Texas A&M."

Bree took out her phone, and Luca knew what she was doing. A couple of moments later, he got confirmation when she showed him the hospital information page with Nathan's bio. There it was.

He'd attended the Texas A&M School of Medicine.

Again, that was nowhere near proof that Nathan had murdered Brighton, but it was a connection that needed further investigation. They already knew from the receipts that Nathan had been at the bar the night Brighton was murdered, and if he had been involved in a volatile relationship with Brighton, then that would give him motive.

"Any reason you didn't tell us sooner about seeing those bruises on Brighton?" Duncan asked.

"Because I forgot about it. Hell, it's been five years, and I'd moved on with my life. Or rather I had moved on before you guys started trying to accuse me of things I didn't do."

"Then why didn't you tell the original investigating officer?" Duncan pressed. "You hear about a woman you claim to have loved had been murdered, and you know someone bruised her up just a month earlier, and you didn't think that was something the cops should know?"

Some of the color drained from Manny's face, and he shook his head. "Her death gutted me, and I wasn't thinking about anything but my own grief."

Duncan made a sound to indicate he wasn't totally convinced of that. Neither was Luca. Manny had had plenty of time to work out what to say so he didn't sound like a killer. And maybe he wasn't. But Luca wasn't taking him off the suspect list, and he doubted Duncan or Bree would either.

"I need to have a word with my client," the lawyer said.

Duncan nodded, stood, and Luca, Bree and he went back into the hall. "I want to get old work schedules for the hospital," Duncan said, keeping his voice low. "I need to see if Nathan was possibly on duty when Brighton was murdered. We know he was at the bar that night, but we don't have an exact time of death for her. I want to know where he was in the hours leading up to and after she was killed."

"Good idea," Bree muttered. "If he wasn't on the schedule, then he can't claim that as an alibi." She paused. "Nathan could have murdered her," she added. "Not premeditated but in the heat of the moment."

Luca turned to her so fast, he heard his neck pop. "You said Nathan never got violent with you."

"He didn't," she insisted, "but I thought maybe the potential was there because of his temper. It was always there, simmering just beneath the surface."

Luca had to rein in his own temper over hearing that. Not anger aimed at Bree but at the SOB Nathan. And anger wasn't going to help solve this investigation.

"Did you ever see Nathan wearing a Texas A&M ring?" Duncan asked her.

Bree shook her head. "And I think I would have noticed. Those class rings are usually big, and since I went to A&M's rival school, University of Texas, I probably would have made some kind of joke about it."

Luca considered that for a moment. "You dated Nathan long after Brighton had been murdered so maybe he quit wearing the ring after he killed her. He might have believed the ring had left a mark on her. Like the bruise on her arm."

Both Duncan and Bree made quick sounds of agreement. "Nathan might not have thrown the ring away," Bree added. "He could have just stopped wearing it." She looked at Duncan. "What are the chances of getting a search warrant to go through Nathan's house?"

"Nil on the evidence we have." Duncan groaned, shook his head. "Which as you know isn't much. Yes, he was in the bar the night Brighton was murdered, but with her estimated time of death, she wasn't killed until about four to six hours or so after she left Hush, Hush. Nathan could have been home. Or at work."

Bree groaned as well, not because she was disagreeing with Duncan, but because she knew all of this was true. It also wasn't a mark of guilt that two people had seen Nathan talking to Brighton. Neither was Manny's speculation that Nathan had put those bruises on her.

So, yeah, nil chances on the search warrant.

"We can't just ask Nathan if he has a ring like that," Luca spelled out, "because if he's guilty, he could toss it. If he hasn't already done it, that is."

They all went quiet, and Luca knew they were trying to figure out a way around this.

"I can pay Nathan a visit and try to have a discreet look around," Bree threw out there.

Luca gave her a flat look and was sure Duncan was doing the same. They both voiced a firm "no" together.

"I wouldn't take the ring if I spotted it," she went on. "I could leave it in place and then you could get a warrant. If the ring is still there, it could have Brighton's DNA on it since she was stabbed to death."

"No," Duncan repeated, and Luca shifted his flat look to a narrow-eyed stare.

"You're not going into the house of a potential killer," Luca insisted. "And even if he didn't murder Brighton, Nathan has a temper and a short fuse. You could be hurt. Or worse."

"I could have my phone on," she suggested. "And Duncan and you could be waiting nearby to run inside the house if anything goes wrong." She stopped and shut her eyes for a moment. "Look, I don't want to be around Nathan, but these attacks have got to stop, and this might be the way to do it."

"No," Duncan said for a third time.

Bree clearly didn't like that because she huffed. "Then, what? We can't just ask around to see if anyone recalls Nathan wearing a ring because it'd get back to him and he'd ditch it."

True, but an idea flashed into Luca's head. "We can search

through social media and look for any photos of Nathan that might have been posted of him wearing a ring. Coupled with Manny's statement, that might be enough to get a warrant."

Duncan didn't look convinced, but he nodded. "Let's do that." He took out his phone. "I can get Joelle started on it right now. She's been chomping at the bit to get more involved in the investigation."

Yes, she had, and when Bree and Luca got back to the ranch, they could search as well. Newspaper archives might have something as well.

At the sound of footsteps, they turned to see Brandon making his way to them, and the deputy had his attention on a laptop he was carrying.

"We just got back the footage from the bank camera," Brandon explained, turning the laptop toward them and hitting Play.

Luca watched as Main Street came into view. Not the sheriff's office since it was tucked just out of sight of the camera, but as the feed advanced, he saw the smoke billowing out of the parking lot.

He soon spotted the woman.

Luca instantly recognized her because he'd seen her driver's license photo. It was Aubrey. She was on the sidewalk, moving in the opposite direction of the sheriff's office and the fire, but she was glancing over her shoulder.

And she smiled.

Luca cursed. The woman was actually happy that she'd put them in danger like that.

"I want an arrest warrant for her," Duncan snarled.

"I'll make that happen," Brandon assured him. "For now, keep watching," he instructed, though he sounded just as angry at the smile as the rest of them were.

Someone had already zoomed in on Aubrey so they

watched as she lifted her phone that was already in her hand, and she made a call right before she walked out of camera range.

"The techs believe they can enhance the footage and get the number she called," Brandon said. "What do you bet she was calling her boss to let him or her know the job was done?"

There were no bets because that would have almost certainly been what she'd done.

"What are the odds they can get the number?" Duncan asked.

"Good," Brandon verified. "In a couple of hours, we might know the name of the killer."

Chapter Thirteen

Back at the ranch, Bree glanced around the living room and saw nothing but frustrated expressions. Her own expression fell into that category as well. For the past four hours while the nannies and Sandra had watched the babies, Luca, Joelle, Slater and she had been digging through social media and newspaper archives to try to find a photo of Nathan wearing the ring.

They'd all struck out.

There'd been plenty of pictures of Nathan, but so far, his hands hadn't been visible in any of them. So, Bree had moved on to a different approach. She was calling jewelers who specialized in making and selling rings for the A&M School of Medicine. So far, she wasn't having much luck with that either, even though she had introduced herself on the calls as legal counsel for the Texas Rangers and was looking for information pertinent to an investigation. The people she'd spoken to had all been cooperative, but none had a record of Nathan purchasing such a ring.

Duncan was clearly getting some frustrating news as well because he'd started pacing and muttering under his breath while he listened to the latest call he'd received. Bree seriously doubted he was hearing anything that would give them hope that this case would soon be solved.

And that's why she would have to push the visit to Nathan.

Duncan, Slater and Luca weren't just going to agree so she needed to come up with an angle to convince them. She considered that while she made a call to the next jeweler on her list. As with the other calls, it took her a couple of minutes to work her way through to speak to the manager, and then a perky-sounding woman who introduced herself as Laine Martinez came on the line. Bree went through her spiel again, and as she'd done with the others, she gave the woman three names to search. Nathan's and two others that Bree had plucked from A&M class rosters. That way, the person wouldn't solely home in on Nathan's name and try to contact him.

"The ring would have been purchased about eight or nine years ago," Bree explained. "But please check for a couple of years in either direction in case—"

"Nathan Bagley," Laine confirmed. "Yes, he did purchase a ring from us."

Bree practically sprang to her feet, and it got the attention of the others, except for Duncan who was still on the phone. Slater, Luca and Joelle, however, came closer.

"I'm putting you on Speaker," Bree informed the woman. "I have three police officers with me who'll want to hear this. You can verify that Nathan Bagley bought a ring from you?"

"He did. The ring had the Texas A&M School of Medicine logo and is fourteen-karat yellow gold with a full carat diamond in the center. A custom design," she went on. "And because of the design, it was priced higher than most class rings. He paid just under five thousand dollars for it."

Not a fortune but still expensive. Maybe so expensive that Nathan hadn't been able to part with it.

"Do you have a receipt for the purchase?" Bree asked.

"Not a paper one, but all the information is here in my computer files. Would you like me to send you a copy?"

"Yes," Bree couldn't say fast enough, and she gave the woman her email address. The moment Bree saw the info pop into her inbox, she thanked Laine, ended the call and pinned her attention to Luca.

"No, I don't want you going into Nathan's house to look for the ring," Luca snapped, and then he sighed, and his expression softened. "It's too dangerous."

"It is," Duncan verified, having obviously heard the gist of what Bree had learned. He put away his phone and joined them. "We'll get to the ring and Nathan, but first, I need to tell you about Aubrey. The tech's got the number she called, but it was made to a burner. The recipient of the call was in Saddle Ridge."

Bree wasn't sure whether to groan or curse so she did both. "All three of our suspects were in Saddle Ridge at the time of the call," she pointed out.

Duncan did some groaning and cursing of his own. "They were, which means the footage didn't help us narrow down anything. Well, nothing except Aubrey being responsible for the fire, and there's no sign of her."

Bree had to hope that would soon change since there was an APB out on the woman. Of course, Aubrey might have already fled.

"I went ahead and told Brandon to cut Manny loose," Duncan added. "His lawyer was squawking about no evidence to hold him, and he's right. So, I told Brandon to let him go with the warning that he not leave the state."

If he was truly guilty, Manny might run, but Bree figured he'd just stand his ground and fight any charges. Nathan would no doubt do the same, which was why they needed more proof. Or something they could use to exclude them as suspects.

Duncan took out his phone again. "I'm calling the hospital to see if Nathan is on duty." They waited, and like her calls to the jewelers, it took him several connections to get to someone who knew the answer. "He went home about an hour ago."

"I have an idea of how to deal with Nathan," Joelle said. She didn't continue until everyone faced her, and she kept her attention on her husband, maybe because she knew she'd have to convince him to go along with any sort of plan. "Since we now have proof that he bought a ring, I could go to his place with backup," she quickly added, "and ask him about it."

This time there were three negative responses. Luca, Slater and Duncan. Duncan's was the loudest.

"Hear me out," Joelle demanded, and Bree noticed her sister instantly switch to cop mode. "We aren't going to get a search warrant, not without alerting Nathan that we could be onto him being a killer. He'd just toss the ring before we got there and maybe say he lost it. But if I show up in an official capacity, with backup," she added again, "then I could question him about the ring. If he denies owning it, then you could use his lie to get a warrant and come straight over before he has the chance to dispose of it."

"And if he attacks you?" Duncan snarled. In contrast, he sounded more like a worried husband than a cop.

Joelle sighed. "He won't because Bree and Slater will be with me."

A hushed silence fell over the room. But it was short-lived. Then, the grumbles and complaints came.

"Nathan could be behind the attacks on Bree," Luca was quick to point out.

"Yes," Joelle admitted, "but he's also smitten with her. Mercy, what a word," she muttered. "But it's the truth. He'll be on his best behavior if Bree is there because he's trying to win her over."

"That's true," Bree said, earning sharp looks from Duncan, Slater and Luca. She went to Luca and ran her hand down the length of his arm while she met him eye to eye. "The attacks have to stop, and Aubrey is still at large. If I can do something to prevent Gabriel from being in danger, then I'll do it. And I'll go in armed," she said. "With Joelle and Slater."

Judging from the tight sets of their jaws, Luca and Duncan weren't convinced. Slater, however, seemed to be seeing the logic of this so Bree continued with the argument.

"The three of us can just show up at Nathan's," Bree spelled out. "Joelle or Slater could read him his rights, and I could hang back, looking sympathetic and acting as if he's being railroaded. That'll make him less defensive and more inclined to play nice. More inclined to lie, too, since he won't want to admit he has anything that can be linked to Brighton."

"I'll use my phone to record him," Joelle said, taking up the cause, "and if he lies, you get the warrant. Slater and I will detain him so he can't leave the room and toss the ring. If he admits he has the ring, then I'll ask him to let me take it into evidence for processing. If he refuses, get the warrant. This can work," she insisted.

Luca looked as if he wanted to curse a blue streak. Probably because he knew it could work as well. But he was also aware of something else.

"Yes, it's a risk," Bree admitted. "We could be attacked going to or from Nathan's house, but we could be attacked anywhere. Including here." Mercy, it twisted at her to voice that last part, but it was true.

"Maternity leave hasn't made me forget how to be a cop," Joelle pointed out to Duncan. "And I'm a good cop. I'll keep my eyes on Nathan the entire time, and if he tries to pull a gun, he'll have three people pulling theirs." She shifted to Luca. "I'm not going to let that scumbag lay one finger on Bree."

The silence came again, and the moments crawled by before Duncan sighed. Bree could tell from his expression that they had convinced him, but he turned to Luca, no doubt to get his take on the plan.

"I could go in with Bree and Joelle," Luca said, but then he immediately waved that off. "No, because Nathan would just get defensive. But I'm going to his house," he insisted. "I'll wait outside in the cruiser."

Bree would feel safer with Luca that close, but that left them with a big problem. "The babies have to be protected," she stated, though she was certain no one had forgotten that.

"I'll stay here," Duncan said, taking out his phone again. "And I'll have Woodrow and Sonya come and stay as backup. I'll have them drive by Nathan's place on the way here to make sure he's actually home." He made the call to get that started.

"You're okay with this plan?" Joelle asked, glancing first at Slater and then Luca before her attention settled on Bree.

Slater shrugged. "This could definitely shake things up. Maybe it'll shake in the right direction."

Luca settled for a nod, and Bree could practically see the nerves tightening in every part of his body. "Give us a minute," Bree said, taking hold of Luca's hand, and she led him out of the living room.

Since Sandra, the nannies and babies were using the family room and adjoining kitchen, she didn't head there. Instead, she took Luca to Duncan's home office, a room that had once been her father's. Yes, there were memories of him here, but at least it was private. She stepped inside with Luca and shut the door.

Then, she kissed him.

Bree hadn't actually intended to do that, but her body was calling the shots here so she kissed him long and deep. Kissed him until she felt some of those nerves start to settle. It worked for her, too, though she knew there'd be a price to pay for this. She could end up with a broken heart since she was falling for Luca all over again. For now, she just enjoyed the moment. The heat.

And Luca.

Definitely an enjoyment, and her body went a little slack in places. The man certainly had a calming effect on her. A surprise since at the same time, he could make her want him more than her next breath.

It had been like this that last time when they'd ended up in bed. The night she'd gotten pregnant with Gabriel. And it stunned her to consider they could easily end up in bed again. Things certainly seemed to be moving that way, and even though she'd been the one to initiate the kiss, Bree didn't think she was ready for that big of a step.

Especially now.

When their son was possibly still in danger.

She eased back, immediately feeling the loss of the heat, and she stared into his eyes. "I can apologize since I shouldn't have done that."

"No apology needed or wanted," Luca let her know. "Did you kiss me to distract me from this plan?" he asked.

"No. But maybe I did it to try to level myself out. I want to do this," she was quick to add. "I need to do this, but I know things can go wrong." He groaned, but she cut him off. "Trust me when I say I'll do everything to stay safe. So will Joelle and Slater."

Luca stared at her for a couple of seconds and then let out a slow breath. "I do know it, but that doesn't stop me from worrying."

She nodded. "And I'll be worrying about you since you'll be parked outside Nathan's house. We'll both be worried about Gabriel," she added before she stepped back. "I need to go upstairs and get my gun." She'd put it on the top shelf of the closet when Slater had brought it over for her with some clothes and her toiletries.

"I'll check with Duncan to see if he wants to put any more security measures in place, and then I'll meet you in the cruiser," Luca said, and they headed off in different directions.

After Bree had gotten the gun and headed back downstairs, she saw Woodrow and Sonya pull to a stop in front of the house. It was showtime, and just as Sonya and Woodrow came inside, Joelle gave Duncan a quick kiss before Slater, Bree and she headed out to Duncan's cruiser. Bree took the back seat, and Slater got behind the wheel. Joelle was shotgun.

"Does Luca know you're in love with him?" Joelle asked.

Bree frowned at her sister. "Who says I am?"

"Me," Joelle and Slater said in unison.

Bree extended the frown to her brother, though he probably couldn't see her face since his focus was on keeping watch around them. "It's my guess you kissed Luca when you carted him off like that," Slater went on. "And it's also my guess that the two of you enjoyed that kiss way too much."

"Is there a point to this?" Bree asked, huffing.

Slater glanced back at her just long enough to flash her

one of his cocky smiles. "Yeah, the point is love, little sister, and that's what you're in when it comes to Luca."

Bree wanted to dispute that. Couldn't. Because, heck, Slater and Joelle could be right. But even if they were, she had no intentions of trying to work out her feelings right now.

"I'm looking for gunmen," she muttered, pinning her attention to their surroundings.

Thankfully, Joelle and Slater did the same. Also thankfully, Luca hurried out of the house and into the cruiser, and Bree hoped he wasn't picking up on the vibe that was still lingering around because of the short conversation she'd just had with her siblings. There was no need for Luca to be distracted with thoughts of how they felt or didn't feel about each other.

Slater immediately drove away, not exactly speeding but not dawdling either. They were all on edge. All bracing for the worst to happen. However, there were no signs of a gunman or any other vehicles for that matter.

They made it all the way into town before they encountered any traffic, and it was minimal. Slater took the turn off Main Street and drove the two blocks to come to a stop in front of Nathan's place. As the deputies had said, Nathan's car was in the driveway, indicating he was home.

The two-story white Victorian wasn't the biggest or most impressive in Saddle Ridge, but it did have an old money air about it, and Bree knew it was one of the first houses built in the area. At least one hundred and fifty years ago. And it'd been in Nathan's family the whole time. He'd inherited it from his parents after their deaths when Nathan had been in his twenties.

"See anyone hell-bent on trying to kill us?" Luca asked, his gaze combing both sides of the street.

Bree was about to say no, but then her attention landed on

the front window, and she saw Nathan standing there, staring out at them. Maybe he'd heard the sound of the cruiser approaching, but it didn't seem to Bree that he'd been expecting them.

Just the opposite.

He was scowling, possibly the cold, hard stare of someone who wanted them dead. Nathan moved away from the window, and a couple of seconds later, the front door opened.

"Let me phone Duncan so he can listen in," Joelle said, making the call, and when he answered, she reached for the door handle.

Bree reached for hers, too, but she also gave Luca a look. She didn't repeat that she'd be careful, and he held back on anything verbal. But both of those things passed between them, and then Bree got out to go to the house with Slater and Joelle.

"What's this about?" Nathan asked, clearly directing the question to Bree. "What happened?"

"May we come in?" Bree tried to keep any wariness and emotion out of her voice. She probably failed though because there was plenty of emotion since Nathan could indeed be a killer.

Nathan wasn't quick to agree to invite them in, but he finally stepped back. Not before shooting Luca a glare in the cruiser though. "What's this about?" he repeated.

"We have a few questions for you," Joelle said. She, too, had leveled her voice, and she was actually attempting a pleasant expression. "And we didn't want you to have to go into the sheriff's office." She took out her phone and lifted it to show him that it was connected to a call. "Sheriff Holder is listening."

Nathan eyed her with suspicion. "So, you brought the sheriff's office here to me, and that includes backup waiting in the cruiser," he grumbled, and he shifted his attention back to Bree. "Are you all right?"

There it was. That creepy concern that Bree in no way wanted from this man. "I'm holding up," she settled for saying.

He continued to study her. "I'm here for you," Nathan murmured. "You know that, right?"

His words made that icky feeling skyrocket, but Bree held back on saying anything. She didn't want Nathan on the defensive before they even got started.

"We don't want to take up too much of your time," Joelle interjected. "But since this is an official visit, I'm going to remind you of your rights." She didn't wait for Nathan to agree. Joelle just went ahead and recited the Miranda.

Nathan's eyes narrowed, and he whipped his gaze to Slater. "Have you come here to try to pin something on me?"

Again, it was Joelle who responded. "Actually, we were hoping you could help us clear up something. Something that could eliminate you as a possible suspect."

"I haven't done anything to make me a suspect," Nathan snapped. "What the hell is it you think I've done now?"

Bree's skin was practically crawling from being in the same space as Nathan, but she pushed that aside and went closer to him. Not too close but she wanted to do something to diffuse the anger she could see building inside him. She knew Joelle and Slater wouldn't be able to do that, but she could.

"We were hoping you'd help with the investigation," Bree said. "There's been some accusations, and while we're not at liberty to divulge specific information about the case, we need your help."

Nathan blinked, and just like that, the bulk of the anger

faded. Probably because he might think if he did help, then it might earn him some brownie points in her eyes.

"What kind of help?" he asked.

Bree waited until Joelle gave her a slight nod before she continued. "We need to know if you have a Texas A&M class ring."

Clearly, Nathan hadn't been expecting that because his eyes widened. "What does a ring have to do with the investigation?"

"Maybe nothing," she managed, "but it was just something that came up. Again, we can't spell out the specifics."

Nathan's gaze stayed pinned to her. "This has something to do with Brighton's murder? And with you being run off the road?"

"Possibly," Bree admitted. Then, she waited for what she was certain would be the denial.

The moments crawled by. Nathan's intense stare was making her stomach knot and twist. Her breathing and heart rate weren't faring much better either. But once he lied, she could stop the pretense of being nice to him—

"I have a Texas A&M ring," Nathan said.

Bree's heart dropped. This definitely wasn't what she'd expected him to say. They'd needed the lie to get the warrant.

Had Nathan figured that out?

Or was his admission simply the truth with no ulterior motive?

Bree didn't want to believe that, but she had to admit her personal feelings for Nathan were playing into this. She despised the man, and she'd maybe let that convince her that he was a killer.

"Uh, may we see the ring?" Bree managed to ask.

Again, Nathan didn't jump to agree, but he finally muttered some profanity. "I don't wear it often because it's bulky and could scratch a patient during an exam."

Or leave bruises on a woman. But Bree didn't voice that.

"I keep it in a safe in my bedroom." Nathan paused, continued to stare at Bree "Do you want to go upstairs with me while I get it?" he asked.

Bree figured that Duncan was silently yelling for her to say no, but she had no intentions of going anywhere alone with Nathan. Slater, however, quickly volunteered.

"I'll go," her brother said, causing Nathan's scowl to return in full force, but he didn't refuse.

Joelle and she paused in the foyer, watching as Nathan and Slater went up the stairs. Bree knew her brother was a good cop, but she felt the instant sense of worry and dread. She didn't want Slater alone with Nathan in case he tried to attack him and run.

"We'll come, too," Bree insisted.

That caused Nathan to stop, and he looked down at Joelle and her. Nathan wasn't doing a good job of covering up his anger, but there was also a touch of that ickiness, too, as if a small part of him was pleased that she'd be in his bedroom.

They all went up the steep stairs to a large bedroom at the front of a narrow hall. The door was open, and Bree could see the king-sized bed. Not antique. Nathan had gone for modern here, and nothing seemed out of place. Still, she continued to look around as Nathan went to a landscape painting on the wall and slid it to the side to reveal the safe.

While Nathan put in the combination, Bree looked around and knew that Slater and Joelle were both doing the same thing. They didn't have a search warrant and were not able to get one, but that didn't mean they couldn't spot something obvious that would link Nathan to Brighton and maybe the attacks. Of course, if there had been such a thing lying around, Nathan almost certainly wouldn't have invited them into the room.

The safe door made a clicking noise when Nathan opened it, and he took out a wooden box that he set on the foot of his bed. There was no lid so it was easy to see the contents. Assorted rings, watches and cuff links. Nathan plucked out the ring and tried to hand it to Bree. She looked at it but didn't touch it.

"May we take this into custody for a while?" Slater asked, pulling out a plastic evidence bag from his pocket.

"Custody?" Nathan challenged. The anger had risen again. "What the hell is this? Who said something about me and this ring that would make you want to take it?" He stopped, stared at Bree. "What do you think you'll find on this ring?"

"We're not at liberty to say," Joelle stated before Bree had to come up with a response.

Nathan did more staring, and then he cursed. For a moment, Bree thought he was going to refuse to give Slater the ring. He didn't though. He practically shoved it into Slater's waiting hand and then they all headed back downstairs.

"Was it Manny or Tara who lied to you?" Nathan came out and asked once they'd returned to the living room.

"What exactly would they lie about?" Joelle countered.

Nathan huffed. "Well, I'm guessing it's about the ring, and that's why you want to take it and send it to a lab. You're expecting to find something. Maybe DNA. Maybe gunshot residue." He leaned closer to Bree. "You won't. You won't find anything because I've done nothing wrong."

Both Manny and Tara had said pretty much the same thing about their innocence. And maybe they were innocent. Heck, maybe Nathan was as well, but someone was responsible for the nightmare that had been set in motion.

"I hope you're taking Manny's jewelry in for processing," Nathan went on. "Or arresting him. The man's a liar, and he's dangerous."

"How so?" Bree asked.

Nathan smirked. "How many lies has he told you? I'm betting a lot," he quickly tacked on to that. "Yet, he, or maybe Tara, convinced you that I had something to hide and that you'd find it on that ring. Don't you see what he's trying to do?" But he waved that off. "No, of course you don't. You have trouble seeing what's right in front of you."

Bree frowned. "What does that mean?"

He tipped his head to the front of his house. "Luca," he said and leaned toward her again. "Has it occurred to you that if you're dead, he gets custody of your son? Sole custody," he emphasized.

Bree had to bite back a whole lot of profanity, and she didn't take the bait he'd just tossed at her. Nathan could want her angry. Or scared. He could want her to say or do something that would compromise the investigation. Then again, maybe he was delusional enough to believe he could put a wedge between Luca and her.

He couldn't.

And as long as she knew that, there was no need for her to unleash some venom on him.

"Thank you for your cooperation," Bree said, using her lawyer's tone.

She glanced at Joelle and Slater to see if they had all they'd come for, and both gave her confirming nods. That was all Bree needed to turn and get the heck out of there. She didn't glance back to see Nathan's reaction. She just left out the front door with her siblings.

Luca had his gaze pinned to the house, but he was also on the phone with someone. One look at his face, and Bree knew that he was aware of what had happened in the house.

Well, maybe not aware of that last part that Nathan had hurled toward her.

"Woodrow was listening to Duncan's phone," Luca explained as she slid into the back seat with him. "And he called me to tell me that Nathan fessed up to owning the ring."

She nodded, but that was all she managed to do because Luca's shoulders suddenly snapped back in reaction to something Woodrow had said. "Where?" Luca demanded.

That one-word question and his expression were more than enough to send a jolt of fear through her. The fear only intensified when Luca snapped, "Drive," to Slater. "One of the hands just spotted Aubrey near the ranch."

Chapter Fourteen

Luca tried to tamp down the panic. Tried not to think the worst could be happening. But it might be.

"Gotta go," Woodrow said, ending the call.

Luca wanted him to go, wanted him to do something to stop Aubrey from attacking them, but it meant Luca now had no way of knowing what was going on.

"Where was Aubrey spotted?" Bree asked, her voice already a tangle of nerves and adrenaline.

"By the back fence. A ranch hand using binoculars saw her, but then she ducked out of sight. He's sure it was Aubrey because Duncan had given all the hands photos of her so they'd recognize her if they saw her."

The back fence was about a quarter of a mile from the house, but a good marksman could hit a target from that distance. Luca didn't know if the target was the house—and those inside it—or if Aubrey had been getting herself into a position so she could shoot them.

"If Aubrey had the ranch under surveillance," Bree said, "she might have seen us leave and could be waiting for us to get back."

Yeah, that was a strong possibility. Well, it was if Bree and he were her intended victims. If Gabriel was, then Aubrey could be working her way to the house right now, and heaven knew how many people she'd shoot or kill to get to him.

Slater was already driving fast, probably too fast, considering the narrow country road, but Luca wished they could break speed records to get there. His son could be in danger. Everyone in the house and on the grounds could be, and he needed to be there to stop this woman.

Since it occurred to him that Aubrey could be some kind of decoy, Luca kept watch. He also gave Bree's hand a gentle squeeze. It wouldn't help. Nothing would at this point other than arriving at the ranch and finding everyone safe. But he needed the contact with her. Needed her touch to steady him some. Apparently though, she needed something from him as well because she looked at him with tear-filled eyes.

"We'll stop Aubrey," he swore to her. Luca didn't know how, but he would stop her. And her boss, too, once this threat had been neutralized.

But who exactly was her boss?

They still didn't know, and with Nathan volunteering to give them the ring, it might not be him. That left Tara and Manny. Hell, it might not be one of them either. It could be someone who wasn't even on their radar, but if so, they'd have to find that person. No way could Luca let Gabriel and Bree continue to be in danger like this.

Luca already had his gun drawn, but he readjusted his position when the ranch came into view. And his heart dropped. The two ranch hands who were guarding the driveway were still there, but they were on the ground behind their truck where they'd obviously taken cover.

Not merely a precaution, either.

Because Luca heard the crack of the gunshot.

The back fence wasn't anywhere near this spot, but if Aubrey had climbed into a tree, she could have fired pretty much anywhere on the ranch. Maybe she'd decided to take out the hands first, one by one, and from that range she could maybe manage to do it.

More shots came, tearing through the truck. Aubrey probably couldn't actually see the men on the ground, but the gunfire was keeping them pinned down. Preventing them from returning shots. The same might be happening to the other ranch hands as well.

"I'm going closer," Slater said. "It'll maybe draw the gunfire away from them."

Since the cruiser was bullet resistant, that was the right decision. However, that didn't mean shots couldn't get through to Bree. Luca wanted to ask her to get down, but she was already taking out her own gun.

"I need to protect Gabriel, too," she muttered. She met Luca's gaze, and he could see the fierce determination there. A determination he fully understood.

"If you get a shot, shoot to kill," he advised her, hoping it wouldn't come down to that. Right now, anything and everything was a possibility, including the fact that Aubrey might not be alone. Another hired gun could be with her.

Or her boss.

If so, Luca hoped he got to take a kill shot. Everything inside him was shouting for him to take out the SOB who'd put babies in danger like this.

Slater pulled up behind the hands' truck, and he motioned for them to move to the side of the cruiser where they'd be better protected. They did while the shots continued. The truck and the hands were no longer the target though.

The cruiser was.

A bullet slammed into the rear window, right where Bree was sitting, but thankfully the glass held. For now. It might not if shots continued to hit that same spot.

"Trade places with me," Luca said, not waiting for Bree to agree to that. He wanted to be on that side in case the glass gave way. Because then he might be able to return fire and get Aubrey to back off.

"Should I open the door and let the hands in?" Bree asked.

"Not yet," Joelle said. "They're safer on the ground where they are. Besides, there could be a shooter waiting for you to open it."

Bree didn't gasp, didn't make any sharp sound of surprise, which meant those kind of scenarios had already occurred to her.

Slater's phone rang, the sound slicing through the noise of the stream of gunfire, and after he answered it, Luca heard Duncan's voice.

"Everyone inside the house is okay," Duncan was quick to say. "No shots have been fired at us. Lenny's spotted Aubrey though," he added, referring to one of the hands. "And she's no longer by the back fence. As you've probably guessed from the direction of the gunfire, she's taken up position near the back edge of the property by the road."

Luca immediately looked in that direction. And cursed. Because there was nothing but trees there. Thick clusters of them where Aubrey could be hiding.

"Lenny doesn't have a clear shot, but he can fire into the trees to distract her. I would suggest you just get yourself and the ranch hands to the house—" Duncan continued.

"No," Bree interrupted. "If we do that, she'll just try to shoot us there."

Duncan didn't dispute that. Couldn't. Because it was exactly what would happen.

"The hands here both have rifles," Luca said. "I might be able to take Aubrey out."

Bree was frantically shaking her head, but she stopped when Luca met her gaze again. This had to be done.

"I'll tell Lenny to fire those shots," Duncan said after a long sigh. "If it flushes her out, then put an end to her."

Luca gave Bree one last look, trying to reassure. Knowing he failed. Then, he moved back to the side with the hands just as he heard the new rounds of shots. From Lenny, no doubt.

"I need your rifle," Luca said, getting out of the cruiser. "Both of you get in the back seat."

The hands did as he'd instructed, and Luca took aim over the top of the cruiser. Not exactly the safest position, but he had to see if he could spot Aubrey. He didn't. Not at first anyway. But then, there was an exchange of gunfire, and Luca saw the movement in the trees. Aubrey was in one of the large oaks, and she was moving out onto a thick limb, probably so she could kill Lenny.

Luca didn't let that happen.

He took his own advice that he'd given to Bree. Shoot to kill. Even if that meant Aubrey wouldn't be able to tell them who'd hired her. He took aim. Fired.

And put two bullets in the woman trying to murder them.

BREE CONTINUED TO hold Gabriel even though the baby was asleep and had been for nearly a half hour. It was his bedtime, and she should have already put him in his crib for what would likely be a three-or four-hour stretch of sleep, but she needed to have him near her a few moments longer.

Those moments ended when Luca came into the guest room, and she could tell from his body language and expression that he needed to be near her as well. Along with that, he probably had updates on Aubrey. Updates she wanted to hear. So, she eased Gabriel into his crib, went to Luca and pulled him into her arms.

Bree hadn't planned to kiss him. But that's what she did, and the moment her mouth landed on his, she realized she needed this as much as he obviously did. Luca sank right into the kiss, stretching it out for several long moments before he ended it and pulled her close against him.

"There was nothing on Aubrey's body to indicate who hired her," Luca whispered. His voice was strained with fatigue, spent adrenaline and worry. "She had a burner phone, but she'd used that only to call another burner. We tried to call it, but no one answered."

Bree had expected that. Aubrey's boss likely would have demanded that she use a burner so Aubrey couldn't be linked back to him or her. But Aubrey's boss had almost certainly wanted her to kill or kidnap Gabriel, Luca or her, and the woman had failed. In fact, no one on the ranch had ended up getting shot except for Aubrey.

"Are you okay?" Bree asked him. She could only guess at the emotional toll this was taking on him.

He nodded, but she figured that was a lie. None of them were going to be okay until the killer was caught. The only thing they could do was make the ranch as safe as possible, but they all knew that might not be safe enough. Now that it was night, the killer could use the darkness to get close to the house. Bree tried to imagine which of their suspects could manage to do that. Maybe all of them.

Or none.

It was just as possible the killer would send another hired gun like Aubrey.

"I need a shower," Luca said, stepping back from her. "I, uh, have blood on my clothes. After the CSIs had photographed the scene, I helped them move the body into a bag," he explained.

Aubrey's blood. Bree hadn't seen for herself how that'd

happened, but once she was secure in the house, Slater and he had gone to check the body, to make sure Aubrey was truly dead and no longer a threat.

Bree took Luca by the arm and led him into the bathroom. She left the door open to the bedroom so she could hear Gabriel and turned on the shower. When Luca just stood there, staring at her, she unbuckled his holster and laid it and his gun on the vanity.

He kept his gaze on her.

Bree didn't shy away from that. After she pulled off his shirt, her eyes locked with his—those incredible brown eyes that always seem to drown her in heat—and she considered her options. She could go back into the bedroom and let Luca have that shower. Or she could do something about those raw nerves. Not just his but her own.

She went with option two.

So did Luca.

He slid his arm around the back of her neck and kissed her. Not exactly a kiss of comfort either since it was long, deep and filled with need. Still, his mouth did the trick of firing enough heat through her that the raw nerves just melted. Heck, she melted, but then she always did when Luca kissed her.

Maybe because his jeans had blood on them, he moved his hands between them to undo his belt and unzip. The touching added to the flames, especially since Luca didn't break the kiss to do that. It took some maneuvering, some dipping down and moving to the side with him, but their mouths continued to pleasure each other while he rid himself of his jeans and boots.

Bree took full advantage of having a nearly naked Luca. She touched him, sliding her hands down his back over all those muscles. The man was certainly built. And even though she knew the feel of every one of those muscles, this moment, this now felt new, as if she'd never had him before. That was probably because her body was starved for him, and that's why Bree didn't hold anything back. She kissed and touched until Luca was cursing her.

Cursing her clothes, too.

That's when she realized that unlike him, she was fully dressed. Luca did something about that. He yanked off her top, immediately kissing the skin he'd just bared. Her neck. Then, the tops of her breasts. He stopped though. Just stopped, and his gaze fired to hers.

"Is it okay?" he asked, nearly stopping her heart because she thought he might, well, be stopping. "I mean, Gabriel's two months old."

Her heart revved up again. "Yes, it's more than okay." Except now, she had to pause. "Well, it is if you have a condom."

He pulled away from her, located his jeans and fumbled through his wallet until he came up with the foil wrapper. She'd known he usually carried one, but Bree had never been more thankful to see it.

Luca smiled, probably because of her obvious relief, and he launched back into another kiss. Not solely that, though. He was obviously a man on a mission, and that mission was to get her naked because he unzipped her jeans and push them down until they dropped around her feet. He lifted her, turning her so she was sitting on the vanity.

Then, he kissed her again.

This slam of heat was so hard and fast that she couldn't catch her breath. Soon, though, she didn't care if she ever caught it again because all she could think of was what Luca was doing to her. He was taking her on one wild ride all the while firing up the need until it became a throbbing ache in the center of her body.

Luca didn't ease away that ache but added to it when he stepped between her legs and pressed them center to center.

He was hard as stone and pushed against just the right spot to make the need skyrocket.

Bree wanted him naked, and she wanted it now so she went after his boxers. Luca went after her panties and bra, but he clearly wasn't in the frantic *now* mode. Not yet anyway. She did something about that by closing her fingers around his erection.

He cursed her, and the sound that rumbled in his chest was all male, all need. All now. Finally.

It was Bree who did some cursing when it seemed to take a couple of lifetimes to get the condom on, and she might have cursed, too, at the immense pleasure when he pushed into her. She didn't have breath to form words. The only thing she could do was feel, and she was having no trouble with that.

Luca and she had been lovers for a long time so she knew the familiarity of this rhythm they found. And because he knew every inch of her body, he knew how to draw out the pleasure. He knew how to take her to the peak, right to the edge and then bring her back down so it could last a little longer.

He kissed her again but then pulled back, spearing her gaze as he made those now frantic thrusts inside her. Bree couldn't have come down from the peak now even if he stopped. She was past the point of no return, and Luca knew it. That's why he gave her exactly what she needed to feel the climax slam through her.

Bree let herself shatter, let the sensations wrack her body and wash over her. And when it was Luca's turn to take that fall, she gathered him into her arms and held on.

Chapter Fifteen

Luca eased Gabriel back into his crib, and he hoped now that the baby was fed and dry he would sleep for another four-hour stretch. A stretch that might give Bree some rest and him as well.

They'd managed a couple of catnaps, but they needed more. Despite being revved from the incredible sex, Luca knew they were both exhausted. That's why he'd done the midnight feeding and diaper change.

Luca slid back into bed, and Bree made a sleepy sound of satisfaction and automatically snuggled against him. She was warm and naked, and he wished they didn't have the threat of danger hanging over their heads so they could truly enjoy every moment of this night. It was still amazing, but Luca figured this was just a short reprieve. Tomorrow, they'd need to dive back into the investigation, and maybe they'd finally get the break they desperately needed.

After that, after the killer was caught, well… Luca wasn't sure what would happen, but he sure as hell wanted the chance to have some time to try to work out things with Bree. Unfortunately, that working out might mean they still continued to be apart, but he thought this night was a good start in repairing their relationship.

"Thanks for giving Gabriel the bottle," she murmured.

He sighed because Bree obviously wasn't asleep as he'd thought. Of course, that only gave him an excuse to brush a kiss on her mouth. She brushed one right back, causing him to smile. A kiss from Bree was something to be savored despite everything else going on.

Luca didn't have a second condom or he might have pushed the kiss to something deeper, but the deeper didn't get a chance to happen. Bree and he both groaned when his phone vibrated. He'd turned off the ringer so it wouldn't wake Gabriel, but his phone was practically skittering across the surface of the nightstand, which meant it was making plenty of noise. Luca snatched it up and saw Slater's name on the screen.

Hell.

This couldn't be good. Not at this hour. The ranch should have been locked down for the night.

"What's wrong?" Luca answered in a whisper. He didn't put the call on Speaker, but Bree moved closer to him.

"Two of the ranch hands aren't responding," Slater quickly said. "We've been doing check-ins every hour, and they both missed the midnight one. I've tried to call them, but they aren't answering."

Luca mentally repeated his, *Hell*. "Where were they positioned?"

"Both by the back fence. One on the east corner, the other one the west. Yeah," Slater muttered when Luca groaned. If someone was going to try to sneak onto the ranch, those'd be the places to do it.

Luca got up and started dressing. Bree did the same. "I've got thermal imaging binoculars," Luca explained. He'd brought several back to the ranch from the sheriff's office, and Duncan had arranged for more to be delivered so the hands could use them. "Let me go to the window and see if I can spot anything."

"I've asked another of the hands, Mike Travers, to use his binoculars to see if he can locate them," Slater explained. "Mike's not at the best angle for that, but I don't want to pull him away from his area since he's guarding the spot near the road."

Luca made a quick sound of agreement. The road was a vulnerable part, too. Heck, there were lots of places that a killer could use to gain access to the house.

"The security system is on, right?" Luca asked, already knowing the answer, and Slater gave him instant confirmation.

"Woodrow's monitoring that," Slater explained. "He's trying to get some sleep, but he's got it set to alert him if there's any movement in or around the house."

The perimeter security and cameras were a new addition, put in just hours earlier. A series of motion-activated sensors had been staked into the ground around the entire house, and some had been positioned in the backyard.

"Good," Luca said, putting on the rest of his clothes and hurrying to the window that would give him a somewhat limited view of the east back corner of the pasture. Limited because of trees and the outbuildings.

Luca handed his phone to Bree who'd joined him at the window, and he looked out with the binoculars. He got a jolt when he saw the glowing eyes but then realized it was a deer. He picked up the livestock, too, and a couple of raccoons. What he didn't immediately see was a ranch hand or anyone else.

He shifted his view, panning the binoculars over the grounds, and he caught just a flash of a heat source. For a moment, he thought it was another animal, but then Luca realized the red blob was a torso. The person was on the ground, partially hidden by a tree, and he or she wasn't moving.

"I think someone's down," Luca relayed just as he saw another slash of red. He muttered a single word of profanity because he had no idea if this was one of the hands or a killer coming their way. "I'm pretty sure we've got a breach," he said, figuring the guy on the ground was indeed one of the hands.

Slater cursed, too, just as there was a knock on the bedroom door. Bree hurried to open it, and Duncan stuck in his head.

"The security camera has likely been compromised," Duncan immediately said. "Woodrow just told me he thinks the camera feed's on a loop."

Luca's stomach dropped because that was the same thing that'd happened to the baby monitor.

"I think we've got a hand down and someone already on the grounds," Luca explained, handing Duncan the binoculars so he could see for himself.

It took a couple of seconds with Duncan moving the binoculars around, but his muttered profanity told Luca plenty. "Someone's coming across the pasture, and I don't think it's one of the hands." His attention slashed to Bree. "Grab Gabriel because you need to take cover now."

THE FEAR AND adrenaline slammed through Bree. Oh, God. No.

Please not this again.

She hurried across the room to scoop up Gabriel. She prayed this would turn out to be nothing, that her baby wasn't in danger yet again. But she had the sickening feeling that a killer was coming for them. And they still didn't know who was after them. Whoever it was, the person was relentless.

"Take Gabriel to the main bedroom," Duncan instructed. "Joelle and Sandra are there with Izzie. I want all of you in the bathroom. It's bigger than the one in here, and the shower stall is all tiled."

Tiled and therefore more resistant to bullets than a wall would be. Bree had to tamp down images of bullets slamming into the house, the way they had when they'd all been huddled in the barn. She had to tamp down a lot of things and focus on keeping Gabriel safe.

Bree glanced at Luca, and their gazes connected for just a second. He was checking his primary weapon and backup, obviously gearing up for a fight. One where he could be shot.

Or worse.

Yes, that was another image she had to shove to the side because she couldn't give in to the fear and panic. She had to do whatever it took to keep their baby safe.

Clutching Gabriel to her chest, Bree hurried down the hall. Unfortunately, the jerky movement woke him up, and he started to cry. She soon learned Izzie was doing the same thing as Joelle and her mother maneuvered them into the shower. The shower stall was plenty large enough, but her mother was trying to make it more comfortable by placing heaps of towels on the floor so they wouldn't have to sit on the tiles.

"I didn't grab Izzie's pacifier," Joelle muttered, handing off Izzie to their mother so she could run back into the bedroom.

Gabriel didn't use a pacifier, so Bree tried to rock him to soothe him. That wasn't working though, and she figured Gabriel had to be picking up on her racing breath and accelerated heartbeat. He was too young to understand the danger, but he likely sensed something was wrong.

When Joelle hurried back, she saw that her sister not only had the pacifier and a small stuffed animal but also her holster and gun. It was a reminder for Bree that she hadn't grabbed her gun from the closet. And she wanted it. If the killer managed to get into the house, she needed to be able to defend Gabriel and her family. Definitely not something she wanted to do because it would mean the killer had gotten way too close to them, but Bree didn't want to risk being unarmed.

Once Joelle had taken Izzie, Bree eased Gabriel into her mother's arms. "I'll be right back. I just want to get my gun and a bottle for Gabriel." He wouldn't be hungry, but a few sips might allow him to settle down enough to fall asleep.

As she'd done with Luca, Bree met her mother's gaze for a second. Of course, there was fear there. Plenty of it. But she also thankfully saw a resolve that Bree figured was in her own eyes and Joelle's. They weren't going to let a killer get near the babies.

Bree rushed back out into the hall and spotted Duncan and Luca on the stairs landing. Duncan went ahead down, but Luca stayed put while she made her way to him.

"What happened?" she asked because she could tell from his expression he'd gotten yet more bad news.

"Duncan's not sure how long the security system's been compromised," he said, the worry flaring in his eyes. "He checked the doors and windows, and they're all still locked, but he can't be sure someone didn't manage to get inside."

It felt as if someone had sucked all the air out of her body. She fired glances around as if someone might be ready to jump out at them. But she heard and saw no one other than Luca.

"I want to get my gun and a bottle for Gabriel," she managed to say.

Luca nodded. "Do that, and then go straight back into the bathroom. Lock both the bedroom and bathroom doors and turn off the lights. I don't want anyone watching the house to be able to pinpoint our locations."

She nodded and tried not to look ready to curse. But she was. It was heart crushing to know the danger could be so close to them.

Luca's phone vibrated, and when he took it from his pocket, she saw Woodrow's name on the screen. "Go ahead and get the gun and bottle. Duncan and I are going to do a room-by-room search downstairs and up here, but I won't do that until you're safe in the bathroom."

A horrible thought occurred to her, and Luca must have known what put the terror on her face. "The killer didn't sneak into our guest room or the main bedroom. If so, we would have heard it."

That restarted her breath because he was right. It was probably the same for her mother's room. That left the hall bathroom and the nursery. It was right next to the main bedroom and was empty since Duncan and Joelle had moved Izzie into their room.

Bree hurried into the guest room, grabbing a premade bottle of formula and the diaper bag since she wasn't sure how long they'd be stuck in the bathroom. She took her gun, shoved it into the back waist of her jeans and went back into the hall. Luca was still there, talking on the phone to Woodrow. He had his back to her and was peering down the stairs, no doubt looking for any signs of trouble. Judging from his body language, he wasn't seeing any.

Not until he turned toward her.

"Watch out!" Luca yelled.

Bree heard the sound of running footsteps behind her, and she whirled around to see the figure dressed all in black charging right at her. She dropped the diaper bag and bottle, reaching for her gun.

But it was too late.

She felt someone latch on to her, knocking away her gun and dragging her hands behind her back. The person slapped plastic cuffs on her before pressing a gun to her head.

LUCA SHOUTED BREE'S NAME, but she didn't get the chance to run. Couldn't. That's because the person who'd run up behind her from the nursery hooked his left arm around her throat and put her in a choke hold. He pressed a gun directly to her temple.

Hell.

This had been exactly what they'd tried to avoid. What they'd been avoiding since the attacks had started. And now, the killer or one of his henchmen had Bree.

Her captor was probably a man, one several inches taller than Bree since he was hunching down behind her. He was dressed all in black, including a ski mask that covered everything but his eyes.

"What's going on?" Duncan shouted, and there were the sounds of movement at the bottom of the stairs.

Luca brought up his gun to take aim even though he wouldn't have a clean shot, but when the attacker turned his own gun in Luca's direction, Luca had no choice but to dive into the open door of the guest room. He landed hard on the floor, the fall knocking the breath out of him so he had to struggle just to get to his knees.

"Stay back," Bree yelled. "Everyone stay back." Which was no doubt what her captor had told her to say.

The man didn't come after Luca and follow up with what

would have likely been a kill shot. But he did move. Luca heard the footsteps, heard the sounds of Bree struggling to get away.

And then she went quiet.

That got Luca hurrying to the doorway, ready to launch himself at her captor, but Bree was still alive and she shook her head.

"He says if I fight that he'll shoot into the bathroom," she muttered. There was terror in her eyes, and it came through in her voice. She reached in her pocket, pulled out her phone and dropped it on the floor. No doubt something else the man had instructed her to do.

"Who is he? Who has you?" Luca whispered.

"I'm not sure. He's using something to alter his voice. Probably because he was worried we'd recognize who he was."

Which meant this thug had come prepared. Of course, he had. He'd compromised the security system and then had gotten in and hidden until the time was right to launch this attack.

The masked thug leaned in closer to Bree's ear and said something, but Luca couldn't make out what.

"He wants you to stay put," she said, her voice cracking. "You, too, Duncan," she added, shifting her attention toward the stair landing. "I'm going with him."

"To hell you are," Luca snarled.

There was no telling what this SOB would do to Bree if he got her alone. But then something occurred to him. If he'd wanted Bree dead, he could have just killed her on the spot. So, he wanted her alive, maybe solely as a human shield.

Maybe for something else.

"Trade her for me," Luca bargained.

The guy laughed, and the sound was like a cartoon

through the voice distorter. A sick sound that ate away at Luca like acid. Somehow, he had to stop this from happening. He couldn't lose Bree, but he also didn't want this armed snake so close to the bathroom where the babies were. He had to hope that Joelle had already locked the door and was ready to stop anyone who tried to get in.

Bullets could still get through.

And that was probably why Bree didn't put up any kind of struggle when the man started toward the stairs with her.

"Duncan, move back," Bree instructed.

The masked man turned, angling Bree so that she was not only in front of him but so he was pressed hard against her with his back against the wall. That would ensure no one would be able to get a clean shot, not with him plastered to her.

Staying low and prepared to dive again for cover, Luca came out of the guest room, his gun ready. He figured Duncan and maybe Slater and Woodrow were doing the same in the foyer.

"Duncan, he wants you to open the front door," Bree relayed.

Luca could see her glancing around, no doubt looking for a way out. He prayed she would find one. If she could just manage to drop down, he would be able to send this snake straight to hell.

There was more movement in the foyer, and Luca heard the front door opening. He crept forward, peering down the stairs just as Bree and the thug reached the last step. Lightning fast, the masked man turned his gun toward Luca.

And fired.

For a couple of heart-stopping seconds, Luca thought he'd been hit. But the bullet missed, smacking into the wall above his head.

"Stay back!" Bree shouted. "All of you please stay back," she added, her voice a strained plea.

Luca couldn't do that. He couldn't stay behind cover while she was in immediate danger, but he also had to time it so the masked man couldn't get off a shot inside the house. He inched forward again and saw the gunman and Bree had already reached the now open front door. Duncan, Woodrow and Slater were indeed all there. All had their weapons drawn and were peering out behind the arched opening that led into the family room.

The thug looked up at Luca, and even though he still couldn't see the guy's face, their eyes met for a moment. Luca couldn't tell for sure, but it seemed to him that the SOB was smirking. The rage knifed through Luca, but he didn't allow it to trigger him into doing something reckless. It definitely wouldn't help matters if he got shot. Or if he did something to cause Bree to be hurt.

The thug moved her onto the porch, and that got Luca hurrying down the stairs. Woodrow, Slater and Duncan all came out from cover, too.

And the sound of a gunshot blasted through the house.

It took Luca a moment to realize it hadn't come from the thug dragging out Bree but rather it'd come from the direction of the kitchen. Every muscle inside him turned to iron when he saw someone. Another person dressed all in black and wearing a ski mask. He or she had a gun and fired again.

This shot, too, missed, slamming into the wall and sending Woodrow, Slater and Duncan scurrying back. Luca didn't head back up the stairs. Instead, he bolted out through the front door and onto the porch.

He cursed when he realized he still didn't have a clean

shot. And worse. The thug was dragging Bree toward one of the ranch hand's trucks that was parked behind a cruiser.

Luca could only watch as the man shoved Bree into the truck. Seconds later, he started the engine and sped away.

Chapter Sixteen

The moment her captor started driving away, Bree tried to figure out how to escape. She hadn't wanted to fight before now and risk him shooting into the house. Or shooting Luca, Woodrow, Slater or Duncan.

But someone inside the house had fired a shot.

Probably a hired gun, and she prayed that everyone had stayed out of the path of the bullet. Prayed, too, that she could figure a way out of this truck.

Her hands were cuffed, but her legs and feet were free, and she tried to swivel around in the seat and kick the driver in the face. She landed a blow on the steering wheel that caused the truck to jerk to the side, but before she could regroup, the driver landed a blow of his own. He bashed the gun against her head, the barrel cutting through her stitches. Had she been standing, the pain would have brought her to her knees.

She fell back on the seat, gasping for air, trying to tamp down the searing pain. But it was overwhelming, and her chest was so tight, she couldn't draw in a full breath.

"There are still people I can shoot," her captor snarled in that fake voice. "If you want them to live, stop fighting."

She immediately spotted two ranch hands running toward the truck as it reached the end of the driveway. They would indeed be easy shots, so she pulled back. Temporarily. She had to regroup. Had to push away the pain, so Bree waited until the truck was on the road before she geared up to try to land another kick.

"One wrong move, and your baby will pay," he snapped.

That got her attention all right, and she stopped again. Even though her head was pounding and making it next to impossible for her to think, she recalled the shooter inside the house.

Maybe more than one of them.

Maybe enough to overpower Luca, Duncan, Woodrow and Slater and get upstairs to the babies. Of course, an attacker would have to get through Joelle, but her sister could be gunned down. If so, Gabriel could be taken.

Or hurt.

Oh, God. That couldn't happen.

She couldn't lose Luca, her son and her family like this.

Bree cursed the tears that instantly burned in her eyes. Cursed that she didn't know what to do to save her little boy. Or even who had kidnapped her. She tried to pick through what she could see of him, but every inch of him was covered, and since he wasn't even using his real voice, she had no idea if this was Nathan or Manny. Or maybe neither. This could be another hired gun taking her to his boss.

"What do you want with me?" she demanded, hoping she'd be able to get answers that would help.

He didn't answer, but he was looking around for something. There were no other actual roads on this stretch, but he was still firing glances to his left. Maybe hunting for somewhere to stop. She had no idea though why he would want to do that.

The man continued to glance around, and this time he looked over his shoulder and ground out some harsh profanity. She soon saw why. There was a cruiser in pursuit.

Somehow, Luca had managed to get away from that shooter in the house. He was coming after her.

That was both good and bad.

Because Bree very much wanted to be away from this killer, but she didn't want Luca or anyone else dying in the process. The odds were Luca would be able to catch up with them in the cruiser and follow them to wherever they were going. There could be a shoot-out, and she had no doubts that her captor would use her as a shield again so he could fire at Luca.

She turned back to her captor who was volleying glances ahead on the dark road and in the rearview mirror. And she thought of a ploy. Probably not a good one, but she tried it anyway.

"Are you taking me to Nathan?" she asked.

The driver's shoulders went stiff. Not a huge reaction. But she noticed it.

"Nathan wouldn't want you to hurt me," she tacked on to that.

He didn't respond, verbally or otherwise, but she thought maybe she'd hit a nerve. The man had recognized the name. Did that mean Nathan had hired him?

Maybe.

Or was this Nathan?

"If this is about Brighton's murder," she tried again, "then it's all for nothing. Silencing me won't stop the investigation."

He cursed again, maybe the sign of another raw nerve. But then, it could also be because the cruiser was quickly gaining ground. Bree saw in the side mirror as the driver pulled out into the lane next to the truck.

It was Luca, and Slater was with him.

Her captor saw them, too, because he belted out more of that profanity and jerked the steering wheel to the right.

There was the sound of metal slicing into metal, and the bottom part of the passenger's door started to cave in. Bree scrambled away from it so her foot wouldn't get trapped if the door collapsed.

"Finally," her captor muttered.

He twisted the steering wheel again, bashing into the cruiser. Bree watched in horror as the impact sent the cruiser into a ditch. She immediately geared up to try to kick her captor, but he must have seen it coming because he hit her with the gun again. Bree fell against the door, the back of her head hitting the window, and then she was immediately slung into the dash when he made a sharp turn onto a ranch trail.

Bree knew most of the trails in this area and was aware this one had gullies on each side caused by rain and erosion. She lunged across the seat and caught hold of the steering wheel to get them off the trail. The man cursed her and tried to knock her away with the gun, but Bree kept fighting. The truck finally veered off the narrow dirt path, and the front end plunged into the ditch.

The impact was like a collision, and Bree jolted forward. The airbags deployed, slamming into her captor and her and spewing a cloud of powder over the entire cab of the truck. Bree didn't waste a second. She dove toward the passenger's side door while the man tried to catch on to her. He had the disadvantage of being trapped behind the steering wheel by the airbag, but she had a huge disadvantage too. Since she was cuffed, she had to turn her back to the door to open it.

And her heart dropped when she realized it was jammed.

Pain shot through her shoulder and back, but she rammed against the door, all the while trying to kick her captor. When the door finally opened, she tumbled out onto the ground. She heard the man curse again, and he must have managed to bat down the airbag because he was there. Right behind her.

She kicked out again, somehow managing to get to her feet, and she started running toward the blue cruiser lights that were slicing through the darkness.

She didn't get far.

The man tackled her, both of them falling onto the ground, and he landed on top of her. She continued to fight. So did he. And in the struggle, the mask hiked up enough for her to see his chin and mouth. Even in the darkness, she recognized him.

Nathan.

LUCA RAN AS if his life depended on it. Bree's life certainly did, and he sprinted away from the cruiser and toward the trail where he'd seen the truck turn. He couldn't let the vehicle get out of sight.

He had to get to Bree in time to stop her from being driven off somewhere.

Slater was out of the cruiser, too, and running behind him, but he was also calling to get the status of the immediate backup they'd already requested. They needed a vehicle here now if he stood a chance of catching the SOB who'd taken Bree.

Still at a full sprint, Luca turned onto the trail and nearly skidded to a stop when he saw the truck.

And Bree.

She was running or rather she was trying to do that, but the thug tackled her, both of them dropping to the ground. Luca started running again, and when the thug pulled back his hand, Luca saw that he was trying to aim the gun at Bree.

The snake was going to shoot her.

"Stop!" Luca yelled, already bringing up his own gun. He didn't have a clean shot so he fired over the guy's head to get his attention.

It got it all right.

The man rolled to the side, dragging up Bree in front of him so he could cower behind her.

"Coward," Luca snarled plenty loud enough for her captor to hear him, and then he had to drop down into the ditch when the guy took aim at him.

He fired, too, and while the shot didn't come anywhere near Luca, he shouted for Slater to be careful. Luca definitely didn't want Slater to take a bullet meant for him. Hell, he didn't want anyone other than this thug dying tonight.

"It's Nathan," Bree managed to yell. "He's the one who took me."

Luca spat out the name like profanity, "Nathan." So, he was their attacker.

Nathan did some actual cursing, and he whipped off the mask and the voice alternator he had against his throat. He also latched on to Bree's hair and pulled her up so that his face was right against hers.

"It's too late for you to save her, *hero*," Nathan taunted. "Too late for Bree to choose the right man."

"You're not the right man," Bree snapped, and she tried to elbow Nathan in the gut.

Luca admired the fact that she wasn't giving up, but he didn't want her to fight right now. He didn't want Nathan to have any reason to kill her. At this point, though, her knowing his identity was probably the only motive Nathan needed to end her life. That's why Luca got down as low as he could and continued toward Bree. Maybe he'd get that clean shot he needed to take out this SOB.

"I've already told him if this is about Brighton, the investigation isn't going away," Bree said, straining against the grip he had on her hair.

"I don't need it to go away," Nathan was quick to say. "I just need the cops looking at someone else."

Luca mentally replayed the words while he glanced over his shoulder at the sound of the movement. Slater was in the ditch, crouched down and making his way toward Luca.

"You're going to set someone up for Brighton's murder?" Luca asked. "Another cowardly thing," he added in a mutter.

"I'm not going to jail for what happened to her," Nathan practically yelled. "It wasn't my fault." If he had any composure left, he seemed to be losing it fast. If he snapped, he just might start shooting before Luca could figure out a way to get Bree out of this alive.

"Are you saying it was an accident?" Luca asked.

Nathan jumped right on that. "Yes, an accident."

That didn't convince Luca one bit. Then again, there wasn't anything Nathan could say that would make Luca believe he was innocent. After all, he was holding Bree at gunpoint.

"Things just got out of hand," Nathan said, and then he made a hoarse sob as if he was about to break down and cry.

"Did things get out of hand with my mother, too?" Bree demanded. "Is that why you kidnapped her?"

"She was insurance, that's all," Nathan readily admitted. "Leverage. If the investigation had turned bad, then she would have been of use to lure out Bree. Or you."

"Me?" Luca questioned. "Why the hell would you want Bree or me?"

"Because Sandra had an alibi for the night of Brighton's murder. We didn't know that at first, but then we found a photo of her on Facebook that would have proved she couldn't have killed her. We couldn't set her up to take the blame."

Luca was surprised Nathan had admitted that since it also implicated him not only in Sandra's kidnapping but also

Brighton's and Shannon's murders. So, why would he spill it? And why wasn't he just trying to get away with Bree?

Was Nathan waiting for a hired gun to show up?

Maybe the one at the ranch who'd fired those shots at Woodrow, Duncan and Slater?

When Luca and Slater had run out of the house to go in pursuit of Nathan, they'd left Woodrow and Duncan to deal with that. And Luca had to hope they had. It'd been two against one. Well, unless there had been others lurking around, but there'd been no choice about coming after Bree and trusting that Duncan and Woodrow would eliminate any threat at the ranch.

But maybe Nathan thought that person would escape and come to help him.

It wouldn't happen because Slater and he would hear an approaching vehicle and would prevent the person from getting to Nathan. Nathan should have realized that by now. He should be panicking and trying to run. Unless…

A thought flashed into Luca's head. A bad one. Nathan had turned onto this trail, and that might be because he knew help would be nearby.

Luca tried to pick through the darkness and look ahead on the trail. He couldn't see another vehicle, but that didn't mean one wasn't there. In fact, there almost certainly was since this particular trail fed out to a road.

"What? No questions for me?" Nathan shouted. "You don't want to know if I killed Bree's father? I didn't," he was quick to add.

Luca tuned him out because he was certain that Nathan was talking to try to distract him. It didn't work. Luca heard the sound of something or someone moving in the ditch on the other side of the trail. He pivoted in that direction and got just a glimpse of the man. Someone he instantly recognized.

Because it was Manny.

And Manny fired a shot at him.

BREE HEARD THE blast of a gun being fired, and for a heart-stopping moment, she thought Nathan had shot her. Or Luca.

But he hadn't.

The sound had come from her right, and she tried to turn in that direction. Nathan didn't let her. He tightened the chokehold, much harder this time, so she quit struggling so she could breath.

And pray.

That gunshot couldn't have hit Luca or her brother. And soon she got confirmation they were alive.

"Manny," Luca yelled, and she saw both Luca and Slater drop back down into the ditch.

"Manny?" she muttered.

What was he doing here? Had he come to help? Maybe he'd followed Nathan so he could try to clear his name.

But that wasn't it. If it had been, Nathan would have dropped flat on the ground with her, or he would have moved her so she'd be facing the direction of the shot. He didn't do either of those things.

"About time you got here," Nathan snarled.

"I was waiting up the trail where I was supposed to be," Manny snarled right back. "You're the one who messed up by wrecking the truck."

Bree heard every word they said, but it took her a couple of seconds to process it. Manny and Nathan were in this together. There hadn't been one killer but two.

"You tried to pin the blame on each other," Bree muttered.

"To muddy the waters of the investigation," Nathan readily admitted. "And now we've got to get out of here. Sorry,

Bree, but you can't die here," he added in a mutter. "We haven't finished setting you up yet."

So, that's why they wanted her. Manny and Nathan were going to try to pin all of this on her. Unlike her mother, Bree didn't have an alibi, but that didn't mean anyone would believe she would kill the woman and then launch into these attacks to cover it up.

"I had no motive to murder Brighton," Bree managed.

"There'll be the motive," Nathan said. "There will be texts to prove how much you loved me and how jealous you were of Brighton. They'll be an eyewitness who saw you go into Brighton's place that night. By the time we're done, even your darling Luca will have thought you did it."

Luca. Bree tried not to think of what he might be doing right now. He was no doubt trying to get into a position to save her. Slater, too. But what they wouldn't be doing was believing she'd had anything to do with Brighton's murder.

And that's why Nathan would try to kill them, too.

"Why are you helping him, Manny?" Bree asked. "Why are you doing this?"

Nathan chuckled. "Oh, Manny has just as much to lose as I do. Don't you, Manny?" He put his mouth to her ear as if telling a secret. "Because you see, Manny was there when Brighton died. In fact, he was the one who set all of this in motion."

Manny didn't address that other than to huff. "Nathan, we need to get out of here. More cops will be coming soon."

"You don't think I know that!" Nathan snapped. "I'm not an idiot. I know they called for backup, and they'll be here soon. Two minutes. If we haven't gotten the text by then, we both start shooting."

"What text?" Bree asked.

"More leverage. The best kind," he added with that despicable taunting in his voice.

Bree had to fight the panic. Had to fight the groan that was trying to claw its way past her throat. She couldn't handle worst-case scenario right now. She had to focus on getting Luca, Slater and her out of this alive.

"I thought you wanted me back," Bree said to Nathan. "I thought you cared about me."

"I despise you," he admitted through what had to be clenched teeth. "You took my love for you and threw it back in my face. It sickened me to act all moony-eyed around you, but I endured because I knew one day I'd make you pay."

In the distance, she heard the wail of sirens. A welcome sound for her, but it caused Nathan to curse and tense even more. He laughed though when his phone dinged with a text.

"Well, the payment you owe me is about to start," Nathan boasted.

Bree pushed aside any thoughts of what the text might be. Pushed aside everything but what she had to do. She gathered her strength and waited for Nathan to take out his phone so he could read the message.

Nathan kept his arm around her neck, kept the pressure so tight that she could barely breathe. But he finally lowered his hand, and therefore the gun, to his pocket. That's when she moved.

"Now!" she shouted to warn Luca and Slater, and she rammed her elbow into Nathan's stomach.

She didn't stop there. Bree scrambled away from him, landing on her back so she could kick him. She landed a hard blow to his face, and she heard the satisfying crunch of his nose breaking. Her satisfaction didn't last long though.

Cursing her, Nathan turned the gun toward her. Ready to kill her.

And the shot came.

The sound of it blasted through the air, and Bree waited for the pain. Waited for her own death.

But it didn't come.

Nathan stopped, his head or torso freezing while his arms dropped limply to his sides. The rest of him dropped, too, and that's when she saw the gunshot wound to the center of his head.

Bree snapped toward the ditch and spotted Luca. He still had his gun aimed at Nathan and had obviously been the one to shoot him.

"Stay down, Bree," Slater yelled.

"Manny," she muttered on a rise of breath. He was there, and he could finish the job that Nathan had started.

Before she could even look in Manny's direction, she heard the shots. Two back-to-backs that caused the fear to slam through her. Oh, God. Had Manny managed to shoot Luca and Slater?

Bree was terrified of what she might see, but she forced herself to look at Luca. He was still standing. So was Slater, and her brother had his gun on Manny. Or rather what was left of Manny anyway. Like Nathan, he was on the ground, and his lifeless eyes were staring up at the night sky.

The relief rushed through her so fast that Bree lost her breath again, but she still tried to get to her feet so she could go to Luca. He made it to her first though and pulled her into his arms.

"Are you all right?" he asked, fishing through his pocket to come up with a small knife. He used it to cut the plastic cuffs and then pulled her right back to him for another hug.

"I'm okay," she said. It was a lie. She was shaking and maybe in shock.

Because this wasn't over.

"The text," Bree managed to say. "We need to see what was in that text."

Luca was already steps ahead of her on that, too, and he snatched out Nathan's phone. The screen was still lit with the message.

"Hell," Luca cursed. "Let's go." He took hold of Bree's hand and started running toward the road.

"What's wrong?" Slater asked, hurrying after them. "Who was that text from?"

"Tara," Luca blurted while he ran, the world of emotion in his voice. "She said she has Gabriel."

Chapter Seventeen

Tara.

The woman's name hammered through Bree's head as Luca, Slater and she ran. Tara had Gabriel. And that meant Tara had likely been the person who'd fired those shots inside the house at the ranch. She was in on this with Nathan and Manny.

All three had worked together to create this nightmare.

She didn't ask why Duncan, Joelle, her mother or Woodrow hadn't stopped Tara from taking Gabriel. Because Bree couldn't deal with the sickening dread that they were all now dead. If Tara had Gabriel, then she'd managed to neutralize them in some way.

No, she couldn't ask about that.

She could only focus on getting to the ranch so she could find Tara and get her son.

They ran out onto the road just as a cruiser braked to a loud stop next to them. Sonya was behind the wheel with Carmen in the passenger's seat.

"What the hell happened?" Sonya asked.

Luca didn't answer. He threw open the back door, and Slater, Bree and he all piled in. "Get to the ranch now," Luca demanded.

Sonya didn't hesitate. She gunned the engine, the tires

squealing against the asphalt, and she got them moving while Luca yanked out his phone. Bree saw that he was trying to call Duncan. If she'd had her phone, she would be trying to call Joelle or her mother.

Luca cursed when Duncan didn't answer, and Bree nearly lost it. She wanted to scream. She wanted to tear the world apart to get to her son, but losing it wouldn't help. They had to focus. They had to get to the ranch and find Gabriel.

Slater took out his phone, too, and he called Joelle. Since he put it on Speaker, Bree could hear the rings as she watched the scenery fly past the window. Her heart crushed with each unanswered ring.

And then Joelle answered.

"I'm a little busy here," Joelle said, sounding out of breath but very much alive. "Are you all okay? Did you get Bree?"

Bree didn't want to respond to those questions. Not when she only wanted to know one thing. "Gabriel," she blurted. "Did Tara take him?"

"She tried," Joelle confirmed. "But she didn't succeed."

Bree went limp with relief, and she sent up a thousand prayers. "But Tara sent a message saying she'd taken him."

"Sorry about that. The text was already composed on her phone, just waiting there, and during the scuffle to retain her, it was accidentally sent. We didn't know who the recipient was since it was being sent to a burner."

Bree was beyond thankful that was how things had played out. "Is Gabriel hurt?"

"No," Joelle was quick to assure her. "No one here is. Well, except for Tara. She's got some cuts and bruises from Duncan and Woodrow tackling her to get that gun and phone away from her. Duncan's cuffing her now." Joelle paused. "Please tell me Luca, Slater and you took care of Manny and Nathan."

So, her sister knew. "They're both dead." That prompted Carmen to make a call to dispatch to get someone out to the scene to secure the bodies.

"Good," Joelle murmured, and she repeated that as if trying to steady herself. "Tara's talking, and she said Nathan and Manny put this plan together."

Soon, Bree would want to hear all about that plan, but for now, she just needed to see her baby. Sonya was trying to make that happen. She was driving as fast as possible while Carmen continued her call to coordinate the efforts to secure the crime scene.

"They were all three in on this," Bree managed to say.

"Yeah." That was all Joelle said for a long time. "How far out are you?"

"Under a minute," Bree said after she glanced around. A minute that was already feeling like an eternity.

Joelle made what sounded to be a sigh of relief. "Mom's still in the bathroom with both babies, and Woodrow is there standing guard."

Bree didn't ask why he was doing that. She knew there could be other hired guns around.

"Some of the ranch hands are searching every inch of the house while others are going over the grounds," Joelle explained. "Every available deputy and reserve deputy will be here soon to help us make sure everything is secure."

"Thank you," Bree managed.

"You're more than welcome. Just get here," Joelle said. "I'm signing off so I can better aim my gun at Tara in case she thinks about trying to escape."

Her sister ended the call, and Bree turned to Luca. She hadn't allowed herself to really look at him because she'd known what an emotional punch it would be. And it was.

She couldn't fight back a sob any longer, and she practically tumbled into his arms.

"It'll be okay," he murmured, brushing a kiss on her head.

She winced a little because she realized she probably had some bruises there from being manhandled by Nathan. It felt as if she'd popped a couple of stitches as well. But that was minor stuff. They were all alive, and Gabriel was safe.

"I'm sorry," Luca said, and she got the feeling he wasn't apologizing because of the pain that had caused her to wince. No. Luca was putting all of this nightmare on his shoulders.

Bree eased back, caught onto his chin and kissed him. She made it long, hard and deep, and when she ended it, she looked him straight in the eyes.

"You did everything to put a stop to the danger," she told him. "You saved me."

Bree would have added more. So much more. But Sonya took the turn to the ranch, and both Luca and Bree readied themselves to jump out. That's what they did even before the cruiser was at a full stop, and they ran into the house.

Duncan and Joelle were indeed there, and Joelle had a gun aimed at Tara who was cuffed and belly-down on the floor. Duncan was in the process of bagging her phone and gun.

"I want a deal," Tara shouted when her attention landed on Bree. "Immunity for testifying against Nathan. He's the one who got me into this, and Nathan killed my sister."

"Manny and Nathan are both dead," Luca snarled, and he hurried up the stairs with Bree.

Tara continued to shout, but they ignored her and went to the bathroom door where Woodrow was indeed standing guard. He quickly let them in to the quiet room. Emphasis on *quiet*. Her mother was still in the shower stall with a baby in each arm, but both Gabriel and Izzie were sound asleep.

"Thank you," Bree told her mother and figured she'd be saying that a lot tonight.

Bree went to the shower and eased Gabriel into her arms. She immediately pressed against Luca so he could get in on kissing their son and making sure he was okay. There was so much relief in that moment. Relief that likely would have brought her to her knees had she not been leaning against Luca.

They both examined their little boy, making sure there were no injuries. Physically he was fine. And he thankfully wasn't showing any obvious signs of trauma because he continued to sleep.

Bree wanted to just stand there and hold him until some of the raw nerves had settled in her body, but there were still a few loose ends to wrap up. Added to that, she wasn't sure the hands had finished their search of the house.

"Just stay in here a little while longer," Bree told her mother and put Gabriel back in her arms. "As soon as Duncan gives us the all clear, we'll be back up to get you."

Her mother nodded, blinking away tears, but Bree thought they were definitely of relief. They'd all had a horrible scare tonight. A scare brought on by three people who'd joined forces to create a living hell.

Bree wanted Tara to pay for that.

Luca slipped his arm around Bree as they headed out of the bathroom and toward the stairs. He stopped on the landing, and even though they could hear Tara cursing and sobbing below, Luca still took a moment to kiss her. That helped with the nerves. Helped generate some heat, too, but she could practically feel the apology coming off him.

"Not your fault," she reminded him.

"I should have realized they were lying," he argued.

"You did realize it. You just didn't know what they were lying about. You need to request to be issued a crystal ball."

He gave her a flat look. "I needed to have been a better cop."

She could have reminded him that none of them had seen this unholy alliance between all of their suspects, but Bree figured a kiss was the way to go here. She kissed, and kissed and kissed until she finally felt some of the tension slide right off her. She might have continued but she heard Tara break into a sob. On heavy sighs, Luca and she went down to see what was going on.

"Manny's really dead?" Tara asked. Duncan had moved her to a sitting position, and both Carmen and Sonya were getting the cruiser ready to take her into custody.

"He is," Luca verified.

That brought on more sobbing from Tara. "He's dead," the woman said and she kept babbling it. "You didn't have to kill him."

"I beg to differ," Slater spoke up. "He was about to shoot Luca and me."

Tara sucked in a hard breath, nearly choking on it, and she shook her head while tears streamed down her cheeks. "This is all Nathan's fault. Manny and I wouldn't have gotten mixed up in this if it weren't for him."

"She's been Mirandized," Duncan informed them. "And she'd obviously decided not to remain silent."

"I want the world to know what Nathan did," Tara snarled. "All of this is his fault."

"How so?" Bree asked.

"Because he started up things with that woman. Brighton," she snapped out like profanity. "Nathan must have known that Manny was still sniffing around her, but that didn't stop him. So, Manny decided to go to Brighton's place to confront her. I followed him because, well, because."

"You were in love with him," Bree provided.

"Yes," Tara readily admitted, "and I was hoping once Manny saw Nathan and Brighton together that it would get her out of his system. It didn't." Her voice broke and she began to cry again. "Everything got messed up."

"How?" This time it was Luca who pressed for more details.

"A heated argument. Brighton said some horrible things about both Manny and Nathan." She paused. "Nathan slapped her, and Manny stepped in. A fight broke out, but then Brighton attacked Manny. She was punching, and I tried to stop her."

"Who actually killed her?" Bree asked.

"Nathan," she snapped but then shook her head. "Both Manny and Nathan. It was awful. Everything was out of control, and Brighton wouldn't hush. She just kept telling Nathan and Manny that they were pathetic losers. She said she was going to file charges against both of them for assault and stalking."

"Only one of them stabbed her to death," Duncan snapped.

Tara shook her head. "Both of them did. Manny lost it. He just lost it, and he grabbed a knife from her kitchen counter. It seemed to go on forever, and she didn't die. She just kept fighting and clawing at them. Then, Nathan shoved Manny aside and finished it."

So, Nathan was the killer. But Manny and Tara were accessories.

"Nathan said Manny and I would be charged with murder if we went to the cops," Tara went on. "He said as accomplices that we'd get the same sentence as if we'd actually killed her. I looked it up, and it's true."

Yes, it was. And while it likely wouldn't have been a capital murder charge had they reported it, they still would have ended up with life sentences.

"Nathan took Brighton's top because he said it would have all of our DNA on it," Tara added. "He said that was his assurance that we wouldn't try to save our own skins."

Bree shook her head. "So, you created a pact of silence. How did my mother fit into that? And my father?"

Tara's denial was fast and frantic. "We didn't kill your father. I swear. We were all stunned when it happened."

Maybe. But it was possible that Nathan was faking his reaction. Then again, he had denied killing her father when he'd been holding her at gunpoint.

"Your mother, well, we took her," Tara said. "Or rather Shannon and Aubrey did. Manny set that up, but he messed up by using Nathan's real name. Nathan was so mad and threatened Manny and me until Manny fixed it by linking it to some offshore account deal."

Manny had hidden those steps well. His business experience had likely helped with that.

"Your mother was continuing to dig and had made the connection between Brighton and the bar," Tara went on. "Manny and Nathan were worried she might learn the truth. So, we took her and thought we could somehow set her up for Brighton's murder, but we found out she had an iron-clad alibi."

Hearing that gave Bree a fresh slam of fury. "So, you what…just decided to hold her captive?"

Tara nodded. "Nathan knew you were digging, too, and he wanted to be able to use your mother as leverage." She swallowed hard. "Your son, too. He said you'd cooperate with anything if we had your son."

This time, it was more than fury. It was a whirl of sick-

ening disgust at this trio who hadn't wanted to take respon-
sibly for what they'd done.

"But Nathan wanted more than my cooperation," Bree
pointed out. "He told me he was going to frame me for Brighton's murder."

Tara gave another nod. "It was all supposed to be over tonight. We'd have the baby to make you confess to the murder, and the investigation would all go away. We'd be in the
clear." She shook her head. "But now they're both dead.
Shannon, too. Manny killed her when she screwed up and
let your mother escape."

So, Nathan and Manny had murdered at least two people, and they'd orchestrated a whole litany of other crimes.

"I didn't want to do any of this," Tara insisted. "But Nathan drew up the plan and said I'd go to jail if I didn't do
everything he told me. Manny and I were to lie and point
the finger at each other. Nathan said that way, it would mess
with the investigation."

It had done that. All the lies. All the accusations. Pep-
pered with attacks. In hindsight, those attacks hadn't been
meant to kill her, but they could have. In fact, all of them
could have been killed.

"You gave us that video of Manny," Luca reminded Tara.

Tara lowered her head. "Because I was so angry that
Manny had killed Shannon. I thought, well, I wasn't thinking straight, but I couldn't come and say Manny had killed
her so I'd hoped you'd arrest him for Brighton's murder. I
figured Manny would accuse Nathan and me of helping him
do that, but there wouldn't be any proof. Manny would end
up paying."

"So, why'd you go through with the plan tonight?" Bree
demanded.

"Because I was scared of Nathan. Of what he might do.

I'm not a killer like Manny and him. I'm not. I was supposed to kill the hands when we sneaked onto the ranch," Tara murmured. "I just couldn't. I used a stun gun on them instead, tied them up and took their keys so we could escape in their trucks. That counts for something, right? It counts that I didn't kill them?"

Disgusted, Bree only shook her head and stepped back. Luca was right there to take hold of her and walk with her into the dining room when Sonya and Carmen began to walk Tara out to the waiting cruiser.

"She'll spend the rest of her life behind bars, and that doesn't feel nearly enough," Bree muttered.

She felt the anger taking over, and she quickly shoved it aside. The anger was justified and would maybe always be there, but she didn't want this moment to be about that. Luca, their baby and she were all alive, and that's what she wanted to latch on to. Later, she'd deal with her feelings for Tara, but for now, she needed Luca.

Bree pulled Luca to her and dropped her head on his shoulder. Instant relief and comfort. Everything about it felt right.

Because it was.

Luca and she were right together.

Part of her had always known that, and it was why she'd found herself going back to him time and time again. It was why she wanted to be with him now.

"You know I'm in love with you," she admitted.

He eased back, lifted his eyebrow. "Really? You never said."

"Well, I'm saying it now. I'm in love with you, and I don't want to co-parent our son. I want the whole parent deal with you with us for, well, everything."

Now, he smiled and brushed his mouth over hers. "Good."

He kissed her. Really kissed her. And she felt the remnants of the anger and fear just vanish. The man could certainly work miracles. But he stopped the miracle kiss and stared down at her.

"You know I'm in love with you," he said, giving her back her own words.

She mimicked his gesture of a raised eyebrow. "Really?"

"Really," he verified, and he finished that off with exactly what she needed to hear. "And everything is exactly what I want with Gabriel and you, too."

* * * * *

WYOMING
CHRISTMAS
CONSPIRACY

JUNO RUSHDAN

For Amber M, a caring, dedicated educator.
While you were the principal at my children's elementary
school, you became one of my personal heroes.
Thank you for your service.

Chapter One

Amber Reyes sped down the snow-covered road, clenching the steering wheel so tight her fingers grew numb. Even though it was freezing outside—30 degrees, which wasn't too bad for December in Wyoming—she was hot under the collar and not from the heat blasting out of the vent in her 4x4. She was headed to her half sister's place.

A half sister whose existence she hadn't been aware of until August, at the reading of her father's will when the details of a legal trust he'd established had been explained. Amber, along with everyone else in the small town, knew of Pandora Frye—the beautiful, eccentric, arrogant, wild child.

But she'd been shocked to discover Pandora was also the beautiful, eccentric, arrogant, illegitimate child of Carlos Reyes, the product of an extramarital affair twenty-two years ago.

Amber believed her mother had never known that her father had cheated. They'd always had a loving, picture-perfect marriage until her mother died ten years ago of cancer. Then everything had changed. At nineteen, Amber had learned the people closest to her couldn't be trusted.

Primarily her father. So she'd run from home to make her own way in the world. And that was before she found out about her half sibling.

A decade later, she hadn't thought her father could top his previous conniving efforts to manipulate her into an arranged marriage—much less from the grave.

How wrong I was.

Though her father had bequeathed Amber most of the land, including the valuable river that ran through it, and the cattle, he had also stipulated ironclad conditions for her to receive it. The betrayal, his indomitable will to have things his way continued after his death.

But then came the real shocker. Her father had not only named Pandora in his living trust, claiming her as his daughter, but he had also given her the Reyes family home and one acre of land surrounding it, which she'd take ownership of at the beginning of the new year following his death. Giving Amber and her brother, Chance, one final holiday season in their home.

Thinking about it made Amber's blood boil. The house her parents had been married in. The house she and her brother had been born in. Land they had been raised on. The house that had been in the family for generations would soon belong to a virtual stranger.

Not if I have anything to say about it.

A wave of nausea swept over her. Slowing down and keeping her eyes on the road, she kept driving as she unzipped her purse in the passenger seat of her Jeep Wrangler. Inside the handbag, her fingers skimmed over the unopened letter from her father, but she didn't find what she was looking for. The saltine crackers were probably still sitting on the kitchen counter. She'd been in such a rush to speak with her sister—*half sister*—that she'd forgotten them.

Maybe she should've listened to her brother and stayed home.

But that was the problem. If she didn't convince Pandora to sell them the house and the acre of land around it, she and Chance wouldn't have a family home for much longer.

Her cell phone rang. The caller ID showed up on the Bluetooth screen on the dash. Sometimes she thought she had a psychic link with her big brother.

She hit the Accept button, putting the call on speaker in the rugged SUV. "What is it? I'm almost there."

"You forgot your crackers."

Despite her anger, she smiled. "I just realized. I'm pretty nauseous."

"Pregnancy will do that to you," Chance said.

She put a hand to her belly. Only four months along, but if not for the baggy sweaters she'd started wearing, the rounded bump that had emerged one morning like magic would be visible to everyone. One careless, reckless night, swamped by grief, she'd given in to a moment of weakness and slept with Montgomery Powell. "We agreed not to use the P-word."

"Which one, Pandora, pregnancy or Powell? I can't keep track."

"Don't use any of them," she demanded, putting both hands back on the wheel. Best for things to be simple.

"You're going to have to tell Monty sooner or later. I think you should've done it by now."

"Thankfully it's not up to you and I choose later." *Much, much later.* "This is my body, my timeline. I won't be harassed or bullied by Monty or his family or you."

"Okay." Chance's snippy tone signaled he thought she was making a mistake.

Her death grip on the steering wheel made her forearms cramp. "I'd like to put out one dumpster fire before dealing with the next."

She switched on the wipers to prevent the falling snowflakes from sticking to the windshield. This time of year, it was typical to get several inches. She'd been gone so long, she'd forgotten how early the winter storms started here in Wyoming, in the valley where the small towns of Laramie and Bison Ridge were nestled.

"You're wasting your time," Chance said.

"I am not. She agreed to hear my proposal." Pandora, the leech, just as vicious as her mother, Fiona, had texted last night, telling Amber to come by for coffee at ten this morning. With flagrant disregard to the fact that Amber was filling in as a substitute teacher at the local elementary school and class started at nine. She had been up since five and decided to throw the young woman off-balance by showing up early. Inappropriately early. Outright rude, truth be told, but Amber didn't care.

"Only to see your face when she rejects it. The girl was over the moon at the reading of the will and so was her mother. The house isn't worth much, but she was ecstatic to get her grubby hands on it because it's ours. Or was. At least Dad left you everything of value with the land and cattle."

Everything but only one way to keep it, or lose all that, too, to Pandora.

"With that unconscionable proviso," she said through gritted teeth. "Why aren't you fuming? He left you nothing."

"Dad set me up for success. He paid for my bachelor's and law degrees, and I didn't have to work through school. I was able to focus on being the top of my class and got hired by a powerhouse company."

In a way, Chance was right. The day he started practicing, he did so debt-free. Not many of his colleagues had the privilege to say the same. Now he worked for Ironside Protection Services, earning a high six-figure salary, which was substantial compared to what she made as a schoolteacher.

A profession she'd chosen out of desperation after she fled the ranch, but surprisingly a rewarding one. "Still, he shouldn't have left you nothing."

"The simple watch he wore every day and his old rodeo buckles aren't nothing. They meant a great deal to him. Besides, I read the letter he wrote for me. I'm at peace with his decision. You should read yours. It might change how you feel."

Glancing at her purse, she seethed. "I have half a mind to burn mine."

"You'd regret it. Just like you're about to regret seeing Pandora."

She sighed, hoping he was wrong. For once. Though Chance seldom was. A fact that grated on her like sandpaper scraping her skin. "I'm almost at the harpy's abode. I'll call you afterward to tell you how it went." A long breath eased from her tight throat as she let up a bit on the accelerator.

"Don't bother calling me back. But would you mind grabbing us breakfast from Divine Treats? I'll take a bear claw. Also, one of those savory croissants. Ham and cheese."

Amber pulled up to the block of a recently constructed town house complex, consisting of ten units, in the center of downtown Laramie. Why their father had felt the need to buy Pandora one of these sleek, newly built places as well as give her the family home, too, was beyond Amber. She'd been here once after the funeral, in a failed attempt to get to know the young woman better. The finishes were top-notch, with custom cabinets and furnished with whimsical luxury. Stunning eye candy filled the interior. Their father had spared no expense.

"Don't you want the details on the meeting?" she asked.

"You can wait until you get home to fill me in," Chance said. "That way I can say *I told you so* to your face."

Shaking her head with irritation, she drove around the back to the parking lot. "You're unbelievable. Instead of being the annoying, know-it-all big brother, why can't you—" She lost the power of speech for a moment as her gut clenched.

"Amber? Are you all right? What's wrong?"

She slammed on the brakes, fixing her attention on the vehicle parked beside Pandora's sporty car behind her unit.

"Monty's truck is here." The words left a foul taste in her mouth.

For him to be here at seven forty-five in the morning could only mean one thing. He'd spent the night.

"Are you sure?" Chance sounded skeptical. "At least half the guys in town probably drive a Ford F-150."

She stared past the swirls of white flakes in disbelief at the truck. "How many drive one that's antimatter blue and has the vanity plate PWEL3?"

Buck Powell had a similar plate with the number one. Holly, domestic goddess extraordinaire and now mayor, had the designation number two. Their eldest son had the plate Amber was staring at right now.

Chance swore.

"That calculating, spiteful…" Amber swallowed the ugly words dancing on her tongue. "Is this the reason she agreed to meet me? Only to rub my face in the fact that she's bedding Monty."

"You're so early. Maybe it's coincidence." Her brother's words were comforting, but his tone full of doubt.

Unexpected tears filled her eyes. She didn't know what hurt more, her heart or her pride. "How could he?" she asked, her voice cracking.

"Not to sound like a callous guy on this one, but you two hadn't seen each other for almost ten years. You came home for the funeral, still angry over how things imploded between you two, and had a one-time slipup with him. Four months ago, might I add? You've avoided him ever since then, right?"

"Yeah, I guess so." Even though Monty had called, asking to see her, she'd rebuffed his attempts at contact because she didn't trust his motives and she didn't trust herself around him. With the unalterable stipulation in her father's living trust—Amber had to marry Monty within five months of her dad's death and stay hitched for two years, or everything, the entire property, the cattle, the money, went to Pandora—how could she believe anything he said? Especially if it was all the things her heart longed to hear.

"Plus," Chance added, "Pandora is easy on the eyes and comes across as, quite frankly, a floozy. It's probably nothing more than a one-night stand."

"But he didn't simply have sex and leave." Which would have been bad enough. "He spent the night." *With Pandora!*

Amber had only had the pleasure of a few nights with Monty herself. Even a lifetime ago, before she learned the horrible truth about why he'd taken a sudden interest in her, he had never stayed and cuddled until the sun came up with her.

She squeezed her eyes closed and saw Montgomery Beaumont Powell, six feet three inches of pure sex appeal. Tawny hair, the same as his father's. Intense brown eyes. A strong jaw with the perfect amount of stubble all the time, like he didn't even have to try. And a sweeping landscape of muscle. His sculpted physique was created by hard work on his family's ranch that was adjacent to hers, in addition to the extra effort he put into staying fit for his full-time job with the state police as a trooper. With his swagger and confidence, the man could've been a Hollywood heartthrob. Women swooned after him from Laramie to Jackson Hole. Not only for his heartbreaker looks, but also his status as heir apparent to the Powell fortune.

And Pandora Frye had sunk her claws into him.

The woman was taking everything that didn't belong to her.

Amber opened her eyes. She stared at the antimatter blue truck parked beside the cherry red Alfa Romeo Stelvio and slapped the steering wheel, letting a small scream slip.

"Get a grip," her brother muttered. "It's only sex. Even if he spent the night."

"He can sleep with whomever he likes. Except for her!" She whisked the tears from her eyes. *I will not cry.* Stupid hormones. "This may be a small town, but I'm sure there are tons of women willing to crawl into bed with him." Monty had never had a problem in that department. "He didn't have to sleep with *her.*" The living embodiment of her father's broken marital vow. The woman who would move into her family's house. "Yes, she's classically beautiful and nubile—" in fact, they were exact opposites: Pandora was slender, sophisticated, with creamy skin and red hair, whereas Amber was curvy and simple, and a brunette with brown skin "—but he knows something like this would bother me."

More like wound her to the marrow.

"Getting upset won't solve anything. You need to calm down, Tinker."

Tinker Bell. How she despised the nickname. It stopped being cute once she'd turned thirteen. At twenty-nine, it made her sound as ridiculous as she felt being back home.

Still pining for Monty Powell, the veritable Peter Pan, who was only interested in using her for her pixie dust.

Straightening, she threw the truck in Park, blocking Monty's and Pandora's vehicles. No quick, clean exits for either party. "You're right. It doesn't matter what they do."

"It really doesn't so long as you marry Monty in twenty-nine days."

The five-month deadline was creeping up on her. One dumpster fire at a time, starting with this. "I'll show Pandora and him that I don't give two figs they're sleeping together. I just need her to agree to sell us back the house," she said in a voice so strained she almost didn't sound like herself.

"You're not still going in there, are you?"

Amber grabbed her purse, slinging it over her shoulder. "I most certainly am. I'm done running from things. This time I'm going to confront it head-on."

"Says the woman running from telling the father of her child that she's four months pregnant and wearing baggy clothes to conceal her burgeoning bump."

"Instead of lecturing me—"

"Reasoning with you."

She huffed. "You should be supporting me."

"You mean enabling you to make poor choices you'll regret."

Why was it so hard for him to be in her corner for once? "Before you can try to talk me out of it, I'm hanging up." She jabbed the red icon, ending the call.

Killing the engine, she pressed her door open against the frigid thrust of the wind. Another thing she'd forgotten about home: it was the second windiest state in the country. The town was in the perfect, or worst, spot depending on perspective. Rather than the mountains surrounding the valley blocking the wind, they made the jet stream faster. Add in high pressure from the Great Basin and low pressure from the plains and the town got squeezed, making the winters harsh.

Cold slapped her face as she climbed out. Icy flakes stung her cheeks. Crisp, clean air moved in the blustery wind, smelling of winter and snow and pine. Zipping up the oversize coat she'd recently purchased to hide that she was expecting, she marched up to the back door. Beside it a sign on the window read Pandora's Box Photography.

Her half sister was a glamour and boudoir photographer. The profession seemed better suited for a big city, but when one's father paid for their lifestyle in hush money, Amber supposed it didn't matter whether their career was profitable.

Bitterness welled inside her. She struggled to tamp it down. Since the day she left home, she hadn't taken one cent from her father or even spoken to him. Everything she had she'd earned and paid for herself, on a meager teacher's salary.

The name, *Pandora's Box*, was apropos, considering the seven deadly sins seemed tied to the woman. She was the product of lust, had seduced Monty—unless there was some other explanation for him being here—was envious of their status as legitimate Reyes offspring and had, driven by greed, held on to their family home. The Reyes home.

What great evil was next?

Amber raised her fist, wanting to bang out her frustration rather than ring the bell, and knocked—only once because the door swung open on contact.

It must've been slightly ajar. She hadn't noticed. A gust of wind sprayed snow inside the entrance.

"Pandora!" she called out, crossing the threshold. She closed the door, keeping more cold air and snow from seeping in.

Music came from the first-floor bonus room Pandora used as her photography studio. A sultry Kacey Musgraves song just ended and a soulful one by Shawn Mendes started as Amber stood there.

A hopeful thought sprang to mind. Maybe Monty was here for some other reason. To get a portrait taken.

But at seven something in the morning with soft pop music playing?

Hope quickly withered. In its place, anxiety swelled, twisting through her.

Amber had no claim on Monty and no longer wanted any. Not after he'd deceived her right along with her father.

Only the house matters right now.

The door to the studio was cracked open. "Pandora!"

Still no answer. Hesitating at the entrance, Amber braced to encounter some tawdry scene inside, the two of them asleep or, worse, intimate. She set her mind to show no reaction.

Steeling her spine, she pushed on the door and strode inside.

She faltered to a stop and gasped. The blood in her veins froze, her stomach giving an acid twinge. A familiar copper scent wafted in the air.

Monty lay, utterly still, on his stomach on a curved, emerald colored velvet sofa, wearing nothing but black boxer briefs. His eyes were closed, his face slack. One long, muscular arm hung off the side, his knuckles on the floor.

A knife. An open butterfly knife was beside his hand. Covered in blood.

Her breath hitched in her lungs, but she forced herself to breathe as she shifted toward her half sister.

Pandora was sprawled on the floor in the center of the room, eyes frozen open and vacant, expression locked in an unnatural contortion, bruises on her pale face, her throat slit.

Squeezing her eyes shut, Amber turned away. Her mind spun. Steadying herself, she looked over the room.

Clothes were scattered about as though they had undressed in a hurry.

A bottle of whiskey was open on a side table next to the sofa along with a tumbler half-full of liquor. Another was broken on the floor. Lines of white powder were on a small mirror on top of a speaker from which music poured into the room.

Alcohol. Drugs.

Murder.

Sickening dread pooled in her chest.

This couldn't be happening, but it was. Blackness edged her vision and she swayed. For a second, she stood there, hyperventilating. Shaking. Trying to make sense of the sordid, horrible scene.

Grim urgency punched through the paralyzing fear. "Monty?" Why wasn't he moving? Was he dead, too?

Please be alive.

Snapping into action, she rushed to him. Red-lipstick kiss marks were on his cheek and neck. Along with some kind of rash. Hands trembling, she tugged off one of her leather gloves and pressed two fingers to the side of his throat.

He had a pulse. Thready and slow. But he was alive.

There was a strange sound. Was it coming from him?

She tipped her ear closer to his mouth. A wheeze came from him on every exhale.

Amber had never seen him like this, blacked out, wheezing, with a rash. What was wrong with him? And what had happened here?

Her gaze dropped to the bloody knife near his hand and then she looked back at Pandora.

Nausea churned her stomach. Amber had wanted this

young woman out of her life from the second she became aware they were related, but not like this. Not murdered, dead, at twenty-two.

This was awful. She needed to call the police. Report it, and say what?

Monty was many things—a liar, a manipulative woman-izer— but every cell in her body, every instinct in her gut, told her that he was not a killer.

She'd known him her entire life, once adored him, had kissed him, made love to him, created a baby together and still cared for him far more than she wanted to admit.

In spite of how this looked, and it did look as though he had killed Pandora, Amber knew he wasn't capable of such a thing.

She crouched beside the curved sofa and cupped his face, gripping his chin. "Monty." When he gave no response, she shook his shoulder. "Wake up."

Moaning, he stirred slightly.

"Monty!" She gave him a harder shake, rolling him onto his side. The wheeze became more pronounced and the rash covered his torso. "Please, wake up," she said, sick with worry.

His eyelids fluttered as if they might open but didn't.

Her mind spun like a carousel.

Think, Amber. Think.

All of Monty's brothers, even his cousin who also lived on the Powell ranch, were law enforcement. Any one of them would know exactly what to do and would protect Monty with his life. She took her phone from her purse, but she only had one of their cell phone numbers.

She dialed Logan, thankful he'd given her his number at her father's funeral. He was with the Wyoming State Attorney General's Office, Division of Criminal Investigation.

She only prayed she'd catch him before he left Laramie to get on the road to Cheyenne, where he worked.

The line rang four times before he answered. "Powell."

"This is Amber." Her voice broke as she stared at Pandora's lifeless body again. "Where are you?"

Never in a million years had she thought she'd ever call him—the one Powell who had always been in love with her and would've married her in a heartbeat, happily, proudly, if she had felt the same.

"Leaving Divine Treats." Keys jangled over the line. "I had to satisfy my sweet tooth. I'm happy to hear from you. Finally."

The Divine Treats bakery was within easy walking distance, three blocks away. "I need you."

"What is it?" His voice tightened. "What's wrong?"

"It's Monty. You have to come, quickly."

"Did something happen to him? Where are you?"

"At Pandora Frye's." She rattled off the address. "Monty is out. I can't get him to wake up." Her voice was shaky, and she took a steadying breath to control it. "But Pandora…" Hot bile rose in her throat. "There's blood and a knife."

"Is she alive?"

Amber shook her head and then realized she had to use her voice. "No. She's dead."

"Are you sure?"

"Yes." Her gaze trained on the lifeless body, and she had to fight the urge to cover the poor woman. "I'm positive. You have to hurry."

"I'm climbing in my truck now. I'll be there in less than two minutes." A beat of silence. "Did you call 911?"

"No." She wasn't sure what to do. The right thing and the best thing might be different in this situation. Not once had she ever broken the law and she wasn't considering doing so now, but when it came to Monty, she never could think straight. One thing was certain. He needed someone on his side out in front of this. "Not yet."

"Okay. We have to hang up," he said, the sound of a car starting in the background. "Then you need to call 911."

But he didn't fully understand what he was about to walk into. What he was about to see. The bloody knife. The alcohol. The drugs. Pandora—naked, slain.

Oh, God. "Logan, the way this looks—"

"Whatever you're staring at will appear far worse if they pull our phone records and piece together the delay in calling 911." Another pause. "We've been on the line for too long already. I'll be there shortly."

Logan disconnected.

Had she made a mistake in phoning his brother first? She hadn't thought about the police looking at phone records. Would her actions make Monty look more guilty?

She only wanted to help, not hurt him.

A rush of mixed emotions battered Amber. She glanced back at Monty and desperately tried to rouse him. Heart pounding in her chest, she flicked another shocked look at Pandora.

No way Monty would've hurt her, much less kill her.

But someone had. Would anyone besides his family, her and Chance believe in his innocence? Half the town loved the Powells. The other half longed for their ruin.

Amber shook off the thought. The who and why behind this didn't matter at the moment. How many would stand beside Monty or stand against him didn't either. The only thing that did matter was proving his innocence and making sure Monty didn't go down for this murder.

She dialed 911.

Chapter Two

Monty opened his eyes to glaring light and closed them again. His head was thick and throbbing, his throat dry as cotton. A bad taste was in his mouth.

"Mr. Powell! Can you open your eyes?" a strange male voice asked.

Pain thundered through his skull. Something was wrong. If only he could think.

Where was he? Why was someone shaking him? And shouting his name?

At least he was sitting up. Groaning, he forced his eyes open.

The room spun. Music played in the background. His breathing was strained to the point of wheezing. His fuzzy gaze veered past the stranger in front of him and locked onto Amber. She was blurry and then the sight of her cleared up. "What's going on?" he said, his voice low, his throat raw and scratchy.

Was she real? Was he dreaming?

"It's going to be okay, Monty." A warm, gentle palm pressed to his cheek. "You didn't do it. You couldn't have killed her."

Someone was dead.

None of the words coming from her made a lick of sense. "Killed…w-who?"

He was exhausted, like his brain and body were wading through sludge.

"Ma'am, we've already told you to step away from the suspect and to go back into the hall," a stern voice said.

Suspect. He refocused on the man in front of him. A police officer. Laramie PD.

"W-what's happening?" Monty asked, trying to piece things together. But his memories were jumbled.

"Get your hands off me!" Logan's voice was sharp, but his brother was out of sight. "Can't you see he needs help? At least let the EMT check him out."

"Sir, can you look at me?" a woman asked.

He was so thirsty. "Water."

"They need to take him to the hospital," Logan demanded.

The woman knelt in front of him. An EMT. She shone a penlight in his eyes, making him squint.

It felt like a jackhammer chiseled away in his head. "I need water."

"In a minute, sir." She lifted a gloved hand in front of his face, raising her index finger. "Please follow my finger." She moved it to the right and he dropped his head. "Do you know what day it is?"

He struggled to keep his eyes open, to come up with an answer. "S-Saturday? No. Friday. I think."

"What's the month?"

"December."

The EMT pressed something to his mouth. "I need you to blow, sir," she said, and Monty did his best until a strong wheeze forced him to stop. She slipped something on his arm that tightened. A blood pressure cuff. Once she finished, the EMT stepped aside. "He's not drunk. Blood alcohol level is zero. But his blood pressure is quite low and he appears to be having an allergic reaction to whatever drugs he took."

"No drugs," Monty said with a harsh wheeze. He'd never done drugs once in his life.

"He's not in anaphylactic shock and could be hauled in, but we'd advise against it. We should take him to the hospital to be examined," the EMT said.

"If he passes out in a holding cell or worse," Logan said, "it'll be on you. Do you want to risk suspension? Or losing your badge?"

"I'll take the chance to make sure a *Powell* doesn't wiggle out of this one," a cop said. "He's practically been caught red-handed, but your family has a lot of influence."

"He didn't do this." Amber's voice carried from the hall.

The other officer grabbed Monty by the arm and tugged him up, but he wasn't sure he could stand.

Monty swayed on his feet. His arms were wrenched at his lower back and cold cuffs were slapped on his wrists, the sound of metal ratcheting in his ears.

His blurry gaze drifted, landing on a pale body lying on the floor. A nude woman. Pandora Frye.

Dead.

Disbelief and confusion twisted together, spiraling and spreading in his brain.

"It's freezing outside." Amber rushed back into the room. "He needs shoes and a jacket."

One of the officers raised a palm, stopping her. "His clothes are evidence."

"Give him a minute," Logan said from the hall. "He can wear my boots. I can help him put them on."

The officer holding his arm in a vise grip yanked him forward. Monty took two steps. Swirling lights danced in front of his eyes. Then his legs gave out as everything faded to black.

10:35 a.m.

Voices murmured nearby.

Amber?

Confusion fogged Monty's brain. Was he dreaming?

His throat ached as his eyelids slowly lifted. The fluorescent light overhead was painfully bright, blinding him for a moment. His thoughts scrambled like eggs in a sizzling hot pan.

The room came into focus. He was wearing a medical gown, lying in a hospital bed with several instruments attached to him, including an IV. A machine beeped nearby.

Amber hovered close to his bedside.

"You're real," Monty rasped. Jerking fully awake, he tried to sit up but winced when pain cut into his wrists and metal clanged.

"Take it easy." She put a palm on his chest.

His head pounded so hard he thought he might throw up. Closing his eyes and swallowing, he concentrated on breathing to help the dizziness pass.

"Do you want some water?" a familiar voice asked.

He turned his head to see Logan on the other side of the bed. His brother had been in his dream, too. With Amber. No, not a dream. A nightmare. "Yeah."

Logan grabbed a cup from a table and put the straw to his lips. "You're looking much better."

Better than what?

Monty drank, taking long, hard gulps, draining the cup of water.

"You're not wheezing anymore either," Amber said.

His gaze dropped to the metal bracelet on his wrist. "Why am I handcuffed? What am I doing in the hospital?" Taking another steady breath, he tried to calm his raging heart. He stared into Amber's hazel eyes and then at Logan's worried face. "What happened to me?"

The room door creaked opened. Both Amber and Logan shifted focus away from him in unison and moved closer to the bed, bodyguards shielding him from whatever was coming.

Hannah Delaney walked in. She was the fiancée of his cousin, Matt Granger.

Logan visibly relaxed. "They put you on the case?"

"What case?" Monty asked. "Would someone please tell me what's going on?"

Furtive glances were exchanged.

"Monty." Hannah stepped closer. She was petite, blonde and deceptively pretty, like a Disney princess but also tough as nails and capable of taking down a guy twice her size. Only a fool would underestimate her. "You should know I'm here in an official capacity."

Official. She was a detective. Worked mostly homicides.

"I'm assigned to the case for now," Hannah continued. "I could be pulled due to conflict of interest, but if I'm not, I won't be working this alone. Waylon Wright was put on it, too. He *asked* me to leave the scene and to come here." Her tone was sharp, and Monty gathered that she'd been kicked out. "He'll be here shortly."

Monty groaned. There was no love lost between him and the egotistical, caustic detective. They'd had an altercation as teens. Over the years, the animosity had only festered.

Hannah folded her arms. "Anything you say, I'll have to report."

"Then he has nothing to say until his lawyer gets here," Amber said.

Monty shook his head, trying to clear out the fog. "But I don't have a lawyer."

Amber took his hand. Her fingers wrapped tight around his. "Chance is on the way."

"But he's not a criminal lawyer," Logan whispered.

Amber pressed her lips into a tight line. "Chance will do until we can get the best attorney for this kind of thing."

"Explain what's happening." Monty squeezed Amber's hand.

"I found you at Pandora's place." Amber hesitated, swallowed hard. "She's dead. You were unconscious at first. Had difficulty breathing and a rash. They brought you here."

The words awakened a memory. Pandora on the floor. Pale. Still. Blood.

Not a dream or a nightmare.

A shudder ran through him.

"Turns out you were drugged," Logan said. "They're not sure with what yet. They're running tests, but whatever it was you had a bad allergic reaction. The doctor says you got lucky you didn't go into anaphylactic shock. They've had you on an IV drip of meds to counteract it. Your breathing is better. The rash is gone."

"I was at Pandora's," Monty said in a low voice, a statement, not a question, but everything was still cloudy. "But how? Why? What happened?"

Hannah eased closer to the foot of the bed. "You really can't remember?"

He shook his head, ready to expound.

Amber slid her hand over his lips. "That's enough. We need to wait for Chance to get here."

"You should be careful what you say." Hannah's face was neutral, her voice grim. "You're as good as family to me, but I will do my job." She looked over at Amber. "What were you doing at Pandora's this morning?"

Amber opened her mouth as if to answer but then pursed her lips tight.

"I can't help if I don't know." Hannah slid her gaze to Logan. "What were either of you doing there? Do you have any idea how this will look to Waylon?"

"Yes, I do." Logan sighed. "Are you here to help or to do your job?"

"Hopefully, both," Hannah said. "If you believe Monty is innocent and neither of you did anything wrong while at Pandora's, then you've got to talk to me."

Why had they been there?

An ugly thought crossed his mind. What if they had done something wrong, tampered with the crime scene, to help him?

But he shook off the idea. Logan was a sworn officer. His brother would never compromise his integrity. Not even for him.

At least Monty didn't think he would.

A woman wearing scrubs strode into the room. "You're awake. That's good." She checked his IV bag. "I'm Nurse Shelby. How are you feeling, Mr. Powell?"

"Like I've run a marathon, slept for days and still need more rest. And my head is pounding like it's going to split in two. Everything is foggy. I'm having trouble remembering."

"The doctor thinks you were dosed with a date rape drug and a boatload of it, too. We'll know for sure as soon as your blood work comes back." Nurse Shelby took his vitals. "But the mixture of the antihistamines and cortisone with whatever else is in your system is probably amplifying the drowsiness. Don't worry, it'll pass."

"How long until he can remember?" Hannah asked.

"Things will come back to him in a few hours, but he'll

never recall what happened while he was blacked out if it was one of the drugs that we suspect."

Logan turned to the nurse. "Does the doctor think it was GHB?"

The nurse shrugged. "Could be. It's one of the most common date rape drugs right along with Rohypnol and ketamine."

But who had drugged him? And why?

"Monty, will you consent to have your medical record released to us?" Hannah asked.

Amber stiffened, tightening her grip on his hand. "Chance can advise us on what to do. If I had thought to call him sooner, he'd already be here. It's still hard to believe that you even need a lawyer."

"I only ask because based on what I've heard I think it will help," Hannah said. "Not hurt you."

Logan nodded. "I agree. I think it'll be the fastest way to get you out of these cuffs." His brother glanced down at the restraints on his wrists.

"Actually, I can take care of that now." Hannah took a handcuff key from her pocket and unshackled him.

"We told the officer who accompanied him here that he shouldn't be restrained in his condition," the nurse said.

"O'Brien." Logan huffed. "The man wouldn't listen to reason because he wants Monty to be guilty. End of story. Forget about due process."

"I'm sorry you went through that." Hannah frowned. "But there are quite a few on the force who'll feel that way simply because you're a Powell."

Monty rubbed his wrists. "Waylon will be one of them."

"No red flags in his record that I'm aware of," Hannah said. "He usually acts first and asks questions later, but a salt-of-the-earth straight shooter. I've known him to be a fair guy."

Logan swore. "Not when it comes to my brother."

Hannah's brow furrowed. "If they keep me on this, I'll make sure everything is handled aboveboard. The medical release?" she asked again.

"Okay." Monty rested back in bed. "If you think it'll help."

"I can see to it for you." Nurse Shelby headed for the door.

"Have it sent directly to the chief of police, Wilhelmina Nelson, as soon as possible," Hannah said.

"Sure. I'll do it right now." The nurse left the room.

Monty looked at his soon-to-be cousin-in-law. "Hey, Hannah. I want you to know, as family and as a detective, that I don't know what happened to Pandora, but I'm sure I didn't kill her."

"Not another word to the police," Amber whispered fiercely and then eyed Hannah with caution.

Everything he'd been told sounded bad. His hazy recollection of Pandora's studio, her dead on the floor, him incoherent, looked even worse. He simply needed Hannah to know that he wasn't guilty of something so heinous. Amber didn't understand how close he was to Hannah. His cousin Matt had been raised alongside him, like a brother, and Amber was aware he considered him as such. But that also meant Hannah was practically the sister he'd never had.

"You should listen to her." Hannah studied his face, her expression one of genuine concern. "If Matt were in your position, I'd advise the same."

He looked up at Amber—his pretty, sweet, fiery Tinker—grateful she was here with him. He'd spent thousands of sleepless nights aching to apologize for the way he'd treated her all those years back. Beg her forgiveness. The worst part, what he regretted most, was making love to her without telling her the truth first—that he'd intended for it to be a marriage of convenience for the land.

During their time together as a couple, everything had changed for him. He'd fallen for her so deeply, so unimaginably hard, he'd wanted forever with her. But when she found out his initial reasons for going after her, it had broken her heart and she'd run from him, from her family, from Wyoming. And it had crushed him.

At her father's funeral, he'd tried to voice the emotions slamming through him. For a moment, they'd gotten close, the clumsy words on the tip of his tongue, but her anger had turned into a different kind of heat, and he'd messed it all up by falling into bed with her instead. Seeing her, touching her, tasting her again was a gut-wrenching reminder of the grave error he'd made. Then she refused to see him anymore and stopped taking his calls.

He would've given anything for a chance to explain. Even though there wasn't any good justification for his actions. But he'd grown up since then. Not a day went by that he didn't hate himself for hurting her. Watching his younger brothers Holden Sawyer and Matt fall in love, with two of them now married and starting families—while he lived alone in the house he was supposed to share with Amber—had forced him to reassess his own empty life, opened his eyes to the fact that the only way to fill the gaping void plaguing him was to win Amber back.

But he'd never imagined that under such dire circumstances, where he might appear guilty of murder, she would support him rather than spit nails at him. A true testament to her character.

The nurse returned, coming into the room carrying a tablet. "I sent what we have so far over to the chief and made a note to have the results forwarded as soon as they're in."

She handed Monty the electronic device. "Just need you to sign two forms. Also, there's someone at the nurses' station looking for you. Tall, commanding voice, ruggedly handsome and a rather abrasive man with a badge."

"That'd be Waylon." Monty finished signing the forms and returned the tablet.

"I think I'll leave before he gets in here." Nurse Shelby hurried out of the room.

"What's the deal between you two?" Hannah asked. "And how far back does it go?"

Monty glanced up at the ceiling. "Started in high school and never ended." It was too complicated to say more than that in the time they had.

The door swung open.

Waylon Wright strode in with all the swagger of a man on a mission, sucking the oxygen from the room.

Chapter Three

Friday, December 6
11:50 a.m.

Waylon shoved into the hospital room and clenched his jaw at the sight of Monty Powell, propped up in a hospital bed, playing the part of the victim when first glance of the damning crime scene made him look guilty as sin.

He tipped his Cutter-style hat to Amber Reyes, glossed over Logan Powell and briefly shifted his gaze to Detective Delaney. If common sense prevailed, she would be removed from the case post haste. But he wasn't going to hold his breath waiting for that to happen. In all likelihood, favoritism would continue to be showered on the powerful, wealthy Powells.

"I believe introductions are unnecessary," Waylon said, "so, let's cut to the chase, Monty. Yeah, you're a Powell and you also happen to be law enforcement." The latter Waylon respected, provided the cop was clean, but the influence and presence of the Powells was ubiquitous. They had enough money to buy senators and governors. Their spawn had infiltrated every corner of law enforcement. Monty was a state trooper. Logan was with the Wyoming Division of Criminal Investigation. Holden was the chief deputy of the sheriff's

department. Sawyer was a fire marshal. Matt Granger—
their cousin who they treated more like a brother—was the
chief of the campus police at SWU, Southeastern Wyoming
University. And the youngest, Jackson, was a US marshal
in another state. Always craving more power, their mother,
Holly, had been recently elected mayor. It was enough to
make Waylon raise an eyebrow and wonder at their motives,
if it wasn't the desire for control. Unfortunately for them,
Waylon wasn't the kind of man who could be bought or easily swayed. "But I have no intention of doing you any favors
in this investigation."

"Wouldn't expect you to," Monty said.

Waylon glanced down at his unrestrained wrists. Apparently, the favors had already started. He came to stand at
the foot of the bed and eyed Delaney. "Why isn't he handcuffed?"

"The medical staff advised Officer O'Brien when he was
brought in that he shouldn't be restrained in his current condition."

"Which at the moment is conscious," Waylon pointed out,
"able to speak and quite possibly capable of running."

Delaney scoffed. "Give me a break. He's not going anywhere, and I was present the entire time they were off."

Waylon nudged the brim of his hat up with a knuckle and
put a hand on his hip. "Is he a murder suspect?"

"I thought you were going to cut to it," Delaney said flatly,
her face deadpan.

"Treat him as such. If you weren't sleeping with his
cousin, he'd be in cuffs." When she narrowed her eyes and
opened her mouth to respond, he raised a palm stopping
her. "A woman is dead, throat slit practically from ear to
ear. That man," he said, pointing at Monty while staying
laser-focused on Delaney, "was at the scene of the crime, is

our only suspect in the homicide, and his prints are on the murder weapon."

Amber Reyes gasped. Concern flooded Logan's face.

But there was only confusion in Monty's expression as he shook his head. "That can't be—"

"Say nothing," Amber said in a harsh whisper, cutting him off.

"I didn't know the prints came back already." Delaney lowered her gaze. "Listen, the cuffs were hurting him and like I said, I was here, watching him the entire time."

"I need everyone to leave the room." Waylon pivoted on his bootheel and glanced between Logan and Amber, but he also meant for Delaney to step outside, too. "I have some questions for the *suspect*."

Amber put a protective hand on Monty's shoulder. "Not without his lawyer present," she said, her voice tart, her cheeks reddening.

"Am I under arrest?" Monty asked, quietly.

"No," Waylon said, wishing that wasn't the case. "Not yet." As much as he'd love to see Monty behind bars, paying the price for any of his wrongdoings, his main concern was getting justice for the victim. Unfortunately, more than a few troubling elements to the case made him question whether Monty had actually committed this crime. It was by no means open-and-shut. He needed all his ducks in a nice, neat row before arresting a member of the Powell family. Especially the heir apparent. "But it doesn't look good for you."

"Looks can be deceiving," Chance Reyes said, sweeping into the room, wearing a crisp power suit and confidence like armor. "I'm Monty's attorney and this conversation is finished." He set down winter clothes and a pair of boots he'd been carrying, presumably for Monty.

"I'm only getting started." Waylon crossed his arms over

his chest, irked that they were already preparing to get him out of the hospital. "I have questions for your client that need answering."

Chance plastered on a smug smile. "According to his doctor, it'll be hours before the effects of whatever he was drugged with will wear off completely and his memory will be restored. She suspects some kind of date rape drug. The results should be in this afternoon."

If that were true, it would take quite a lot to knock out a guy Monty's size. But what reason would Pandora Frye have for drugging him?

"There are still a few questions that he's capable of answering right now," Waylon said. "Such as his whereabouts last night before he went to Ms. Frye's residence."

Chance stood beside his sister. "Is my client under arrest?"

Waylon shook his head. "No."

"Is he being taken into custody?" Chance asked.

They could only hold him for seventy-two hours. Then they'd have to charge and arraign him or release him. Based on everything they had so far, the district attorney would only insist on cutting him loose.

"Not at the moment," Waylon said, but he was a patient guy.

"Then this conversation is done because I'm advising Mr. Powell not to answer any questions and to exercise his right to remain silent."

"Let's make it official." Waylon redirected his gaze to Monty. "Are you willing to answer any of my questions at this time?"

Monty shook his head. "I invoke my right to remain silent."

"Satisfied?" Chance asked. "As soon as he is medically able to be released, he'll be at home."

"Don't try to leave town." Waylon turned for the door. "You'll be under surveillance."

"The heads-up is appreciated," Monty said. "Unexpectedly gracious of you."

"Grace has got nothing to do with it." Waylon flicked a glance at the other detective. "You'd know anyhow." And there was more than one way to get off a ranch that was thousands of acres without being seen by one cop parked at the front gate. In all honesty, the measure was simply procedural. "Delaney, a word in the hall."

Waylon stepped out of the room and waited for her. He had questions for Amber Reyes and Logan, too. An officer at the scene of the crime had stated that both parties had been present when the authorities arrived and made things difficult.

With Chance present, Amber already acting cagey, Logan being tightlipped and not knowing if Delaney had already helped them get their stories straight, he figured it best to catch them off guard separately without a lawyer around. Sooner rather than later he'd find out exactly why they had been at Pandora Frye's home and no attorney was going to shut down the conversation.

Delaney joined him in the hall and looked him in the eye, shoulders squared and hands clenched at her sides like she was ready for a fist fight. "Do you have more griping to do over the removal of the handcuffs?"

"No. I want you off this case."

Delaney reeled back. "Why?"

"It's obvious, isn't it. You can't be impartial."

"The same could be said of you. I heard about the bad blood between you and the suspect."

He shrugged. "Grievances of teenagers. Nothing more to it than that," he said lightly, trying to dismiss it.

"Felt like a lot more in there to me. You were practically radiating rancor."

"Then you got your wires crossed. Sure, I don't like him, but I don't have to. What happened is ancient history unlike your current romantic relationship with a relative of the suspect. In fact, don't you live on the Shooting Star Ranch, making you a tenant of his parents?"

Her chin rose at that. "The house I live in with Matt and the land it's on belongs to him. I'm not the tenant of any Powell."

"Did he buy it from his aunt and uncle or was it given to him?"

"That's irrelevant and has no bearing on whether or not I should be working this case," she said, not answering the question, which told him everything he needed to know.

"Then you're not only lying to me, but also to yourself."

"Matt's property is legally separate and considered the Little Shooting Star. Some of the income from his ranch goes to the family. But it's his choice. He's under no financial obligation to do so."

"Still sounds like a relevant conflict of interest."

"The decision isn't your call to make. It's up to the chief."

His cell phone rang. He took it from his pocket and glanced at the caller ID. "Speak of the devil."

"Mind if I'm a part of the call?" Delaney asked.

Waylon didn't care. Whatever he had to say to the chief he could say in front of her. He answered, "Wright. I'm with Delaney. Putting you on speaker, Chief."

"Good to catch you both together."

"Speaking of together," Waylon said. "I believe it's best if I work this case alone or with another detective for reasons that you're already aware of, but I'm happy to list them in writing if necessary."

Delaney appeared unfazed.

"That won't be necessary," Chief Nelson said. "This case is rightfully hers. She was the first detective able to respond. I also assigned you to alleviate any possible concerns regarding impartiality. As for a conflict of interest, I believe she's far enough removed from the suspect to do her job and see justice served."

Waylon let a bitter chuckle slip out. "I'm not surprised you think that, Chief."

"What is that supposed to mean?" Nelson snapped.

His laughter curdled in his throat as he realized, though his comment was rooted in fact, he had overstepped with a superior officer.

The truth was the chief had almost as much reason to give the Powells preferential treatment as Delaney. Chief Nelson was married to the sheriff. The sheriff's sister was Holden Powell's wife. To muddy the waters further, Logan had assisted Wilhelmina Nelson with cleaning up the LPD, cracking a huge case wide open and cementing her as the police chief. Forget about six degrees of separation. In this small town, when it came to the Powell clan, it was more like two.

"One might say you have a possible conflict of interest as well, ma'am," Waylon admitted.

"One might, but are you saying it?"

Waylon met Delaney's prying gaze "I am. Not only are you family for all intents and purposes, but your boss, the mayor, is also the suspect's mother."

Chief Nelson cleared her throat. "I notified Mayor Powell of the situation and informed her that I'll report directly to the governor regarding this case. She emphatically agreed and then assured me that she would in no way meddle in how this was investigated. In fact, she stated that she wouldn't even go to the hospital to check in on her son because she didn't want her presence to be a distraction. I handpicked you to be the lead detective on this homicide because your reputation is above reproach and your character is unimpeachable. So I'm going to let your comment slide. Just this once. Do we understand one another?"

He clenched his jaw at the hint of a grin on Delaney's face. "We do."

"Now that all that's settled, I'm aware the suspect's fingerprints are on the knife found at the scene of the crime. But the medical examiner gave us an estimated time of death between four and seven in the morning. According to Monty's medical record, it doesn't seem that he would have been in any condition to commit the murder. He couldn't even stand up when the EMTs evaluated him."

"Another theory is he was faking it," Waylon said. "Or perhaps he killed the victim first and then took whatever drug he was strung out on."

Delaney raised an eyebrow. "Well, he didn't fake a full-blown allergic reaction."

"This is such a high-profile case I ran it by Assistant District Attorney Merritt," Chief Nelson said. "She believes the DA won't touch this case with a ten-foot pole based on what we have so far. Once his blood work comes in and we know more, we'll reevaluate."

"Speaking of which, how do you have his medical file so fast?" Waylon asked. "The warrant hasn't even been signed yet."

"I asked the suspect to release them to us," Delaney said.

Only because she thought it would help him look less guilty. And so far, it had.

"The warrant just came through," the chief said. "I called the judge and asked him to expedite it."

Now, that was surprising, and also reassuring to see the

chief doing everything possible to handle this properly. With the one exception of keeping Delaney assigned.

"I noticed a security camera mounted outside above the door of the victim's residence," Delaney said. "But I wasn't given a chance to see if there was any footage."

She referred to him booting her from the crime scene.

He'd made the right choice and would make it again given the chance. "We'll have to crack her password to access her main hub, but the camera had a micro SD card. Forensics happened to have a card reader. Everything had been deleted except for footage of the night prior showing Montgomery Powell parking beside her and entering the residence along with Pandora Frye at ten thirty. Then nothing else until Amber Reyes arrived the next morning at seven forty-eight. Followed by Logan Powell at seven fifty-two. Then the ambulance and squad car shortly thereafter."

"Odd that everything else was deleted," Delaney said.

His thoughts exactly. "I figure the victim might've had it set to automatically back up to cloud storage. If so, we'll have access to the entire history in a day or two."

"On the footage, what was the dynamic between Pandora and Monty?" Delaney asked.

"She was smiling, excited, chatted almost nonstop while she unlocked the door. Monty on the other hand didn't look too pleased to be there, but he followed her inside. The camera on the front door was missing a micro SD card."

"Get access to the cloud storage as quickly as possible," the chief said. "And, Waylon, if you have any future concerns of corruption, malfeasance or whatever doesn't smell right to you, feel free to file a report with Internal Affairs in Cheyenne. Otherwise, no more crying about who your partner is. Get the job done and keep me updated. Are we clear?"

"Crystal."

The chief hung up.

He slipped his phone back in his pocket. "We may be partners on this, but I outrank you."

"That you do, Detective *Lieutenant*. Planning to pull rank?"

A detective lieutenant wasn't typical in a large city, but with smaller departments such as theirs, not only was he senior in the investigations division, but he also needed to remain hands-on. He found it easier and simpler to be referred to as a detective while working cases and dealing with others in the division unless circumstances required him to throw his weight around.

"Not at all." Delaney was an excellent cop but had a reputation for not working well with others and a habit of going rogue. It was the only reason she hadn't been promoted a long time ago. "I only bring it up because I don't want you to give me a reason to feel like I have to. That means no coloring outside the lines. You do this by the book, work it with me, every step of the way. If Monty or anyone in that family says a single word to incriminate him or another Powell, you've got to keep me in the loop."

She hesitated for a moment.

A moment too long for his liking. "Don't forget the oath you swore. Your loyalty has to be to the badge." Waylon blew out a heavy breath. "Or you should get out of my way, do the right thing by passing on this one."

"I'm clear on my loyalties."

No doubt she was, but since she neglected to clarify, he still wasn't clear on whether her loyalty was to the Laramie Police Department or to the Powells.

"The last thing I need is an IA investigation into my conduct," she added. "They'll go through my entire history with the department and I don't need that kind of headache."

True. IA would love nothing more than to dig into her file. They'd have a field day.

Delaney straightened her shoulders. "I'll do it by the book. If I learn anything incriminating, you'll know."

He wanted to believe her. Only time would tell.

Waylon nodded and started down the hall. "Pandora Frye's parents need to be notified. Let's find out who they are and see what they have to say."

"In the spirit of an honest partnership, I need to tell you something about her parents and some land she recently inherited. This is much bigger and complicated than you realize because it gives Monty a motive. Not just him, but most of the Powells."

"Sharing is caring." Waylon couldn't wait to hear this. Maybe Delaney would prove to be more a help than a hindrance. "I'm all ears."

Chapter Four

The cell phone on her desk rang. Valentina's heart leaped with expectation at seeing the name of her enforcer whom she'd made a lieutenant on the caller ID. "Please tell me it's done, and that SOB is in jail."

"There's been a problem," Roman said. "He's in the hospital."

"I don't understand." Valentina glanced at her Rolex. "The ketamine would have worn off by the time he was arrested. He should've appeared hungover but alert."

"I had to call the police sooner than intended. I watched them carry him out, handcuffed to a stretcher, and load him into an ambulance shortly after eight."

Eight! Her chest constricted. "That was way ahead of schedule. Why would you do that? What happened?"

"Not what. Who. Amber Reyes happened. She messed up everything."

Valentina sucked in a calming breath. "Explain."

"The Reyes woman showed up more than two hours early, throwing off the timing of things," Roman said. "I had gotten out of there just before she arrived. It's a good thing I spotted her before I left. At least I called 911 right after she went inside. I'm fairly certain I made the call before she did, *if she did*, but I'm not sure if the plan will still work."

Valentina restrained impulsive words of aggravation. "You assured me you had things under control."

"And I did. Until Reyes decided to ignore the time set in the text message that I had Pandora send to her. She also must have called one of the brothers because Logan Powell showed up there, too."

So many brothers and a cousin to boot. "Remind me, which one is Logan? Is he the fire marshal?" She knew that Holden was the sheriff's deputy but couldn't keep track of the rest.

"No, that's Sawyer. Logan is with DCI."

Valentina rolled her eyes. How was it possible for them to all be in law enforcement? "Did you take pictures of everything? Time stamps on their arrival?"

"Of course. Never know if we could use something later."

She shoved back from behind her desk and paced in the office that was once her beloved father's. "This could work to our advantage. Maybe Amber Reyes and Logan Powell might have done something stupid in an effort to help Montgomery." If anyone knew how to tamper with a crime scene, it was a cop. If so, then things would work out even better than she had originally hoped. She would not only take him down, but his law enforcement brother and former fiancée, too.

"If they tried, they wouldn't have had long," Roman said. "The police were on the scene only moments after Logan stepped foot inside. Not enough time to dispose of evidence that would point to Monty. Only enough rope to hang themselves."

"Their presence will be incriminating once the detective

on the case finds out they were there before the authorities, especially if you were the only one to call 911. It'll beg the question of whether they corrupted the crime scene. Do you know who's assigned to the case?"

"I do. You won't like it."

She was never one to be coddled, not even as a child. Always ready to have the Band-Aid ripped off no matter how much it would hurt. "Tell me."

"Hannah Delaney was first on the scene and they're leaving her on the case."

Valentina had never heard of the detective. "What am I missing?"

"Delaney recently started a relationship with the cousin. Matt Granger. It's serious. They're engaged. Live together on the family ranch."

Letting out a growl of frustration, she picked up her coffee cup and threw it against the wall, smashing the mug to pieces. For a reckless second, she considered ordering Roman to shoot Montgomery Powell in the head. But then she remembered the promise she'd made to her father—his dying wish for Montgomery to suffer the way her brother had—and stopped herself.

"There is good news," Roman said. "Waylon Wright was made the lead detective. From what I've heard, he hates the Powells. Any shred of evidence that points to Montgomery being guilty, he'll chase it. The man is a bloodhound. Nothing and no one will get in his way."

One small consolation in the face of this unmitigated disaster. "Why did that wretched woman have to show up so early and ruin months of meticulous planning?" Amber Reyes would have to pay.

"It was way too soon for the authorities to find Montgomery. We needed at least another ninety minutes. Possibly two hours. I gave him a precise dose for his body weight. He would've been awake on his own by then. The authorities only would've run a general tox screen to check his blood alcohol content and to see if he did any of the cocaine that I left in the studio, but now they'll order a full panel. They'll find the ketamine in his system."

I should've taken care of it myself.

She dropped down in her chair. Tapping her long finger-nails—painted the color of blackened berries—on her desk, she considered the situation. Forced herself to focus on the things going in their favor. "This is simply a hiccup." Concentrating on the positives and how to maximize them was the only way forward. She never wallowed.

"No. This is worse than that. There's more. It's my under-standing that he had a reaction to ketamine. I couldn't have known he'd be allergic, but it's still my fault. *Perdóname.*"

Roman—once her father's right-hand man and now hers—made it difficult to remain angry with him. He was fiercely loyal. Took responsibility for his mistakes, which were rare. When they did occur, he always asked for forgiveness.

He was also quite attractive. Slick bald head and a touch of stubble, giving him that rough appeal she found alluring. An excellent lover, too. She'd sampled his goods herself. If only she didn't need him for the dirty work, like seduc-ing Pandora Frye and killing her, she might've given him a place at her side. As her partner. Not as equals, of course. She would remain in charge of her father's empire, as queen, while he could've been her prince consort.

It was lonely at the top. The seat of power was never meant to fall to her. Santiago was supposed to take over the cartel, but with her brother's brutal death, she was the only one left to reign.

Her heart ached. She could use her father's wise counsel now. He would know precisely what to do to avenge Santiago.

All she could do was trust in the plan. And in Roman. The one person she could count on.

"You're taking great risks for me," she said. *For her father. For Santiago.* Far beyond the scope of anyone else in her organization. "Thank you. Now we have to do damage control."

"I don't know how it'll play out," Roman said, "but I don't think they're going to arrest him just yet."

Focus on the endgame. "Whether or not he ends up in jail today matters little." Ultimately, his final destination would be a cell behind bars, where he would watch, helpless to do anything, while she tore apart his family. Only then would he die. While incarcerated. Painfully. Slowly. The way her brother had. "The first seed of doubt has been planted. His character and motives will be questioned. Opportunity, means and motive are clearly there. He won't be allowed to return to his position with the state police unless this is resolved in his favor. This will give us the chance we need for the next step."

"I won't be able to be your eyes and ears at the hospital. I'm not sure when he'll be discharged."

Roman was working on something else equally important for her.

"Never mind that. I'll send Leo to get an update. It'll be easier for him to contact me." Her driver was a capable man, interested in taking on a larger role in the organization.

"I'm sorry. If this murder doesn't stick to him—"

"We can't wait to find out. We need to expedite the rest of the plan. Starting today."

"Move up the timeline on everything?"

"Yes."

"Are you sure that's wise? It could raise unwanted suspicion."

"We have no choice now. Do your part. On my end, I'll get Leo to help me. It'll be the perfect test for him," Valentina said. There was more than one way to make a person suffer. "I've got to go. I need to reach out to our contact inside the highway patrol."

The day after Montgomery hit her family's radar, she'd begun her search for the perfect person to infiltrate the state troopers. One thing her father taught her was to never underestimate the power of an inside man.

"You're going to have the phone planted?" Roman asked.

"Yes. Go handle the remaining things on your end. Don't fail me again." Before he made any promises, she hung up. Then she dialed Officer Nicholas Foley. "It's me. I need to put you in play."

"Yes, ma'am. How may I be of service?"

"The item I sent for you to hold until I gave further instructions," she said, referring to the burner phone, "needs to be found in Montgomery Powell's locker when it's searched." The phone was Roman's suggestion. Once he explained his rationale behind the idea, she'd wholeheartedly agreed that planting the phone at the right time would be genius.

"You're sure it will be searched?" Foley asked.

If the LPD was doing their job, his locker would definitely be searched. She couldn't give any guarantees, but, if necessary, she'd get Nicholas to whisper a suggestion in the right ear. "I'm sure this must be done."

"It might prove difficult."

"You're not being paid double what you're making wearing the badge because you were going to be asked to do something easy. Get it done. Within the hour."

"I'm on patrol. I can't just leave and waltz into the station."

Excuses were number two on her list of things she hated,

right after failure. "Figure it out. Quickly. Or I have no further use for you. Or your wife." Both were her employees. Both would suffer the consequences. "Do you understand what I'm saying?"

"Yes, ma'am. I'll see that it's done."

"You had better. For your wife's sake, if not for your own." She hung up and had one of her guards posted near her office fetch Leo.

He knocked twice.

"Come in," she said.

Leo entered, eyeing the broken mug on the floor. "Would you like me to have someone clean it up?"

"No." The maid would take care of it later. She beckoned him forward.

Dressed in his usual simple, off-the-rack, black suit and white shirt with a skinny necktie, he stopped right in front of her desk, hands clasped behind his back like a good little soldier still in the army. He followed orders so well, sometimes she found it hard to believe he had ever been dishonorably discharged.

"Time to get your hands dirty," Valentina said. "Go to Laramie. Montgomery Powell is in the hospital. Send me updates on his status. I want to know when he's released and who his visitors are. Then I need you to put your sniper skills to use." She removed a folder from her top desk drawer and opened it. Sifting through the photos, she found the one she wanted and slid the glossy 4x6 across the desk to him. "This is your target."

His dark eyes widened. "Really? Him?"

She gave a single nod.

"Do you want him injured or—"

"Dead. A bullet to the stomach would be better than the heart." When he raised an eyebrow, she explained. "Nice slow bleed-out over an instant kill shot." *To give loved ones false hope.* "And I'd prefer you to do it in front of Montgomery, if at all possible. They live on a compound. You'll have to get creative. There'd be a sweet bonus in it for the personal touch provided you can pull it off where Montgomery can see it."

Leo grinned. "I'll head out now."

"Max will go with you," she said, deciding on the guard with the hulking chest and goatee to accompany him. Max would keep an eye on Leo and report back on how he handled himself.

Leo picked up the picture and stared at the target. "What have you got against Montgomery Powell, if you don't mind me asking?"

An eye for an eye. She wanted that man to suffer unimaginably. Before he died, he'd feel the same heart-wrenching pain that she had endured. The thought of her brother, beaten and stabbed in jail, and her father's subsequent stroke had her chest constricting again. She had to concentrate to take a simple breath.

"I do mind," she said. "All you need to know is that you begged for this opportunity to prove yourself. Don't waste it."

Leo slid the picture into his pocket. As he opened the office door, her nephew bolted into the room faster than a rocket. He was holding Legos and a piece fell off, clattering to the floor. A harried nanny ran in after him, and Leo left, closing the door.

"Auntie Val, Auntie Val! Look what I made." The four-year-old leaped into her lap.

"Let's see it."

Julian held up the toy.

She scrutinized it for a moment. "Is it a gun?"

"No, silly." He giggled. "It's an airplane."

"Of course, it is, but it's lost a wing." Not her fault he held it like a gun and a piece was missing. "You're so smart and creative." She ruffled his dark curls and hugged him tight. Every time she held her brother's son, she felt a little closer to Santiago.

"I'm sorry, madam." The nanny wrung her hands as her face creased with worry. "He got away from me."

"I was about to take a break anyway. Julian, how about we have lunch together today?"

"Yippee!" He hopped down. "Can we have pizza and carrots?"

"Of course." Valentina closed the file, covering the pictures of the rest of the Powell family and tucked it back in her desk.

One way or another, Montgomery was going to get what was coming to him.

Of that, she would make certain.

Chapter Five

Friday, December 6
4:20 p.m.

Amber walked through the lobby of the hospital alongside Logan and Monty, who sat in a wheelchair, pushed by Nurse Shelby. Chance had left a couple of hours earlier to go over the case with the top criminal defense attorney in Cheyenne and was planning to meet them at the Shooting Star Ranch for a family meeting.

As they neared the exit, she slowed to a stop. "That vile reporter, Erica Egan, is waiting outside. She even has a camera guy."

"I thought she was bad before," Logan said, "but her promotion to the KLBR TV station has only emboldened her."

"Are they here because of Mr. Powell?" Shelby asked.

"Yeah, they are." Logan's voice sounded tight and annoyed. "No way they've been waiting out there in the cold for hours. Someone must've tipped them off that you were being discharged."

"I can take you to a different exit. Most people don't know about it. We use it for mothers with newborns, so they don't have to encounter as many folks."

"That'd be great," Logan said.

Monty nodded. "Much appreciated."

"It's this way." Shelby turned down a hall on the right.

"I'll use the main exit to distract them," Amber said. Her father's death had been big news in the area. Reporters jumped at the opportunity to remind everyone how close the Powell and Reyes families were. She'd caught her picture in the paper and on TV more than once since she'd been home. "I'll meet you at the house."

"See you soon." Logan flashed her a sad smile. "Thanks for everything."

Down the hall, Monty grumbled, "I'm fine to walk on my own. I don't need a wheelchair."

"Sorry, it's policy," Shelby said. "You're free to do as you please once you leave the hospital."

Amber stood still, giving them time to reach the less frequented exit. Once they disappeared from sight, she headed for the sliding doors.

"Ms. Reyes." Erica Egan rushed toward her, holding up a microphone. Her colleague pointed the camera at Amber. "Were you here at the hospital to see Montgomery Powell?"

Although Amber wanted to run to her vehicle, she forced herself to slow down. "I was here for personal reasons." Over the shoulders of Egan and the cameraman, she spotted Logan and Monty hurrying across the parking lot.

"Would those reasons have anything to do with Mr. Powell?" Egan asked.

"As I've already stated, it was personal."

"What to do you think of Monty Powell being the prime suspect in the murder of Pandora Frye?"

Stopping, she gathered her thoughts. "First, the murder is a horrific tragedy. Second, I believe the evidence will eventually show that Monty is innocent."

"Are you saying he isn't capable of murder?" Egan thrust the mic back in Amber's face.

"Yes, I am."

Logan's truck zipped out of the lot and turned onto the road.

"A source has told me that the two were lovers and this was a crime of passion," Egan said. "How long were they sleeping together?"

Amber's cheeks burned, her chest tightening. All she could do was shake her head at the accusation.

"Would you care to comment, Ms. Reyes?"

"Yes. Get better sources. Please excuse me." Amber pushed past them and hustled toward her Jeep. She dug into her purse, rifling through it for her keys. Why hadn't she simply put them in her pocket?

Finally, she found them. She hit the key fob, unlocking the door, and rushed around the rear to get to the driver's-side door.

"Ms. Reyes." Waylon Wright tipped his hat at her. "I have a couple of quick questions for you."

He'd been waiting to ambush her.

She looked around. No sign of Hannah. "I'm sorry, but I need to go. I'm expected somewhere."

"At the Shooting Star Ranch for a big Powell meeting? I figure they'd be keen to circle the wagons since Monty has been discharged."

She swallowed past the lump in her throat. "I don't have time to talk right now." She reached for the door.

But he stepped in the way, blocking the handle. "This won't take long. Make time. Unless you have something to hide. See, I'm starting to get the sneaking suspicion that you might. Considering how you insisted that Monty not talk to me. An innocent person has nothing to fear."

"Monty is innocent, but I believe he has a great deal to fear from you. As for insisting that he wait for his lawyer before answering questions, it was common sense. He wasn't in a good state of mind since he was under the influence of—"

"Ketamine. Yes, I'm aware. His blood work came back." He pulled out a notepad and pen. "Still doesn't explain your reluctance to answer a few questions yourself. Might that have something to do with the terms of your father's trust?"

She stiffened. "What do you mean?"

"It's simple. The land you stand to inherit has a river running through it. A river that is vital to the Shooting Star Ranch because their cattle depend on it. Your father had a neighborly agreement with the Powells, giving them access to the water until his death. If you don't marry Monty Powell in a little less than a month, then you'd lose everything and Pandora Frye stood to inherit it all. It would explain why he was sleeping with her," Waylon said, and the fire in her cheeks spread to her chest. "As an insurance policy in case things didn't work out with you. But maybe things turned sour last night, giving him a motive to kill her."

Amber shook her head. "The amount of ketamine in his system would've been too high."

"He could've killed her and then taken ketamine."

"Why would he do such a thing?"

"To put reasonable doubt in the mind of a jury." He rested his forearm on her 4x4. "A cop planning a murder would think of that kind of thing."

"Not Monty."

"You seem certain. If he's such a great guy, why haven't you married him? Based on your father's will, I'm sure he'd make an eager husband."

Fiddling with her keys, she averted his keen gaze. "Marriage should be based on love. Not money." But she couldn't squeeze blood from stone. She never wanted any man to feel forced to marry her. "Monty is flawed, but he isn't a murderer."

"For the Powells, that river and your land it's on are priceless. Even if he didn't kill her, it still gives every member of his family a motive. Also gives you a pretty big one, too."

Amber staggered back a step, shocked at the redirection of his line of questioning. "Are you accusing me?"

"Why were you at your half sister's house this morning? And if you even think of stonewalling me, I'll cross this parking lot and give Erica Egan the scoop of her life. She'd gladly swallow every crumb I threw her way, particularly the part about you being at the scene of the crime. This can play out in the court of public opinion if you want."

Egan would paint a story that was thirteen shades of ugly, portraying Monty or even her as a cold-blooded, greedy murderer. Amber sighed, her breath crystallizing in the chilly air. "I assume you know that she also inherited my family home."

Waylon gave a single, slow nod. "I do."

"I wanted her to sell it to me and Chance. She agreed to meet me. To discuss it. She texted me last night, telling me to come over this morning."

"May I see the text?"

He already seemed to know so much. What harm could it do?

She pulled out her phone and brought it up.

Waylon took her cell, glanced at it and scrolled through several other messages. "You've had some heated exchanges back and forth."

Lowering her head, she did her best to tamp down the spurt of anger. "I didn't know I had a half sister until the reading of the will. Not the best way to find out. I just lost my father and I didn't want to lose our family home, too."

"The message told you to come at ten. Why did you arrive so early?"

She huffed out a breath. "It was silly. I've been working as a substitute teacher while I'm in town. School starts at nine. I felt like inconveniencing her rather than be the one inconvenienced."

"Are you involved with Monty?"

Blood drained from her face, her entire body growing heavy as stone. "W-w-we aren't a couple."

The corner of his mouth hitched up. "Have you ever been romantically involved?"

She clenched her fingers around her keys. "Years ago."

"What about since you've been home, after the reading of the will and he learned about the trust?"

Everything inside her went numb. She glanced past him at the door. "This is taking too long. I need to go."

"When you arrived early at your sister's place and discovered that Monty was with her, did it anger you?"

"Half sister." She looked up at him. "If you're asking me whether or not I killed her, I didn't. I swear it. The front door wasn't closed all the way. It swung open after I knocked. She was already dead."

"I believe you," he said, quickly, easily.

Relief crept through her. "You do?"

Waylon nodded. "You got there at seven forty-eight. You didn't kill her. But I think you were worried that Monty had. Why else would you call Logan?"

She grimaced. How did he know that?

"This looks bad," Waylon said. "Your phone call could get Logan into a lot of trouble, legally, professionally, but an honest answer could make it better."

The last thing she wanted was to incriminate Logan in some way or make this worse. "I freaked out." She shrugged.

"He popped to mind because I realized he would know what to do."

"What did he tell you?"

She hesitated.

"I only want the truth," he said, his tone comforting and sincere, "and you've got nothing to hide, right?"

"He told me that he was at Divine Treats and would come straight over, but to hang up and call 911."

"Logan told you to call right away *before* he got there?"

She nodded. "He insisted on it."

Waylon handed over her phone.

The screen was on her recent calls. He'd toggled over and had already seen how long they'd spoken and that she'd called the authorities right after. "Were you testing me?"

"I prefer to think of it as poking around to get a good sense of a person." He stepped away from her Jeep. "You never answered my question. Have you been romantically involved with Monty since you've been home?"

This man kept finding ways to corner her and squeeze out answers. "You lied, Detective Wright." She opened her door.

He narrowed his eyes. "That's the first time anyone has ever accused me of lying. About what exactly?"

She climbed inside the Jeep. "You said this wasn't going to take long. Now, I'm late for an important meeting."

"Apologies, ma'am. I stand corrected. And that's twice you've dodged the same question about the nature of your relationship with Monty since the reading of the will. Some might consider that an answer."

Amber closed the door, cranked the engine and peeled out of the lot.

Chapter Six

A hundred different things crawled through Monty's head with his brain still pounding as he rested his eyes during the drive to the ranch. He was grateful for the silence.

In a few minutes there would be nonstop chatter and strategizing.

"We're here," Logan said far too soon.

Monty opened his eyes. "This is a nightmare."

His brother gave a grunt of assent and put the truck in Park.

"Thanks for having my back, looking out for me."

"Always. You're my brother." Logan pressed his lips in a firm line, his jaw tightening.

Clearly, his brother was weighing his words, deciding if he should give voice to them. "Are you going to spit it out or keep it to yourself?"

"Most of what I have to say should probably wait until we're all together."

"And the rest of it, you want to get off your chest now?"

"This isn't about whether you're guilty. I know you didn't kill anyone."

"Thanks. I'm sensing a *but* there."

"But sleeping with Pandora, the fact that Amber had to see you with her, like that." Logan shook his head. "Her of all people."

"I don't even know why Amber was there, but that's beside the point. I didn't—"

"I'm not finished," Logan said, cutting him off. "You really hurt her bad with the engagement, scheming with Dad and Mom, lying to her the way you did. When are you going to stop being a source of pain for her?" He clenched his hand into a fist. "Enough is enough. I won't stand by and watch you do it again. So help me, I'll knock your head off myself first. Do you hear me?" Logan jumped out, slamming the door closed behind him.

Monty scrubbed a hand over his face, wanting to disregard Logan's anger. After all, Logan was his least favorite brother and that included Matt in that count. Yet, the brutally honest words rang true in his head.

To many, his history with Amber looked black-and-white. Simple. It was anything but.

He stared up at his family home. His parents had meticulously crafted the house. Floor-to-ceiling windows, ten bedrooms, twelve bathrooms, gourmet kitchen, gym, movie room and state-of-the-art automation. They had designed it to entice their children to stay close. They often talked about their legacy, the importance of the ranch, about all the weddings, holiday celebrations and big birthdays they wanted to have here. With plenty of room for grandkids, extended family, in-laws and friends to stay.

More than a home, more than a ranch, this sanctuary embodied their hopes and dreams. And those of many Powells before them who had sacrificed so much in the hope it would be passed to the next generation.

He'd never wanted the responsibility of that legacy. Fought against it for as long and as hard as he could until that fateful day in the kitchen with his folks.

He could still hear his parents like it was yesterday.

"All I've ever wanted was for my sons to take up the mantle," Dad said. *"Do what my father and his father before him has done. Hold tight to the ranch, grow, prosper. I have five boys and a nephew I love like a son. Six of you. I figured at least one of you would surely want to run this place."*

"I can't speak for the others," Monty said. *"I want to be my own man. Make my own choices. Live my own life. Not one you've decreed."* He turned to his mother. *"You claim all you want is for us to be happy."*

"That's true," she said. *"But you seem miserable being a state trooper. Driving around handing out speeding tickets half the time. Like you picked that job just to spite us."*

Monty heaved a breath. "You're missing the point. I picked it. It was my choice."

"This land, being a part of the ranch, working with the cattle makes you happy," she said. *"It's what you were born to do. I've seen how you thrive."* She sighed. *"Amber has been in love with you forever and I know that if you open your heart to her, you're bound to fall in love. And unlike most of those fast fillies you usually go after, Amber will stand up to you and not let you treat like her garbage, which is what you need. A woman with a backbone."*

Monty chuckled. He'd pay to see that. The reality was Amber doted on him every chance she got. He could do no wrong in her eyes.

He didn't want a doormat. Even if she was perfect for him, which she wasn't, he still wouldn't want her—a woman picked for him by his parents, a bride he was expected to marry.

Like this ranch that he was expected to love and oversee until the day he died.

No, thank you.

"The two of you are opposite sides of the same coin." Mom took his hands in hers and met his eyes. "You could have a wonderful marriage with Amber. Just give it a chance. Put the work in and really try. You'll see."

Pulling away, he turned his back on her. "No."

"Yes! You, insolent son of a gun!" his father said, his eyes filled with anger and...pain. "I have never asked anything of you. We have never asked. If we don't control that land with the river, anything could happen to it. You don't marry her, the land will go to someone else. A person with no love for our family. Someone who might one day decide to dam it."

"Whoever it is, we could buy from them," Monty said, suggesting a reasonable solution.

"We can't tell you who." His father clenched his jaw. "But trust me. That person won't take our money. Their ears have been poisoned against the idea. They'll sell it, perhaps to someone who wants to build a big, noisy resort. Frightened cattle with no access to water means the end of this ranch. You don't do this, everything we've built will be lost."

Monty grimaced, his heart throbbing like an open wound.

"For once in your spoiled life, you're going to put this family ahead of yourself!" Dad jabbed a finger in his chest. "We need the river and you're the only one who can get it for us. You'll marry that girl. Get yourself a sidepiece if need be."

Mom gasped. "Buck! How dare you. Amber deserves a real husband."

"A cheating husband is still a real one," Dad said.

Monty imagined sex with Amber as vanilla. Boring. She was so young, seven years his junior. He'd never seen her *go out with anyone, and she was probably a virgin. He pre-ferred spicy girls with more experience, but he would never humiliate her or any wife by treating her like that. "I'm not the cheating kind."*

"Even better." Dad threw his hands up. "We need you to do this, son."

As much as Monty despised the idea, the pressure was unrelenting, making him consider it. "If I did do this, I'd have to tell her up-front that it's just for convenience only."

"You can't." Mom shook her head, her eyes weary. She looked bone-tired. "Carlos made it very clear. He doesn't want her to know. That's why he's putting things into motion now, long before he dies, and she learns she'll inherit all the land."

Of course, Mr. Reyes wanted this to feel organic for Amber rather than orchestrated. He'd like to give that man a piece of his mind, trying to dictate whom Monty should marry, whom he should love, how he should live. Just as bad and manipulative as his parents.

"Don't tell her. Woo her. Get hitched," Dad said. "Give it a solid go for two years, putting in the work like your mother said. Those are the rules. After that, you can decide about forever and it'll be whatever life you want. Free from the legacy that you're too good to carry on, and may I live long enough to have a grandchild who'll do so."

Monty felt like a block of stone split in two, cracked right down the middle, but keeping the truth from Amber made him sick to his stomach. "No. I won't do it."

A week later his father had a heart attack. At his bedside, his mother begged Monty to agree.

Was it weakness? Fear? Love? Duty? All Monty knew was he'd caved.

He courted Amber and proposed. For the land. For the river. To make everyone, other than himself, happy.

They all thought he'd told Amber some great lie.

But he never said those three little words, *I love you.* Not once. He never painted a rosy picture of happily-ever-after. Never whispered sweet things in her ear. Never wooed her. Never seduced her. He didn't have to do any of that stuff. Plainly asked her out and things went from there. She had been the one to initiate sex. As he'd guessed, she'd been a virgin. He'd underestimated the power of that experience on both sides. To be her first everything—not something he took lightly.

The truth was, he didn't have to put in much effort to get the relationship to bloom. She got caught up in a fantasy of her own making, and he let her.

He let her because it made her happy. He let her because his parents had promised his duty would be done. No more pressure for him to take over the ranch if only he married Amber Reyes. He let her because he reached a point where he believed he could make it work. Make it real. Give her what she needed. Saw she was what he wanted after all. As much as he'd been loath to admit it, his mother had been right about him and Amber. Forced together, a collision of smashing pieces, they fit and became easily entangled.

They had just found their footing as a couple, enjoying the discovery of one another, with him surprisingly excited for the future. A future with her. Instead of feeling he had settled for someone else's choice, he simply felt settled. Delighted by how deeply, madly he'd fallen for her. How she knew him better than he knew himself. Like they were really meant to be.

Then it fell apart. Because he hadn't been honest.

Still, he'd been wrong to do it. After she left, he missed

her something awful. A lot more than he ever thought possible. There was a hole in his life, where she had always been. Sometimes he lay awake at night, especially during the past four months—thinking about Amber, about the time they'd spent together, about how right she felt in his arms, about how the sex had been vanilla sweet and spicy hot, the best of both—and he tossed and turned. Sick down in his soul with regret.

Now everyone probably thought history was repeating itself and he'd lured Pandora Frye into some romantic web.

What a fool he'd been to go to her place last night only to talk about a potential deal they could make for the land if Amber didn't marry him. His mountain of mistakes kept growing higher.

He had a sinking feeling that he was playing right into someone's hands. Whoever had killed Pandora was trying to frame him for murder.

But why? Did it have something to do with the Reyes land? The river? Or was there another reason?

Until he had answers, he might have a tough time proving his innocence.

Chapter Seven

By the time she pulled up to the sprawling Shooting Star Ranch, which was really a compound, and waited for the grand wrought iron gate to open, she was fuming.

Where was Hannah? How did Waylon find out the details of the trust so fast? Had Detective Delaney told her new partner?

The main house came into sight with a mesmerizing backdrop of the mountains. A modest term for the massive estate that was a haven of luxury.

A lifetime ago, this had been a place that Amber loved. Not for the amenities or upgrades that the Reyes house lacked. Once, in a dream never meant to be, she'd thought this ranch was going to be home.

She pulled into the circular driveway behind a long line of vehicles. The only two people who wouldn't be at the meeting were Jackson and Sawyer. They'd both come to her father's funeral. It had been nice to catch up with them and to discover Sawyer had married his high school sweetheart, Liz. Theirs was a tragic story but one with a happy ending. It would be nice to see them again in a couple of weeks for Christmas.

The rest of the boys lived on the ranch. Holly and Buck had built Monty a cottage farther back from the main house after he had proposed to her. Meant for the two of them. Holden and his wife had their own cottage now, with a fourteen-month-old son and another baby on the way. The kind of life Amber had once fantasized about having with Monty, being his wife, living on this ranch. Even though her dream had crumbled to ash because of his lie, he'd still decided to move into the house that was supposed to be theirs, where they were going to have a family and raise their children.

Climbing the stone steps of the main house, she put her hand on her belly one last time. Once she walked through those doors, she didn't dare call any attention to the life growing inside her.

She didn't bother to knock. They never locked the front door and already expected her.

"You made it," Buck called out to her as he came down the stairs. At sixty-five with salt-and-pepper hair, he exuded the virility and indomitable strength of a man half his age. After his heart attack, he'd cut back on drinking and stopped eating red meat. He was still handsome in the fit and tailored way of the wealthy. In his arms, he carried his first grandchild, Kayce, and his daughter-in-law was beside him.

Grace was a nurse and the nicest person, caring and thoughtful, making sure that Amber had everything she needed the week of her father's funeral, though they barely knew each other. Since then, she called regularly to check on Amber and invite her to lunch.

Not only was Grace easy to like but also a natural beauty. Flawless brown complexion and sparkling eyes. At eight months pregnant, she glowed, her belly round and tight under the empire waist of her dress, hair falling in long, dark curls around her shoulders. All soft curves and fertility. Somehow, she had only gained weight in her stomach. While Amber was practically subsisting on crackers and already packing on the pounds. But Grace's mother was the famous supermodel Selene Beauvais, which was like hitting the genetic lottery.

"They're in the great room talking now." Grace gave her a warm embrace. The best hugger, too. "Kayce was napping in a guest room and woke up. Buck insisted on coming with me to get him."

"I was so focused on ranching when my own were young that I didn't realize how much I missed until this little fellow was born." Beaming, Buck kissed the boy's forehead. "They grow so fast. I don't want to miss a single minute this time around." He stared into the boy's bright brown eyes. "You're going to grow up to be a rancher like your grandpa. Aren't you? Say yes, yes, I am," he said with a smile for the child in his arms. "As soon as you're old enough to ride, I'm buying you a pony."

"You're going to spoil him," Grace said.

"That's what grandfathers are supposed to do."

Kayce was the perfect mix of Holden and Grace. Tan with curly blond hair and a calm temperament, and he'd slept through the night since he was three months old. Amber had only seen him fussy if he was hungry.

"Do you want to hold him?" Buck offered.

Amber loved holding babies, the way they smelled, how their warmth soothed something in her soul, but with her hormones all over the place today she worried touching Kayce might bring tears to her eyes.

"I wouldn't dare deny you the pleasure," Amber said. "I'll get a chance the next time Grace and I have lunch."

"Which I hope will be soon." Grace took her arm and ushered her deeper into the house. "Since I'm on leave from the hospital until this one comes," she said, rubbing her belly, "I have free time. We better make the most of it while we can."

Smiling, Amber nodded. "With two under two, you're going to have your hands full."

Grace flashed her a weary expression. "That's an understatement."

"Your mom is flying out soon from Los Angeles to help, right?"

Buck and Grace laughed in unison.

"My mom is coming, but it'll be like having a third child to take care of. She can be pretty high maintenance."

"Holly is on it," Buck said. "She's already spoken to Selene and is putting her up in the main house this time. She also hired one of the best night nurses in the area to help you and Holden for the first few weeks."

"Wow." Grace put a hand to her chest. "But they're so expensive. I can manage. Women do it all the time."

Buck clasped her shoulder. "What's the money for, sweetie, if not to make your lives easier. It's a Christmas gift. Please don't tell her I spoiled the surprise, or I'll never hear the end of it."

Grace smiled. "I won't. Promise."

Raised voices carried from the great room around the corner.

"Waylon thinks you were sleeping with Pandora to get your hands on the land," Hannah said.

"It wouldn't be the first time you've done something like that." Logan's voice held a bitter note that Amber knew was on her behalf.

"If you were," Holden said, "we'd understand, but we need to know."

"I wasn't." Monty's tone was sharp. "She's not my type."

"Are you sure you weren't lovers?" Chance asked. "We all know you've compromised your integrity before to do your duty to this family, regardless of the woman not being your type or who got hurt in the end."

Another person on her side.

"I made a mistake with your sister. I regret ever laying a finger on her wit—"

Buck let out a loud, whooping cough, drawing everyone's attention to them as they entered. Silence descended like a foul odor.

Humiliation burned Amber's cheeks as her stomach sank. Taking a seat in a chair on the far side of the room, she avoided eye contact with the others. She slipped off her gloves and coat, wanting to disappear into the furniture. Maybe she shouldn't have come. But Pandora's murder affected both their families and the prime suspect was the father of her unborn child.

Tension hung over the room, finally eased by a tiny squeal of pleasure coming from Kayce as he smacked his grandpa's cheeks.

She dared look up and found Monty staring at her with a mix of sadness and something else she couldn't quite name. Maybe pity. She was pitiable right then after his declaration about her to all of them.

He stood and took a step in her direction when Holly waltzed into the room. Her presence had him shuffling back and sitting down.

His mother came from the opposite hall and entrance, accompanied by her assistant, Eddie Porter, and her campaign manager turned chief of staff, Brianne Mallard—a woman who never stopped managing Holly's public image.

"Why are you all so silent and still?" Holly asked. "What

happened?" Her gaze scanned the room, landing on Amber, and the new mayor pursed her lips. "Oh. I see everyone has arrived. What did I miss?"

"We're discussing whether Monty was sleeping with Pandora," Logan said. "Because it definitely looks that way."

Amber's stomach lurched.

"And I've already told them that I wasn't." Monty leaned forward and rested his forearms on his thighs. "But they don't believe me."

"It's understandable if you're reluctant to admit to it. We just need to be sure." Hannah scooted to the edge of her seat beside Matt. "Waylon is going to look for proof that you're lying about this because it makes the most sense in light of the terms of the Reyes trust."

Staring at the detective, Amber fumed all over again. The woman was a newcomer to this inner circle. She and Matt had been together less than a year. Although they were engaged, she didn't wear a ring, there was no talk of marriage, or a wedding or kids, and it was plain to see that his uncle Buck and aunt Holly didn't know what to make of it. Amber had asked Matt about it once while casually chatting and he'd intimated that he didn't want to *push* the detective and was happy simply living together. Another thing that raised eyebrows in this circle.

No telling where Delaney's loyalties rested. Amber couldn't hold her tongue a second longer. "How did Waylon find out the details of the trust so fast? He knew everything and interrogated me about it in the hospital parking lot. He only stopped short of accusing me of murdering her, too. Did you tell him?"

The full force of everyone's scrutiny swung to the traitor in their midst. "We spoke to Fiona Frye. She's in Arizona, visiting family. We had to inform her about her daughter's murder over the phone." She hung her head like that had been the hardest task in the world. "She's flying back sometime late tomorrow. We'll get an official statement from her in person on Sunday, but she didn't hesitate to accuse this family of murdering her daughter. Because of the land." Hannah turned to Monty. "She claims she has proof that you were sleeping together."

Monty turned pale as a ghost and looked like he'd just been slapped upside the head by one. "That's impossible."

"She said Pandora was seeing someone," Hannah said, "but her daughter couldn't talk about it yet until things were official. Legally. That by the time her mother got back from Arizona it would be and she'd be able to tell her everything. Apparently, Pandora also gave her a flash drive as insurance."

"What's on the drive?" Monty asked.

Hannah shook her head. "She never looked. Fiona says her desktop computer is thirty years old and doesn't even have a USB port on it, but she's confident it'll prove you two were in a relationship."

"I can dig up dirt on Pandora Frye and her mother," Brianne said, with a spark in her eyes. "Feed it to the press. Change the narrative. Get us control of the story."

A horrified look crossed Holly's face. "We're not talking about an opponent in an election. Fiona is grieving the loss of her only child. We won't get dirty by tarnishing Pandora's reputation. Or hers."

"Not even if it helps Monty?" Eddie pushed his glasses up the bridge of his nose and smoothed back his hair. "And in turn the whole family? Guilt by association is a real thing for the constituents." He was a mild-mannered, soft-spoken man, at Holly's beck and call.

"He's right." Brianne typed away with one hand on her tablet. "We need to think of your public image."

"No," Holly said, with a wag of her finger. "Not another word about it."

Everyone was just going to let Hannah Delaney skate by without answering the question. Cops and lawyers were good at that, but Amber was equally good at catching it. "Did you tell Waylon about the trust?" Amber asked. "Yes or no."

The detective's gaze flashed up, meeting hers. "Yes, I did."

Matt sighed with a shake of his head. "We should go."

"No." Hannah turned, angling toward her fiancé. "I'm not scurrying out the door with my tail between my legs. They need to understand I made the right call."

"Explain it, then," Buck demanded. "Why you'd hand Waylon a motive on a silver platter?"

"Because as soon as we spoke to the mother, he was going to find out anyway. Figured it was better to use it to my advantage. Before I told him, he was certain he wanted me removed from this case and now he's not so sure. If I'm not on it, then I can't pass along information."

"Such as?" Buck handed the baby to Grace and put his hands on his hips.

"The direction the case is headed."

"Go on," Amber said. "We're going to need more than that."

The detective narrowed her eyes. "The warrant was approved. Monty's truck, house, even his locker at work is going to be searched. Tomorrow, once they have enough officers available to handle it. Since he lives here, they'll have access to the whole ranch. Waylon is planning to use that full authority."

Buck pivoted on his heel and glanced over his shoulder. "You got anything to hide, son?"

"No, sir."

Amber huffed a breath. "Don't say anything else."

Monty rubbed his temples like his head still ached. "But I don't have anything to hide."

"This information sharing is a two-way street," Amber said. "Everything we say, she's going to report."

"Is that true?" Buck asked the detective.

But Logan answered, "It is."

The traitor nodded. "Yes, I have to. I'm still a cop working this case and Waylon is the lead on it."

"We can't talk freely. She shouldn't stay." Amber jumped to her feet. The room spun. She reached out for the closest thing to steady herself and sent a lamp crashing to the floor. Stumbling, she headed for a face-plant, but Chance and Monty leaped up and were at her side. They each grabbed hold of one of her arms.

"Are you okay?" Monty asked.

A new twinge in her stomach around her belly button stole her breath. "Fine." Amber shook her head, trying to ward off the dizziness. "Low blood sugar. I haven't eaten today. Shouldn't have moved so fast."

"How does a piece of lasagna and a glass of wine sound?" Holly asked. "I'm sure you could use a drink after the day you've had."

Her stomach roiled. "Crackers and ginger ale would be perfect."

"You need to hydrate," Chance whispered.

Holly crossed the room, took hold of her arm and shooed the others away. "Let's go to the kitchen. Grace, darling, please join us."

"Matt," Buck snapped.

"I know, sir." Matt rose from the love seat. "Come on," he said to the detective. "We're leaving. Now."

Grace passed the baby to her husband and trailed them to the kitchen, along with Brianne and Eddie.

Holly sat Amber in a chair at the long wooden table near the marble island. "Grace, please make sure she's all right." Holly whispered something to Eddie, who ducked inside the walk-in pantry.

Grace poured a glass of water, handed it to her before the nurse took a seat beside her and proceeded to take her pulse.

Clutching her tablet, Brianne leaned against the wall, looking bored.

"Here you go." Holly took something from Eddie and shoved it in Amber's face.

A plate with a peeled banana.

The smell made Amber gag. "I think I'm going to be sick."

Holly handed the plate back to Eddie. "You're pregnant."

"What?" Amber stared up at her, horrified by the emphatic statement.

"You haven't eaten all day, but the only thing you want is crackers and ginger ale." Holly glanced at Eddie. "Please get that for her and applesauce and lemon wedges."

Pam, the housekeeper and cook, stopped what she was doing at the stove. "I'll handle it."

"When your mother was pregnant with you and Chance," Holly said, "the doctor told her to try eating bananas to quell the nausea, but the smell of them always made her want to retch."

Amber considered concocting a story as to why she was sick.

"Those wheels are spinning so fast in your head that I can practically see smoke coming from your ears." Holly sat across from her. "You always did wear your heart on your sleeve and your thoughts were easy to read in your face. Please don't insult me by denying the pregnancy."

What would be the point? Soon enough they would all know the truth. "I am," Amber said.

"Congratulations," Grace said softly and covered her hand with a warm palm. "I've known for a while. You threw up at our last few lunches and you're starting to show. I figured that's why you began wearing baggy clothes. But I thought it best to let you tell me when you were ready." Grace cast a scolding glance at her mother-in-law.

Holly cut her gaze from Grace, sliding it back to Amber. "Is the child Monty's?"

Amber stiffened at the invasive question. "This is very personal and I'm not ready to discuss it." Especially around people she didn't know well. Everyone in the Powell household might have been used to Brianne and Eddie's constant presence, but she wasn't.

"You don't have to say another word about it," Grace said, with a reassuring squeeze of her fingers.

"Please excuse us," Holly said to her assistant and campaign manager as if reading Amber's thoughts on her face. "And, Eddie, call Vera, tell her that since I've been out of the office today for personal reasons, and with me being busy in town all day tomorrow, we'll have to work on Sunday. I'll be in after the eight-thirty church service and will need her in the office by then. I've got so much work to catch up on."

Vera was Holly's secretary. Amber had met her a couple of times. Nice, hardworking lady.

"Sure thing," Eddie said. "Should I tell her to expect you there by ten?"

Holly nodded. Once they were gone, she put her clasped hands on the table. "I don't wish to be indelicate, but in less than thirty days, land that we need will go to Pandora's next living relative. Her mother. If the child is Monty's, when he finds out, he'll insist on marrying you. Why drag this out any longer? Is the baby his?"

Amber was really going to be sick now.

This kind of pressure was one reason she didn't want anyone besides her brother to know the truth. She also didn't want further humiliation. Unrequited love, the duped former fiancée, the man who broke her heart sleeping with her again out of pity, the unplanned pregnancy. It was the plot of some melodramatic movie or a soap opera storyline.

"If I wanted Monty to marry me out of obligation, I could've had him as a husband ten years ago. The entire room heard him say that I was a mistake and that he regrets touching me." Unwelcome tears sprang up, blurring her vision. "Yes, the child is his. But *I* will let him know when I'm ready." Her eyes burned and she closed them. Still, more tears escaped, and she quickly dashed them away. She refused to let Holly think this was a moment of weakness that she could exploit. Opening her eyes, she pinned the formidable older woman with an unwavering stare. "If you tell him or get one of your flunkies to let it slip or try to push me in the slightest, so help me, I'll disappear. *Unmarried.* Unconcerned what happens to the land or the river running through it. And there's no telling when you'll see this baby. Understand?"

"All right. Calm down, dear," Holly said in an easy-breezy tone. "I think we understand each other quite well."

Pam set a tray in front of her with crackers, applesauce, lemon wedges, a can of ginger ale and a glass of ice.

"Thank you," Amber said to Pam. "What's the lemon for?"

"Take a wedge." Holly pointed to the slices. "Sniff it."

She did and the refreshing, citrusy scent immediately tempered her nausea.

"Worked like a charm for your mother. The applesauce helped, too. See if it works for you."

Willing to give anything a try, Amber spooned a little into her mouth and was surprised she wanted more.

"Right after you ran away all those years back, everyone blamed me and Buck, and of course Monty. But it was your father's decision to write that will and trust that started it. Truth be told, this entire mess is really your fault," Holly said.

Amber almost choked on the applesauce. "Is that some kind of sick joke?"

"After your mother died, and with Chance living in a different state, on the road to becoming a bigwig lawyer, your father was worried about you being alone once he passed eventually. He wanted to give you your greatest, deepest desire. *Monty.* So he hatched this twisted scheme with the trust, playing games with hearts, like people were pawns. *For you.*"

"I thought he was only thinking about leaving me the land back then. He'd already written the trust, with Pandora in it?" Amber asked.

Holly nodded. "As soon as he finished and made it legal, he couldn't wait to tell us all about it on the back porch over a glass of whiskey. About Pandora, too, using her as leverage in the trust. Of course, he knew we'd steer Monty toward you," she said. Amber believed it more possible they shoved him toward her. "And it blew up in our faces when you ran away."

It blew up when she overheard Monty admitting to one of his brothers, Sawyer, that he was only marrying her to get the land for his family because she'd one day inherit it. She had been nothing more than an obligation. A chore on his to-do list.

"I thought Carlos might change his mind and rip up the

trust," Holly said. "He might've if you had ever married or moved on with someone new."

Goodness knows, she had tried hard to do so, but no man ever measured up to Peter Pan.

"When that baby is born, you'll understand the desire to see him or her happy, to give them what their heart wants," Holly said. "Too bad you didn't love Logan instead, huh?"

It would've made things easier for everyone if she had.

Grace patted her hand. "Finish eating, then you should go home, rest and hydrate. Nurse's orders. Chance can fill you in on the meeting."

Starving, Amber stuffed a cracker in her mouth.

"Yes, rest up." Holly stood. "I'll be expecting you at the Holiday Tree Lighting ceremony tomorrow. It's from noon to six. I need you there by four thirty. We're lighting the tree with fireworks promptly at five. Your father was meant to have the honor of pressing the button. You'll do it in his stead."

A command. Not a request. *Typical.* "You can't seriously be planning to go through with attending the ceremony," Amber said while chewing on a second cracker. "The police are coming to execute the search warrant tomorrow."

"All the more reason for the entire family to be out of the way," Holly said. "Besides, this is a town function that everyone from Laramie to Bison Ridge looks forward to each year. We've expanded the activities—a children's craft center, petting zoo, pop-up holiday markets, live music and food trucks. It's grown into a big deal. As mayor I've organized everything and it's my duty to be there. The show must go on, my dear." She turned to head out of the kitchen.

"Holly," Amber said. "You won't say anything, not even to Buck?" She wasn't concerned about Grace spilling the beans to Holden. They'd become fast friends, and if Grace had already known Amber was pregnant for weeks, she'd more than proven she could be trusted.

"Your secret is not mine to tell. I won't say anything," Holly said. "We meddled once before and look how that turned out." She glanced up at the ceiling with a faraway look for a moment. "I want to be in the lives of my grandchildren. All of them. The boys, the women they love, the grandbabies and their mothers—that's all that really matters in the end."

"Thank you." Amber truly meant that. Holly Powell could've made it much harder.

"If you need anything," Holly said, "absolutely anything, please don't hesitate to let me know."

Amber nodded, wanting to feel relieved at not having to deal with future pressure from Holly. Instead, dread filled her in anticipation of the moment when she would have to tell Monty the truth.

Chapter Eight

Saturday, December 7
4:40 p.m.

Are you at the ceremony with Amber, yet? I need to speak to her.

Hoping he'd finally get a reply, Monty sent a third text to Chance. He stood on the fringe of the crowd, far from his family, sandwiched between a Belgian waffle food truck and another selling doughnuts and warm apple cider. The delectable aroma was enticing but he wasn't in the mood for sweets or revelry, or to put on a show of a united front with the rest of the Powell clan, pretending everything was fine.

Yesterday, the family meeting had turned into an inquisition. Even Hannah had been under fire when she was only doing her best to walk a fine line. Being a part of his big, bossy, overbearing and close-knit family could be a lot for someone unaccustomed to it. Heck, plenty of times it overwhelmed him and was part of the reason he spent so much time off the ranch. He understood the precarious position Matt's fiancée was in and respected her efforts to help. The rest of the family should have done the same since he was innocent. None of them needed to compromise their integrity for his sake.

For some reason, the people closest to him doubted him. Not that it had dampened their staunch support of him.

Sure, he'd made plenty of mistakes, chief among them deciding to talk to Pandora on her terms, but the only thing he was guilty of was being a foolish, insensitive jerk to Amber years ago. Downright reprehensible.

I'm a horrible person.

But he was *not* a murderer.

Looking up from his phone, which still hadn't chimed with a reply from Chance, he caught an elderly couple giving him sidelong glances, whispering and pointing at him. A child leaving a food truck line with a loaded waffle piled high with fruit and Nutella waltzed in front of him. Her mother cringed at the sight of Monty and snatched the little girl away, drawing her close, like he posed a serious threat.

Mrs. Sanders from the Ranch and Feed Supply store noticed him and got out of the line for the doughnut food truck. She'd always been kind to everyone. His family had used their store forever, making them not only loyal customers but substantial ones.

He plastered on a soft smile. "Hello, Mrs. Sanders. How's your husband?"

"You should be ashamed of yourself." She pointed an accusatory finger at his face. "What you did to that girl." Mrs. Sanders reeled back with a disgusted expression, drawing attention from passersby. "I can't believe your mother let you show your face here tonight."

Stiffening, he reminded himself that he wasn't guilty, and the truth would come to light. At least, he hoped it would. "For the record, I haven't been charged because I'm innocent."

"Likely story. Or is the real reason because your mama is

mayor?" Her voice rose along with the number of onlookers. Some of whom nodded in agreement. "There are kids around here. This is a family-friendly event. Do the rest of us a favor, go back to your ranch and stay there."

Perhaps standing idle in a spot that drew so much foot traffic, with a uniformed officer babysitting him since he was under surveillance, wasn't the wisest idea after his picture had been splashed across the evening and morning news. All day, he'd dealt with much of the same.

His mother had insisted that he be here with the family to help finish setting up and that his attendance during the remainder of the festivities was mandatory. The least he could do since they were here publicly supporting him. It had been a day of walking around feeling like he wore a scarlet letter branded on his forehead.

Shifting his black Cattleman-style hat forward to shield more of his face, he moved on, deciding it best to circulate. Might be the only way to find Amber before she had to go up for the tree lighting. He was sure she'd disappear after she pushed the button.

With the cop following him, Monty strode by a giant, inflatable snow globe, a line for free horse-drawn hay wagon rides around the town center, a decorated drop box for unwrapped presents to donate to local children in need and the largest Christmas light display in the state with more than a hundred individual pieces. Santa, Mrs. Claus and their elves had arrived by firetruck ten minutes ago and were setting up to hear wishes and take photos in the gazebo. A table beside it offered free cookies and hot chocolate—courtesy of the mayor.

This was the biggest Laramie–Bison Ridge Holiday Tree Lighting celebration ever. His mother had transformed downtown into a winter wonderland fit for a postcard.

He looked over at the stage. His mother stood with his father by her side, both smiling as the women's auxiliary choir sang holiday carols. The children's chorus had already performed and the Cowboy Harmony Group, an all-male singing society, was up later.

His mother was in her element, bringing people together, hosting the ceremony, working the crowd, shoring up Powell defenses by trying to garner public support. Managing anything from a staff to a ranch, to finances, to an entire town, came naturally to her. Hard to believe that at one time she'd wanted to be a federal law enforcement officer like her dad and grandfather. She even had a degree in criminal justice. Then Monty's grandfather got sick, and his parents had decided to take over the ranch. Their duty. Their honor.

He stared at his mother, so proud of her.

Being mayor suited Holly Powell, like she was always meant to have the job. In the same way being a rancher suited his father. The Shooting Star had been a part of his family for six generations.

A legacy Monty still didn't want. One of his other brothers was welcome to have it and run the place. Not that being a state trooper fulfilled him. Quite the opposite in fact. Law enforcement was in his DNA on his mother's side, but every time he put on the uniform, he felt like a fraud living the wrong life.

At least it was a life of his own choosing. A man should have the right to that, even if he messed it up.

Moving through the crowd, he spotted Amber. Chance was on one side of her and Logan on the other, his arm slung around her shoulder.

Gritting his teeth, Monty took out his phone and sent another text to her brother.

Chance dug out his cell, looked at the screen and shoved the phone back in his pocket.

He was being deliberately ignored. First by Amber and now her brother.

Giving her space, allowing her to decide when and where they spoke, hadn't worked for months. He was done using that tactic. Ever since he woke up in the hospital yesterday, a clock ticked in his soul, making him feel time was running out. He couldn't afford to wait any longer.

Monty cut through the crowd, weaving around people. "Excuse me," he said several times, drawing closer to the front near the stage, where Amber was headed. He pushed through gently, ignoring the wary glances he drew once people recognized him.

Under normal circumstances, he loved living in a small town where everyone knew each other, but once he was suspected of murder, those friendly neighbors, some of whom had known him since he was a child, had turned on him quicker than a pack of wolves on a wounded stag.

For a second he lost them, but then he homed in on the group standing a bit taller than most. Matt, Holden, Logan and Chance stood out clustered together. He made his way over to them.

Grace was next to Holden, who held Kayce. Matt was singing along with the choir to the baby and making funny hand gestures that had the little one giggling. Hannah was off at the ranch, searching it from top to bottom with Waylon and as many officers as they could muster.

Narrowing his eyes at Chance, he slipped an arm past him and caught Amber's elbow, drawing her gaze. "Hey, can we talk? I really need to speak with you."

Logan flashed him a surly expression that he wanted to

knock off his face, but his brother was only being protective of Amber. How could he not respect him for that?

"Talk about what?" she asked, like she didn't have the foggiest idea.

"Everything. Yesterday morning and the way it looked." Monty glanced around, needing to be discreet, but the crowd made it a challenge. "What's happening to me," he said, in code for the fact he was accused of murder. But they also had other things to discuss. "About us. That thing after your father's funeral." Namely, the hot sex they'd had and how the thought of it, of her, had been torturing him for months until he woke up with a dead body yesterday morning, changing the priority of his concerns. "Just give me a minute."

She didn't look amenable.

Then Logan dared to add, "You don't owe him anything. In fact, it's the other way around."

Fighting hard to ignore his brother, he stayed focused on the person who mattered right now. "Please. I'm begging." Something he never did.

She held up a finger. "One minute."

Cupping her arm, he glared at his brother before he led her to the side of the stage by the stairs she would have to use in a few minutes when his mother called her up.

It wasn't ideal. Brianne and Eddie were standing close. The chief of staff mooned over his mom's assistant. She fed him a piece of a doughnut and brushed crumbs from his mustache. He thanked her with a peck on the lips.

"Would you mind giving us a minute?" he asked them.

Brianne pursed her lips at the intrusion into the space they had occupied first, but Eddie smiled and ushered her off in the direction of the food trucks.

"I'm not sure what you could possibly have to say about

sleeping with Pandora," Amber said, "but I know you didn't kill her."

"But there was nothing between me and Pandora. I've never slept with her. I need you to know that."

"Really? You expect me to believe that?" Amber shook her head, pursing her rosy, bow-shaped lips. "Please don't try to spoon-feed me the same hogwash you used with your family about her not being your type. I know better. Svelte blondes and redheads, who only need you to look their way and smile to spread their legs, is precisely what you like."

He loved the fire in her, even when it burned in his direction hot enough to scorch, especially when it burned in his direction.

"Sleeping with her would've hurt you. That's why she wasn't my type," he said. Her gulp was audible. Maybe he was getting through to her. "I'd never do that to you. Never. I promise."

Those striking hazel eyes that were an intriguing mix of brown, green and amber framed by inky, thick lashes widened, boring into his. Her tongue darted out, wetting her pink lips.

And he was struck by how pretty she was. Not drop-dead gorgeous, but the kind of face that only got better with age. That caught and held his attention. Always had. A head full of dark curly hair that she kept wild and free. A soft brown complexion, dimples when she smiled, and when she did, her face glowed with an intoxicating enthusiasm that made him grin, too.

Averting her gaze, she shoved hair behind her ear with a trembling hand. Was her blood sugar low again? Or was he to blame, making her nervous?

But that look of vulnerability, the complete lack of guile in her, the dichotomy of sweet and sassy, had won him over.

"Please, Amber. I need you." Now more than ever and he wasn't going to get her, not really, not the in the way he wanted until they hashed things out.

"Need me for what?" She stared at her boots. "You've got your family. And Chance found one of the best criminal attorneys for you."

He wanted her friendship. Her support. Her affection. And so much more. "It's difficult to explain."

"Now isn't the right time to talk."

The choir finished their song.

His mother went up to the microphone at the podium. "Everyone, let's show the women's auxiliary choir how much we enjoyed their performance."

The crowd broke into a raucous round of applause.

"I agree," he said to Amber, unable to disregard the stares he garnered, ranging from leery to hateful. "We should speak somewhere quiet. In private." Without the prying eyes of the entire town. "But you've ghosted me for weeks. Months. When I called you last night, you sent it straight to voice mail. How about after you light the tree we go somewhere together?"

She looked around. "I can't. I'm exhausted and not feeling well," she said, still not meeting his eyes. "I need to go home and get some sleep."

"Then when?"

Amber shrugged. "I don't know." The fear in her voice was clear.

She was scared he would hurt her again and she had every reason to be guarded, but he had grown up while she was gone. Made changes. The old him was a bull in a china shop when it came to going after something or someone he wanted.

Maybe she was expecting that from him.

With her, he didn't want to come on too strong and have her thinking it was because of the land. He'd learned from his mistakes and would never mislead her, never let her believe something that wasn't true ever again.

"Listen, I've been a very patient man." Too patient. Too passive.

"Good for you. Would you like a trophy with your name engraved on it?"

He swallowed back a groan.

His mother was talking about Christmas, gearing up to bring Amber onto the stage.

"Your son is a murderer!" a man called out from somewhere in the crowd. "He should be in jail! Why hasn't he been arrested?"

Monty spotted the guy. Barrel-chested. Goatee. Stood out like a sore thumb. But several in the crowd echoed the man's sentiments.

"My son has not been charged with any crime," his mother said. "Every single person is innocent until *proven guilty*. Let's get back to the festivities and the reason we've all gathered here as neighbors, friends, a community that stands strong together, united in any adversity."

Needing to get out of the public eye, he turned back to Amber to pin her down on a place and time. "This is important. Come on. You can't avoid me forever, Tinker."

Her head whipped up at him, her angry eyes locking with his. "That's how you still see me, isn't it? An overly emotional fairy, stuck in never-never land, in love with Peter Pan, destined to only be his sidekick. Well, I have news for you. I have a life waiting for me back in Texas, and I deserve more, I deserve better, than the likes of you, Montgomery Beaumont Powell," she said, knocking the wind from his lungs.

"Now it's time for the moment you've all been waiting

for," his mother announced over the mic. "The lighting of the holiday tree. Amber Sofia Reyes, the daughter of Carlos Reyes, a pillar of the community who recently lost his long battle with cancer, will do the honor. Come on up here, honey."

Amber spun away from him, hurried up the stairs and joined his mother at the podium.

Monty turned, scanning the crowd for the man who had shouted accusations and riled up the crowd, but he was gone.

"Three!" His mother began the countdown as Amber's hand hovered over the big red button, ready to push it. "Two. One."

Amber pressed the button.

The tree lit up in a dazzling blaze of color in tandem with fireworks going off. But over the "oohs" and "aahs" a sharp crack punctured the air. Monty's mind registered the danger as reflex took over.

A gunshot.

"Get down! Gunfire!" Monty was already up the stairs, bolting across the stage.

His father grabbed his mother, rushing her to safety. From the corner of his eye, he spotted the rest of his family, scrambling for cover as the crowd dispersed in screaming chaos.

Pop! Pop!

Monty lunged for Amber and threw her to the ground behind the podium, pinning her underneath him to protect her.

The sound of the shots echoed in his head. He remained in that position, shielding her, waiting, listening.

"Monty, I need to move," she said in a strained breath, like he was crushing her.

He hadn't realized he'd put so much of his weight on her, and rolled off. "Stay down." He peered out from behind the podium, looking to see if the gunman was still out there.

Then it occurred to him that with all the accusations and hateful glares, whoever had opened fire had probably been targeting him. Maybe by trying to protect Amber, he was the one endangering her. He scanned the area to make sure it was safe for her to get up.

Police were fanning out. His family were all okay. Grace, the baby, his brothers, Chance—no one appeared injured. *Thank goodness.*

It looked all clear.

His mother broke free from his father and dashed out from behind a position of safety, rushing toward him. He was about to tell her that he was fine, but she ran right past him and dropped to her knees beside Amber.

"Are you all right?" his mother asked.

"I think so," Amber said, but her voice sounded pained and exhausted to the point of tears.

Monty knelt to help her up, taking her hand.

Wincing, Amber groaned.

"What's wrong?" He checked her visually, making sure she hadn't been hit.

"She needs to go to the hospital," his mother said.

Amber shook her head. "No." She glanced at Monty before looking back at his mother. "I'm fine." She stood, using his assistance. Once she got upright, she doubled over with another grimace and held her stomach.

"Oh, God. Buck! Get the car!" his mother called out. "We'll go to the hospital and get you checked out. Just the two of us, honey, okay?"

"What's wrong?" Monty asked. "Were you hit?" He didn't see any blood. "Where were you shot?"

"I don't feel well." Amber grimaced. "Something's wrong."

"I'll go with you," Monty said.

Her eyes widened in alarm.

"No, no," his mother said, waving him off. "She's sick with a woman thing. We'll go without you. Buck! Where's your father with the car?"

As if she'd willed it, his father sped up in his mother's Hummer and screeched to halt near the curb. Thankfully, as mayor, she had a reserved spot close by.

Pain wrenched across Amber's face, and she squeezed his hand hard. "On second thought, you should come to the hospital."

"Are you sure?" he asked, panic gripping him.

She nodded. "Just in case everything isn't okay." She curled her arm around her stomach. "I'm not sick. I'm pregnant."

"Pregnant?" Monty stared at her in stunned surprise. But they hadn't slept together in months. Was she that far along? Four months?

His mother smacked the back of his head, nearly knocking off his hat. "Get her to the car."

A protective rush seized Monty's chest like a vise. He bent over and, sweeping an arm under Amber's legs, lifted her up from the stage. Then, holding her tight against him, he ran to the waiting vehicle.

Chapter Nine

Saturday, December 7
5:55 p.m.

Lying on a hospital bed in the Laramie emergency room, Amber groaned as another sharp pain sliced through her pelvic area.

Please, let the baby be all right. Please.

Monty was at her side, holding her hand.

"Is it still the same?" Holly asked, pacing back and forth. "Changed any? Worse or better?"

"It's the same. Something is wrong." Tears welled in Amber's eyes, blurring her vision. "I'm scared."

Amber had lost her mother, her father, and even Monty once. Losing this baby, too, would be more than she could be bear.

Monty brushed hair back from her face and kissed her forehead. "It's going to be all right."

"Now is not the time for empty platitudes, son, as well-meaning as they may be. We need a doctor. Right now." Holly yanked aside the curtain that afforded her a modicum of privacy in the ER bay. "I'm going to find one." She closed it and padded off.

"My mom is about to get scary and make a scene," Monty said.

Amber expected no less from Holly Powell. The woman was a force to be reckoned with. "She has my blessing. How long have we been waiting?"

He glanced at his watch. "Twenty minutes." He peered down at her and flashed a sad smile. "Don't worry, she's going to get someone in here lickety-split." His tone was off somehow. He sounded distant, filtered.

She couldn't quite put it into words, but she didn't like it. "Monty, I want you to be here with me through this, but you're acting weird. It's making it worse."

He frowned. "Do you want me to leave?"

"No." Another pain lanced her and she hissed, breathing through it.

He kissed the back of her hand. "Is there anything I can do?" he asked, tightening his grip on her.

"I'm scared, terrified I might lose this baby. I need *you*. To act normal. To sound like you."

"I'm sorry." His brow furrowed, his face taking on the expression he got when he was thinking hard, trying to work out a problem, solve some puzzle.

"What are you thinking?" she asked. He hadn't uttered a word about the baby or the fact that she'd hidden it. Hadn't asked her a single question. "I need you to be honest." For once. "Please."

He hesitated, staring at her, looking completely lost.

"If you're angry I didn't tell you or disappointed that I'm pregnant, I'd understand." She stared down at her belly bump.

Once she discovered she was pregnant and got over the initial surprise, there had never been any doubt in her mind that she would keep this child. Raise it. Cherish it. She'd loved Monty since she was twelve, dreamed of marrying him, but after he'd conspired with her father to trick her into marriage so the Powells could have the land they always coveted, she hated him in equal measure. But if she were to ever have a child, it might as well be Monty's. That didn't mean he wanted this baby.

"I'm not angry. I'm not disappointed." He hesitated again.

"Then what is it? What aren't you saying? What are you thinking?" She squeezed his hand so hard he probably thought she wanted to break it. "You need to tell me the truth. Or I'll imagine the worst."

"I'm freaking out. Okay? I know that's not what you want to hear. It sure isn't what you need. Give me gunfire and deranged criminals and I'm fine. Give me fifteen thousand cattle to brand and herd and I'm great. But I woke up drugged with Pandora dead on the floor yesterday. I came this close to getting arrested. We were shot at tonight. Now I find out that I'm going to be a father. Possibly. Because I don't know what's happening with you, if the baby, my baby, *our baby*, is all right. I'm worried I hurt the two of you when I was trying to get you down behind some cover. Maybe I hit your stomach by accident." He scrubbed a hand over his face. "So I've been trying to be quiet, to be supportive, to give you what you need, not that I know what that is, and not make this about me when it has to be all about you and…" He pressed a tentative hand to her belly. "Why didn't you tell me?"

"You know why." She looked away from him and at the pale yellow curtain.

Fluorescent bulbs flickered overhead. The smell of antiseptic made her nausea flare.

"My daughter-in-law needs to be seen right this second!" Holly yelled at someone in the hall. "I know every single person sitting on the board of directors at this hospital. If a doctor isn't in bay four in the next two minutes, examining her and making sure that my unborn grandchild is okay, after we were just shot at, I'm going to start making some unpleasant phone calls."

Monty sighed. "You should've told me about the baby," he said, his tone gentle, his voice soft. "From the way my mom acted on the stage, she already knew. Didn't you think I had a right to know, too?"

"I was going to tell you. And your mom only found out at the house yesterday."

"I get that you needed time and space." He kept using that tone of gentle compassion that made her want to dissolve into a puddle of emotion. "But I've been calling, texting, leaving notes on your front door, and you've been ghosting me for four months, using Chance as an intermediary. When were you going to tell me?"

She couldn't trust the sweet things he said. Couldn't trust his affection. Most importantly, she couldn't trust herself around him. "When the time was right."

The curtain was drawn aside. Holly stood there, letting someone pass her.

A man wearing green scrubs and a white lab coat entered the bay. He had light brown hair that was receding. Busy chewing, he held a sandwich in one hand and raised a finger from the other, indicating he needed a moment. "Sorry for the delay," he said around the food in his mouth. "The ER doctor heard the mayor's frustration and was afraid to examine you. Dr. Plinsky thought it best for an expert to come down. I'm Dr. Kevin. Like to keep it informal. I'm the head of OB-GYN."

Amber glanced at the partially eaten sandwich in his hand. "Do you need to finish eating?"

With a shake of his head, Dr. Kevin stuffed the rest of the food in his mouth and went to the sink to wash his hands. "I just finished delivering two babies back-to-back. This was my first chance to grab a bite to eat." He dried his hands, pulled on latex gloves and turned to her. "What seems to be the problem, Mrs. Powell?"

Her cheeks were suddenly on fire. "We're not married. I'm Amber Reyes."

"Oh, I see. I must've misunderstood. Everyone else can step outside and go to the waiting room if you'd like."

"I'm staying," Monty said.

Holly nodded. "Me, too."

The doctor frowned. "That's up to Ms. Reyes to decide, sir, and Mayor. We're sticklers about privacy here at the hospital. Amber, it's important that you feel free to speak openly during the examination. Clearing the bay of everyone else might be in the best interest of your health and that of your baby."

Now that Monty knew about the baby and was here beside her, she didn't want him to leave. "No, no." She shook her head. "It's okay." She tightened her grip on Monty. "If they stay, it'll save me the hassle of updating them on everything."

They might as well hear it firsthand.

"I'm afraid only one of you can stay," the doctor said.

Amber looked at Monty.

The corner of his mouth hitched in a small grin. "I'm not going anywhere."

"Mayor." Dr. Kevin turned to Holly. "You can step out to the waiting room." He drew the curtain closed. "Tell me what's going on, Amber."

"I've been having sharp pains, some dull ones, too, right around my pelvic area and belly button. At times it feels like stabbing and other moments like a tight pull."

Dr. Kevin put a blood pressure cuff on her and started the machine. "How long has this been going on?"

"There was a shooting at the tree lighting ceremony," Monty said. "I knocked her to the ground, trying to protect her, and then she was in pain." The guilt in his voice tugged at her heart.

"It actually started yesterday. I got lightheaded at the house. The room spun. And I felt a new twinge, a sort of pulling, in the lower part of my belly here." She showed him the location of the pain. "As the day wore on, it's gotten worse and I've still been a bit dizzy. I thought it was low blood sugar. I nibbled on something, but the twinge turned into a slight stabbing. Then when I fell—"

"When I knocked you down." His voice rumbled with something that sounded like fear.

"When Monty saved me from getting shot, I protected my belly and fell on my back. But the stabbing pain has gotten bad. So has the pulling sensation. Feels like I'm having contractions."

It was far too soon for that. The baby didn't have a chance of survival outside the womb until she was at least six months.

Amber rubbed her belly. *You have to be all right, peanut.*

She wanted this child more than anything. Not for a second had it been unwelcome. She would never think of this baby as a mistake even if loving its father might have been. The conception had been completely unplanned, but a blessing in disguise. Endometriosis and surgery for it had caused scarring that blocked one of her fallopian tubes. Doctors had told her it might be extremely difficult if not next to impossible to conceive when she was ready.

In a way, the child growing inside her was really a miracle.

"Your blood pressure is elevated." Dr. Kevin removed the cuff from her arm. "Along with your heart rate. But you've just been through something stressful. How far along are you?"

"Seventeen weeks, four days."

"Any vaginal bleeding?" the doctor asked.

"No," she said, thankful for that. "I checked again when we got to the ER."

"Mind if I take a look?" He indicated her belly.

"Please do."

Dr. Kevin lifted her oversize sweater and started prodding her stomach, working clockwise.

"You've gotten so big," Monty said. "That's why you wouldn't see me."

"I honestly didn't think you'd notice," she said. "Figured you'd assume I was simply getting fatter."

"You're not fat. You're voluptuous." He flashed her a warm smile. "I like your curves."

She twisted her mouth, swallowing the word *liar*.

"It's true." Monty leaned over and brought his lips close to her ear. "Believe it or not, a man likes a woman with some meat on her bones," he whispered. "I didn't become attracted to you until you filled out in all the right places. I remember the day I first noticed. We went to the town's spring dance. You wore that skimpy sundress that revealed far too much leg and cleavage. With straps so thin I was tempted to pluck them with a finger to see if they'd snap. And that dress had bright red, plump cherries all over it. Fitted like a second skin. You didn't even wear a bra underneath. Teetered on indecent." He purred in her ear, sending tingles dancing over her skin. "Paired it with cowboy boots and a straw hat. You looked ripe enough to eat, even though you were jailbait," he drawled, his voice dipping low, making her toes curl. "I remember like it was yesterday."

This time her cheeks heated for a different reason. She'd

worn it just for him. Her mother had called the dress *scandalous* and *inappropriate*, worried it would set tongues wagging in the small town, and forbade her going to the dance with it on. But her father had intervened, having the final word. He'd even sent Chance on ahead dreadfully early and called Buck, asking him if Monty could give her a ride.

She had been on cloud nine, squealing her thanks to her dad, hugging him tight, so excited to ride alone with Monty Powell in his truck. Until he showed up. Along with all his brothers—the lost boys. The guys whooped and whistled. Except for Monty. He was stone-faced, not cracking a smile, eyes hidden behind dark sunglasses, not uttering a word about the dress, barely giving her a second glance.

"Nice boots, Tinker," was all Monty had said.

And only Logan wanted to dance with her.

A stab of pain had her gripping her lower belly.

Concern etched Monty's face. He pressed a palm to her cheek, and she couldn't help but turn into his touch. What she wouldn't have given for a hug.

"Tell me, Amber, have you had much to eat or drink today?" Dr. Kevin pulled her sweater down, covering her belly.

"Crackers. A little applesauce. Lots of ginger ale. Soup for lunch."

Dr. Kevin nodded as though he was thinking. His face was inscrutable. "I have good news and bad news."

Fear jolted through her. She exchanged a worried glance with Monty.

She braced for the worst and Monty moved his palm from her cheek to grip her shoulder as if to steady her.

Dr. Kevin peeled off his gloves and tossed them in the trash. "The good news is I think it's only dehydration and the usual discomfort that comes as your uterus grows and stretches the supporting ligaments."

A breath of relief punched from her lips. Her little peanut was going to be okay. Monty smiled down at her and kissed the top of her head.

"Thank goodness," Holly said from the other side of the curtain.

Dr. Kevin raised an eyebrow. "I can't believe she's still here," he whispered.

"That's because you don't know my mother."

"Dehydration can be problematic any time, but it's especially concerning during pregnancy," the doctor said. "Not only do you need more water than usual, but your baby needs water, too. Not staying properly hydrated can lead to serious complications. Neural tube defects. Low amniotic fluid. Premature labor. Poor production of breast milk. But even something as mild as dizziness can be an issue if you were to faint."

The number of things that could go wrong was staggering. She should have known better. Three different baby books were on her nightstand, and she had read through two of them. She'd found an OB-GYN in Cheyenne to keep it quiet, and was taking prenatal vitamins, going on long walks for exercise, and had cut out fatty foods and desserts. Well, most desserts. When she could tolerate them, she was guilty of indulging.

"What's the bad news?" Holly asked from the hall.

Dr. Kevin shook his head and mouthed, *unbelievable.* "The bad news is you need to carry a water bottle around and constantly sip on it. That means you're going to run to the bathroom a lot. Especially as the baby gets bigger and presses down on your bladder."

A small price to pay for a healthy child. "Okay. I'll buy one tomorrow." She would do whatever was necessary.

"No need, honey," Holly said. "I'm texting Buck now to go get one before the store closes. Thirty-two ounces with time markers to help you remember."

Dr. Kevin blew out a breath. "The time markers are a good idea to help you remember," he said with a thread of annoyance. "I also want you to try to eat more. Get in some protein, plenty of veggies and fruit. If you don't, a baby will suck its mother dry of nutrients in order to survive."

He made an unborn child sound like a vampire.

"Does she need to be on bed rest?" Monty asked.

"No. I don't see any reason for that. But stress should be kept to an absolute minimum. I would like to take a look at the baby because of your fall. To be certain everything is okay and that there's no placenta abruption. I'll get you started on an IV to replenish your system. Then we can do an ultrasound, if you'd like."

"Yes," she and Monty said in unison.

The doctor got to work setting up the IV drip.

She met Monty's gaze and swore more than affection was reflected in his eyes.

He would finally get to see the baby growing inside her. A joy she had denied him by not telling him.

All she wanted was to protect herself and this child, but maybe she had done more harm than good by giving him the cold shoulder. No matter what happened between them, they were going to be parents, and she wanted him to start bonding with and loving this baby as soon as possible.

But she couldn't help but wonder whether a part of him might resent her for getting pregnant.

"This should help you start to feel better quickly, in a

manner of minutes. I'll go get the ultrasound machine." Dr. Kevin left.

In the hall, Holly said to the doctor, "I have some questions for you." Her voice faded as she followed him away.

"I need to ask you something," she said, not quite sure how to put the words together. Typical questions like if he wanted to be a father, to have a baby with her, wouldn't work.

The man was a paradox. Half of him driven by duty and honor. In that regard, he'd give the right answers to conventional questions. Declare he was going to marry her. Do right by the child. But the other half of him was compelled to act in the opposite manner of what was expected of him.

If he felt forced, he'd only be miserable.

She wanted this child to be a source of happiness for both its parents. Not one of obligation. And certainly not a convenient way for the Powells to get their hands on the Reyes land.

"Ask me anything," he said, his voice soft, his expression open, his eyes warm.

"Why did you sleep me with after the funeral? Don't worry, you can be honest. You won't hurt my feelings." Not any more than he already had.

He looked taken aback. "Nature, I guess."

Her throat went tight, and she cursed how wrong she was about the depths to which he was capable of wounding her. The nonchalance of his three-word response broke her heart.

This was torture. Loving someone, desperate to have him love her back and want the life she desired when he didn't.

"Nature?" she asked. Like she had been a mare in heat and him a stallion, following instinct.

Monty shrugged. "Yeah. What are you getting at? If this is about the land, it had nothing to do with that."

"Because it was nature." Sounded so much better. Frustration welled. She shook her head and clenched her hands. "Just say it. You were only comforting me that night." She struggled to hold back tears. "It was pity sex. Yes, you do want the land, for your family, but you didn't sign up for a kid." The terms of the trust were that the marriage had to last two years, no children required. Then he could bail. "You didn't want to be tied to me for the rest of your life. I know you regret sleeping with me."

"What?" A low chuckle rolled from him. "That's not true."

"Stop lying to me. I heard you at the house. You specifically used the words *mistake* and *regret* in the context of having sex with me." *In front of everyone!*

The wound in her heart opened anew at the same time another pang jabbed her pelvis, but the intensity was less than earlier.

Monty sat on the edge of the bed, pressed a palm to her cheek and cupped her jaw, drawing her gaze to his. "I never got to finish what was on my mind because someone interrupted me. I did make a mistake with you. A big one. I regret ever laying a finger on you without telling you the truth first. It was one thing to take you out and spend time with you, but quite another to get intimate. I should've been honest before we made love much less before I proposed. I'm sorry I hurt you. I ruined everything. Blew up the life we could've had." He heaved a breath. "You've got a right to believe what you want. Except for one thing. I didn't sleep with you after your father's funeral out of pity."

She squeezed her eyes shut to keep tears from falling. "Then you did it because of his will." She hated that land and the river on it.

"I am not a manipulator."

"Oh, no?" Tightness pulled at her belly. Wincing, she rubbed the bump. "Could've fooled me. Ten years ago, you made me believe that you loved me. That you wanted to marry me."

"Made you believe?" he asked. "Or let you?"

She glared at him. "Are you trying to spin this back onto me somehow?"

"It takes two, sweetie. You have some culpability in what happened. Not much. Maybe the size of a mustard seed while I'm responsible for the bushel, but it's there."

Amber rolled her eyes. "You misled me. How is that my fault?"

"Did I ever tell you I loved you?"

She thought about it and squirmed. "Well, no."

"Did you ever ask yourself, or me, why would a man who's never said those words propose to you?"

She'd gotten so caught up in the butterflies and the romance and the fairy tale she'd dreamed of finally coming true that she didn't want to ask. "But you made me feel like you loved me."

"I've always had deep feelings for you." He brushed her jaw with his knuckles. "I only hid it well."

"Why? If that's true, why would you hide how you felt?"

He took off his hat and sat it on a table, which meant this was going to get serious. Real.

"Two reasons," he said. "First, Logan was in love with you. I was the eldest. The one who gave up toys, clothes, the extra dessert, who took tasks that the younger ones didn't want to do. If there was something we both wanted, I let whichever brother who desired it have it. No way, no how, was I going to flirt with you or date you and rub his nose in it. No, sirree. That might not make sense to you because you're the youngest and a girl, the apple of Carlos Reyes's eye, and always got everything you wanted."

Except for you.

"It makes sense, in a weird way," she said grudgingly. "What's the second reason?"

"That one's personal."

The only thing stopping her from screaming her frustration was this baby. Her lungs burned as she inhaled. "Hiding things from me is how you ruined everything before. I need the truth."

"This is true." He leaned in, gently gripping her chin between his thumb and forefinger. "Back then, when we were going out, the more time we spent alone, talking, having fun, *having sex*, taking long drives with no destination and enjoying the journey together, the more I felt for you until I loved you, so deeply. More than anything. But then I lost you."

She dropped her head back on the pillow, wanting to believe him. But how could she? Only someone glutton for punishment would. "Fool me once shame on you. Fool me twice shame on me."

Monty sighed. "After your father's funeral, I found you in the barn, brushing his horse." He put a palm on her wrist and leaned in close, sending a rush of warmth spreading through her chest. "I hugged you and you started crying. I was wiping away your tears, feeling sorry for your loss."

So it was *pity*. The man was an incorrigible liar.

"But…" His voice trailed off. "This is going to sound selfish—I felt more sorry for myself because I'd let you go and didn't run after you. I've regretted it every day, every single second, of these past ten years. When we were in the barn, alone, I held you and looked down into your face and I wanted you. The way a man wants a woman. *Nature.* Wanted to kiss you, to hold you, to be inside you again," he said, and her stomach swooped.

She swallowed, blinking through a shimmer of tears. Why was he doing this? Saying everything she wanted to hear?

Reeling her in when she was vulnerable? She didn't know if she could go down this path again. It had taken years of therapy to recover from the betrayal. She wanted to trust the father of her child, the man she desperately loved, but she didn't want to get hurt again.

Meeting his gaze, she was thunderstruck by what she saw in his eyes. Regret. Anguish. Desire.

"Amber." He cupped her face with his hands. "That night I needed to show you what you meant to me and how much I still love you."

And then he kissed her.

She squeezed her thighs together to ease the ache of longing that spread in an instant.

His lips were hot and firm and certain. A mix of fire and hunger. He kissed her like he was starving. Drinking her in with each stroke of his tongue that plunged deeper, sliding against hers in the sweetest heat, melting her to pieces.

Chapter Ten

This was his woman. His future wife. The mother of his unborn child. And Monty let her know it the only way he could. With this kiss, he told her all the things he couldn't say because she wouldn't believe him. All the things he wanted—to devour her, to take her to his bed, to have her body beneath his. To lose himself in her. To hear her cry out his name.

To hold her. To love her.

To have a second chance.

A chance to get it right.

The sound of the curtain being drawn had them jerking apart.

The doctor cleared his throat as he wheeled the ultrasound machine into the bay. Based on the wide grin on his mother's face, she had also seen them.

He looked down at Amber and swallowed, his mouth going dry again. In her eyes, he saw lust and desire and possibly the spark of forgiveness. Everything he'd hoped to see.

Hell, that kiss should have taken away some of her doubts. The chemistry they had—he'd never experienced anything like it. And right then, he'd never wanted anything so much in his life as he wanted to kiss her again.

"How are you feeling?" Dr. Kevin closed the curtain in Holly's face. "Any better?"

"Much better actually. The twinges and pangs are less frequent. The intensity decreased, too."

"Good. That's exactly what I was hoping to hear. Are we ready to do an ultrasound?"

She nodded.

"Yes," Monty said. He needed to make sure Amber and the baby were okay.

The doctor turned on the machine and washed his hands again.

"I'm sorry you missed the first one," she said, looking up at him. "You had a right to be there. It's your baby, too."

"It's okay." He understood why she'd kept the truth from him. "When did you do it?"

"The doctor recommended at seven weeks. The baby is due May sixteenth."

A May baby. "Did you go alone?"

"Chance came with me."

Of course, her brother had the whole time. It explained why he had agreed to act as a go-between, not letting him in the house, but passing on his messages. Normally, Chance didn't like to get involved in other people's affairs. Not that Monty could be angry with him for supporting his sister. She had needed someone to be there for her when she probably worried she'd have to contend with the full force of the Powell clan.

"Well, I'm here now." He took her hand in his. From here on out, they were going to do this together. He couldn't wait to see his baby for the first time.

Dr. Kevin put on gloves. "Pull your sweater up for me and lower your waistband. Sorry, the gel is going to be cold."

As Amber adjusted her clothes, Monty noticed her hands trembling slightly. "Are you hungry?"

"Yeah. I find it easier to eat a little bit at a time."

"Craving anything?" he asked, knowing his mother was still eavesdropping.

"This IV must be doing the trick because I'm craving a hamburger smothered in ketchup. And ice cream. A chocolate milkshake. But I know I shouldn't have it."

Dr. Kevin picked up the gel. "Sounds like you haven't been eating much lately. A burger is perfect. Full of protein, iron, zinc and several B vitamins. And there is nothing wrong with a milkshake as long as you're not drinking one every day. You and the baby both need the calcium."

Monty leaned in close to her ear. "How much do you want to bet that a burger and chocolate shake will be waiting for you once you're done here?" He gestured to the curtain with his head.

She smiled bright and warm, full of pure joy, and his heart danced in his chest as he grinned back at her.

The doctor moved the sweater higher and her waistband even lower.

Monty hadn't been lying about loving her figure. Full curves in all the right places that he couldn't get enough of. He wondered what she would look like with her belly big and round, heavy with his child and her breasts too full for his hands. Even sexier was his guess.

He stroked her hair, running his fingers through the lustrous, soft strands.

Dr. Kevin squirted goo on her abdomen. Amber gasped.

"Sorry, I know it's cold," he said.

"It's all right. You did warn me. I just hadn't been prepared for how cold. The gel my OB uses is warm."

"Who's your doctor?"

"Jennie Jankowski."

"Out in Cheyenne?" Dr. Kevin asked, and Amber nodded. "She's great, but if you're planning to have this baby around here, you should find someone local. Otherwise, although you may develop a good, trusting relationship with Jennie, she probably won't be the one to deliver the baby. Having a stranger help you bring your child into the world can be disconcerting."

"I guess I'm not sure where I'll be when this peanut is born."

She wasn't thinking of going back to Texas, was she?

Not pregnant with his kid and alone.

The doctor pressed the probe to her belly and moved it around while staring at the screen until a weird throbbing noise echoed in the room as a grainy image flickered on the screen.

"Looks good so far," Dr. Kevin said. "Nice, strong heartbeat, this one. No worries there."

"Is it supposed to be that fast?" Monty wondered.

"One hundred forty-five beats per minute is perfectly normal." The doctor grinned. "Should be almost twice the mother's heart rate."

"Is everything else okay?" Amber asked.

Dr. Kevin moved the probe around her belly, staring at the screen. "There's the head, the arms, legs," he said.

It looked like a baby. Not just some peanut-shaped blob the way he'd expected.

A perfectly shaped, tiny hand came into view. Monty leaned in toward the screen, his chest coming close to Amber's head. If his mother peered in now to catch a glimpse of the scene, she might naturally assume there was no question this would work out, the two of them as a happy couple, and for a wild, hopeful moment he wished with all his heart it would be that easy.

Even though her father had thought his last legal wishes would bring them together, and it had ten years ago, it kept them apart now.

"Everything looks normal. Very healthy. I'm not seeing any issues with the placenta," Dr. Kevin said, and Monty heard his mother exhale in relief. "Your baby is a little over five and a half inches long and almost seven ounces. Hey, fun fact, your baby's fingerprints are now formed."

Amber grinned from ear to ear, and Monty lit up. They were going to have a baby. The specifics still had to be worked out, but they were a family. Despite everything else going on, this was something to be celebrated.

"Would you like to know the baby's gender?"

Tipping her head back, she smiled at him and shrugged. "I don't know. This could be a once-in-a-lifetime surprise. Maybe we should wait. What do you think?"

He was chomping at the bit to know, but it was Amber's decision. "Whatever you want to do, that's what I want. A once-in-a-lifetime surprise sounds nice."

"You're disappointed," she said. "I can hear it in your voice. You want to know."

"This isn't about me. I'm happy to wait."

"Be honest. Please." She studied his face. "What do you want?"

This was a test. In his gut, he knew it. He had to be honest in all things. "Whether it's a boy or girl doesn't matter. Either way, I'll be thrilled, but I do want to know. I just don't want to spoil a surprise for you. Ruin it for you."

"This baby is healthy. As long as he or she stays that way, nothing is ruined." She looked at the doctor. "Tell us."

Dr. Kevin moved the probe again, making some adjustments. "Sure you want to know? You can always wait for a later appointment."

"I'm sure. We're together now. I don't know about the next ultrasound," she said, and something in his chest pinched.

She still doubted him. Much more than he thought.

The doctor pointed to the screen. "There you go. Can you see the package?"

"Do you mean…" Excitement competed with anticipation, leaving him speechless. He waited for confirmation.

Dr. Kevin nodded.

Monty's eyes watered. "A boy." His voice was choked. "Amber, we're going to have a son."

Her bottom lip trembled and tears welled in her eyes. "A son," she echoed, in amazement or disbelief, or perhaps a bit of both. Pressing her hands to her chest, she stared at the monitor before turning back to him. She sent him a tremulous smile.

Monty didn't hesitate to bend over and give her a gentle kiss on her lips.

"Buck, it's a boy!" his mother squealed. She must've called his father on the phone.

Monty pulled away, beaming at Amber, and they both laughed.

The doctor raised his eyebrows. "I forgot she was there," he whispered.

Staring deep into her eyes, Monty wished he could name all the emotions flooding his heart. He looked back at the screen, awestruck. The baby was so tiny. So fragile.

And someone had fired a gun several times, endangering Amber and his little one.

He needed to figure out what was going on and fast. It was the only way to keep them safe.

"Would you like me to print a picture?" Dr. Kevin asked.

"Yes," they said in unison.

"One for each of us," Amber clarified. "We're not together."

Dr. Kevin's smile deflated right along with Monty's hope. He had more work to do than he realized. Regret siphoned some of his elation, but he hid it well, not wanting to dampen Amber's spirits.

"Please print an extra one for me," his mother called out.

The doctor handed one to each of them along with some paper towels for Amber. "The IV should be finished in another fifteen to twenty minutes. I'll have Dr. Plinsky get your discharge paperwork ready for you."

"Thank you." Amber wiped the gel from her belly. "We appreciate you rushing through your late dinner."

"I'm happy to assuage your worries. Be sure to eat, drink lots of water and get plenty of rest."

"I will."

Smiling, the doctor handed his mother an ultrasound picture on the way out.

Monty took the paper towels from Amber and tossed them in the trash. "Go to the waiting room, Mom." His tone brooked no argument. "I'm serious."

"I'm going," she said, with a smile and a nod. "We got you a burger and milkshake, honey. Do you want me to bring it to you?"

"Thank you," Amber said. "But I'll wait to eat on the way home."

"Okay. If you change your mind, text me." His mom waved and shut the curtain.

Monty sat back down on the bed next to her. "I want us to be together," he said, plainly.

Cringing, she squeezed her eyes shut. "Don't. Please don't." She huffed a breath. "Monty, don't do this—talk about marriage. I should've known better. You can't just be happy that the baby is healthy. That's it's going to be a boy. Can you? You're never satisfied with halfway. You always want it all. This is why I've dreaded telling you, because I knew you'd go caveman on me when I can't trust a single word that comes out of your lying mouth."

"I love you, Amber Reyes."

Her wary gaze flashed up to him and she looked as though she was holding her breath.

His timing was wrong. No, it sucked. But he'd put it out there and now he had to double down. "Did you hear me? I've never said that before to anyone."

"I heard you." Her voice was soft, her tone skeptical. "Want a trophy for that, too, *Peter Pan*?"

Frustration bubbled in Monty's gut. Enough was enough. "Listen, woman, this stops right here. You're not Tinker Bell. I'm not Peter Pan and I'm not some crude Neanderthal from the Stone Age either." He was a cowboy who'd finally gotten his head screwed on straight. "This isn't a fairy tale. It's messy. It's ugly. People make mistakes. Goodness knows I've made a lot of them. But this is also beautiful. And it's real. This is us, for better or for worse. We're going to have a baby. That makes us family. For life. Whether we get married or not. But I *want* to marry you. And not out of duty or honor or to get the land."

"Then why? Why do you love me? Why do you want to marry me?"

He had an answer at the ready because he'd spent many a night, tossing and turning, pondering the same thing. "I think of my life in terms of B.A.R. and A.A.R. Before Amber Reyes and after Amber Reyes. Before we got together, I was fine. Thought I was, anyway, content with my life just as it was. After you left, there was a gaping hole. Like a sucking chest wound. I became painfully aware that I was lonely. Miserable, if I'm being honest."

Raw emotion gleamed in her eyes, but she still looked dubious.

Silence stretched between them.

Taking a breath, he resolved to try harder. "It was kind of like watching the *Wizard of Oz*. Everything is black-and-white and looks pretty good until it changes to Technicolor. That's what you are for me. Every color of the spectrum in high definition, brightening and enriching my life. I'd be lying if I said I tried to move on. I didn't even bother. In my gut, I knew it'd be futile. I've just been existing. Passing time. Waiting for you. Now you're back." He put a hand to her belly. "Pregnant with my son. I need you, sweetheart. I'm miserable, sick down in my soul, without you."

Tears streamed from her eyes and her bottom lip trembled once more. "Before my father made the land become an issue and you asked me out, you claim you had feelings for me."

He nodded. "I did. Took a while for me to realize it was more than lust. It was in the way I tried to look after you. Protect you. Help you with anything that you needed. Just wanting to be near you. It was coming from a place of me loving you for years." All along. Way before their parents meddled.

"Then what's the second reason, besides Logan, why you never acted on those feelings? No more secrets. No hiding anything from me."

For her to believe, he was going to have to open up and lay himself bare. He got to his feet and peeked through the curtain into the hall, checking to make sure his mother was gone.

Satisfied she wasn't lurking within earshot, he sat back down beside Amber.

He wasn't proud of his reason, which wasn't anything noble, and that was why he classified it as personal.

Lowering his head, he pinched the bridge of his nose. "Since I was little, I was told who I was and what I was going to be. Buck and Holly Powell's eldest. Born to be a rancher. Destined to carry on the legacy. I'm sure you've noticed I don't like to be told what to do."

"I have. Kind of hard not to."

He took her hand. "I had an eye for you something fierce since you wore that cherry sundress, but Logan's interest forced me to keep my cool and my distance, like I said. But one day I overheard our parents talking about how you fancied me and how good we'd be together. How wonderful it would be if we got married and had kids. The Reyes and Powell land becoming one since neither you nor Chance wanted to be ranchers. They had my whole life mapped out for me. Choosing my vocation, choosing my wife. Then I found myself pushing against that, too. *Real hard.*" From an early age, since he could ride a horse, he'd decided for himself who he was going to be. What he was going to do. "I set my mind against being with you. Told myself all sorts of lies, like you were too young, sex with you would be boring." His eyes flew up and he stared at her, horrified to see hurt in her gaze. "Idiotic nonsense I tried to believe to stay away from you. Making love with you is perfect. Sometimes sweet and slow. Sometimes dirty, hot and wild." She brought him such pleasure, opening herself, holding nothing back, and he endeavored to do likewise. "I dream about it. A lot. Anyway, I couldn't see past those two reasons—

Logan's feelings and being told I should be with you—until we were actually forced together. Sounds foolish, I know."

"It doesn't." She whisked the tears from her eyes. "Simply sounds like you."

Drawing in a breath of relief, he was glad she knew him so well. "You believe me?"

"I want to. Really, I do. More than you know. But…" She shook her head. "How can I?"

The land. The river. *The trust.*

Pain lodged in his chest. He would do anything to reassure her. "I can prove it to you. In less than thirty days, if we're not married, the land will go to Pandora's next of kin. Her mother. We let it happen. Then when you believe in my feelings, when you're ready to say yes, I'll propose again. Whether that's in two months, two years, or twenty."

Her mouth fell open, and she reeled back. "You can't be serious. You wouldn't give up everything for me. You love that land. And it means so much to your family. It would devastate your parents."

The land he'd grown up on was like gravity for him. Grounding him. Keeping him steady. Calling him always. Being out there on horseback, wrangling cattle, gave him a sense of satisfaction, of purpose, like nothing else ever had. "I love my parents. I love that ranch. But I love you more. You and this baby are everything to me. All that matters."

Staring at him, she looked stunned. "They'd never allow it. Buck and Holly would coerce and push and plead until we got married just to keep that land from going to Fiona and you know it."

A valid point. Buck and Holly were resourceful. Persuasive, too.

An idea came to him. His parents would hate him for it, but it might be the only solution. "Once we figure out what's going on and clear my name of any suspicion of murder, we leave town together. Go to Texas. Without telling anyone anything. I mean no one. Not even Chance." If word got out, they'd be in a pressure cooker. "Simply pack our bags and leave one night. And if you think that they'd follow us and harass us, then we go somewhere else until the deadline passes and it's too late."

"Monty." Amber stiffened. "I can't ask you to make that kind of sacrifice."

"You didn't ask. I need to do this to prove to you this is real and how much I love you."

"They'll never understand. They'll never forgive us. Forgive me."

He gave her a sad smile. "Yes, they will."

She shook her head slowly, unconvinced.

"Once the dust settles, after they've sold the cattle, and thousands of acres of our land since they won't need it, they will forgive us. Because of the baby you're carrying." He rubbed her belly. "They'll want to see him. They can only do that if they're nice to both of us." Might be asking a bit much. "At least civil. I won't have them giving you the stink eye or saying a cross word about you." They could curse his name if it made them feel any better.

She tore her gaze from him. Wringing her hands, she considered it.

"Give me this chance and I won't let you down." He cupped her face. "Not ever again. Take this leap with me. What do you say?"

Her swallow was audible, her cheeks going rosy, her eyes luminous. "Yes."

"Yes?"

She nodded. "I love you. I want us to be family."

Growling with soul-deep satisfaction and relief, he pulled

her close and crushed his mouth to hers. He closed his eyes and reveled in the kiss, in the sultry jasmine scent of her, in the feel of her rounded baby bump pressed against his abdomen. Luxuriated in the moment. This was bliss—the quiet connection to the one woman who'd always been meant for him.

His heart drummed a frenzied rhythm against his ribs. Every muscle in his body went taut, vibrating with anticipation, straining with need so strong he ached down to his bones.

But thoughts of Pandora and the shots fired sprang to mind. He clung tighter to Amber, unable to fight the sense of helplessness rolling through him. In the pit of his stomach, he felt this might be the calm before the storm.

Chapter Eleven

Saturday, December 7
8:08 p.m.

The Shooting Star Ranch had been turned upside down and inside out and Waylon had nothing to show for it. He climbed behind the steering wheel of his truck. Hannah jumped into the passenger seat. They'd driven over together since they had to go back to the station to fill out paperwork.

He pulled out, leading the caravan of LPD cops off the ranch.

"That was a complete waste of time," Hannah said.

The hint of smugness in her tone irked him. "Maybe the flip phone the state police found in his locker and delivered to us will have something on it."

"And maybe it's just a spare phone." Hannah shook her head. "The guys didn't have to leave such a mess back there. Looks like a tornado ripped through every residence."

"I'm sure they have people to clean things up. Right? Staff? Servants?"

"No, they don't. Not in the way you mean."

He scoffed. "You expect me to believe that Holly Powell is scrubbing toilets?" he asked with a chuckle.

"There was a time when she did, but Buck and Holly have

help now that they're older. Monty is going to have to clean his own cottage."

"Boo-hoo. Cry me a river."

She shifted toward him. "What about Holden and Grace? They'll have to clean their place, too, since you insisted on executing the full scope of the warrant. She's eight, almost nine months pregnant and they have a fourteen-month-old baby."

"Put your violin away, Delaney. The lawful search was a part of the job, and the mess came with the territory. You were standing right next to me when I issued the orders. I didn't tell anyone to get nasty about it." Though he did feel bad for Grace, who was pregnant and had a toddler to contend with, and Holden, whom he liked.

Holden lacked pretense and didn't have the same egotistical swagger as Monty.

"True, but you did seem to pick every available officer with a grudge against the Powells," she said. "You knew what was going to happen."

"I think they'll survive." He switched the radio on low. "You didn't happen to give them a heads-up about the search, did you?" He quirked an eyebrow at her.

"Monty was found with a dead body. A reasonable, rational expectation would be for a search warrant to be executed. Do you really think they needed me to do the math, two plus two equals four? Simple enough without my help."

Popping a piece of gum in his mouth, he restrained a chuckle at her continued avoidance of answering his questions regarding that family. "Do you want to know what I think?"

"Of course, I do, partner."

Sarcasm duly noted. "I think you told them that the search was going to happen before they gave you the heave-ho from the family meeting yesterday." He would've moved the timeline up if he'd had the necessary personnel available.

Delaney had extended the courtesy of giving him a heads-up about the meeting, which he appreciated, but he wasn't a fool.

"If I was so helpful to them, why do you suppose they kicked me out?"

"Because you're conflicted. They can smell it on you, the same way I can."

She straightened in her seat and opened another energy drink. "I know where I stand."

"Want to enlighten me as to which side that's on?"

"The side of truth." Her phone chimed. She took it out. "Monty's financials are in."

He gave her time to scroll through it. The silence was welcome. Trading barbs with her was exhausting.

"Anything of interest?" Regardless of her answer, he'd comb through it himself later.

"Possibly." She looked over at him. "What time did the outdoor security camera at Pandora's show her and Monty arriving?"

"Ten thirty."

"He used his debit card to pay at the Howling Wolf Roadhouse just before that."

"Time?"

"Four minutes past ten."

"We've got ourselves a lead. Get on the radio and let the others know we're going to peel off." The turn for the street that led to the roadhouse was about to come up soon.

Hannah passed along the message.

Once they made their turn, the others continued to the police station. The parking lot at the Howling Wolf was half-full. Security cameras mounted on the outside covered the lot and probably the road in front as well.

They climbed out and headed inside. Typical dive bar. Dim lighting. Shabby decor. Darts. Pool. Food and drink. He preferred to grab beer outside of town in Wayward Bluffs where he lived.

He wouldn't call the place seedy but wouldn't be surprised if drugs were sold out of it either.

They approached the bartender. A lanky guy covered in tattoos drying a glass.

"I'm Detective Wright. This is Detective Delaney. Were you working Thursday night?" he asked, and the guy nodded. "What's your name?"

"Finn."

"Was this guy in here that evening?" Hannah whipped out a photo of Monty on her phone.

"Yeah. Monty is in here every Thursday like clockwork."

"Oh, yeah." Waylon leaned against the bar. "Describe a regular Thursday night for him. What time does he arrive and leave? What does he do while he's here?"

"Gets in around nine. After his shift ends at eight." Finn put a tall glass under a spout and filled it with beer. "Orders dinner. Eats. Usually leaves with a woman. Rarely the same one."

Sounded like one of Waylon's Friday nights.

"Or I should say he used to leave with someone," Finn said.

"What do you mean used to?" Hannah asked.

"He stared eating alone and leaving alone."

Waylon scratched his chin. "When did the change start?"

"I don't know," the bartender said with a shrug. "Been a while. A few months back I guess. Maybe in August."

When Amber Reyes came back to town for her father's funeral. "And he only comes in on Thursdays?"

"Yep. Like clockwork."

"What about last Thursday?" Hannah asked. "Was he by himself?"

Finn laughed and set the beer down in front of a customer. "Nah, he wasn't alone. A hot redhead came in as he was finishing dinner. She was draped all over him, coming on strong."

"And how did he respond?" Waylon asked.

"Oh, he was into it. Feeling her up, stroking her leg. Smiling at her. Looked like those two were ready to get a room."

Hannah narrowed her eyes. "Really?"

That was the same question on Waylon's lips. The footage at Pandora's had showed a different sort of interplay in which Monty wasn't a happy camper. Maybe something had soured between them by the time they got to her place.

"Yeah," Finn said. "I guess he was looking for some action the other night and she was ready to show him a good time."

Hannah turned in a slow circle, scanning the place before looking back at the bartender. "We'd like to see the security footage from that night."

Finn ran a hand through his greasy-looking hair. "I wish I could show it to you, but we've been having problems with the system. It's on the fritz."

"That's convenient." Waylon exchanged a furtive glance with Hannah. "How about the cameras outside? Those aren't working either?"

After a moment of hesitation, Finn shook his head. "Nope. The whole system is down." He rubbed the back of his neck.

"Let me show you something." Waylon beckoned to him with a finger. The guy leaned across the bar and Waylon pointed to one of the cameras. "You see that little green light at the bottom? That says different. Tells us the cameras are operational and that you're lying."

The question was why.

Finn reeled back. "Nah. I'm not lying. You misunderstood me. They're working now. But they weren't Thursday."

Hannah raised an eyebrow. "Just got them fixed?"

"Yep. Sure did. Friday."

"Do you have a work order? A receipt?" Waylon folded his arms across his chest. "What company repaired the system?"

"My cousin fixed it," Finn said, easily. "He tinkers with electrical stuff. Really handy."

Hannah smiled. "If you're not lying, then you won't have any problem taking us to the office and showing us the footage that doesn't exist. Come on, sport." She hiked a thumb toward the hall.

"I've got customers. I can't just leave the bar and register unattended."

"Get moving," Waylon said. "Or I'll get you moving."

Hannah grimaced at the bartender. "Trust me, you don't want that."

"All right." Finn wiped his hands on a dish towel and led the way to the office in the back. He sat down behind a desk and logged into the computer.

Waylon and Hannah stood on either side of him, peering over his shoulder at the screen. He toggled over to the folder for the indoor cameras. Clicked one labeled Main Bar. Then December.

Footage for Thursday, December 5, was missing.

"Get up." Hannah tugged on his collar and the guy moved, letting her sit down. She got out of that folder and went to the recycle bin—a temporary storage location for items recently deleted, whether by mistake or purposefully. People often forgot to clear it.

The recycle bin was empty.

Her shoulders tensed but her face was deadpan.

Finn grinned. "See. I told you. This proves I wasn't lying."

Waylon shook his head. It was the exact opposite.

If the surveillance camera had been experiencing glitches, there would be footage that showed some problems throughout the day. Pieces missing. This proved the entire day had simply been deleted.

"Check the footage for the outside cameras," he said, and Finn stiffened, his premature smile falling from his face.

Hannah moved the mouse, sliding the cursor to the folder for the outside cameras. There were two. He pointed to the one that he thought offered the best view of the parking lot. She opened it and went to the night in question.

There was footage available. Waylon smiled.

Finn didn't move a step, but his gaze kept flying to the door like he wanted to run.

Waylon pinned him with a look and pointed a finger at him. "I hope you're not thinking of going anywhere."

"I'm just worried about my customers, that's all."

Hannah brought up the footage, sped to the point where Monty arrived and parked.

Shortly before ten a red Alfa Romeo Stelvio pulled into the lot. Pandora hopped out of her sporty SUV, wearing a short dress, leather boots and a fur jacket. The young woman put on lipstick and fluffed her hair before strutting inside the bar.

Carefully easing the footage forward, Hannah took the video to three minutes after ten. She let it play.

Waylon leaned in and watched alongside her.

Minutes later, Pandora sauntered out alone. She sashayed over to her vehicle and leaned against the hood, waiting. It wasn't long, a few seconds, until Monty left the bar, too.

With his hands stuffed in his pockets, he strode up to her. He nodded as he said something.

A bright smile spread across Pandora's face. She stepped closer and ran her hand up his chest, but he backed away, ending the physical contact, and got in his truck. She pulled out of the lot first and he followed behind her.

Hannah sighed, her disappointment palpable.

This didn't confirm Finn's version of events. It also didn't prove that they weren't romantically involved either.

"Why did you lie about the security cameras glitching?" Waylon asked Finn.

"I don't know what you're talking about." The guy rubbed his arm, his gaze shifting. "There was no footage inside the bar. I guess I got it wrong about outside."

"The redhead who was in here the other night is dead. This is a murder investigation, understand?" Waylon stalked over to him, and Finn's eyes grew big as hubcaps. "I'm going to give you a choice. You can give us honest answers and we'll leave you alone. Or we get one of our techies in here and it'll be easy enough to prove you deleted the file. That's obstruction of justice, buddy. Continue to lie and it'll only make this worse. Also, it'll just tick me off. Means I'm going haul you in. Did you know you could get up to a year in jail?"

Hannah stood and went around the desk. "And because we don't appreciate having our time wasted, this place is going to be raided, regularly. We'll be sure to use a narcotics detection canine."

"So, I'm going to ask you one more time." Waylon got up close and had to peer down in his face since the bartender was a head shorter than him. "Why did you lie?"

Finn's gaze fell for a long a moment, then he looked back up at them. A fixed gleam in his eyes. "I didn't lie. Monty was hot and heavy with that woman."

"Lied about deleting the footage," Delaney said, clarifying for him. "*That woman* is dead, remember?"

"Sorry she's dead but it's not my fault," Finn snapped.

"Watch your tone." Waylon pointed a finger at him. "That's no way to talk to a lady."

"Thanks. But I'm no lady. I'm a detective."

A thought occurred to Waylon. "Maybe you deleted the video footage because it shows you slipping a roofie into Monty's drink. Maybe the redhead paid you to do it. Maybe you were in cahoots together and now that she's dead you're worried we'll think you killed her."

Finn's eyes grew big and he shook his head. "No. No way."

Hannah's face hardened. "Are you sure? If we find out that you're lying, you're going to regret it."

"I'm sure. It wouldn't have worked anyway. No way to slip him a roofie. Monty only orders bottled beer while sitting at the bar. Always wants to open it himself. Never leaves his drink unattended. He'll chug it before going to the bathroom."

Sounded paranoid. But with everything going on, maybe the man had justified cause. If he was so cautious, it begged the question of whether he was indeed roofied or took the drug himself to cast reasonable doubt. "What about the redhead, was she ever in here before?"

"I'd never seen in here until last Thursday."

How did Pandora know to find Monty at the Howling Wolf on Thursday night at the right time?

"The file. Why did you really erase it?" Hannah demanded.

"I deleted the file because it was useless from going in and out. Real glitchy. You couldn't see anything. I've only got so much storage space on the drive. It made sense to get rid of it."

That was his *story,* and he was sticking to it for now.

"If something comes back to you and you remember things differently, let us know." Waylon handed him a business card, itching to take another go at this guy. But not now. Later, when they had more information. Use a lot more pressure and put the fear of God in the man.

Finn snatched the card. "Sure. I'll do that."

They went back out through the bar and left.

After they got in his truck, Hannah turned to him. "What do you make of it?"

"He's lying. About deleting the file for certain. Not so sure about his replay of how things went between Monty and Pandora inside the bar, though."

"I agree about the footage." Hannah nodded. "But do you still think Monty was sleeping with Pandora?"

He gave a one-shoulder shrug. The more he learned, the more he suspected Monty might not be guilty of murder. Didn't mean he wasn't sleeping with her. "I wouldn't put it past him." Monty was selfish, arrogant and tended to take what he wanted. "Do you have any idea what that ranch is worth with the cattle and access to the river?"

"No idea."

"Millions. Tens of millions. I've known men who have slept with two women at the same time for a heck of a lot less. And if he was bedding both of them, it would explain why he'd want it to keep it secret. So it doesn't upset the one who is still alive. He had to be extremely careful with Amber, didn't he? I mean with the engagement falling through ten years ago. Him using her to get the land way back then and now once again."

"I don't think it's that straightforward. He lied to her and proposed to get the land, but I think he's always truly cared about her. Monty isn't a typical user. He's not a womanizing manipulator. Not the way you want to believe."

The whole town had heard about the engagement. Two powerful, wealthy families about to be united. Then Amber Reyes fled in the night. Never to be seen again until her father's funeral. Waylon had no idea why it had fallen apart.

Or that Monty had lied, seduced her and proposed only to get the land for his family. It simply had been a connect-the-dots suspicion of his.

But thanks to Hannah Delaney's little slipup, he knew for certain now.

His phone rang. "It's the medical examiner." He put it on the Bluetooth speaker in the truck. "Hey, Roger. Delaney is with me. What do you have for us?"

"You'll have my full report in the morning, but I wanted to give you a quick update. I've narrowed the time of death to between six and seven in the morning. And she didn't die from exsanguination. The victim was strangled to death first. The perp waited before slitting her throat. Based on the low amount of blood flow I'd estimate twenty minutes."

"Maybe he was busy setting the scene," Hannah said, "and saved cutting her throat for last to keep from tracking blood around."

"I was thinking the same possibility. Anything else, Roger?"

"The victim recently had intercourse. My guess is fairly close to the time of death."

"Consensual," Hannah said, "not rape, right, Doc?"

"Yes. But he didn't leave behind any bodily fluids. That's about it. Wanted you to know straight away. The rest will be in my report."

"Thanks, Roger." Waylon disconnected. "We need more

answers. Fiona Frye is supposed to come at nine. Something she said keeps bothering me."

"About the proof that Pandora was seeing Monty?"

"No, not that, but it is odd. Right? I mean if she was seeing Monty or someone she trusted, why would she need insurance? The part that bugs me is when she told us her daughter was waiting until things were 'official' before she could tell anyone." The word kept turning over in his head.

"Like a deal for the land?"

Rubbing his eyes, Waylon fought a yawn. "Maybe. There's a whole lot about this case that I don't like." Things niggling at the back of his mind. "A puzzle with too many missing pieces." He started the engine. "Too many things just don't add up. The missing micro SD card in the security camera at Pandora's. The techies cracked into her hub and everything before that night was deleted. Her entire place was wiped clean of prints, except for the studio where she and Monty were found. The ketamine in his system. This story from the bartender about deleting a bad file to save on storage space. Now no bodily fluids left in the victim."

"What's odd about the last part Roger told us?"

He pulled out of the lot and hit the road. "There were no used condoms found in her home. If Monty slept with her, he didn't run out to dispose of it, only to go back, drug himself and wait to be found. Whoever she did sleep with right before she was murdered was careful." Waylon shook his head. "We can't discount what the bartender told us either about Monty and Pandora getting hot and heavy in the bar. What reason would he have to make up something like that?"

Delaney sighed.

A similar frustration pounded in Waylon's temples. "It's time Monty filled in some of the blanks for us. Talking to him after we speak to Ms. Frye would be best. Can you arrange for him to come in, with his lawyer if he insists, for a chat at eleven?" Plenty of time. There shouldn't be any excuses.

"Sure." She took out her cell and fired off a text. "I'll follow up with a phone call and convince him it's in his best interest to cooperate and simply talk to us already. Stonewalling is not helping him."

Although Waylon was starting to suspect that Monty wasn't the murderer, he still expected the eldest Powell son to be tight-lipped and lawyered up.

Sometimes he had to rattle a cage and poke the bear, get it angry to get progress. And one thing he knew about Montgomery Powell was that when he was angry, he ranted, at times even saying things that he shouldn't.

Tomorrow, Waylon would see if it'd work.

Chapter Twelve

Saturday, December 7
11:00 p.m.

The text message was unexpected.

Tapping her fingernails on her desk, Valentina wasn't sure what to do with the news she had just received. Tying up loose ends was always a good thing. But there was a bigger opportunity here. She simply had to see how to use it.

A knock on her office door pulled her from her thoughts. "Enter."

Max and Leo shuffled inside the room. From their hung heads and wary expressions, they'd failed.

Valentina crossed her legs and leaned back in her chair. "I'm going to ask you something, Leo, in a way that you can understand. What is the maximum effective range of an excuse?" The US Army was fond of that question, or so Roman had told her when she hired Leo. Back then she'd seen such potential in the young man, to prove himself, rise through the ranks of her drug empire. Staring at him now, she was no longer so sure. If he couldn't kill one man, how could he be trusted with the inner workings of the cartel?

"Zero meters is the maximum effective range of an excuse, ma'am," Leo said, hands clasped behind his back, standing at attention.

"Remember that and think carefully before you answer my next question. Why isn't Holden Powell dead?"

He looked up at her. "The family was finally out in the open at the tree lighting ceremony in the center of town. I had him in my sights. But he was holding a baby the entire time and had his pregnant wife next to him."

Valentina wrinkled her brow. "I'm not hearing a reason."

Confusion took over Leo's face. "I couldn't get a clear, clean shot. He—he had a baby in his arms."

"I understood the words the first time."

Anger sparked in his eyes. "I could've hit the kid by accident. If I took a head shot, the child would've fallen. Might've cracked his skull on the pavement. They're fragile as eggs when they're that little. Did you want me to hurt a baby?"

Her thoughts careened to Julian. His laughter. His smile. His warmth. "No. I only wanted the brother dead. Him first. The one with a kid." Like her own brother, who had to leave his son fatherless.

Because of Montgomery Powell.

Seemed fair.

"First, ma'am? Who would you like me to kill second?"

"Buck," she said, the name spilling from her lips with bitterness. "The leader of that clan. But I want the dominoes to fall in the proper order until I've destroyed everything Montgomery holds dear. Not that you've proven yourself capable of helping me." She slid her gaze to her burly guard. "And what did you do, Max? Simply stand there and watch this failure unfold?"

"No, *jefa*. Leo asked me to stir up the crowd. That way after there were gunshots, it would appear random. Unplanned. In-the-heat-of-the-moment kind of thing and not like an assassination."

She hadn't considered that. "Smart. Still doesn't change the fact that an opportunity was wasted."

Leo dared to step forward. "But it wasn't, ma'am," he said, his voice rippling with confidence.

Maybe she wouldn't kill him today if he redeemed himself. "Explain."

"After the gunshots, Montgomery Powell picked up a woman and rushed her to a vehicle. The entire family raced to the hospital. We followed them over. I slipped inside and hung around in the waiting room, eavesdropping. The woman, Amber Reyes, is pregnant. And the baby is Monty's. It's going to be a boy. They were all overjoyed."

A sweet smile spread across her face. Now she knew precisely what to do with the information she'd received in the text message. "There's something I want you both to do."

Leo straightened. "Anything, ma'am."

She grabbed a notepad, pen and the folder from her top desk drawer. "First, I want you to go to this address." She copied it from the text that had been sent to her. "You'll find a dead body in the house. I want you to take it and put it in the trunk of another vehicle." She wrote down the second address, along with the make, model and license of the car. "Stealth will be required. People will be at home and asleep at the second house." She handed him the paper. "You're not to be noticed."

"That's it?" Leo asked. "You don't want me to kill anyone?"

"Well, I did, but you messed that up, didn't you? For this task, the blood has already been spilled. Get this errand right. No mistakes."

Both Leo and Max nodded.

"You may go." She waved them out, picked up her phone and dialed Officer Nicholas Foley.

He answered on the fourth ring. "Yes, ma'am. The Laramie PD has the cell phone that was *found* in Montgomery's locker."

"Good boy," she said, like he was a dog. "I have another mission for you. Tomorrow morning, I need you to do your job and make a traffic stop."

"Who am I pulling over?" he asked.

"Amber Reyes. She lives on the big ranch on Longhorn River Road. She will have an appointment in town at ten. There's only one route for her to take. Expect her to leave her home sometime between nine fifteen and nine thirty. She likes to arrive early. During the traffic stop, you need to search her trunk."

"Want to tell me what I'm looking for?"

Valentina grinned. "Don't you like surprises?"

"No, ma'am. Not when I'm working for you."

She chuckled. "Once the trunk is open it'll be obvious. Trust me on that."

"Are you sure she'll be going that way around that time? I can't sit out on the road forever. Someone will notice me. This appointment is set, and she'll keep it?"

"No, not yet. But if you pass the phone to your wife, she can help me arrange that part."

"Sure. One second."

There was a rustling sound. "Hello, Ms. Sandoval. What do you need from me?" the wife asked.

"Two things. Both are equally important. Contact Amber Reyes. Set up some kind of urgent meeting in the morning somewhere in town. Tell her she needs to be there by ten. You will not accept 'no' for answer. Ensure Ms. Reyes is in the right place at the right time."

"What else?"

"The project you worked on regarding Holly Powell. Activate it as soon as possible."

"I could reach out to Erica Egan tonight. Get the ball rolling. That woman will answer the phone no matter what time it is. But she'll want the proof tonight as well. Or would you like me to wait until tomorrow morning?"

"Which one is as soon as possible? Tonight? Or tomorrow?"

"Okay. I understand. I'll call her right now and arrange everything tonight. You should see it on the news about Holly before lunch."

Valentina ended the call.

Never underestimate the power of an inside man. Or woman.

Chapter Thirteen

The next morning, Amber stared absently through the windshield of her Jeep, feeling unsettled as she drove into town. Vera, Holly's secretary, had called, insisting that she come down to the mayor's office by nine. To talk with Holly away from the house in private.

She cringed on the inside over how that discussion was going to go.

Hold your ground. Create boundaries. It'll be fine.

She'd already decided there would be no talk of marriage or the status of her relationship with Monty at all. Baby talk was fine. Nothing more.

The one bright spot was that Vera promised to have a wide selection of munchies from Divine Treats. A boiled egg, applesauce and toast for a quick breakfast wouldn't hold her long. She was ready for a mouthwatering, sugary treat. Then she crossed her fingers her appetite would last.

She took a sip from the new water bottle Holly had gotten Buck to purchase last night. Already it had made a huge difference in her water consumption. Monty's family was overbearing and intrusive, but they meant well and looked out for those in their inner circle.

Rubbing her belly, with one hand on the steering wheel, she thought she'd be overjoyed to know that Monty loved her, to have proof she mattered more than the land and the river. And a big part of her was, but the only way to know for sure was to let him lose it all.

The idea of taking away the ranch, the land, generations of hard work from him, from her unborn son, from Kayce, from the child Grace was carrying now, made her heart weep.

As much as Monty didn't want to admit it, he was born to be a rancher. One day he'd come to realize it. But she couldn't let that happen with him working on someone else's land.

The next generation of Powells being born might have a love for ranching in their souls. Wouldn't that be something? The operation was large enough to share among so many, especially once it was combined with the Reyes land, and Matt was expanding the business further. Offering wild game hunting for tourists. Cabins were being built on the Little Shooting Star. She'd heard all the boys had pitched in, helping to build the cabins that would be rented out.

She made a right onto Route 207, which turned into Third Street, the main road into town.

Who was she to steal such a thing from everyone just to be 100 percent positive Monty's feelings for her were real? That she mattered more?

In the end, would he resent her? Would her son, after he learned about the incredible legacy that should've been passed to him?

A siren whooped once behind her.

Amber looked up in the rearview mirror. Red and blue lights flashed on a state police cruiser. Sighing, she pulled over, came to a stop and put the SUV in Park.

An officer strolled up to the driver's side and gestured for her to roll down the window with a gloved hand.

"I'm sorry, Officer. Was I speeding?" She had a tendency to do that. A bad habit she needed to break.

No more speeding with baby on board.

"License and registration." A rough voice rumbled in that authoritative way cops had. He hooked his thumbs on his utility belt and waited.

"Oh." She reached over to her glove compartment. Found the registration and handed it to him.

"License."

She opened her purse and stared at the envelope she still hadn't opened. Her father's letter. Bypassing it, she grabbed her wallet and gave him her license. "I know I was going too fast. If you let me off with a warning, I promise not to do it anymore."

He looked over her documentation. "Your registration from Texas expired last month."

She cringed. "My father died in August. I came here for his funeral and after the reading of his will things got topsy-turvy. I wasn't expecting to stay this long, but then I did. I didn't forward my mail and didn't realize the expiration was coming up. Once my brother pointed out to me that it had in fact expired, I didn't know if I should renew the registration in Texas or get a new one here. Everything in my life is changing so fast. It's so complicated and messy. I might stay. I might go. But I'll know for sure in a couple of weeks and figured I would take care of it then. In January. Once I knew if I was getting married or not. Or staying here. Or going back to Texas. Do you see what I'm saying?"

The cop grimaced.

"That was long-winded. I apologize…" She looked at his name tag. "Officer Foley." She looked over his state police uniform and made the connection. "Do you know Monty Powell? You two probably work together. We're very close."

"Ma'am, please step out of the vehicle."

"Come again?"

He put his hand on the hilt of his weapon. "Please step out of the vehicle."

She stiffened. "Yes, Officer." She did as he instructed, and her legs shook. Something like this had never happened to her before. Sure, she'd gotten a ticket before. Okay, lots of speeding tickets, but the police had never asked her to get out like she was a criminal.

He peered inside her vehicle and looked around. "Ma'am, please open your trunk."

"Is this really necessary?" she asked, incredulously. A bit excessive, wasn't it?

His features tightened to stone. His jaw set as he put his hand back on the hilt of his gun.

A flutter zipped through her chest. "Of course." Amber tapped her coat pocket, checking to make sure the key fob was inside, raised her palms and walked around to the rear of the Jeep. "This seems silly, if you ask me. I only have an emergency kit in there. Flares. Jumper cables. And a spare tire." Since the key fob was on her, she just moved her foot under the rear bumper in a straight kicking motion, activating the hands-free sensor.

The hazard lights flashed and the liftgate opened.

Her heart dropped to her stomach and the ground beneath her feet seemed to crumble away like the earth had split open wide. She staggered back. "No," she choked out.

Fiona Frye was dead. In her trunk.

"Ma'am, put your hands on your head. You're under arrest." The officer wrenched her wrists behind her back and slapped handcuffs on her while reciting her Miranda rights.

He steered her to his vehicle and put a hand on the top of her head, helping her inside.

Her pulse was pounding a mile of minute, but a weird calm stole over her. "Can you please grab my purse and water bottle? I'm pregnant. The doctor said I had to stay hydrated."

The officer hesitated a second. "Sure. But you've got to wait until after you're booked to get the water bottle."

"Can I be booked at the sheriff's department?" she asked. The sheriff was in California helping his and Grace's mother with something, leaving Holden in charge.

Holden would sort this out. She'd be okay there.

At the Laramie Police Department, with Waylon Wright eager to believe in this dreadful conspiracy spreading like a disease, there was no telling what would happen to her.

"I do know Monty, ma'am," the officer said. "His brother is chief deputy at the sheriff's. Sorry, but I'll be taking you to LPD." He slammed the door shut.

Oh, my God. Fiona, the next person who stood to inherit the land, was dead, and she was about to be booked for her murder. If she hadn't been sitting, she would've collapsed.

First Monty.

Now her.

Who would be the next person to die? And who would be blamed?

Chapter Fourteen

Done prepping for his upcoming interview with Monty, Waylon closed the folder he planned to bring inside the room with him. He couldn't believe what they'd found on Monty's flip phone that had been seized from his work locker.

Montgomery Powell had a lot of explaining to do, and Hannah Delaney wasn't going to be there to help him. When Fiona Frye never showed up for their appointment, he'd sent her to go check on Ms. Frye and to take another crack at questioning Pandora's neighbors. Neither who lived on either side of the young woman had been at home when they'd tried before. They could get lucky. A neighbor might have seen Pandora with Monty or with some other man.

"Hey, Wright." One of the officers who had participated in the execution of the search warrant last night came over to him. "Maybe we searched the wrong ranch last night?"

He sipped his coffee. "What are you talking about?"

"I guess you haven't heard. Amber Reyes was just booked for the murder of Fiona Frye and is sitting in a holding cell right now."

That caught his attention. "Do you mean for the murder of

Pandora Frye?" he asked, but that still didn't make a lick of sense. Instinct told him that she wasn't a murderer. Besides, based on the security camera footage, she wasn't guilty.

"No. The mother. Fiona Frye."

His gut twisted. Waylon shot him a confused look. "Who was the arresting officer?"

"A guy with the state police. He's still here doing the paperwork." The cop pointed to him.

Familiar face. "Thanks," Waylon said to the cop. Grabbing the folder for his interview, he got out of his chair and waltzed over to the state trooper. "Officer Foley. Two times in two days that you're here. First, you dropped off the phone from Powell's locker."

"Yeah, they figured it made sense for me to run it by since I live in the area."

"What brings you here today?"

"Routine traffic stop turned into something more. There was a dead body in the trunk."

In mock surprise, Waylon raised both brows. "Wow, you don't see that every day. Especially not around here in our small town."

Foley flashed an easy smile. "I know, right?"

Waylon sat on the edge of the desk the guy was using. "Walk me through how it happened. The specifics."

"I was on my way to work when my wife called. So I pulled over to see what the Mrs. needed."

"Where were you?"

"Oh, I was on Route 207 near the intersection of Longhorn River Road. Anyway, this woman—"

"Name?"

"Amber Reyes. She failed to come to a complete stop at the intersection where there was a red light and didn't use her signal when you make a right turn. Turns out her registration has been expired for weeks. Then she started rambling incoherently. I asked her to step out of the vehicle. She didn't want to do it. Tried to talk her way out of it, still not making any sense. I got a weird feeling, you know, a cop's sixth sense," he said, and Waylon nodded. "With all those violations and how suspicious she was acting. So I asked to see the inside of her trunk. Bingo! Dead body."

"Golly. That's some story." A lot of stories were flying around lately. Waylon stood. "Hey, tell me something. Where do you live?"

Foley spouted out his address. The trooper lived on the western outskirts of town while the Reyes ranch was in the northeast, nowhere near town.

"Huh? That's clear on the other side. Do you drive past Longhorn River Road every day?"

"No. I was craving one of those Cronuts from Divine Treats and decided to take the scenic route to enjoy it on the drive. Pure coincidence what happened."

"Yeah, three things I love. Scenic routes. Perfect timing. And coincidence." Waylon clapped the trooper on the back. "You keep up the fine work."

Foley's smile brightened. "Will do, sir."

Waylon made his way back to the holding cells, where he found Amber Reyes looking pale, rigid and unwell. "Ms. Reyes."

She met his gaze with tired eyes. "Detective Wright. Are you here to gloat?"

"No, ma'am. I admit I'm guilty of schadenfreude when it comes to the Powells, but please believe that I take no enjoyment from the troubles of anyone else outside that family. Especially when it involves another murder."

"I didn't do it. I don't know how Fiona's body got into the trunk of my car."

"You're entitled to have a lawyer present."

"They told me I had to wait to make my phone call. But I'd tell you the same thing with an attorney present. I didn't like Fiona or Pandora. But I didn't hate either woman. I didn't wish them ill. I certainly didn't kill them."

He believed her. "Speaking of ill, that's how you look. Can I get you anything?"

"The officer who arrested me brought my water bottle and my purse. Can I have them and something to eat?" She put a hand to her stomach and rubbed it. It almost seemed an unconscious movement. "I had to go the ER last night. The doctor said I need to stay hydrated and eat. I missed breakfast."

The way she sat, hunched like the weight of the world rested on her shoulders, highlighted the outline of her belly bump. "Are you pregnant?"

Her eyes widened, but she nodded.

"Is it Monty's?"

She licked her lips and bit the inside of her cheek. "Yes."

"I'll make sure you get your phone call, the water bottle and something to eat. I can't give you your purse. Was there something inside you wanted?" Maybe she had prenatal vitamins or something for nausea.

"There's a sealed letter. From my father. I think I'm finally ready to read it."

"I'll get you taken care of, ma'am." He turned to leave, but then looked back at her. "Don't worry, Ms. Reyes. You won't be in here long. Just be patient. I don't think you killed Fiona Frye any more than you did Pandora."

"As you've already pointed out, I stand to gain if those two are gone. Why do you think I'm innocent?"

"Because I don't believe in coincidence. No such thing. And when people start using it to explain something that doesn't add up, it sets my teeth on edge. I'm going to get to the bottom of this. You can trust that."

On his way to the interrogation rooms, another officer stopped him.

"Montgomery Powell is in room one with his lawyer waiting for you."

"Thanks. Do me a favor. Ms. Reyes is in holding. Let her make her phone call ASAP. Also, see that she gets plenty of water, let her order whatever she wants to eat from Delgado's Bar and Grill—I'll cover the charge—and find her purse. There's a sealed envelope inside. Supposedly a letter. Check it to be sure and then let her have it."

"No problem."

Waylon went to room one and grabbed the handle. Taking a breath, he considered how to play this. *Poke the bear or good cop?*

Today felt like the perfect day to rattle a cage. "Poke the bear it is," he whispered to himself.

He entered the room and sat down.

Across the metal table was Monty, wearing a button-down under his shearling jacket, jeans and his black cowboy hat. His lawyer sat stiff as a board in a suit, sipping a coffee.

Waylon slapped the folder down and put his hand on top of it. "I see someone has already offered you something to drink."

"Let's get on with it," Monty said.

"I'm Tim Lemke, Mr. Powell's attorney. He has graciously agreed to cooperate with you today. We only ask that you be respectful of his time."

"Certainly." Waylon nodded. "Walk me through the events of Thursday evening."

Monty opened his mouth, but Lemke put a hand on his forearm, stopping him.

"Could you please be more specific?" the attorney asked.

"Sure." Waylon shrugged. "Where were you at nine p.m. on Thursday night?"

"The Howling Wolf Roadhouse. I have dinner there—"

Lemke leaned over to his client. "Only answer the question asked. Don't offer any additional information."

"Look," Waylon said, "this will take all day unless he fills in the blanks by offering additional information, which is the reason he's here. I thought you wanted me to be respectful of his time. Either you killed Pandora Frye or you didn't. So, if you want to get on with it, start talking."

"I have dinner there on Thursdays," Monty said.

"Why Thursdays?" Waylon wondered. "Why not Fridays?"

"I have seniority. I only work Monday through Thursday. That's my Friday, the night I want to unwind. The other three days I spend working on the ranch. Long, hard hours and I don't feel like driving to a bar afterward."

Satisfied, Waylon nodded. "Do you only eat dinner there? Do you ever pick up women?"

Monty clenched his jaw. "I used to."

"What changed?"

Monty looked at his attorney.

"I don't see the relevance," Lemke said. "How does this pertain to last Thursday? Why don't we stick to that?"

Everyone had secrets, the guilty and innocent alike. But Waylon needed to know why Monty wanted to hide his relationship with Amber if he wasn't sleeping with Pandora.

"Okay. Did you see and speak with Pandora Frye at the Howling Wolf that evening?" Waylon asked.

"I did."

"And?"

Monty looked to his attorney and got the okay before going on. "She approached me as I was finishing dinner."

"Did she make any amorous overtures that you welcomed or encouraged?"

"She tried to touch me a couple of times. Pandora is—*was*—a handsy person. I didn't take it as her hitting on me or anything, but I also let her know that I didn't like it."

"Let her know how?"

"I removed her hands from my body."

"Interesting. The bartender at the Howling Wolf, Finn, told us that you two were all over each other and looked like you—and I quote—'needed to get a room.' Any idea why he would tell us that if it wasn't true?"

"None at all. I think you should go back and ask him again."

That was on Waylon's list of things to do for this afternoon. They needed to squeeze the bartender and get to the bottom of why his story felt off. "Why did Pandora approach you?"

"Told me she didn't think Amber was going to marry me. But once Pandora inherited the land, that we could strike a deal where I could get it."

"What were the terms of this deal?"

"She refused to talk about it at the Howling Wolf. Told me that I had to do it at her place over a drink or there would be no deal. Then she left."

"What happened next?"

"I paid the bill. Went outside to find her waiting. I agreed since I didn't see the harm in hearing what she had to say."

"You drove yourself to her place?"

Monty nodded. "I followed her over. She let me in and showed me into her studio, where she worked. I took a seat. She poured me a drink. Then she made small talk for a bit.

The conversation turned to Amber and Chance. Pandora told me that she would never give up the Reyes family home, but she didn't want that to put her at odds with her half siblings. She wanted to get to know them. And then." He shook his head. "I don't remember anything clearly until I woke up in the hospital."

"Did you watch Pandora pour your drink?"

Lowering his head, Monty looked like he was thinking about it. "No. She handed me one of her portfolio books and asked me what I thought of her work while she poured the drinks."

Maybe he had let his guard down around her. What danger would he have assumed a woman weighing one hundred twenty pounds would've posed to him? How was he supposed to know where the night was headed?

One possible theory.

But there were others and they all needed to be explored. "The portion of the Reyes land that might've gone to Pandora is extremely valuable to your family, isn't it?"

"It is."

"Valuable enough for you to have started a romantic relationship with Pandora. To have seduced her. Perhaps promised marriage to her."

Monty's eyes hardened. "No."

"That's impossible?" Waylon gave a light, incredulous chuckle. "You wouldn't seduce a woman for the land? Or should I say once more. The way you seduced a young and vulnerable Amber Reyes when she was only nineteen years old shortly after losing her mother."

"Watch it," Monty said, through gritted teeth.

"Did I strike a nerve?" *Good.* Waylon was only getting started. "In your locker at work, a burner phone was found. I printed out screenshots of some of the texts." He pulled a couple of sheets from the folder and slid them across the table.

Monty picked up the papers. He and his lawyer read through them. Alarm washed over Monty's face.

"Steamy stuff in there," Waylon said. "Kinky, too. A lot of talk about what you liked and how much she enjoyed giving it to you. How much she loved you. How she couldn't wait to marry you."

"I've never seen these texts." Monty finally looked scared. "I didn't write them or receive them."

"My client's name is never mentioned," Lemke said, stabbing the paper. "Nor that of Ms. Frye. Only McDreamy, Lover, Bubba and Cupcake. These texts could be between any two people."

Waylon frowned. "The problem is that the phone was found in your client's locker and the number he texted did in fact belong to Pandora Frye. There were also some racy photos that you took of Pandora that were found on the phone." He took blown-up copies of the pictures from the folder and slid those over next.

Monty peered down at them and his jaw dropped.

"Looks like you're into bondage," Waylon said, his stomach turning. That was not his thing. "And asphyxiation during sex." There were photos of Pandora tied up, nude, someone with a gloved hand choking her. The person had worn long sleeves. In some of the photos pleasure was on her face, either real or feigned. But in the rest the fear in her eyes was clear. All the pictures and texts were from last month. "Maybe you got too rough during sex on Thursday night. Choked her to death by accident." Most crimes of passion were violent, such as strangulation or a stabbing, a hands-on act done in the heat of the moment. "Then you got desperate and needed to cover it up." He shoved a picture of Pandora, lying on the floor, naked and murdered, in his face.

"Go to hell!" Monty threw the photos at him and jumped to his feet. "We're done here!"

"You're going to sit back down," Waylon said calmly.

Monty narrowed his eyes and clenched his hands. "Or else what?"

"Or else I'm going to have a little chat with Amber Reyes. Who, by the way, is sitting in a holding cell right now because a dead body was found in her trunk this morning."

"What?" Monty reeled back. "Whose body?" he demanded.

But Waylon was on a roll and ignored the question. "And when I talk to the mother of your unborn child, I'm going to show her those racy photos and tell her my theory about your kinky side."

A ferocious expression darkened Monty's face, and he cocked back his fist, ready to pound into Waylon.

His attorney jumped between him and the table. "Don't do it. You can't."

"No, let him," Waylon said with a grin. Gone were their high school days where he'd been smaller than Monty. Now he was two inches taller, outweighed him by about twenty pounds of solid muscle and still had sharp reflexes. He could've stopped him if he wanted, but he welcomed the punch. "I'd love to charge him with assault of a police officer. I can put you in a cell next to Amber's."

"You sick son of a—"

"Stop and get control of yourself," his lawyer warned. "This is what he wants. You acting like a crazed animal with anger management issues." The lawyer faced Waylon. "My client's face was not in any of the photos. You can't prove it was him."

"The phone they found isn't mine," Monty said.

"Then how did it get in your locker?"

"I don't know, but the only reason you're doing this is because of what happened in high school." Monty lowered his fist. "I'm sorry, okay? I didn't know Tara was your girl-friend when I asked her to homecoming."

This wasn't about some gripe from high school, but since Monty had brought it up, he was willing to discuss it. "I told you she was and that the only reason she said yes to you was because your father and hers were in business. That she thought she had to agree."

"And I thought you were a lying, sore loser! It wasn't until I didn't end up going to homecoming and she confessed to me that she was relieved not to go with me that I learned the truth."

"Take what you want, regardless of who gets hurt," Way-lon said. "That's your motto. That's the code you live by. And as if that wasn't enough, you had to break my hand."

Indignation twisted Monty's features, reddening his cheeks as he shook his head. "You picked a fight after foot-ball practice. I was holding my helmet and used it to block your fist. I didn't mean to break your hand and end your football season."

"I guess you didn't mean to throw me into the trophy dis-play case either, shredding my face with glass." He had fallen face-first. Took thirty stitches. Not to mention the pain. For the rest of his senior year, everyone called him *Scarface*.

"It was an accident. I never intended for you to get hurt. Not like that. And I came to your home and apologized."

"Only because your father made you." The gall. Monty could've shoved that artificial, hollow apology where the sun didn't shine for all Waylon had cared. "What really burns me to the core is that after the stitches and getting a cast, I was the one sentenced to detention for fighting. Not you. Oh, no, a Powell was too good for detention. That was beneath the son of the almighty Buck and Holly."

A roar of angry laughter rolled out of Monty. "You're right, I didn't get detention because I'm a Powell. But what you don't know is that my father whipped me with a leather strap until I bled because you were smaller than me at that time and got hurt so badly. I didn't get to go to homecoming. I didn't get to finish the football season either. My father pulled me from the team. And I'm the one who had to pay for a new display case by working on the ranch well before dawn prior to school and after until midnight. Every day for months. He came down on me particularly hard because I was to be made the example for my brothers. The cautionary tale of what not to do. So, yeah, I'm sorry I didn't get two weeks of detention, but there was ranch justice exacted on your behalf. Take some consolation in that."

Waylon had no idea his father had been so harsh on him. If he had known, it would've been water under the bridge eons ago.

"No matter what you think of me," Monty said, "I'm not a murderer and I have never slept with Pandora. And I won't tolerate you hurting Amber to get to me."

"Then why were you hiding your relationship with Amber?"

"It all looks bad! Having a relationship with her makes it look worse, especially if you think I was sleeping with Pandora, too. But I wasn't and never would."

Waylon spotted another opening and pushed. "Why *never*? Why such an impossibility? She was a very pretty girl and you had a lot to gain by doing so."

"Sleeping with Pandora Frye, hell, looking at her the wrong way would have hurt Amber. I broke her heart once.

I love her. I want to win her back. Last night I told her the land doesn't matter. We can wait to get married to prove it to her. Fiona Frye can have it for all I care. Even if it means my family's legacy has to die. Amber, our baby, that's all that matters."

Waylon leaned back in his chair. "The dead body in Amber's trunk was Fiona Frye."

Monty spit out a curse. "I don't believe this." Heaving a ragged breath, he scrubbed his face with his hands. "This can't be happening. Amber didn't do it. You probably figure the same. Why would she drive around with a dead body in the trunk? Unless you think I did it and asked her to take the body somewhere?"

"I don't think you did it." Waylon stood. "There's a bigger game at play here. I needed you to be honest. I'm talking bare-your-soul-in-a-confessional kind of honest to fill in some of the blanks. I need to get to the bottom of this before any more dead bodies turn up. No hard feelings. Right?"

"To clarify," Lemke said, "you're not charging my client?"

Waylon took a deep cleansing breath. "No, I'm not charging him."

"You're going to release Amber?" Monty asked.

"She will be. There's a procedure. I need to talk to the chief and explain."

"I want to see her," Monty said. "Make sure she's all right. She needs to eat and drink water."

"I made sure she's being taken care of."

An urgent rap on the door interrupted them before a cop poked his head inside. "Assistant District Attorney Melanie Merritt is on the phone for you. Says it can't wait. You can pick up line two in the next room."

A tingle zipped down Waylon's spine. "I'll be right back."

He hurried next door and answered the phone. "Howdy, darling, please tell me this call is of a personal nature."

Two and a half years ago, when Melanie moved to the area, before he knew she was going to be the new ADA, they'd run into each other at a bar in Wayward Bluffs. One thing had led to another, and they'd slept together.

Since then, they'd been in a quasi-relationship. Unofficially and under wraps. Always on her terms. They usually met at his place or hers three to four times a week. Sometimes in the middle of the day for a hot quickie. Strictly sex had become sentimental and even sweet. But he was ready to take things to the next level. Exclusivity in secret was no longer enough. He wanted to go from quasi to serious. Surprising her with tickets to the Caribbean for Christmas was either going to get him what he wanted or scare her off.

"Sorry to disappoint you, cowboy," she said, her tone all business, and the spark of anticipatory joy in him fizzled. "Next time watch it, I could've had you on speaker."

The line between personal and professional were critical to her. He got it and had to if he wanted to see her whenever she fancied herself in the mood.

"Are you not alone?" he asked.

"Yes and no. Someone unexpected is paying me a visit. I waited until he went to get coffee to call you because you tend to be unpredictable on the phone. I never know what filthy thing might come out of your mouth. I need to see you, Delaney and Montgomery Powell right now."

"Delaney is wrapped up at the moment, but I'm with Powell. I've got him in the next room."

"Good. I'm sure you've been scratching your head over the Pandora Frye case."

"As a matter of fact, I have. The pieces don't add up." He had the feeling Monty was being framed.

"I think I have some answers for you. Get him over to my office on the double. This can't wait for any reason." She hung up before he could respond.

"Yes, ma'am," he said to himself. He pulled out his phone and called Delaney. "Hey, Fiona Frye is dead."

"I figured as much. I'm at her place now. Looks like a tornado went through here."

"The body was found in Amber Reyes's vehicle."

"You've got to be kidding me."

"Wish I was. Hey, Monty claims he wasn't sleeping with Pandora and that their discussion at the bar was all business. Funny thing is, I believe him. Which means the bartender is lying. Go back and talk to him again. Find out why. Tell him we've got a witness who was in the bar that night contradicting his story. Lean hard on him."

"Are you mansplaining to me how to do my job, Lieutenant?"

Waylon cleared his throat. "Apologies. You've got this. I'm heading to the ADA's office with Monty."

"Why?"

"Don't know. She wants to see us about the case. I'll text you with an update when I know more."

"Okay." They hung up, and he ducked back into the interrogation room. "The ADA has information about this case. She needs to see us in her office immediately."

"But I need to see Amber."

"That'll have to wait. Trust me, she's fine." Waylon hurried Monty and his attorney out of the room and down the hall. "Hey, do you know a state trooper by the name of Foley?"

"Yeah. Nick."

"Does he have a grudge against you? Any reason to have it in for you?"

"None that I can think of. Why?"

Waylon shook his head, not ready to get into it any deeper. "Only wondering."

As they crossed through the bullpen, Detective Kent Kramer was ushering in Holly Powell in handcuffs. Her assistant, Eddie Something, was following them, carrying her purse.

"Mom!" Monty rushed over to her. "What's going on?"

"I've been arrested." She held up her hands, wrists cuffed in front of her.

"For what?" her son asked.

"Embezzlement."

The Powell family house of cards was tumbling down today. Waylon approached the other detective. "What's going on, Kent?"

"Erica Egan stopped by to see me earlier as a *courtesy* and handed over proof that Mrs. Powell has been embezzling money from the mayor's office. Twenty-five thousand dollars."

"That's absurd," Monty said. "She doesn't have a need to steal any money."

"I had Eddie call Buck to get our attorney, Corthell," Holly said.

"He's on the way, along with your husband." Eddie stepped forward. "I also asked Brianne to get out in front of this."

"Not Corthell, Mom." Monty shook his head. "You need a criminal attorney." He grabbed Lemke by the arm and shoved him toward his mother. "Use mine."

"Anyway," Kent said, "I think Egan was so generous sharing the information before she broke the story because she wanted to catch us arresting Mrs. Powell on camera. I'm sure it's all over the news by now."

"The world is going to hell in a handbasket, Mom," Monty said. "Amber was arrested, too."

"Oh no! That poor thing," Holly paled, pressing her hands to her chest. "Is she all right?"

"Have them put Mrs. Powell in the cell next to Ms. Reyes," Waylon said to Kent. "We need to go see the ADA. She said it can't wait for any reason." He took Monty by the arm, and the man jerked free of his grip. *Guess there are hard feelings.* "Let's go."

Chapter Fifteen

Sunday, December 8
12:20 p.m.

"What's this all about?" Monty asked, walking into the assistant district attorney's office. Best for them to get straight to it. The sooner they did, the sooner he could see Amber.

"Take a seat," Melanie Merritt said, seated behind her desk. She turned toward a man who was standing in the corner, staring out the window. "This is Agent Welliver. He's with the Drug Enforcement Agency. This is Montgomery Powell and Detective Lieutenant Waylon Wright." The ADA used Waylon's full pompous title that everyone else simply shortened to detective.

The man strolled over to the desk, holding a cup of coffee. Looked to be in his late fifties. Weathered. He wore a crisp black blazer and jeans. He offered a tight smile. "I'd say it's a pleasure to meet you, but I come as the bearer of bad news."

"Related to the homicide case of Pandora Frye?" Waylon asked.

Monty cut his gaze to the detective. He was still simmering over the interrogation but he now had a better understanding of Waylon and was trying to not take the harsh tactics so personally.

But it felt brutally personal.

"I believe so," Agent Welliver said. "We've been working on a case for a long time. Years really. Trying to bring down the Sandoval cartel. Earlier this year, we finally infiltrated them. Got our guy recruited. He's been working as a driver. Feeds us information."

"Some of that information helped us with a local case," Melanie said, "that led to the takedown of Todd Burk and a few Hellhound bikers. We were worried that Rip Lockwood and Ashley Russo had popped up on the Sandoval radar. Consequently, they had to go into hiding."

Monty knew them both. Ashley had worked for the sheriff's department. Her brother had been Holden's best friend in high school, before he was killed. They'd all suspected that Burk had been behind it. Monty had been thrilled when he'd learned of Burk's arrest. Justice finally served. "Yeah, I heard they picked up and disappeared. What does this have to do with me or the murder of Pandora Frye?"

"Welliver contacted me earlier," Melanie said. "Gave me the heads-up he was coming and why."

"Our inside man called me at two this morning. He's been trying to reach me for a couple of days, but he's being watched closely." Welliver sat on the edge of the desk, his expression grim, his eyes predatory, and Monty supposed one had to be a predator when hunting monsters. "Valentina Sandoval, the head of the cartel, has you in her crosshairs." He pointed at Montgomery.

"Me?" He stiffened. "Why?"

"After we talked a few hours ago," Melanie said, "I rushed into the office to see if I could figure out why. I cross-referenced your name with any cases related to the cartel. I got a hit on a big one." She offered the file and Monty took it. "Does the name Santiago Sandoval ring a bell?"

"Not really." He opened the folder. As soon as he saw the picture, it hit him. Dark eyes, slicked back hair, cocksure attitude. "I do remember him. He was speeding in a Mercedes-Benz G-Class. A two-hundred-thousand-dollar car. I expected a hard time. A smooth talker who wouldn't care about a hundred-dollar ticket. You know the type, it's more about the inconvenience. But this guy was different. A nasty piece of work. Real ballsy. He had a woman in the passenger seat, performing a sex act on him. She stopped at the last minute. He had white powder on his nose. There was more on the dash. When I questioned him about it, he offered me money. A lot of money. In cash. Boasted about how it was more than I make in a month. Told me to shut up, take it, get back in my vehicle and forget I ever saw him. Or there would be consequences. Life-and-death consequences."

"Of course you arrested the jerk," Waylon said.

"Of course." Monty nodded. "I did so with great pleasure, too. Turns out he had ten kilos of cocaine and one gram of fentanyl in the trunk. Along with a lot more cash."

"He was the son of Alejandro Sandoval," Melanie said. "Who used to run the cartel. Santiago was sentenced for possession with intent to distribute and received seven years in prison. His wife, who was in the passenger seat, got three years."

"Okay." Monty shrugged. "You do the crime, you do the time."

Welliver grimaced. "Not so simple. In prison there's a system, a code, a manner in which things are handled. Someone inside broke that code. A guard was probably paid off to move Santiago to a cell block where he didn't have protection. He died a very brutal, very violent death. It was slow. Painful. Real ugly. His father suffered a heart attack shortly thereafter, leaving Valentina in charge of the cartel and as guardian of her nephew, Santiago's son."

Ice ran through Monty's veins. "I take it she blames me. Because I didn't take the bribe and let him get away."

"Pretty much, yeah." Welliver sipped his coffee. "The reality is that she could blame Santiago's lawyer. The prosecutor on the case. The judge who sentenced her brother. The guard who was paid off. But you make an easy, simple source for her vehemence because probably in her twisted, dark mind it started with you. Makes it all your fault."

"Did your inside man give you anything else to go on?" Waylon asked. "Specifics?"

Welliver nodded. "Valentina asked him to assassinate your brother Holden. He made it look like he tried during the holiday tree lighting ceremony."

A hot blade of agony stabbed his chest. "She tried to have my brother murdered. But why?"

Welliver shrugged. "Because her brother is dead."

"But I've got a lot of brothers. Why would she single out Holden?"

"We've asked ourselves the same question. Best guess? He's the only one with a child," Melanie said. "I think that might be the reason, as disturbing as it sounds."

He swallowed down the raw bitterness rising in his throat.

"She also told my guy that she wanted him to do it in front of you, where you could watch. Valentina is a sadist. Next, she wants your father, Buck, to be executed. Her plan is to destroy everything you care about. Piece by piece."

Rage prickled his skin. "You think she's responsible for Pandora's murder."

Welliver tipped his head from side to side. "Stands to reason, considering I know she's behind Fiona Frye's death. She had my guy and one of her guards move the body and plant it in Amber Reyes's trunk."

Monty swore. "Why did she have to hurt so many other people? Why not just put a bullet in me and be done with it?"

"Too easy." Welliver smiled. "To her, you probably don't deserve a quick death since her brother didn't have one."

"But why kill Fiona?" Melanie asked. "To compound your guilt and implicate Amber?"

"I think there's more to it." Waylon moved to the edge of his seat. "Pandora was seeing a man. She had intercourse less than an hour before she died. My guess right there in her house, where you were blacked out. I think Pandora didn't fully trust this guy. Rightfully so. She gave her mother a flash drive with proof of who this man is and the nature of their relationship. Proof I'm sure we'll never find now."

"This guy is out there somewhere. In town." Monty stood. "My family isn't safe. None of them."

"I suggest you all go on lockdown at your ranch," the ADA said. "Lie low and wait it out."

"Wait? For how long?" Growing unease curled through his body. "Are you going to arrest Valentina?"

"For this?" Welliver asked.

"Yes!" Monty took a breath, doing his best to control his temper.

"Look, buddy, these are the facts." Welliver crossed his arms over his chest. "We have no proof that she's responsible for Pandora Frye's death. We have no proof that she ordered the murder of Fiona. Only that she had a body moved."

"What about my brother?" Monty asked in disbelief.

"Attempted murder for hire," Melanie said. "Solicitation carries the same potential penalty as the underlying crime. In this case, a conviction would carry a life sentence."

"There we go." He clapped his hands together once. "Make the arrest."

Welliver shook his head.

The ADA sighed. "This is her first offense. The judge will set bail. Probably somewhere between one hundred thousand and a quarter million."

"Chump change for her," Welliver said. "And what do you think she's going to do in the meantime? No need for suspense, I'll tell you. Send the full force of her cartel to slaughter your entire family. And my guy will have been burned by then, so no more information from him. You won't see it coming. Not to mention she'll also put a hit out on my informant so he can't ever testify."

"What are you saying?" Monty asked. "There's nothing I can do?"

"We have to do more than arrest her," Agent Welliver said. "We need to cripple her business. Isolate her. And take down her crew as well."

"My family won't hide out at home indefinitely." Monty shook his head, sick with worry. "My mother is the mayor. My brothers are in law enforcement. They will feel obligated to do their jobs."

"Speaking of your mother," Waylon said. "I guess we should assume the embezzlement case that coincidentally popped up against her today is bogus."

"Based on the timing," the agent said, "in all likelihood."

"Listen, your ranch is a compound." The ADA met his gaze. "Call your family and have them muster there. Lock it down."

Monty nodded. He hated it, but she was right. "I need you to get my mother and Amber released from jail," he said to Waylon. "I'll call my father. He'll make sure they get to the ranch safely and he'll give everyone else a heads-up about what's going on."

"I'm on it. I'll call Chief Nelson. I can see if we can spare any officers to safeguard you guys at the ranch." Waylon took out his phone. "I also need to text Hannah about this."

"Don't ask for any police assistance," the DEA agent said. "We don't know who is in her pocket."

"You make a valid point." Waylon nodded. "Remember when I asked you about Officer Foley," he said to Monty.

"Yeah."

"He's the one who brought us the phone that was found in your locker at work. He was also the one who pulled over Amber on a traffic stop and searched her trunk, where Fiona Frye had conveniently been dumped."

"I know him. I work with him," Monty said, exasperated. "He seemed like a good guy."

"They all do until they don't." The DEA agent strolled back to the window. "That's how it works in the underworld."

"The four of us need to put our heads together and map out how Valentina has done all of this," the ADA said. "She has more than Agent Welliver's inside guy helping her. Officer Foley is a possibility that we need to verify. He could be the tip of the iceberg. Until we figure out how deep this goes and who is involved, we don't know how much danger you or your family are truly in."

"You're right," Monty said. "Without knowing, my family and I are vulnerable, exposed, essentially operating blind." His gut burned.

If he didn't know the extent of the danger, how could he ever hope to keep his family safe?

Chapter Sixteen

Sunday, December 8
2:10 p.m.

To Amber, it was all a vicious blur. Seeing Fiona Frye in the trunk of her car. Being arrested. The mug shot. Having her fingerprints taken. Hauled to this awful cell and locked up.

She couldn't believe that having Holly in the cell next to her was comforting. Even though the accusation of embezzlement was unnerving. It seemed they were all being systematically targeted. But why and to what awful end?

"Honey, you can't keep stalling, sitting there simply holding your father's letter," Holly said.

Amber glanced down at the envelope in her hands. "I'm afraid."

"Of what?"

"I've been mad at him for so long, needing..." Her voice trailed off. She wasn't actually sure of what. "Something." An apology. An explanation that made her feel better. "And I'm scared that he won't give it to me in this letter. That I'll still be angry with him."

"Anger is the second stage of grief. As I see it, you've been grieving the loss of your relationship with him since you left. It's time to work through the other stages."

Amber shook her head. It couldn't possibly be that simple. Read a letter and work through the stages. Could it? "He should have told me that he was sick and given me a chance to fix this broken thing between us. Why would he deny me that closure?"

"Maybe it's in the letter. There's only way to find out." Holly leaned back against the wall. "My dad died on the job. Shot in the line of duty. He was healthy. In his prime. I never got to say goodbye to him either. But I would've given anything to have the kind of letter that you're holding now. It's a rare gift."

Amber swallowed hard. No matter how she felt after reading it, this was her father's final attempt at speaking to her. She owed him the respect of finding out what he had to say. She took a sip from her water bottle and opened the envelope.

Slowly, she removed the handcrafted white wove paper with the Longhorn Ranch logo embossed at the top and read the *handwritten* letter that she'd been carrying four months.

My Dearest Amber Sofia,
If you're reading this, then I have passed and, hopefully, I'm reunited with your mother. She was the love of my life. After hearing my last will and testament and the full terms of the trust, I'm sure you question that. Yes, I had an indiscretion many years ago. I have no excuse for it. Your mother was perfect, far too good for me, while I was a deeply flawed man who gave in to a stupid moment of weakness. The affair was short-lived because I realized that if Sofia ever found out it would break her heart. By that point, Fiona was pregnant and wanted to keep the child.

I provided for them, with the understanding that Sofia would never know the truth and Pandora would only learn I was her father when I was ready. Fiona agreed and waited for years. When your mother died, I was lost. Scared. Terrified about what would happen to you. I didn't want you to be alone and I didn't want you to settle for less than you deserved.

You were my princess. I wanted to give you the world. I thought I could give you Monty. You loved him and I knew that he would love you in return one day. That he would make a strong, caring husband who would be a true partner through life. Also, through your union, our ranches could also be united. I never wanted to push either of you into ranching the way Buck did him. The boy only rebelled.

Buck treated him like he was a wild horse that needed to be broken. Tamed. But I saw something different. Monty is no horse. He's a mule. For one thing, they're smarter and can't be bullied. They need a legitimate reason to do what you want. "Because I said so" isn't good enough reason for them. You can't push them the way you can a horse and you have to have a ton more patience. Instead of using a whip, one must use love, understanding and a good reward system.

That's why I created the terms of the trust, as Machiavellian as it might have seemed. And it worked, too. Only weeks after you two became a couple, he was ready to marry you with a heart full of love, to be a faithful husband, a dedicated father to your children. But you found out about my machinations and split.

I can't say I blame you, my dearest. You have your mother's fire, her pride, her fighting spirit. I respect you for leaving and for turning your back on me.

My one regret is that I didn't apologize. It was the only way to get you to come back home. That or die.

Ha ha! You see, I couldn't give you the apology you wanted, some heartfelt "sorry" because, well, I wasn't truly sorry. How could I be if I was willing to do it again?

And a million times over, I would do it.

You wanted Monty and I aimed to get him for you. Hence the reason I kept the trust as is. You never married. Monty never married. I must have faith in the belief that I have done the right thing and that you shall reap the reward even as I endured the price at not having you by my side in my final days.

Which brings me to Pandora. My child who suffered in my absence from her life, not having a father growing up though I lived in the very same town. She never had the memories and the birthdays, the celebrations, and the words of adoration from me. The hugs and kisses. My support or encouragement. To see the sparkle in my eye the way you did every time I looked at you. I can't ever give her those things. But I can give her the Reyes family home.

I know that one day you will call the Shooting Star Ranch your home. And Chance has moved on from Wyoming, and he doesn't care about the house.

Let Pandy have it with peace in your heart. Call her sister. Embrace her. Welcome her. If you don't, Chance never will.

Do this for me, though I have no right to ask anything of you. Please. I bet you can count on one hand how many times I've used that six-letter word with you and have fingers left over. Don't be angry with me anymore. Let it go.

Remember me. Toast me. Don't put flowers on my

grave. Save those for your mother's. Pour a little whiskey on mine instead. The good stuff.

You are now and will forever be my sunshine.

Your Loving Father

Amber wiped the tears streaming down her face, but she couldn't stop crying. She was a total sobbing mess.

"Oh, honey, I wish I had some tissues for you," Holly said. "How was the letter?"

"You were right," she said, choked up. "A rare gift."

She suddenly missed her father so much and wished she could hug him. Hug him tight and tell him how much she loved him. That she was the one sorry and he was right about Monty. How he'd love to hear that. "You were right, Daddy," she whispered. "You were so right."

If only she had read the letter sooner. Before Pandora was murdered. She could've done as he requested. Maybe it would've made a difference somehow.

An officer came down the hall and stopped at their cells. "You're both free to go."

"Really, why?" Holly asked.

The cop shrugged and unlocked Amber's cell. "Orders from the chief."

Rubbing her swollen eyes, she rose to her feet and stretched her legs.

Next, he let Holly out. "Mr. Powell is waiting for you two."

Which Mr. Powell? Amber wanted to ask. There were so many of them.

Outside of the cells, Holly pulled her close, wrapping her in a warm hug. "You looked like you could use one of those."

She hugged her back, grateful for the affection. Having Holly and Buck as in-laws would be a mixed blessing. The best part was that they could tell her stories about her parents, things she didn't know, like the stuff about the bananas and lemon wedges. Stories that she'd be able to pass on to her own children even though her parents were gone. Their memories would live on.

"Thank you." Amber gave her a sad smile. "Let's get out of here and see who's waiting for us."

"My money is on my husband," Holly said.

Amber was relieved to leave the holding cell area and step into the hall on their way to freedom. "Even though we didn't get a chance to have the morning meeting you wanted, we still got to talk." It had been nice to have Holly there, for support, for comfort, for a friendly ear with no pressurizing discussion of the future and marriage.

"What meeting, honey?"

Amber furrowed her brow. "The one Vera called me about. She said you wanted to talk to me privately, away from the house."

"I didn't ask her to do that. There must be a misunderstanding. Maybe I made an offhand remark about wanting to speak with you and she took the initiative. She's helpful that way. Reading my mind, anticipating my needs."

"Must be nice to have such a helpful staff."

"I couldn't do this job as mayor without my team."

They passed the bullpen and could see the lobby. She spotted Buck and Eddie waiting for them.

As soon as they pushed through the double doors, Buck enveloped Holly in a bear hug and kissed the top of her head. She was a petite woman but looked even smaller and more fragile in her husband's arms.

"Why did they release us?" Holly asked. "Not that I'm complaining."

"Something to do with the Sandoval cartel and a woman named Valentina," Buck said. "Apparently, she's been targeting Monty. Wants to make him pay. All this misery we've been through over the past couple of days has been about a vendetta. She even tried to have Holden killed."

Holly gasped. "No."

Shock filled Amber's chest.

"That's what those shots fired at the tree lighting ceremony were all about," Buck said. "Goons from the cartel trying to take out our boy, Holden. I guess to punish Monty. We need to go to the Shooting Star. Arm up. Get the ranch hands in the bunkhouse to stand guard. And we'll wait for Monty. Once he has more information, we'll decide what to do."

"Where is Monty?" Amber asked. Why wasn't he here?

"He's working with Waylon, the assistant district attorney and a DEA agent. They're trying to figure out how deep this goes and who in town might be involved."

"Why is a DEA agent here?" Eddie asked. "Is it simply because it's about the cartel or are drugs a part of this?"

Buck shook his head. "I'm not entirely sure. Come on. We should get going."

"What about Grace?" Eddie pushed his glasses up his nose. "She and the baby are at the church. She was staying after service to help sort the donated toys for children in need. I hate to think about something horrible happening to her or poor little Kayce."

Holly pressed a hand to her chest. "Oh, no. Buck, we need to pick them up right away. I don't want her on the road alone. Unlike you and me she refuses to carry a gun."

"By the way," Buck said. "Here's your purse." He also handed Amber hers.

Holly took the handbag and checked the contents. "I need to buy her and you," she said, pointing to Amber, "a Beretta like the one I have. Small, but packs a deadly punch. Let's go to the church."

"Why don't you two go and get Grace and Kayce and I can take Amber to the ranch," Eddie said. "It's not best to have everyone clustered and so exposed. Two pregnant women and a baby all together? Makes for a tempting target. These cartel folks could have hired men lurking in every corner of the town."

"That's true." Holly put her purse under her arm. "But they're messing with the wrong family."

"Are you carrying?" Buck asked.

"Always." Eddie flashed the gun in his shoulder holster under his jacket.

"All right." Buck gave a firm nod. "You two go straight to the ranch. We'll be along shortly."

They hustled outside and separated, going toward different vehicles.

"Do you mind if we swing by my house first?" Amber asked. "I need to pick up some things. Clothes. My prenatal vitamins."

Eddie frowned. "Buck told us to go straight to the Shooting Star. We should listen to him."

"But there's no telling how long we'll be on that ranch." It wasn't like she could borrow stuff to wear from Holly or Grace. Neither would have anything that would fit her. Even Grace at almost nine months probably wore a size small in maternity clothing. "Please. I promise I'll be quick."

"Okay. Do you mind driving?" Eddie asked. "I've never been out to your place. That way instead of me focusing on directions, I can keep an eye out for anything suspicious. Worst-case scenario, if we were under attack, it would be hard to shoot at someone while driving."

"As long as it's not a stick. I'm not good with a manual."

"You've got nothing to worry about." He handed her his keys, and they climbed into his Chevy Tahoe.

Watching Buck and Holly speed in the direction of the church, she signaled and pulled out. At the corner, she turned onto Third Street and headed home.

Eddie was vigilant. Checking the rearview and side mirrors. Turning around and looking over his shoulder. Once they made it out of the busy part of town, he settled down.

It was easier to see someone trailing them or racing up behind the vehicle on Route 207.

"I have a small confession to make." A sheepish grin tugged at the corners of his mouth, and his brown eyes sparkled briefly.

"Please don't tell me you don't know how to fire a gun or aren't a very good shot," she said, half joking. She wouldn't have been surprised if that was the case, since he was such a gentle man with a quiet voice, disinterested in typical cowboy things like riding and shooting, but the odds were low. Most people raised in these parts or had lived here for a substantial amount of time learned to shoot and understood gun safety.

"Oh, no, it isn't that," he said. "I'm a rather good shot."

"Then what is it?"

"I wasn't entirely honest."

Longhorn River Road was coming up soon. "About what?"

"That you have nothing to worry about."

She glanced at him, trying to understand what he meant. Eddie pulled his gun from the holster and aimed it at her.

Panic shuddered through her as her mouth fell open. "What are you doing?"

"Incentivizing you to do as I say. You're going to pass Longhorn River Road and make a left onto Big Canyon Way instead. Then we're taking Interstate 80 to I-25 South."

Her heart pounded, and her brain raced a million miles a second. "But why?"

"We need to go to Boulder."

She looked at him in shock, unable to keep her full focus on the road. "What's in Colorado? Why do we need to go there, Eddie?"

Taking a deep breath, he removed his glasses, setting them on the console between the seats. He peeled off his mustache, giving it a little yank that seemed to hurt. With a good, solid tug, he pulled the wig back, revealing a bald head. "Call me Roman. My boss is there," he said, his voice changing, deepening, hardening. His demeanor shifted, too, transforming before her eyes from unassuming into terrifying. "Valentina Sandoval. She's the head of the Sandoval cartel. One of the most powerful and ruthless individuals on the face of the planet." He spoke honestly without any affectation, and every muscle in her body vibrated with fear. "She's also the woman who wants to make Montgomery Powell suffer. Hence the need for you, the mother of his unborn child."

Chapter Seventeen

Sunday, December 8
2:50 p.m.

"Thank you. I appreciate the information." Monty hung up the phone. "My captain said that Nicholas Foley came in off patrol early on Friday afternoon. Claimed he wasn't feeling well. The camera showed him entering the locker room between shifts, when it wasn't busy and most likely empty, where he remained for less than five minutes and then left. But since we don't have cameras inside the locker room, we can't prove that he planted the phone."

"The flip phone had been wiped clean of any prints," Waylon said. "And there's no way it was coincidence that Foley was the same officer to pull over Amber. His story doesn't make sense. The guy lives way on the other side of town."

Monty grabbed one of the steaming hot coffees that had been brought in on a tray. "If Foley is a part of this, then his wife might be, too."

"Who's the wife?" the DEA agent asked.

"Vera. She's my mother's secretary in the mayor's office."

The ADA snapped her fingers. "Explains the neat packet of evidence that landed in Erica Egan's lap and made its way to the LPD. I'm sure that if we explain to her the extenuating circumstances, she might be willing to make an exception to her rule as a reporter and reveal her source for the story on your mother."

"I can light a fire under her," Waylon volunteered.

Monty gave a nod of gratitude. It was so much nicer to have this guy on his side rather than working against him.

There was a brief knock on the door before it opened. Hannah stalked in, shutting it behind her. "The bartender was lying. A guy came to see him on Friday morning after the murder. Broke into his house and woke up from a deep sleep. Terrified him. Paid him a thousand bucks to feed any cops that came sniffing around, asking questions, the story he told us and gave instructions to delete the footage. Threatened to kill him if he didn't."

"Did he give you a name?" Waylon asked.

"No, but he described the guy. Tan. Muscular. Not like a bodybuilder. But someone who works out. The guy could handle himself. Bald. Extremely scary. I showed him a picture of someone and it was the same guy."

"I don't understand," Monty said. "How do you have the guy's picture?"

"I was at Fiona Frye's house. It was ransacked. Someone was clearly looking for something and turned the place over good."

"He was looking for the flash drive." Waylon stood and stretched.

Monty happened to glance at the ADA and caught her watching the detective quite intently with unmistakable interest. Waylon's gaze flickered to Merritt's and a sly grin tugged at the corner of the detective's mouth a split second before the two looked away from each other.

The ADA and Waylon shared a mutual attraction, or they

were discreetly involved. Either way, Monty saw the potential for problems.

"But he didn't find it," Hannah said with a smirk. She pulled out an evidence bag from her pocket. Inside was a flash drive. "I did. Found it hidden in the bottom of a can of vegetable shortening in the pantry. Fiona was careful, too. When I popped the lid, it looked perfect. Brand-new. But something told me to dig."

"And our guy is on there," Waylon said.

"He is. Along with proof that the mystery man and Pandora were involved in a hot and heavy relationship."

"Let's see it." The ADA extended her palm. "We need to take a look at him."

"I can do you one better." She took out a folded-up paper from her jacket pocket and opened it. "I checked out the drive on one of the laptops Forensics had. Found a clear shot of his face and printed it." She slapped the eight-by-eleven-inch photo down. "It's him. That bald head is distinct, and Finn confirmed he was the one who paid him to lie and delete the security footage. The bartender was more afraid of this guy than of going to prison for obstruction of justice."

They all gathered around and peered at the picture.

Agent Welliver groaned. "That's Roman Cardoso. An enforcer turned lieutenant, holding the second highest position in the Sandoval cartel. He was Alejandro's right-hand man and is now Valentina's. If that man is in town," the DEA agent said, pointing to the picture, "then your family is in grave danger. I can't impress upon you how deadly this man is. He's not just a killer. He's clever. A seducer, snake charmer. A chameleon."

Chameleon. Monty stared at the picture. The eyes were familiar. Yet different. And there was something about the shape of the face that he recognized. "Give me a pencil."

Someone handed him one. He drew a pair of classic rectangular frames around the eyes, added a mustache and began filling in hair. A sledgehammer of horror slammed into Monty's chest.

"Dear God," Hannah said in a low voice, seeing exactly what he saw. "That's Eddie Porter. Your mother's assistant."

Eddie was always with his mother, attached at the hip. In the office. At the house. The man had unfettered access. "He's with my family right now." He whipped out his cell phone and hit the first speed dial—his father was number one, at the very top of his contacts. He was barely able to hear the numbers beep over the pounding of his heart in his ears.

"Thank goodness. I was about to call you," his dad said.

"Why? What's happened?"

"I—I—I don't even know how to say it. Monty…" His father's husky voice trailed off, only heightening his alarm.

His pulse quickened as he stared at the carpet. "Tell me what's wrong," he ordered, pressing his suddenly damp palm to his side. He'd never heard his dad, a man who was a stone pillar, unshakable, sound despondent. *"Tell me."*

"Amber's gone."

Monty drew in a sharp breath, his chest squeezing tightly. "What in the hell do you mean she's gone?"

"She left the police station with Eddie and they were supposed to go straight to the ranch, but they never made it here, Monty. I thought the cartel might've gotten to them on the road. But there's no sign of them of them anywhere. I've checked and her phone goes right to voice mail."

Rage churned in his stomach. "How could you let this happen?"

Silence. Sheer deafening silence over the phone.

"Son," his father croaked, with such despair echoing in the single word. "Monty… I'm so sorry."

Monty couldn't remember ever feeling this way, power-less, scared, spiraling out of control. But causing his father pain by blaming him wasn't going to solve anything. Eddie, that cunning viper, had fooled them all.

Focus. For Amber's sake, for the sake of our son. Focus!

He looked at the others in the room. "Eddie—Roman Cardoso—has Amber." He spoke through unbearable pres-sure swelling in his chest. "She's missing." The thought of her at the mercy of some sadistic kidnapper with a vendetta against him made his heart clench like a fist.

Agent Welliver let out a soft curse. "He's probably tak-ing her to Colorado."

"You know where?" Monty asked.

"I don't know, son," his father said. "I'm so sorry."

"No, Dad. Not you. Hold on."

The DEA agent nodded. "Valentina has several places. My inside guy told me that Sandoval is in Boulder. I know the property."

Hope fired in his chest. "Then I'm going. With my broth-ers. We'll get her back."

Welliver shook his head. "You should let us at the DEA handle it."

No way was he waiting for approval and red tape to clear. "She might not have that kind of time. Boulder is a two-hour drive. We can arm up and strategize on the ride. Where is it?"

Welliver raked a hand through his thinning hair. "You and your brothers have no authority across state lines. I'll go with you. I can have some other agents meet us there. Trust me, you'll need every able body you can get. Valen-tina travels with an armed team. They are as capable as any paramilitary unit."

More manpower and more experience. He'd take it if didn't mean unnecessary delays. There wasn't a minute to spare. "No red tape?" Monty asked, wanting to be sure they were clear.

The corner of Welliver's mouth quirked up in a wicked grin. "I color outside the lines. A lot." His eyes flashed a predatory gleam. "I'll go hunting with you. No red tape."

Monty put the phone back to his ear. "Dad, tell my brothers we're going to get Amber. And ask Matt to bring his special toys." When Matt left the military, he took some Special Ops equipment with him. "It might come in handy since we're not entirely sure what we're going to be up against."

"We can cover you with almost anything you'll need, weapons, equipment," Welliver said. "We're used to this kind of thing. Trust me, we're prepared."

Monty gave a nod of thanks.

"I'll let the boys know," his dad said, "and I'm coming, too."

"Nope. You're not coming. You and Chance need to stay with Mom, Grace and the baby. Make sure you keep them safe."

"Chance won't like this anymore than I do," his father grumbled.

"He's the last Reyes male, the one expected to carry on his family name. If anything happened to him, I'd never forgive myself. Do what you can to make him see reason."

"Easy if I go with you and he does the babysitting."

"Mom would have a conniption. You're not going, Dad. You're needed at the ranch. That's final. Got to go." He hung up before his father could argue.

"Got room for one more?" Waylon asked.

Hannah clasped Monty's shoulder. "Make that two."

Monty nodded, the tightness in his chest easing a fraction at the show of support. "The more help the better."

4:35 p.m.

AMBER'S PULSE SKITTERED in her veins. She was in a warehouse filled with drugs and a small army of scary-looking men armed to the teeth. This was bad. Even if Monty was able to figure out where they were holding her, it would make a rescue problematic.

She stumbled into a small room on the second story, pushed by Roman. He shoved her down into a heavy metal chair bolted to the floor and restrained her to it using zip ties. Her gut knotted.

The fact he hadn't blindfolded her once during the trip and allowed her to see the abundance of drugs stored on the lower level didn't bode well at all.

"What do you hope to gain by this?" she asked him.

He sneered at her, and she ached to kick him between the legs, but she was bound and helpless.

"Gain isn't my goal," he said. "It's my pleasure and privilege to be of service. To Sandoval."

High heels click-clacked across the floor, close by, and an elegant woman appeared in the doorway. She wore varying shades of purple, from her silk top to her designer shoes. "You should understand, Ms. Reyes. Roman is talking about loyalty. To family. You're loyal, aren't you? To your brother. To the Powells. To Montgomery, no matter what he does."

"That's not true," she said, wanting to sound brave, but the tremble in her voice gave her away. "Monty hurt me once. I didn't stay with him. I didn't trust him, and I left. Because I deserved better."

"And now you think that's what he is. *Better.* Is that why you climbed back into bed with him? Had unprotected sex? Which requires a high degree of trust in my book. Why you're so excited to have to his child?"

Amber lowered her head. She didn't know how to answer.

The truth would only confirm how much she loved him, putting her in more danger, and a lie would backfire since she wasn't good at pretenses. There was no winning if she played this woman's game.

"I get that you have a vendetta against him," Amber said. "That you want to hurt him. But why did you have to kill Pandora Frye?"

After reading her father's letter, she wished she'd had a chance to fulfill his wishes. To welcome and embrace the woman she had once unjustly hated.

"I didn't kill her." Valentina flashed a smile sweet as saccharine. "Roman did. As to why, well, her murder accomplished two objectives at once."

"First." She raised a single slender finger with a nail long as a talon. "Framing Monty for a crime that would land him behind bars for a considerable amount of time. And second…" Another finger lifted. "Gaining the power to destroy his family's legacy."

The land with the river. "But you lost that power when you killed Pandora."

Valentina quirked a brow. "Did I?"

"If I don't marry Monty—"

"Believe me, you won't live long enough to do that," Valentina said, cruelty radiating from every pore.

Amber drew a shuddering breath. She was scared. For her unborn child. She didn't want this precious life to be collateral damage in this woman's bloodthirsty quest for vengeance. "The land would've gone to Pandora," she continued, steeling her voice. "After you killed her, then it would've gone to her next of kin. Fiona. But for some sick, awful reason, you murdered her, too. Now the land will go to my brother." She thanked God that Chance was safe, far from the clutches of this vile woman. "He'll gladly give it to the

Powells. So, you see, no matter what you do to me, the legacy of Monty's family will live on. It will thrive. It will grow. And there's nothing you can do about it."

Tapping a finger at the corner of her mouth, Valentina gave a mock frown. "Poor thing. You're two steps behind. Your little line of succession would be correct if Fiona had been Pandora's next of kin."

"I don't understand."

"Clearly. I'll spell it out for you." A Cheshire-cat grin spread over her face as she circled closer. "Fiona wasn't Pandora's next of kin. Roman is." She strutted up behind him and rubbed his shoulders.

"We were married last week," he said. "Our secret from everyone. Except *la jefa.*"

This couldn't be happening. "You have a marriage license and had a ceremony?"

He nodded. "The whole shebang."

"A marriage to a fake person, to Eddie Porter, won't count." Monty and the rest of the Powells would piece it together.

He smiled, making him look even more terrifying somehow. "She married the real me. Roman Cardoso. A valid license. A legally binding marriage before her tragic and untimely death."

Amber reeled from the duplicity, the depths of evil. "But then why did you kill Fiona if she wasn't the next of kin?"

"She had evidence I was involved with Pandora. The mother might've been able to identify me."

"Why put her dead body in my trunk?"

"To wreak more havoc in Montgomery's life by framing you for murder and his mother for embezzlement. Next, I have wonderfully creative plans for the land," Valentina said, "none of which include the Powells ever getting their hands on it. Maybe I'll start with poisoning the river. Kill fifteen thousand head of cattle. That'll hurt. But I have so much more planned."

Dread burned up Amber's throat, lodging into a painful lump. "Please don't hurt me. Think of my unborn child. It's innocent in this."

"*He's* innocent," Valentina clarified. "Right? It's a boy. All the Powells are overjoyed."

This monstrous woman knew everything. Amber needed to think of a way out of this or she would be as good as dead. "You could just keep me hostage until January. Then it won't matter. I won't matter. The land will be Roman's."

Valentina tilted her head to the side and gave her a pitiable look that didn't reach her ice-cold eyes. "Aww, but you will matter. Montgomery Powell loves you. Hurting you will hurt him. That makes you a powerful bargaining chip. Whether you live or die will be up to him. I'm going to wait until you're dehydrated, hungry, writhing in pain. Then we're going to make a video. You're going to beg Montgomery to save your life. To save his son. All he has to do is kill an innocent person in public, in broad daylight, and turn himself in for the murder. Afterward you'll be released." Her tone was sincere but, in Amber's gut, she knew she was lying.

A slow, sick misery pooled in her stomach like raw sewage she wanted to expel.

This woman had no honor. And no heart. No matter what she did, Valentina Sandoval was not going to let her live. Fighting a jolt of panic, she took a deep breath. Becoming hysterical wasn't going to help. She had to stay strong.

When it came time for her to make the video, she wouldn't beg Monty to save her. She'd do the unexpected. She'd tell him to survive—that would be the sweetest victory.

If she was going to die, she'd do so without pleading. Fearless. On the outside, if not inside.

The only real chance she had of getting through this by some miracle was if Monty managed to find her before it was too late and came to the rescue.

She ached to wrap her arms around her belly, to protect her child. Shield him from any danger.

Hurry, Monty.

Please!

He had to save them both. It was her only chance.

Chapter Eighteen

Geared for battle, Monty and most of the team stormed the side of the hill overlooking the warehouse in Boulder, where they suspected Valentina Sandoval held Amber captive.

In total, they were ten, including Agent Welliver and three more guys from the DEA.

Two of Welliver's men and Waylon—the Bravo team—were covering the nearby residence, where Valentina was currently located. The inside man had eyes on her and had confirmed her presence as well as chatter about Amber being somewhere on the property. The warehouse looked like the most likely spot since the insider hadn't seen her or heard any mention of her being in the house. If the large building proved to be pay dirt for the DEA, with a cache of drugs, they'd arrest Valentina.

A massive seizure and the arrest of her crew would cripple her operation while she was behind bars. This was a golden opportunity to not only incarcerate her but neutralize her.

That woman had framed him for murder, gone after his brother, set up his mother, planned to kill his father and kidnapped the woman he loved, also endangering his unborn child. Monty needed to put an end to this to protect his entire family.

"Bravo team, this is Alpha. We're getting into position," Welliver said over the Bluetooth comms in their ears to the others waiting near the Sandoval residence, ready to take down Valentina.

Adjacent to the Eldorado Mountains, the grassy ridge was steep and the earth muddy, but they ate up the terrain in steady strides. He needed to clear his mind and focus his energy, but worry for Amber clouded everything.

Monty flattened against the tactical crest of the hill, below the actual peak where they had maximum visibility without advertising their position. Peering through the Eagle Eye scope, he swept the three stories of the warehouse. Cartel foot soldiers in tactical gear crawled throughout each floor. A fleet of black SUVs was parked outside.

"A freaking army down there," Logan said, lying in a prone position.

"We've got this." Matt's confident tone was to be expected.

He used to be Special Forces for years before he had enough of the bloodshed and came back home. This sort of thing had been routine for him.

The only other person with combat experience, DEA aside, was Waylon, but Monty had no idea what the scope and breadth of his skills were, only that he appeared just as at ease as Matt before they had separated.

Holden nudged Agent Welliver. "The size of that crew down there is a little intimidating. We're outnumbered and outmanned. Any chance of getting us some additional backup?"

The seasoned DEA agent chuckled, the sound sharp-edged

and almost homicidal. "Nope. Afraid not. This is the best I could do on short notice with no red tape."

Popping cinnamon gum in his mouth, Matt said, "I only see guns and knives down there. We have a force multiplier." He indicated the grenades the DEA had passed out.

They had three varieties, the primary being smoke. Flash and stun were the other two. The former would act as a great distraction, issuing three to seven loud reports—explosions—each accompanied with a flash. The latter had a more devastating effect. A stun grenade had one huge explosion of up to 185 decibels and an eleven million candlepower flash. Used in a small room it would rupture eardrums and cause temporary blindness.

In a warehouse environment, a stun grenade could buy them anywhere from eight to twelve seconds. Not much time but enough to disarm and incapacitate a gunman if they didn't hesitate.

Welliver had also provided them with top-of-the-line comms, bulletproof vests, helmets and other equipment they needed to help locate Amber. He gave the signal to a younger agent, Jasper Pearse, who deployed the drone fitted with a thermal camera. They were particularly useful for finding a missing person because of their ability to detect heat and temperature differences.

The drone circled the building going one floor at a time from top to bottom until Pearse isolated her probable location. "Look here." Pearse pointed out clusters of men in various sections. Then he brought the drone back around to the second floor, over to a back corner. A solitary heat signature was seated in a small room. "I think that's her."

"Our best bet," Monty said, agreeing with the assessment.

"Let's get this party started." Welliver slung the strap of a grenade launcher over his shoulder. "Once we get close to the building, we should split up. Some go high and some go low. Sweep the building from the bottom up and top down in tandem."

"High," Matt said.

"I'll go with him," Logan volunteered.

Monty flicked off the safety on his personal 9mm, and they swept down the hill in a V-formation with Welliver leading the way. Anxious energy wired him tight.

Off on Monty's left flank, Matt and Logan took out the gunmen on the east side of the building in a controlled sweep of muzzle-suppressed fire.

Once they came within spitting distance, Welliver held up a fist, bringing them to a halt. The team flattened up against the east side of the building while Pearse whipped out two grenades of white phosphorous. Slipping on gas masks, they prepped to breach the building and pop smoke.

Matt and Logan needed time to cut around to the north side of the building to a fire escape before the rest of them entered the building.

Pearse was tracking a countdown on his watch. He gave a vigorous nod once it was time, pulled the pins on two grenades from his pack, yanked open the door and pitched them inside.

A barrage of bullets sprayed the steel door. In ten seconds, thick white smoke would conceal their ingress and throw the Sandoval soldiers off balance.

Pearse gave the go-signal with another sharp nod and opened the door. They rushed inside, peeling off in different directions.

Dense smoke wafted throughout the entry of the industrial space, not quite reaching the high ceiling where metal ductwork ran in heavy rows. On the first level old machinery served as excellent cover for the enemy. Dark figures darted in between concrete pillars and rectangular objects—cases or boxes—digging in for the fight.

The Alpha team fanned out and moved in. Monty was keeping a close watch-out for hostiles in any sniper positions as he maneuvered across the wide warehouse floor. But there was no telling how many of the cartel's foot soldiers lurked. He eased to the far wall, looking for a different angle to exploit.

Wearing a bulletproof vest and sleek tactical helmet, he followed the path of huge ductwork along the ceiling to a wall and series of pipes.

Gunfire came from the far side of the space. Controlled bursts from armed men sweeping in toward the entrance where he'd last spotted Hannah and Holden. They were no doubt picking off targets.

With the chaos and noise of the gunfire, they were operating with limited communication. The one equalizer: the cartel soldiers were functioning under the same conditions.

Monty skirted the wall, scanning for hostile movement, until he hit a barrier. A half wall, maybe an office or, from the heavy industrial look of the space, an old clean-air room used to house special AC equipment.

Testing the stability of a pipe connected to the wall, he shook it. Solid. Risking exposure by climbing up was necessary to find an avenue to gain the upper hand. He holstered his gun and scrabbled up, using the bolted brackets for footholds and handles. Sweat dripped from his forehead under the gas mask, rolled down his temples and pooled under his chin.

His hands found a three-foot-wide gap between the pipe and office-type structure. He pushed off the pipe, gripping onto the top of the self-contained space. Hoisting himself onto the roof, he didn't make a sound. Ten feet of clearance to the ceiling and high above the layer of phosphorous.

Crouching, he stayed low and removed his mask. The smoky air below was dense and heavy in pockets where the grenades had gone off. He scanned the area. Open crates of drugs packaged for possible shipment were lined up in rows.

They had confirmation of drugs. "We've got thousands of kilos in here," he said to Welliver.

Six dark-clad figures circled closer to Hannah and his brother Holden.

An electric energy pumped hot through him. He locked sights on the two closest to them. A couple of soft squeezes on the trigger, and the men dropped. More stun grenades were used. Systematically, they either eliminated or incapacitated the rest of the cartel men on the first floor. Waylon was making his way to a staircase and signaled for them all to advance while Pearse covered the rear.

Confident no more hostiles remained on this floor, Monty jumped from the office structure, landing on the balls of his feet. Pain torpedoed his knees, but he blinked it away, hustling to join the others at the stairs.

They tried to take a furtive peek to see what waited for them on the next floor.

A wave of bullets rang out in a striking clang. Suppressive fire swept over the metal staircase to keep them from ascending.

Backs against the wall, Welliver pointed to his own eyes, then the stairwell. Pulling out a telescoping-wand camera that allowed tactical viewing without getting your head blown off, he ventured to the edge of the staircase to determine the location of the gunmen.

Welliver shifted the wand around the corner for a complete picture. He slipped back beside Monty. "Two shooters.

One at the top of the stairs. The second is leaning over the railing. They're taking turns with bursts of fire."

It would require someone to drop to the ground on their back to take the shot. Someone precise. Decisive. Sharp.

"From what you told me," Welliver said to Monty, "you might be better suited for this. Young back and all." He grinned.

On the ride to Boulder, Monty had told him about the marksmanship training he'd had growing up. He loved ranching and shooting. The more his father had hounded him about legacy, the more Monty had focused on handgun and long-range rifle shooting. As a state police officer, he'd aced marksman sniper training.

No doubt the older agent had a ton of field experience, but Monty was probably a better shot.

Now that they knew the setup of the shooters, he listened. For the pattern and rate of fire. The one at the top, leaning over with a sweeping view of the steps, was the most dangerous and needed to be eliminated first.

Waiting for his blink-of-an-eye window to open, Monty removed his tactical helmet. Not a reckless choice. A calculated one. He couldn't chance the gear getting in his way, throwing him off a centimeter.

The bottom stairs cleared of gunfire for a breath, the shooters prepping to reload. Monty dove, sensing where to aim as much as sighting the targets. He fired, rolled, readjusted and squeezed the trigger again. The first man hit the staircase with a bullet to the head. The second took a slug to the chest.

Monty climbed to his feet. "Did you see all the drugs they've got in crates?" he asked Welliver.

"Yeah. Better than what we could've expected."

"Give the order. Before someone tells Valentina that we're

here and she gets away." He couldn't let that happen. "Do it now. There's no reason to wait."

"Bravo team," Welliver said over comms, "you're cleared hot to take the queen. We've got powder. Lots of powder."

"Roger that," another agent responded. "We're going in."

Monty hoped Waylon and the other agents apprehended Valentina Sandoval fast.

Turning his focus back to finding Amber, he bounded up the steps. Quick. Quiet. The others were right behind him.

The landing opened onto the second floor. No corners, no walls to hide behind immediately. That meant exposure at the top of the stairs. Whatever was waiting could hit them full force.

Bracing against the railing, Monty slipped his helmet on. "Be ready to use flash grenades," he said to the rest of the team. "I don't want Amber getting hurt if we use something more aggressive or her getting caught in the middle of a shoot-out."

Welliver held up a stun grenade. "Bigger impact. It would be better."

"You're probably right," Monty said, understanding the disadvantage it would put them at, "but Amber is pregnant. Flash only around her. I won't take the risk. Got it?"

Everyone nodded.

Pounding footsteps resounded on the first floor, drawing closer. Someone must've called for reinforcements to circle around behind them.

"We'll go hold them off," Hannah said, referring to herself and Holden.

Pearse tapped her on the shoulder. "I'm with you guys."

The three of them took off back down the stairs.

Poised near the top of the landing, Monty was ready to

bolt up and try to get to cover. He glanced back at the senior agent.

"I'll cover you from here," Welliver said. "And make sure no one gets past those three downstairs and sneaks up on your rear." The agent took a defensive posture on the stairs, the only position affording cover.

Glass shattered on the floor above them. A flurry of activity up there followed. Guns were chambered followed by a riot of gunfire. Logan and Matt must've breached the third floor.

Now or never. Monty raced up the last few steps, rushing onto the second-floor landing. Quickly, he got a look, spotting Amber, and ducked to the left, taking cover behind a wall.

The man he had known as Eddie Porter, kind and agreeable and soft-spoken, was gone. In his place was the cruel-looking Roman Cardoso, holding a gun pointed at Amber's head, using her as a shield.

Relief trickled through him. She was alive. Possibly fatigued and dehydrated, but otherwise she didn't appear hurt.

If this got to the point of some feigned negotiation, Monty realized he could lose the woman he loved along with his unborn child. He needed to act first and seize the advantage.

"Come on out, with your hands up!" Roman said. "Or I'll shoot her!"

Monty steeled himself for what he had to do next. He grabbed two flash grenades. Pulled the pins with his teeth. Released the spoons. Counted to two and tossed them into the wide-open space littered with ratty furniture and large crates.

The grenades clanged to the floor. Rolled and detonated.

With the first two pops, he drew his weapon and stormed inside. Roman had released her and was trying to get to cover. Amber had her hands over her ears, with her eyes shut as she crouched beside a stone pillar.

Monty hustled inside and grabbed her by the arm. Shuffling backward, keeping his eyes trained on the room, he ushered her toward the stairs.

Welliver lunged forward, taking hold of her arm. He got her down out of the line of any possible incoming fire.

This wasn't over. No way was he going to leave Roman Cardoso in there to come after his family.

Monty swooped back into the room. He slipped up behind a pillar and then dashed to the next. A figure ran behind one of the crates near the sofa. *Gotcha!* Monty stalked closer to the crate, his weapon up and at the ready.

A man leaped up, holding an AR-15 rifle, and Monty fired, hitting him square in the chest. Just a nameless soldier. As the guy dropped to the floor, another man—packed with lean muscle—lunged, tackling Monty and knocking his gun loose.

Monty let the momentum carry him, flowing into the fall. He drove his knees into Roman's torso, flipping him overhead. Moving fast, Monty spun and sprang upright, sending a blow to the man's forearm, dislodging the weapon. But Roman followed up, throwing a punch toward him. Monty twisted sideways. The fist barely missed his face and rammed into his shoulder, knocking him into a forty-five-degree spin.

Staggering backward, Monty struggled to right himself. Roman bent down, reaching for something on his ankle. Another gun appeared in his hand.

Adrenaline flaring through him, Monty didn't hesitate. He threw a sideways kick into Roman's wrist. The pistol discharged before it flew from his hand, skittering out of reach.

The slug slammed into the concrete pillar beside Monty.

Close. Too close. Another inch or two and the bullet would've hit his abdomen. Not slowing for a beat, Monty kept moving. But Roman was ready for him. Vicious kicks and punches were exchanged back and forth. But Monty couldn't afford to lose, couldn't give this man the slightest advantage.

A brutal punch struck Monty's cheek, another in his ribs, pounding the air from his lungs. The taste of metallic salt hit his tongue.

Monty butted his skull into Roman's head and jabbed a fist into his exposed throat, bringing the guy to his knees. *I've got him!* Now he needed to end this.

A flash of metal glinted.

By the time Monty registered the knife, it was too late. Roman stabbed the large blade into his thigh and twisted it. White-hot agony tore a scream from his lips.

Roman lowered his shoulder and slammed it up into Monty's chest with the force of a battering ram, taking them both to the floor.

A desperate, violent need to shut this man down eclipsed everything else. Monty sent his elbow crashing into the head of the dangerous man who had infiltrated his home and threatened his family. He knocked Roman to the side, but the guy scrambled quicker than lightning. Roman made it up, spotted something on the floor—a gun—and grabbed the pistol.

Breathless and face bleeding, Roman aimed the 9mm at Monty's chest.

His blood chilled at the split-second thought of failing Amber. Of losing her and his baby. Blinking it away, he vaulted at the guy, unarmed, screaming through the gut-wrenching pain in his leg, determined to protect his family. Even if he had to die to do it.

A distinct pop punctured the air, and a shudder ripped through Monty.

The hot slug made Roman's head jerk back on impact. He staggered a step and dropped to his knees and keeled over, dead.

Monty glanced over his shoulder.

Logan stood holding a gun.

The stark fear gripping Monty in a fist-tight hold dissolved as a rush of peace filled him. "I've never been happier to see you."

Logan grinned. "I've got your back. Always."

Yeah, his little brother did. Lucky thing, too, otherwise he'd be the one dead on the floor.

Logan glanced down at Monty's leg, noticing the injury. He hurried to his side.

Monty slung his arm over his brother's shoulder. Matt met them at the landing of the stairs and came up on the other side of him. The two supported Monty, helping him hop down the stairs.

"The queen is dead," Waylon said over comms. "She opened fire. We had to take her out. All of Bravo is fine."

It was over. The nightmare was finally finished. Roman and Valentina were dead. The threats to his family had been eliminated.

His brothers helped Monty limp through the warehouse and outside into the fresh air. Hannah, Pearse and Holden were right behind them. They made their way back to the other side of the hill.

Welliver had gotten Amber to safety and secured inside one of the vehicles they had driven. She spotted him and bolted from the SUV.

He didn't want her to run, but also couldn't wait to hold her in his arms.

She rushed to him, wrapping him in a tight hug, her trembling body crushed to his, and nothing in the world had ever felt better.

Amber pulled back and stared at his leg. "Oh my God. Are you all right?"

"I think I will be." It hurt like hell, but he had Amber, he was on his feet, breathing, and they hadn't sustained any casualties. He couldn't complain.

"We've got to remove it," she said.

"No," several voices said in unison.

He met her frantic gaze. "I could bleed out," he said, with a sad smile. "Best to let a doctor do it."

She threw herself into his arms again, and he basked in the warmth of her embrace, the surety of her touch. No more skepticism. No more hesitation. No more fear.

Raw emotion flooded him, replacing the adrenaline high. He bent down to look into her eyes and smiled at the love shining on her face.

"We need to get him in the vehicle," she said to his brothers.

They helped him hobble over and got him inside. She found a medical kit and climbed in on the other side. The others hung back, giving them a moment alone together.

"Are you all right?" he asked, looking her over.

She nodded as she took gauze out of the kit. "Once I get your leg wrapped to slow the bleeding, I'll grab a bottle of water." She bandaged his thigh as best she could around the Bowie knife lodged in it.

The pain was intense. He'd never felt such agony.

But Amber was all right. His son was all right.

He pressed a palm to her cheek. "I'm so thankful you're not hurt. I imagined horrible things. What they could've been doing to you. I couldn't bear the thought of losing you. Either of you."

She placed her index finger against his lips. "No more imagining the worst. No more regrets. No more looking backward. From this day forward, we're together. A family. No matter what. I love you, Montgomery Beaumont Powell, and I want to marry you as soon as possible."

The words curled around his heart like a warm embrace. He cupped her jaw and gave her a soft kiss. "Are you sure?"

"I'm one hundred percent positive about everything. That I want to marry you. That you truly love me, with or without the land."

"You just went through something horrendous. You might not be thinking straight. We can wait. Stick to the plan. I don't mind."

"We can't stick to that plan because I do mind. It's selfish and rooted in fears that I no longer have." She took his free hand and put it on her rounded belly. "Our son, your brother's children, Kayce and the baby coming in weeks, and all the other little ones on the way deserve their birthright. The Powell and Reyes legacy. We need to protect it, fight for it, not take it away from them."

Joy ballooned in his chest until he could barely breathe. He was in so much pain but had never been happier. "How did I get so lucky to have you?"

"Fate." She shrugged. "Or a wise father's keen insight and persistent machinations."

Smiling, he pulled Amber into his arms and then gave her a heart-pounding kiss that rocked him to his core. "Whether it was fate or your father or both, I know that we were always meant to be together. Joined as one."

Epilogue

Three months later
5:50 p.m.

"What do you think about Beaumont, my grandfather's name?" Monty asked, his voice rough and husky, making her bare skin tingle.

She turned over onto her back, lying in their bed in the cottage that had been built for them a decade ago, and stared at him. "Beau," she whispered, a soft smile surfacing on her face, and nodded. "Could we name him Beaumont Carlos?"

He kissed her on the lips. "Has a great ring to it, but it could be whatever you want. We could name him Peanut if it makes you happy. Peanut Powell has a ring to it also." Then he kissed her full belly and the baby kicked hard. "Oh, I felt that one. A good pop to my mouth. I guess baby says no to being officially named Peanut."

They laughed.

Fully naked, he rolled out of bed and crossed the room, grabbing his boxer briefs from the chair. He still had a slight limp from the knife wound in his thigh and the doctors told him he always would. That made him unfit to continue with the state police, but when he heard the news, a weight lifted from him, and he acted at peace with giving up the badge.

Now he was a full-time rancher in charge of the Shooting Star-Longhorn. His choice. He woke early with a sense of purpose and pride. He went to bed after loving her and cuddling, a happy kind of tired from the work, without a care in the world. Slept blissfully, soundly, with his arm draped over her.

Things on the ranch were delightfully dull. No danger. No dead bodies. After the reporter Erica Egan gave up Vera Foley as her source on the embezzlement case against Holly, Waylon had managed to squeeze a confession out of her. She admitted to forgery, being the one to embezzle money from the city, and working for the Sandoval cartel along with her husband Nicholas.

"There's something I never asked you," she said.

"Fire away."

"Why did you move into this, our house, after I left?"

"Two reasons. One, it was penitence. To be reminded every day, every second I was here of what I did wrong. Two, I was waiting for you."

She smiled. "Did you ever bring anyone here? A woman? You can tell me. I won't be mad."

"Bring another woman to our house? No, sweetheart, I never did that." Monty slipped the boxers on up to his trim waist.

Nibbling her lower lip, she couldn't tear her gaze from his marvelous body, strong legs, sculpted arms, washboard abs, a dusting of hair on his muscular chest. A spectacular specimen of a man. With his tawny hair a beautiful mess from their lovemaking and the evening stubble on his jaw, he looked rugged. Sexy. Perfect.

Squeezing her thighs together, she ached deep in her core to have him again. She glanced down at the diamond wedding band on her finger. Every time she looked at it her heart danced in her chest. *I'm Mrs. Montgomery Powell.*

An uncontrollable rush of pure joy suffused every cell in her body.

"What are you thinking right this second?" he asked, the expression in his eyes dark and alluring.

She loved the way he looked at her. Like she was the most beautiful, precious creature that he'd ever seen.

"About you. How happy I am to be your wife and that we got married on New Year's Eve."

It had been a gorgeous, candlelit evening ceremony at the ranch with the entire family and a few old friends from town. Some new ones too, such as Waylon. It had been small and intimate. She wore an empire-waist dress, her hair full of curls pinned high. He wore a tailored navy suit. They dined on filet mignon and sea bass and had three different flavors of wedding cake. Vanilla with passionfruit curd, a layer of purple huckleberry, and lemon with raspberry filling. Everyone danced until the stroke of midnight when fireworks burst into the sky, ringing in the New Year and celebrating their nuptials.

The only thing missing was her mother helping her get ready and her father walking her down the aisle, but Holly and Chance were pleased to fill in.

She missed her parents and her dad's meddling, but she'd worked through the stages of grief and was finally at the stage of acceptance.

Her life was full and rich and overflowing. She was grateful to be surrounded by so much love and support. To have such a large family where she got to see her nieces and nephews grow up. To be close to them. To have huge dinners where they all gathered, their lives inextricably intertwined.

To call this ranch her home as her father always knew she would. Where their son would be raised.

Monty came back to the bed, leaned in, cupped her breast and gave her a deep, hot kiss. She pulled back and looked at him. Heat flickered in his eyes.

Laughing, she tapped his nose. "Don't even think about it, mister. Holden will be dropping the kids off for us to baby-sit any minute."

Grace had given birth to the most beautiful little girl, Nova. Six pounds, seven ounces. The baby came two weeks early and she was only in labor for three hours. Another easy baby with a sweet temperament.

"You know, we could always get Mom and Dad to watch them." His timber-rough voice sent a shiver along her spine. He cupped her breast again and ran his thumb over her pert nipple.

Hot waves of awareness coursed between them.

"Don't you want to practice being parents, Monty? We're going to have our own soon."

"Oh, I want to practice all right. Practice making babies. This one might be a fluke."

Her smile fell as she realized they still hadn't discussed something.

"What's wrong, sweetheart?" He rubbed her arm. "Was it something I said? I don't want you to feel like I'm always all over you and you can't get a break. It's just you're so sexy." He beamed at her, sending a flutter through her chest.

"No, it's not that." Looking at the bed, she took his hand. "How would you feel if this baby was a fluke?"

"What do you mean?"

"The doctors told me it would be difficult for me to get pregnant. Next to impossible. Because I have a blocked fallopian tube as a result of surgery I had for endometriosis.

What I'm saying is that this little guy is our miracle baby." She lifted her eyes to his. "He might be our only baby. I don't know if I'll be able to give you more children. I'm sorry. You wanted a big family. We should've talked about it before we got married instead of rushing."

He crushed his mouth to hers in a toe-curling, stomach-dropping kiss. "We already have a big family. Proof will be knocking at our door dropping off two babies in a minute. If our son is an only child, I guarantee he'll never be lonely. Not with his cousins living on the ranch." He smiled at her. "No imagining the worst. No regrets. It's you and me and this little one." He rubbed her belly. "No matter what. Right?"

A burst of all-consuming happiness rushed over her.

Monty stroked her cheek so tenderly that tears sprang to her eyes. "Don't be sad, sweetheart. This house is going to be full of kids we love. Trust me."

"I'm not sad. These are happy tears. I promise." She sat up and leaned against his chest.

Wrapping his arms around her, he hugged her tight, and she sank into the embrace, certain he would never let her go.

"Come on," he said. "We've got a reputation to earn. The best uncle and aunt ever. I want that top-dog status of *favorite*. Let's get dressed. We've got to entertain two kids under two until they run us ragged to the bone."

She laughed. "I can't think of anything else I'd rather do."

"Well, I've got a couple of ideas." He winked at her.

* * * * *